The Queen's Companion

The Queen's Companion

Lucy Pick

Cuidono • Brooklyn

/ CHAPTER ONE

Antioch, March 1148

✠

The second time I met Eleanor of Aquitaine, I was on a pier noisy with gulls and stinking of fish guts, on the last leg of a long journey heading for home. The muck-ridden scow I paid to sail me to Jaffa dumped me instead downstream from Antioch, along with my baggage and a monkey named Eve I had picked up along the way. The winds hadn't cooperated, and the crew wouldn't take me any closer to my old home, mumbling excuses about it being unlucky to have a lady on board. Unlucky for me, certainly. May God take all ships and hurl them to the depths of the sea, though preferably without me on them. I had spent three months hop-scotching from port to port across the Mediterranean all the way from Lisbon. I was tired and grubby from my travels, and heartsore, for reasons I will not go into now.

Even before my last bag was hoisted up, I realized onward travel would be a challenge. A disorderly crowd was disembarking from a flotilla of ships bestrewn with gold fleurs-de-lys that told me my arrival had collided with the crusading vessels of France. All I wanted was to curl up and weep on the tarred planks of the pier, but there was no rest to be had. As I counted my bags, a sudden scream, monkey-like, and then the human-sounding squeals of frightened women made me look up.

"Drat that monkey! Where's she got to now?" I muttered. Unlike me, Eve had thrived at sea, climbing up the rigging and begging food from the sailors. I bundled up my skirts and followed the squeals to find my animal perched on Eleanor's shoulder, surrounded by a knot of over-excited, finely-dressed women. Eve had removed the gold circlet that held the queen's veil and placed it around her own head, and was pulling at the queen's hair. Eleanor was trying to dislodge her while her ladies screamed and hovered ineffectually.

"Eve, no!" I called, running up to them. "May I?" I asked, and without waiting for a reply I untangled the little minx from the queen's headgear and slipped her back on her lead. Then I stared in horror at the wreckage of the queen's coiffure. A thousand tiny auburn braids once twisted and looped and coiled; now they were a tangled mess. The ladies hastened to repair the damage while I had my hands full with Eve, who jumped onto my own shoulder and chattered in my ear while I poured out apologies.

"Never mind," said Eleanor straightening her veil, "All's well, and it was an adventure. I've never been assaulted by a monkey before." She smiled at me, brown eyes frank and clear, sizing me up.

Eleanor was the most beautiful woman in Christendom. That's what they said, and it might even have been true. She was certainly the richest—queen of France by marriage but duchess in her own right of wealthy Aquitaine. Her smile could charm, well, even me, and in those days, she was lively and full of fun. She was two decades my junior, just twenty-five, and as vain as I am you might have thought I'd be jealous of her, but I never was, not for a minute. Maybe that's because I came to know her better than most, and saw the suffering under the beauty. And I am happy enough with my own looks, thanks to some walnut hair tint and cucumber face cream. But there were men and women who hated her.

Cued by their mistress's forgiveness, and hair damage concealed best as possible under a white linen coif, her women's anxiety turned to curiosity about my monkey. Always ready to play for an audience, Eve jumped off my shoulder to their feet, and they bent to get a closer look, at first shy and then bolder.

"She's so pretty and sweet, like a little furry person. What's her name?" one of the ladies asked, fear forgotten, as the others cooed and competed to stroke her silky golden fur.

"Eve," I said shortly, "I found her stealing apples."

The queen, the only one more interested in me than in Eve, continued to stare at me with those appraising eyes. Finally, she spoke. "We've met before, haven't we?"

We had — it was how I recognized her right away as Eve's victim — but I never thought she'd remember, especially with me dressed for a sea voyage not a royal audience. I curtsied. "Lady Aude of al-Lawza and Gistel at your service, my queen," I said, "We have met. At Vezelay, two years ago, when you and my lord the king took the cross."

"Of course," she said, clapping her hands together, "I remember. You were the twelfth Amazon."

She was right, I was the twelfth Amazon at Vezelay, when the flower of the nobility of France, Flanders, Normandy and Aquitaine came to the great Easter council to decide the fate of the Holy Land. I was in the entourage of the countess of Flanders, but I had my own interest in travelling to Jerusalem. For me it wasn't just a place to gain salvation and seek adventure fighting our Muslim enemies. It was my home, and I'd been exiled from it since I was a girl. And more than that, I had a pledge to fulfill and a promise long-neglected to keep there.

I belonged there in a way these Franks, who came for a few years, bashed heads, won booty, and prayed in Jerusalem before taking ship for home, never would. My crusader father met my Armenian mother under a warm sky in a fragrant courtyard in Edessa and when the Franks took Jerusalem, he decided to stay and carve out an estate at al-Lawza. They married and then produced me.

Both were long dead, rest their souls, but it was news of the destruction of Edessa filtering back to Europe in hushed tales and horrified letters that caused the great council at Vezelay. All Christendom shuddered at the reports from Edessa, tales of Franks and Armenians slaughtered by the Turks or sold into slavery. If they could take Edessa, what stopped them from attacking Jerusalem itself? And the first stop on their path was Antioch, held by Count Raymond, who just so happened to be Eleanor's uncle.

I became Eleanor's twelfth Amazon at Vezelay after the countess of Flanders refused, feigning illness when she saw the costume Eleanor planned. It was an outrageous rig — a white tunic emblazoned with a huge red cross, plumes to be worn in a kind of soft helmet, and a pair of gilt buskins designed to show off more leg than was the custom for decent women. But my eyes were drawn to the most beautiful pair of cherry-red boots I had ever seen, soft as butter with a high instep and elegant overstitching up the seams. I have always been partial to beautiful footwear, so I volunteered to take the countess's place, earning her gratitude.

We assembled in an open field on the hillside beyond the town walls of Vezelay in the chill and dew of a March morning, ground already churning to mud beneath our feet. From where I stood, surrounded by the company of Flanders, I had a clear view of the dais where the king and queen sat enthroned beside the preacher, Bernard, the frail abbot of Clairvaux, who looked barely able to stand unaided. All the world knew of Bernard, how ladies renounced vice and knights became monks at a word from his lips. He was a champion of the new order of Templar knights, monks dedicated not to prayer but to battling the Muslims in the Holy Land. Several of them stood on the dais behind Bernard and the royal pair, clearly identified by the bold red cross on their surcoats.

My attention was drawn to one Templar in particular, a sandy-haired man with an eye patch who stood close enough to the king to touch him. My eyes narrowed. The intervening years and the eye patch could not conceal from me the fact that it was Thierry de Galeran, a man I hadn't seen since I was fifteen. He'd grown from a callow youth to an imposing figure with the ear of a king, but I didn't care. I had no cause to be a friend of Templars, and de Galeran, who had once done me great wrong, least of all.

Bernard's voice distracted me from my old enemy. All impression of frailty vanished the moment he opened his mouth.

"Behold, brethren," he boomed, "Now is the day of our salvation. The earth itself moves and trembles, because of our sins. The enemies of the Cross have raised their heads, ravaging our Promised Land with the sword, beginning with Edessa. If no one stops them, they will burst into Jerusalem itself."

We shivered at his vision. Were the battles between Christians and Muslims the beginning of the Apocalypse heralded in the Bible? Many said so. A woman beside me began to pray the Our Father under her breath, over and over.

"What will you do then, O brave men?" the abbot's thundering voice rang out over the crowds. "What are you doing now,

O servants of the Cross? How many sinners who weep before me now will sit at home doing nothing while Jerusalem is lost? What a grief, a loss, and a vast disgrace to this most graceless generation."

Someone fainted in the far corner of the field. I clutched the simple cross around my own neck, the cross that was testament to my own weighty crimes and a long-ago pledge to return to Jerusalem that they might be forgiven. I might be able to make good on my vow at last.

Because the abbot also offered hope. "Take the sign of the cross and you shall gain pardon for every sin that you confess with a contrite heart. The physical crosses themselves are worth little; but placed on devout shoulders, they are worth the kingdom of God itself. Take up the cross! Take up YOUR cross!" he finished to huge cheers as throngs pushed towards the dais, hoping to receive their crosses from the abbot's own hands.

First, King Louis prostrated himself before the abbot and pledged his vassals to the cause, receiving in exchange a cross sent for him by the pope himself. But before the barons of France could follow his lead, Queen Eleanor pushed forward and kneeled before the abbot in the place her husband had just vacated.

"My lord abbot," she said in a clear high voice, "I pledge myself to this holy covenant and to the sacred duty of protecting Jerusalem, and I vow to take up the cross. And I pledge my knights, the noble vassals of Aquitaine and Poitou."

Even where I stood, I could tell that Bernard was caught off guard. Enrolling the queen as a crusader was surely no part of his plan. What could a woman do on crusade anyway? But the promise of her vassals could not be rebuffed. Until the king and queen married, Aquitaine had been often at war with France. With the king away on crusade, the threat of more war loomed. But send all the knights to Jerusalem and we could have peace in Christendom and war with the infidels. Bernard gave her a cross and she retreated.

The queen's departure from the platform was our signal to change into costume. I found the tent by the walls that had been set aside for us, thirteen white horses held by their grooms, waiting for us to mount them. The queen was already there, and a woman who identified herself to us as Berthe was making sure we were all present.

"Eight, nine, ten, eleven," Berthe counted, "Wait a minute—who are you? Where's the countess of Flanders?"

"Lady Aude," I answered her first question. "The countess is indisposed so I am taking her place."

"I don't know about that," said Berthe, contemptuous.

"Don't be unfriendly, Berthe, we need her for the numbers," said the queen. "I hope you can ride!" Just then we heard a huge crash and the sound of shouts and cries from the crowd. The hastily-built dais had collapsed. Above the din we heard Abbot Bernard cry, "A miracle! A miracle! The platform fell but all are unharmed. God smiles on our errand."

I had my doubts. Surely the collapse of the dais itself was an evil omen? We in the tent turned back to our task, changing hastily, giggling and helping each other lace up. After we mounted our steeds, each of us was handed a white banner emblazoned with a cross, and a satchel filled with drop-spindles for spinning wool.

"Throw them to the men too cowardly and womanish to join our crusade," Eleanor shouted over her shoulder. "Follow me!" She set off and we followed, while her men blew horns and cried out, "Way, way for Queen Penthesilea and her band of Amazon warriors!" A mob still flocked around Abbot Bernard, who stood blessing and distributing crosses. He had long since run out of those he brought with him, and was tearing them from his own cloak to satisfy the masses.

We circled the crowd while troubadours played and sang about the crusade. The queen shouted gaily, "Don't be cowards! Join us! Take the cross or stay home and spin!" and tossed spindles like favors at the men. It was almost all I could do to keep holding onto the banner without falling off my horse, but I did manage to toss a few spindles. I felt a thrill as we cheered them on, all these men pledging their swords and lives to protect Jerusalem. The crusaders were returning to the Holy Land, and at long last, I was returning too.

It was an experience I wouldn't forget, and all for a pair of cherry-red leather boots. How could I forget? I still had the boots, packed somewhere deep in one of my bags.

"My bags!" I gasped. I had forgotten them in my haste to collect Eve, and when I turned to look, every last one of my bundles was gone. They must have been collected by the porters who were loading all the royal gear onto barges ready for transport up the river. I looked at the boats piled high and knew I'd never find my meager collection among them. But what was I going to do?

The sharp-eyed queen had spotted the problem. "Did they put your belongings with ours? Never mind. Do you have friends waiting for you in Antioch? Lodgings arranged? No? Then why don't you come with us. Several of my women died, rest their souls, on the hard journey through Turkey. We are a sorely reduced company and could use a new face."

At her words, I suddenly saw that the impression Eleanor and her women gave of wealth and luxury was deceptive. There were marks of privation on their faces—tightness around the mouth of the woman I now recognized as Berthe, from Vezelay, and tension in Eleanor's forehead belying her open smile. Their clothes, while fine, were much mended and hung from gaunt frames. These women had been hungry, I realized in shock, and they probably wore every stitch they owned on their backs.

But join the entourage of a queen, when all I wanted was to slump in self-indulgent solitude and nurse my grievances? I knew what courts were like. I would have to sparkle and be entertaining and sing for my supper. Not to mention that it would now be my task to help twist those thousands of little braids. Still, a queen's favor could be useful as I fulfilled the mission that brought me to the Holy Land. I weighed my options and realized I had no better plan than this. And I confess it: already Eleanor's charm had pulled me under her sway, as it did so many. I liked her.

So I stood with the queen's women while the patriarch of Antioch descended from a barge that pulled alongside the pier, greeting us with banners and trumpets and choirs singing hymns of praise. I got my first good view of the king then, reed thin and blond, hemmed in by priests and Templars. He kept glancing over to the queen, as if torn between his duties as Christian king and coming to his wife's side, but he never made a move in our direction and she paid no attention to him at all. My eyes searched for someone else among the ranks of the king's attendants. Yes, there he was. My old enemy, the Templar Thierry de Galeran, as close to the king as he had been at Vezelay.

Another rich barge rowed up and, with a flourish of horns, our host, Raymond of Antioch, bounded onto the jetty to welcome us. Tall, silver, and built like a lion with a devouring grin, his arrival turned a solemn religious moment into a festival. Eleanor walked over to join her husband. Raymond greeted the king with a friendly aggression, and the king responded with royal hauteur and smiling condescension. The two were like matched game cocks, sizing each other up for a fight. I worried we'd see claws and feathers flying, but Eleanor intervened.

"Meu oncle," she said, her face alive with joy. She reached one hand to her husband, and another to her uncle, bringing them together under the shelter of her dazzling smile. "It makes me feel like we have come home at last, to see you here."

I was impressed. Give her a chance, and this woman could rout the Muslim armies on her own with a flash of the dimple in her right cheek. Raymond clearly liked what he saw, too, in the niece half his age. He liked it very much. He put his arm around her and kept her there, while he responded to her in a language I recognized as Occitan, their shared mother tongue spoken in Aquitaine. Eleanor was flattered, I could tell, and not a little charmed by her uncle, but as he continued to speak, and didn't let her go, I thought she began to look a bit bewildered by his attention. From Eleanor's blushes and the stern looks from some of the women, the Occitan I could not understand went beyond the avuncular.

At last, Raymond urged us onto the barges for the trip up the river. He travelled with the king, while Eleanor and all of us ladies were in a separate vessel. One of the men who accompanied us sat on a bundle and pulled out a viol. I was hoping for a song, but he spent the whole journey down the river turning pegs and testing its three strings. I supposed their recent sea voyage had put the instrument well out of tune. Eleanor neglected us, lost in her thoughts. I saw Raymond staring back at our barge from his own.

Once we were moving, oarsmen plying their way against the current of the river, the women quizzed me about my identity and ancestors. After telling them about my father the crusader and my Armenian mother, I cut them off with a question of my own. News travelled poorly around the Mediterranean, and I had heard nothing of the Vezelay crusaders since I left on my own journey. I wanted to know why, when the council at Vezelay was two years before, it had taken them so long to reach Antioch.

One of Eleanor's women began to sob softly at my question and another put an arm around the weeping woman and addressed me. "It took us a year to get started. We didn't leave until the following June, planning to travel by land."

I nodded. That's when my own group left by sea.

"We reached Constantinople by October."

"Constantinople was lovely!" another broke in.

"...But that's when our troubles started. The Greek emperor gave us no assistance at all. No food, no soldiers, and worse, no guides through the mountains. Every step of the way, we were attacked by Muslims and starved by Greeks. Then it grew colder and the rains came. On Christmas day, we lost men, horses, and most of our tents when a river flooded the plain we were camped on."

"That's when Beatrice died. And Marguerite," said the weeping woman in a soft voice, still cradled in the embrace of her friend.

"One day, we were with the queen and her vassals in the vanguard, while King Louis brought up the rear with his men. We found a perfect valley where we could camp for the night, and we hastened down to it. It was not our fault the king's forces were too slow."

"No matter what they say," chimed in another woman.

"They were too slow, and fell behind. The Turks attacked, and slaughtered the king's men, raining arrows down upon them and descending from the heights on their sturdy little ponies. Our men slipped and slid on the narrow mountain paths. Men, horses and carts tumbled into the gorges below. We had no idea what had happened, why they were so late, why they never arrived."

Eve was tugging at my coif as if she hoped I had sprouted braids like Eleanor's. I pulled out a bag of dates to distract her. "What happened next?" I asked.

A different woman took up the story. "Late that night, the king's chaplain, Odo, the stern monk-priest who never leaves the king's side, rode down to us and told us about the attack," she said bitterly. "I'm Mabilie, by the way. From Aquitaine, not France. Anyway, Odo blamed the queen — told her our baggage had slowed down the army, and that she was responsible for the loss of the entire French army and death of the king."

This caught Eleanor's attention. She snorted with disdain and got up and walked to the front of the barge where she stood watching the boat carrying Raymond and the king ply the river ahead of ours. With the sun on her, she looked like the prow of a great ship, the kind that sailed the North Sea.

Mabilie continued. "The next morning we learned the news was less terrible, when the king and a few stragglers turned up. But it was bad. We struggled our way to the port of Atalya all January, eating the last of our horses and mules and trading our clothing for food. Only the wealthiest could afford to take ship for Antioch, those you see here."

"What will the rest do?" I asked. "Eve! Stop that!" She was spitting date pits at one of the women.

"The rest will have to make their way by land," replied Mabilie. "If they're not starved or murdered by Turks and Greeks on the way it will be a miracle. And the journey by sea took us three full weeks."

Three weeks to make a sea journey that should take a few days at the most. This enterprise was surely cursed. I shivered. Now I knew why they looked so threadbare, and why the whole army could fit into a few barges. And why there were no horses.

The woman whom I recalled from the Amazon ride as Berthe asked sharply, "And how about you, Aude? Why did it take you so long to get this far? You were with the queen at Vezelay, so why did you not come with us and share our trials?"

I didn't want to talk about my recent past, but I could not escape a direct question. So I said simply, "I was with the group that took the sea route. I was present at the siege of Lisbon. That delayed me."

"The siege of Lisbon?" one repeated. With these words, I had gone from a traitor who had abandoned the queen to a hero. News of their disaster had not reached Lisbon, but somehow word that the northern crusaders had helped the king of Portugal take the city of Lisbon from the Muslims had reached them. It was to be the only real success of the whole crusade, and they clamored for details.

"Tell us the whole story, Aude. We've only had each other to listen to for months."

"Yes, tell us about Lisbon. We're longing for some good news from a true crusader."

I shuddered. It was too soon to tell that tale. My heart was still raw from what happened after, and I had no desire to share that pain with strangers. I missed the ones I had left behind there, and I was not going back. End of story.

"I'm not a crusader," I said. I had enough of crusading in Lisbon. "I am going home, to Jerusalem."

But this was even more exciting. "Tell us a different tale, then. Tell us about Jerusalem. Is it really as beautiful as they say?"

"Is it as big as Constantinople? And Rome? And do you think of Our Lord every moment you are in the city?" one asked, a pious woman fingering the cross around her neck.

"And will we see camels there?" added another.

"Yes, and if it is your home, tell us why you left it," Eleanor spoke from behind me, making me jump. She had returned to our group while I wasn't looking. "I want to hear that story most of all. Why would anyone leave this lovely, warm country to go north?"

I nodded. I knew I owed these women something for allowing me to travel with them, and if the coin was a story, so be it. It might distract the curious women from more personal and immediate investigations I wished to avoid. "It's a long tale," I warned. "I left many years ago."

"We don't mind," one said and most of the others nodded, though Berthe sniffed.

Why did I leave Jerusalem? Good question. To answer it I'd have to begin with the prince. If I hadn't met Charles when I was but six years old, who knows how my life might have been different? I began to speak, but found myself revealing more than I planned.

✠

Aude's First Tale: Jerusalem, 1109

We lived out in the country, in a manor house called al-Lawza, half a day's ride west of Jerusalem, but off the main road. Father did what knights do, and mother ran the villa, checking up on the dragoman and bossing the servants, mostly Muslim peasant girls from the village who left the moment mother finally had them trained. The dragoman negotiated with the headman of the village to extract the taxes the villagers owed, paid in kind in heaping sacks of wheat, barley, and chickpeas, and brimming vessels of olive oil and fermenting wine. Normally my father would have been in charge of the dragoman, but Father was a Frank and found the whole system of dragoman, headman, and village strange. My mother, Theodosia, an Armenian, was almost a local, more used to manor life in this part of the world, less easily deceived.

My mother was beautiful like an icon, all round dark eyes, soft lips and listening ears. Father adored her, and so did I. I didn't take after her at all, though everyone said I looked more Armenian than Frank. I was bony where she was soft, with a long thin nose and small mouth, and my hair was not her rich, dark brown but a lighter color, like a swallow's wing. My skin was olive and permanently tanned. "If you'd stay indoors where you belong, it would be as fair as mine," she reproved me when I was a child, and though being like her was all I wanted, it was not enough to compete with the lure of the fields and trees and village children. Only our eyes were the same color, though mine darted at every distraction, while hers were still and calm.

I think she would have been content to spend all her days in our courtyard counting sheep and waiting for father to return, but she was constantly summoned to the palace in Jerusalem, to attend Queen Arda, the wife of King Baudoin. Arda was also Armenian and Baudoin had married her in Edessa when the Franks first came to this land to conquer Jerusalem, the same time father married mother. Arda was grumpy and lonesome in Jerusalem, though there was a sizable Armenian community there, and every few weeks she'd send a messenger demanding mother, some kind of distant cousin, come and attend her. Mother made as many excuses as she could, but every second or third time she had to comply.

"Why does she take you away all the time, mother?" I'd say, trying to climb into her lap.

"Get down, Aude. Don't cling so," Mother would reply, then tell me that Arda was lonely so far from her home and needed her. I need you too, I thought, but didn't say. And when they didn't know I was listening, my parents spoke of marriage troubles and fights between Arda and Baudoin. "He's not a man with much use for a wife," said my father. This didn't make sense to me. Every man needed a wife unless he was a monk. Even the old, toothless headman had one. And why was she so unhappy? She was a queen. What more could you want?

I hated when mother went, leaving me behind with my nurse. But one time, a few weeks after Easter when I had just turned six, a messenger came when I was between nurses. I had driven the last one off by filling her hair full of burrs while she slept. It all had to be cut off and she decided that pressing her father's olives day after day was easier than taking care of me.

"You'll have to tell the queen I can't come. I have no one to leave Aude with, and she'll drown in the wadi or fall out of a tree with no one to watch her," she told the messenger.

"The queen was most insistent. She commanded." The queen always commanded.

Mother looked carefully at the messenger's face. She measured how serious the command was by how frightened the messenger looked the first time she refused. Even I could see that this one looked terrified, eyes bulging, forehead sweating, hands and voice shaking.

She took pity on him. "Very well. I'll come." My shoulders slumped and I started to whine. But then, a surprise. "Aude must come with us though, and the queen will have to make do."

I'm not sure who was happier, me or the messenger, and soon we were on our way, with me perched on the front of my mother's horse. The messenger had come with an armed escort. Though Jerusalem was close, the roads were full of bandits and thieves.

The adventure delighted me and I wriggled with glee against my mother until she told me to stop. I had been to Jerusalem before, but so long ago I didn't remember it. Mother pointed out its walls from a distance, glowing and massive in the noonday sun. I didn't see that they were old and crumbling in some places, only that they were many times higher than our villa, which was the biggest building I knew. They were so wide that once we drew close, they seemed to extend from one end of the world to the other. It was grain market day, so as we approached King David's gate we had to negotiate herds of camels laden with sacks, screaming and spitting at their drivers when they were forced to move, and letting loose huge gushers of urine that made me giggle. But camels were ordinary, even in such great numbers as these. I stared up at David's citadel as we entered the gate, seeing the armed men of the garrison watching us from the roof. I waved, and one waved back.

The city was less impressive inside the walls. The Christians had slaughtered most of its original inhabitants when they conquered it almost a decade before. Though King Baudoin had encouraged the local Syrian Christians to move in and settle, it was still largely empty and many buildings were ruined and uninhabited, though I hear it is much restored now. Armed knights, liveried messengers, and busy servants passed us as we rode through the narrow streets to the palace, crossing paths with priests and canons belonging to the Church of the Holy Sepulcher, the ancient shrine over the site of Christ's crucifixion and glorious resurrection, and all the other churches and monasteries that filled the city. I saw black-hatted Armenian priests, monks in cowls and rope-knotted habits, Greek clergy in white and gold, and even turbaned, black-skinned Ethiopians. The streets were so steep, they had steps, and stone vaults over them protected us and the shopkeepers from the vicious sun. The vendors, whose shops opened onto stone verandas right in the road, called us to buy their rugs and painted tiles and brass basins or taste their pomegranates, almonds, or bananas. Their shops looked seductively dark and mysterious when I peered in, but we rode past and didn't stop for so much as a fig.

We crossed straight through the city and then climbed up to the Temple mount. The king's palace was located in Solomon's Temple, and Arda ran to meet us at the great double doors the moment we dismounted, trailing silk garments and a cloud of musk.

"The watchman told me you were arriving. What took you so long, Thea?" she wrung her hands, earrings bobbling and bracelets jangling, "And who is this?" A plump, jewelled finger pointed to where I clung to my mother's skirts.

"This is Aude, my daughter. I couldn't leave her."

Queen Arda tugged on mother's sleeve and drew mother to one side, speaking in a loud whisper I could hear clearly. "But Thea, we have to talk. Terrible things are happening, awful things. I need your advice. And not in front of the——," she gestured her head in my direction.

I knew Mother was torn. The sooner she satisfied Arda, the sooner we could leave. But she wanted to keep her eye on me.

"I know!" the queen clapped her hands together, setting off a new chorus of jangles. "She can stay in my apartment and play. There's a guard at the entrance, so she will come to no harm. And we can talk in the garden." She dashed into the palace, and all we could do was follow her and try to keep up.

When the Muslims held Jerusalem captive, the building had been a mosque and in their day it was a cavernous white expanse divided by four rows of pointed arches which directed all eyes to a domed apse at the back. I have seen the Great Mosque of Lisbon since then, so I can imagine what it must have been like. But when the king made it his palace, he kept the central section open for a great hall where he could welcome visitors, and dine, and his high court could meet. The rest was partitioned into different sized apartments hiding storerooms and kitchens and armories and sleeping quarters. It was a haphazard job and many of the partitions were no more than a length of canvas stretched between two piers. Few went all the way up to the ceiling, so the hubbub of the palace could be heard all over.

Arda took us through a door in one of the more substantial partitions. It was her bedroom. "We can leave her here, Thea. There are some sweets for her and I'll send for some mint tea or a nice cup of salted yoghurt. Your little Ada will be safe and happy."

"Aude," I said. "My name is Aude."

But she didn't listen, and swept my mother out again after her. "Sit quietly like a good girl, Aude," said my mother before being dragged away, "And don't touch anything. Especially not those sweets."

They left and I was alone. Arda's chamber smelled thick with the same scent of musk and frankincense that perfumed her body, layered over less pleasing aromas of dirt and stale clothing. Woven panels of rich wool covered the partitions, Tyrrhean purple shot through with gold thread, dusty where their hems touched the ground. Arda had taken on some European customs while married to Baudoin, and an enormous frame bed dominated the cramped space. This became my perch as I surveyed the room, which was a jumble of bedclothes, linens and blankets, of material and color, twisted and tumbled as if a giant had a nightmare there the previous evening. The room was cramped, not because it was small, but because it was filled with so much furniture: wooden stools and leather hassocks; brass pitchers and basins; side tables with mother of pearl tops, barely visible under a litter of half-burnt candles, small jars, jewelry, and drifts of powder from spilled cosmetics; chests, intricately carved or inlaid with precious woods, spilling over with sleeves, silk scarves, and woolen cloaks woven in red, indigo, and green. I gazed longingly at a tiny table that looked about to collapse from the weight of the sweets it carried: a plate of honey pastries, fruits of all kinds dried or candied in sugar syrup, sweet sesame paste, and jellied rose candy in a haze of powdered sugar—all things Mother never let me eat to protect my teeth. Since Arda's mouth was half rotted, and her breath stank, maybe my mother was right, though this didn't convince me at the time.

I wasn't going to stay cooped up when there was a whole world to explore outside. I grabbed a handful of dates and slipped through the door of Arda's chamber. The guard may have been alert to the danger of assassins sneaking into the queen's chamber but he was busy chatting with a cheerful maidservant so I stole past him, unobserved. Munching on dates, I found my way to the doors of the palace and blinked my eyes in the brilliant sunshine. The color of the sky was the exact match of the walls of the Temple of the Lord in front of me, its golden dome shining in the sun.

My eyes were drawn to a cluster of children, hooting and calling with their backs to me. I went to see what they were looking at. A group of boys close to my own age were standing around a fountain while one of them balanced precariously, walking on its rim. I pushed my way to the front of the group. When he finished his circuit, everyone cheered.

"That's nothing special," I said, "Anyone can do that."

As I planned, they immediately took up the challenge and goaded me into trying. I was good at balancing, and drove my mother to despair by walking along tree branches and ridgepoles at al-Lawza. I handed one of them the last of my stolen dates, then leapt up and made the circuit, pointing my toes as I put one foot in front of the other. When I finished, I jumped down and flung my arms up in an attitude learned from the women dancers who sometimes entertained in our hall. "See? Easy."

"Show off," someone muttered.

I explained. "The rim of the fountain is narrow, but because it is not too high above the ground, it isn't scary, so it is easy to balance on it. If something is high above the ground, it is harder, even if it is wider. Like for instance,"—I scanned the courtyard for something that would be a proper test of my skill—"That wall, up there." I pointed to the crenellated parapet wall that ringed the courtyard. It was high above my head, but wide, and I saw the stone had decayed enough to provide secure hand and footholds for climbing it.

For some reason, this proposal made the boys all very excited, and they chattered to each other. One boy spoke. "You think you could walk along the top of that wall? Say, from here all the way to the corner over there?"

"Of course. No problem." The chattering grew louder.

"Fine. I dare you."

I began climbing right away like a little monkey, cheered on by the boys below. When I got to the top, I pulled myself up to a standing position and looked down the other side of the wall. I hadn't realized that both sides of the wall were not the same height. The side I had climbed was high but not overly so. I could have easily jumped down if there were someone to catch me or something soft to land on. But the Temple mount itself was far above ground level and the far side of the wall was much steeper, many times the height of a man. If I fell, I'd be dead. The boys knew this of course, and I should have realized it too after seeing the walls around David's gate. A thrill of vertigo shot through me and I extended my arms for balance.

"Do you want to come down?" someone called from below.

"Certainly not." I wasn't going to give up. The top of the wall was as wide as I was tall, and even though I was going to have to scramble up and down the crenellations, there was no reason I should fall. I began my trek, one, two, three, four crenellations mastered. Maybe I was getting cocky but I didn't realize that the erosion which had made the wall easy to climb had affected the top of the wall, exposed as it was to every weather. Stepping down into the hollow between two crenellations, I discovered the surface listed steeply. My foot slipped, and I screamed, and slid down the exterior wall. The children below heard my shout, saw me vanish, and started to shriek and yell, "She's fallen! She's dead!"

Two things saved me. First, the wall was not straight but pitched gently outwards, so the bottom of the wall was wider than the top. I slid more than I fell. Second, and most important, the wall was full of growing shrubs and bushes that had taken root in its cracks. My descent was broken by these and halted momentarily by an especially tenacious thorn bush. I was able to scrabble for hand and footholds. I was safe, but I knew I couldn't hold out for long.

"Help, help!" I called. "Bring a rope!" Some brave souls had climbed up to the spot from which I had fallen, and they relayed my cries to those below.

I tried to brace myself and began to cry. The thorn bush beneath me gave way a little. Could I cling to the wall if I lost its support?

It seemed like an eternity before I saw larger figures on the top of the wall and I heard the sounds of men directing a rescue operation. Then one of those above me rappelled down the wall to where I was clinging. "Stop!" he called to those still at the top when he was even with me. There before me, I beheld the tallest and most beautiful man I had ever seen in my life.

"It's a good thing you're small," he said. "Can you hang onto me as tightly as you are clinging to this wall?" His French was softly accented and unfamiliar. I nodded limply, and he took me in one arm. I clung to him, arms tight around his chest and, using both hands on the rope, he pulled us back to the top. When we reached the parapet, two men at the top of the wall hoisted me up. More men were at the bottom, bracing the rope.

Once we were both standing on the top of the parapet wall, I looked way up at my rescuer's face. Eyes blue like the sky, and hair like spun sunshine, he gazed down at me with a look of relief and concern. "You were very brave," he said.

A tight twist of fear in my chest I hadn't known was there swelled and burst into an explosion of stars. Warmth flooded my body and I found I was smiling. I was smitten.

He either didn't notice my adoring look, or was inured through experience to such female gazes. "Let's get you down to the courtyard below. Do you think you can climb down the same way you climbed up, if I go ahead of you?"

I could have flown down if he had asked me to, but I obediently followed him down the wall. When we were both safely on the ground, the crowd of people who had flocked to watch the rescue cheered. My savior was clapped on the shoulder by one man, almost as beautiful, but dark and much shorter who said, "Rescuing damsels in distress again, Charles? It's a lot of trouble to go to for one little urchin."

Charles. So that was my hero's name. I turned it around in my mind, savoring the sound so much I didn't notice my mother run up. She caught that last of the dark man's words.

"Urchin! How dare you. That's my daughter. Aude, Aude, whatever have you done? Can I not leave you for one moment without you causing trouble?" She hugged me tight, then pulled away and slapped my face (but not hard) and then hugged me again, even more tightly. Finally she squeezed me close in one arm while she addressed my rescuer. "Sir, I would thank you for risking yourself to save my wayward daughter, but I do not know whom I am addressing."

Sir. I took a closer look at my rescuer and his dark companion. Charles was rebuckling a sword he must have removed to make climbing the wall easier. He bowed and answered my mother. "My lady, I am Charles, prince of Denmark, and my companion here is William Clito of Normandy. We are lately arrived on pilgrimage, to pray and defend the Holy Land. It was an honor to rescue one small part of it just now."

I could tell my mother was pleased by his gracious response. "I am Theodosia Korikos, wife of Guy, sieur de Lawza. This naughty sprite is my Aude."

Naughty sprite! I was mortified, until Charles bent gracefully, took my hand in his and kissed it.

But then Queen Arda trotted up, puffing slightly, and ruined everything. "Theodosia! That's him," she hissed perfectly audibly, "The man I was telling you about. Both of them. They're the two who are ruining my life."

Charles and William melted away at her approach and the three of us were left alone. Arda looked at me for the first time. "Child, you are filthy. Theodosia, can't you take better care of your daughter than this?" I looked down at myself. My second-best dress was covered with stone dust, twigs and thorns and I'm sure my face had big smears of dirt on it. "Come," Arda continued to mother, "The girl needs a bath. We can all go to the bath house, and I'll tell you more about these terrible men who were with your daughter."

Once we got to the bath house and were stripped down to towels and sandals by the attendants and placed in the hot room to sweat, Arda recounted a tale of woe and betrayal, a tale my mother had already heard, judging by how often she said to the queen, "Yes, you mentioned that," and tried without success to change the subject to something more suitable for my tender ears. Arda had clearly forgot her original reticence about speaking in front of me.

"Of course, King Baudoin has never been much for the ladies," the queen began archly, "but it never caused me problems until those two arrived."

"Shh, Arda, the child!" my mother said.

"She doesn't understand what I'm saying. You're not listening us to us, are you, little girl?"

"Oh no, your majesty," I said. She was partly right. I was listening with all my might, but I didn't understand what she had just said.

Arda continued with her tale. "Ever since the two of them arrived, they and the king have been inseparable. They ride together, hunt together, fight together, dine together. And after. You'd think one or the other would be jealous, but no. Sometimes I think Baudoin likes Charles best, sometimes William. But they both pour bile into his ears about me. Thea—make us more steam."

My mother obediently ladled a cup of water onto the hot stones that provided the room with its heat. The water hissed, almost drowning out Arda's next words.

"Together they've persuaded Baudoin to cast me aside, to repudiate our marriage. The tall one, Charles, he's so pious. Always on his knees in church. He heard those nasty rumors about what went on when I took ship from Armenia to meet Baudoin in Jaffa, seven years ago, and has been telling Baudoin I'm not good enough for him. 'Caesar's wife must be above reproach,' he says, which is ridiculous. Baudoin is no Caesar. And that William; he's a devil. He tempts Baudoin with the thought of a rich new bride. If only my father had finished paying my dowry."

She began to weep, then lashed out at the servant woman who was massaging her indolent bulk. "Not so hard, woman! Do you think I'm a lump of dough? Come, time to wash." She raised herself, and we followed her into the bathing room where more women were waiting to soap and rinse us.

Arda hadn't finished. "It wouldn't be so bad if he would let me go back to mother and father. They're in Constantinople now. Living in reduced circumstances, but still — Constantinople. But no, he insists I enter a monastery. A monastery! Little girl, can you imagine me as a nun?"

"Indeed I cannot, your majesty," I answered truthfully.

"Perhaps it won't be so bad," consoled my mother, "He's not sending you into the desert. You told me he wants you to enter St. Anne's, right here in Jerusalem. You'll still be in the middle of everything and we'll all visit. You've always complained that this palace is more like a barracks than anything else."

But Arda was not to be comforted, and continued complaining until we were dried off and dressed again. By then, it was too late for mother and me to set off for home, so to my glee we spent the night in Jerusalem. That evening at dinner I saw my new hero, Charles, seated on one side of the king, while William was on the other. The king kept passing each one choice tidbits from his own plate. Arda chewed glumly further down the table.

✠

We turned a bend in the river and the towers of Antioch rose before us, pulling me out of my story. I was silent, a bit stunned that I had revealed so much about myself to these strangers. I hadn't thought of Charles for years. Being so close to home had loosened my tongue, I suppose.

"I don't see how you could live here, surrounded by Turks and Saracens, all Muslim," said one of the women. "I'd worry I'd be murdered in my bed."

"Who betrayed you on your way to Antioch, the Muslim Turks or the Christian Greeks?" I asked sharply. That quieted her. I continued, under my breath. "I've seen Christians who pray to the same saints in the same churches do worse to each other than any Muslim."

"Did you see Charles again on that trip? Did you ever talk to him alone?" Eleanor asked. She seemed reluctant to let go of the tale, even though the boatmen were preparing for our landing, and the jetty was just up ahead.

"I saw him one more time while we were still in Jerusalem," I answered. "Arda had said that Charles was pious, so I begged mother to take me to Mass at the Church of the Holy Sepulcher before we left. She was suspicious of this unusual display of piety coming from me, but she complied and I had my reward. Charles was there too, blond hair glowing in the sun that streamed through the windows, making him look like an icon of one of the warrior saints, George maybe, or Sergius and Bacchus. He came over and asked mother if I was well after the previous day's ordeal, then bent his full height down to speak with me. 'No more escapades climbing parapets, Lady Aude,' he said, 'Next time there might not be a rope handy.' And then he was gone."

Eleanor sighed. She was more a romantic girl than a queen at that moment. "Such a true gentleman, he sounds," she said, "And that was it?"

"I didn't see him again for many long years, until I moved to Flanders," I answered. "But how and why I got there is too long a tale for right now."

CHAPTER TWO

Antioch, March 1148

✠

We tumbled out of the barges and I stared at the city rising before us, domes, spires, and towers, and a maze of terraced buildings and gardens climbing the mountain above. I felt a curl of excitement flicker deep inside me for the first time in weeks. In the thirty years since I left this part of the world, Lisbon was the only place that had felt remotely familiar, but this city, with its massive walls and orchards of lemons and oranges through which peeked the remains of ancient temples and crumbling amphitheaters, told me I was getting close to home. Waterfalls crashed down from the heights of the mountain where the citadel stood, and after spying the snaking curve of an aqueduct reaching around the hill, I thought how very nice it would be to have a bath. Soon.

Raymond's guardsmen led us through the great gate of St. George into the walled city. The knights were billeted in mansions through the town, but the king and queen's party made straight for the palace at the town's center. Carried on litters, we passed under colonnaded streets by squat churches, the occasional mosque, and endless dull walls of baked clay. Through the odd door or gate that opened off these unprepossessing exteriors, I glimpsed splendid gardens and tiled porticos supported by marble columns. I kept tight hold on Eve's lead. If she jumped out of the litter now, as she was threatening to do, I'd never find her in the twisting labyrinth of roads and alleys. Sharing the streets with our litters were clean-shaven Franks, merchants from Amalfi, turbaned Turks, capped Jews, bearded Greek and Syriac Christians, and veiled women of all creeds and nations, busy with errands in the crowded shops, bazaars, and roofed marketplaces. It was a typical eastern city. I was home at last, and I felt my shoulders relax as I took in the familiar scents of spices, roasting meat, incense, dust, smoke, and under it all, a hint of sewage.

When we reached the heart of the city, we descended from the litters. We were at one end of a wide forum, an oasis of order amid the tangled streets, with the cathedral on one side and public courts and offices on the other. The seven iron doors of the count's palace loomed above us. Out of the corner of my eye I saw an army of bearers taking baggage through a side door, and I fervently hoped my things were among them.

Raymond took us through the middle door into a massive hall whose roof was carried on the backs of rows of arches patterned in red and white stone. "A quick refreshment?" he asked, and before we could answer, servants appeared out of nowhere bearing cups. Parched and dusty throats soothed by fruits juices cooled with precious mountain snow, we began to return to life.

King Louis, showing more animation than I had yet seen, downed his cup and said, "How wonderful it is to be here in the city of the apostles, the town where for the first time the followers of Jesus took the name 'Christian,' and Saints Paul and Barnabas preached. First of all, we must make a circuit of all the places where their holy feet trod, and give thanks for our safe arrival."

Raymond was aghast. "I thought you might all like a bath first. And then some food."

Oh yes, please, please, bath, bath. I shut my eyes and silently prayed.

Louis was perplexed. "A bath would be very nice. It has been so long. But I don't know. Is that the proper behavior for a crusader?" He looked back for guidance at Odo, his chaplain, stern in the black robes of a monk, and at Thierry de Galeran.

"As Templars, we avoid bathing. It's part of our practice laid down by Abbot Bernard of Clairvaux. But you must do what you think is right," said Thierry. I resolved not to get close enough to smell him. His tone left no doubt about what choice he thought the king should make.

"There can be no real harm to a basin or two of cold water in the king's room," said Odo with the air of one making a great concession.

"Then that's what I'll do, my chaplain. Take us to our rooms and we'll do a quick washing up," said Louis. "But you women should enjoy a nice bath. Gentlewomen cannot be expected to keep such austerities as we men observe."

I was willing to ignore the insult to my sex if it meant I could have a hot bath, but I did wonder how these men would fare if they had to suffer the indignity and pain of childbirth. De Galeran might remain stoic, but I wasn't too sure about the king and I expected Odo would squeal like a snared rabbit.

We were taken to our chambers. I followed the queen and her women to small rooms that ringed an open portico with a garden atrium at the center. The queen was given the biggest chamber, running the whole way along one side of the atrium. We were well lodged here, and I was pleased to see my scruffy belongings were already in one of the rooms. But where was his majesty going to stay? Would they share her room? That was most unusual. I glanced at Raymond and the king, who had come with us.

I was well off the mark. "Your majesty, as you requested, I have arranged rooms for you and your men close to the cathedral. You will be able to have access to the church anytime you wish through a side door. The rooms are in the opposite wing of the palace, so I will send you with my steward," said Raymond.

"Lead on, steward!" said the king, after a quick backward glance at Eleanor.

I stared after the men as they left. While I was glad to see the Templars as far away as possible, it seemed strange that Louis would wish to be so far from his beautiful young wife in the night. Strange, and possibly unwise, I thought, as Raymond began a low-voiced conversation with Eleanor, a conversation that seemed to require him to stand very close to her.

One of the queen's women stood beside me and watched as the king walked away. It was Mabilie, who spoke on the boat, and, as with sharp-tongued Berthe, I vaguely remembered her from the Amazon ride two years before.

"It will be a long walk for the king in the middle of the night," I said.

"A long walk that the king will never make." Mabilie answered drily.

"Oh no? They don't…?"

"No. They don't. Not since Vezelay. The king made a vow that he would remain chaste until he reached Jerusalem. And Odo and his Templar friends have seen to it that he kept his vow. The whole way through Europe and into Turkey, they slept in his tent and we slept with the queen in hers. You saw the man with the eye-patch? That's Thierry de Galeran, the king's bodyguard. He makes sure that no one approaches the king without his consent. And that includes the queen. Day and night."

I gave no sign I already knew de Galeran and concentrated on Mabilie's other revelation. "Not since Vezelay? But that's been two years," I said. No wonder the king and queen were estranged. "Has he no interest? And what about children? The king needs an heir." All they had was a small daughter, I remembered, left at home.

"The king has plenty of interest, but he is torn. He feels he is on a holy mission. You can imagine how the queen feels, a young and beautiful woman ignored by her husband. And she is losing her patience. She thought they'd be partners on this venture, Aquitaine and France, united to protect the Holy Land. But his men keep her out of every decision. That frustrates her as much as the loss of the king's caresses. More perhaps."

So Eleanor had as little reason to admire de Galeran as I did. Another thought struck me. "But what if…" I stopped, thinking I'd better keep my mouth shut, but my eyes involuntarily wandered to where Raymond had taken Eleanor's hand. Starved of attention from her diffident husband, I saw how she opened like a flower under Raymond's bold and appreciative gaze.

Mabilie caught the direction of my stare. "What if she finds someone else who is willing to respond to her charm and give her the attention she needs? Let us hope that doesn't happen. And we must protect her if it does."

This was a complication I had not foreseen when I joined the queen's entourage. Her own uncle. I shuddered. But I could see how the admiration of this confidant, older man might draw her in when her husband offered so little. If her king refused to appreciate her as she deserved, I wagered there would be more than one to take his place.

We couldn't talk more because it was time for our bath. We were escorted there by yet more servants who looked with distaste at our grubby clothing as they undressed us. "These will all have to be burned," the woman in charge of the palace bath house said. I didn't care, as long as they brought us replacements. I brought Eve with me. No one would be glad to see her if she was riddled with fleas, so I asked the bath attendants to wash her with a soap scented with citrus and chrysanthemum to keep the insects away.

Once we had been scrubbed and pummeled and pounded, we lay in the big bath floating in warm water kept hot by a natural spring. It was a chance to relax after a long day that was not yet over. The bath reminded me of the story I had told on the barge of my mother, and how Queen Arda had needed her. It seemed I had acquired my own needy queen, but I was drawn to her in return, something you couldn't say about my mother and Arda. Like those two, Eleanor and I also shared some common background. We both lost our parents at a young age. That was not unusual in our fallen age — mothers succumbed to childbirth and fathers to battle and illness, and a rare child reached adulthood with both parents still living. But most had other family elders to rely on, cousins and uncles and so on. Eleanor had been left at age fifteen mistress of the greatest domain in Christendom with no one to say her nay, and Louis's father as her guardian. Her uncle Raymond was already far away in Antioch when she was left an heiress-orphan. I too had no one of my own to turn to when my parents died.

Our thoughts must have been running in the same direction because Eleanor interrupted my reverie. "I'm thinking about the story you told us this afternoon," she said. "I want to hear more about Charles, and a bath is a good place for a story. Would you continue your tale?"

A bath was a good place for a story because at the very least, it gave us an excuse for sitting in the lovely water doing nothing for a while longer.

✠

Aude's Second Tale: Kingdom of Jerusalem, 1109–1117

I didn't see Charles again before he left the Holy Land, but from time to time word came to al-Lawza of his exploits, and these stories became the stuff of my daydreams under the olive trees. I even begged my mother to arrange a marriage between us, but she only laughed. After William Clito raided the caravan of a wealthy Muslim princess and upset the uneasy peace between Jerusalem and Damascus, he was invited to leave the kingdom and Charles went too, back to Flanders. My heart was broken, but I remained certain my fate was allied with his. In the end I was correct, but I never dreamed that I would go to his land rather than he return to mine.

King Baudoin repudiated Queen Arda and, as threatened, put her in a convent. Arda was inconsolable. Eventually, to my mother's relief and mine, Arda fled to Constantinople and the house of her parents and, I thought, she was no longer our problem.

Mother had new worries. The chickpeas, millet, and wheat we didn't lose to drought and insects fell prey to armed brigands whenever father tried to send them to market. Frustrated, he joined with a group of Frankish lords who all had villas like ours on the road to Jerusalem. They formed a kind of protection service for each other's goods as they went to Jerusalem, and if it had been left at that, mother would have been content. But the ringleader of the men, Bertulf, had bigger ambitions. He wanted everyone travelling this stretch of the Jerusalem road to come under their protection and to pay well for the privilege, and he was willing to use violent means of persuasion. Before long, whenever Father wasn't raiding the Muslims with the king, he was tucked behind a rock on a mountain ridge, waiting with Bertulf and his men to swoop down on a hapless band of Muslim traders, Frankish pilgrims, or Syrian Christian peasants.

"Brigands and thieves, that's all you are. It's not Christian," Mother would protest, patching his wounds when Father arrived home with his men, cheerful and battered. But her hands were deft and gentle as she cleaned and bandaged their injuries.

"Thea, dearest, you know we mostly attack Muslim traders who are lucky to be able to operate in our land at all. They're all enemies of Christ. I'm fulfilling the vow I took back home." Back home? Wasn't this our home, I wondered.

Mother was not impressed. "What of that caravan of wealthy Christian pilgrims you attacked right before Easter? And the two knights on their way to Jerusalem? Were they Muslims? Please, please give it up."

But father was not to be dissuaded. "After all," he said, "We're not the only ones. Every league of the road between Jaffa and Jerusalem is controlled by someone. It's the only way to keep it open. All roads have tolls, and we don't kill anyone unless they refuse to pay."

Mother hated father's new friends and cringed every time she had to entertain Bertulf at dinner. He was big and loud and balding, and I watched his eyes follow her breasts whenever she served the high table of men with the choicest dishes and finest wine we had.

"Nice wife you have there, Guy," he would say loud enough for her to hear, shoving food into his mouth while he spoke. "If I'd gone to Edessa with you lot, I might have found one just as fine for myself. You men had it easy." Me, he never noticed. Even when I left childhood behind, I was too thin and bony to attract attention from anyone. Maybe that's why my dreams of Charles continued as long as they did.

King Baudoin was too poor and too dependent on men like my father to stop their depredations. He would have been lost without the continual stream of Christian knights from abroad who came to Jerusalem to pray each Easter, stayed to fight all summer, and then returned home to their castles and flocks in the autumn, vows fulfilled. After Arda was out of the way, he laid siege to the heart and considerable riches of the dowager countess of Sicily. Despite a summer of eclipses and earthquakes portending doom from their union, she came from Sicily to marry the king in a galley decked in purple and cloth of gold attended by her Arab militia in white robes.

But the portents could not be denied, and this marriage foundered just like Baudoin's previous one. Once the money ran out, he had little use nor time for his bride. He fell deathly ill and, fearing for his immortal soul, he agreed to dismiss his wife and to call Arda back from Constantinople. Once he healed, he sent his new wife packing, though minus the gold, the purple, and the Arab retainers.

The second part was harder. How could he persuade Arda to come back to him? The answer was my mother.

Mother returned one day from a summons to Jerusalem to find father and I nibbling figs in the hall after our midday meal. She ignored my excited greeting and addressed my father.

"As we feared, King Baudoin maintains his exaggerated notion of my influence on his former wife. He wants me to go to Constantinople to fetch Arda and persuade her to return to Jerusalem."

"And you refused? You told him you were needed here?"

"Of course. Then he told me it was a command, not a request, and that he would be very displeased with me, no, with both of us if his command were ignored. And that he could not say what form his very deep displeasure would take."

My father looked defeated. "Then you go to Constantinople, I suppose. I can't go with you. Will you take Aude?"

At this I perked up. Travel on a ship alone with mother all the way to Constantinople? How wonderful! "Yes, mother, do take me! I promise I'll be good. And I can help with Arda."

My mother cut short my pleadings. "Certainly not. You'll fall off the ship and drown or cause all the sailors to mutiny. And I'll have enough to do in Constantinople without tracking your whereabouts."

This was not fair. I wasn't a small girl diving into every sort of mischief any more. My body had recently blossomed (if you could call it that) into womanhood, and I was trying hard to live up to my new adult state. But like any girl in that awful intermediate stage between childhood and marriage, I was prone to grumpy moods and fits of sulks. I fell into one at mother's words. Knowing from experience that changing her mind was impossible, I got up from the table and slammed the door behind me.

I spent most of her last days at home sitting in dark corners feeling sorry for myself, and I was still mopey and silent when we rode to Jaffa to see her off. The grateful king provided her with a princely escort and one of his own ships. We at least had no fear of extortionist bandits as we rode single file to the coast.

Jaffa is a walled citadel on a rocky outcropping overlooking a beach. With no secure harbor, departing crusaders and pilgrims had to brave boardings in small ferry boats, at the mercy of a cruel off-shore wind. The wind was blowing swiftly when we arrived, and the flat-bottomed ferries were waiting.

"Make haste," called the ferry master over the roar of the wind and the waves beating on the shore. "Bad weather moving in. We need to board before it reaches us." He pointed to the sky where black clouds were rolling in from the west, beyond the little ship bobbing in the distance that was to take mother to Constantinople.

Everyone jumped to follow the master's order. I had hoped for a long farewell with Mother crying and wishing she could bring me along. I got a fierce, fast hug and a command to be good and obey Father, and almost before I could respond, Mother was boarding the ferry, bundled skirts in one hand, the other on the arm of the master. She waved a distant goodbye once she sat down, then the oarsmen began rowing with all their strength to escape the pull of waves.

Father and I watched in silence for a few moments as her boat got smaller and smaller.

"She's gone. Shall we go too? It makes me sad to see her so far away." I tugged his arm.

"In a moment. I want to see her reach the ship safely," said my father. For the first time I saw how tight and anxious his face was, eyes fixed on the horizon, as if he could ensure the ferry reached the ship by simple force of his will. I followed his gaze to where mother's boat was straining through the waves. The dark clouds were advancing and the wind and waves picked up. The ferry seemed caught in the onshore wind, no longer making any progress forward, merely struggling to keep the boat heading straight for its destination.

"Are they going to make it, Father? Will they turn around and come back to shore." Maybe I wasn't going to lose my mother that day after all.

"Shhh," he said.

Turning to speak to him, I missed the crucial moment, the instant when a rogue wave, more demanding than the rest, caught the boat broadside, swamping it. I looked back in time to see the boat lurch up, then turtle, spilling out all its passengers.

"Mother! No!" I cried, and made as if to charge forward into the surf to rescue her myself.

Father caught me and held me tight. "Take her!" he barked at one of the attendants, who sprang into action. I found myself in the rough arms of a stranger, as my father and another man ran to a small rowboat abandoned on the shore. They flipped it over and dragged it down to the water. But it was no use. The wind was now so strong that they could make no headway.

My eyes were fixed on the horizon where mother's boat had gone down. Was that an arm I could see, a head? Other, sharper eyes shared this fruitless vigil. After what seemed an age, another man on the shore called to my father in the boat. "Sieur, it is no use. I can see nothing where the ferry was. You'll drown too, and for no purpose." The rowboat was still pathetically close to the shore and both men were clearly already exhausted. They laid their oars down and soon simply drifted in to shore.

We remained standing there on the shore for some time, watching as the dark clouds swallowed the distant ship until we could no longer see it, hoping for I don't know what to drift in on the punishing waves. Nothing came. It started to rain, and finally we turned away.

And that was it. Arda had taken my mother away from me once more, this time for good. That night, when the clouds had cleared enough to see it, the moon turned blood red before our eyes, and then pitch black. But I didn't need the eclipse to know that my world had ended.

When you're an adult, you know how to deal with grief. You pray or light a candle or weep with a friend or curse God. But at scarce fourteen, I didn't know what to do. I slammed doors, wept when someone said the mildest word of reproof, flirted with the Syrians who tended our vines, and sneaked extra wine when father was home for dinner. Which was rare enough. It happened so long ago. I'm now a decade older than my mother was when she drowned. I go for weeks and months without thinking about it at all, but then suddenly I will hear a tune she loved or someone will use a turn of phrase and I am taken right back. I'm a young girl standing on the shore, and she is gone forever.

CHAPTER THREE

Antioch, April 1148

✠

My mother remained in my mind. Raymond sent us dresses from the region to replace the tattered finery of Eleanor and her women. Though the others oohed and ahhed over their unfamiliar beauty, to me they were just elaborate court versions of the clothing Mother wore every day. I felt her beside me when I slipped the close-fitting tunic over my head, admiring its embroidered hem and sleeves. My mother used to embroider her own garments in the hall of al-Lawza on a winter's day. She tried to teach me her stitches but I refused to learn and only picked it up much later. I pulled the silk brocade gown over the tunic, belted it, and looked at myself in the polished silver mirror hanging in my room. I fancied my mother stared back at me. As I admired myself, another face appeared over my shoulder in the mirror. I turned quickly. It was Eleanor.

We hadn't spoken since my story in the bath. After my tale was done, the women cooed condolences, reminding me why I never liked to speak of my mother's death. Only Eleanor had said nothing, her face frozen in pain, and she left quickly.

"Aude," she said now, her face still carrying that pain. "Your mother. Mine too. She drowned crossing the Gironde with my little brother. I wasn't there. I was eight."

We stared at each other, not queen to lady, but woman to woman, sharing a grief we could not put into words, a grief we did not need to put into words because we knew the other understood. Moved, I knelt before her and held my hands out, raised and joined as if in prayer. She clasped them in hers, giving and receiving homage, as a tear rolled down her cheek.

At dinner that night in our fine dresses, we met Raymond's wife, Constance, who had brought him the principality of Antioch. Part Armenian, Frank, and Norman, in her the Norman won out and she was a yellow-haired pale-faced woman with a similarly diluted personality. While we ate our grilled fish gilded with saffron, and rosemary scented roast goat stuffed with leeks, onions, and garlic, one of the men from our barge that afternoon sang, accompanied by the one who had been repairing his viol.

"Ben tenc lo Seigneur per verai, per q'ieu veirai l'amor de loing," he sang. It was in Occitan, so I couldn't understand more than a word here or there, but I knew "amor" meant "love."

I had realized by this time that Eleanor's women were not the homogeneous group they first appeared. Some were Occitan-speakers from her native Aquitaine, while the rest were French. Moreover, they separated themselves along those lines and gathered mostly with their own kind. I whispered to my neighbor, one of those from Aquitaine named Ermine, "I am surprised the king and his Templars permit us to do something so frivolous as listen to a commoner sing love songs at table."

"It's not a love song, at least not one for a flesh and blood woman," Ermine whispered back. She was a plain girl with a serious face. "Louis and his priests forbade such songs before we departed France. We feared we'd have no music at all, until our troubadours decided to sing about the Holy Land itself as a woman, distant and beautiful. Listen to him sing of how he wants to dress as a pilgrim with staff and cape to go meet her. And he's no commoner. That is Jaufré Rudel, the lord of Blaye. In the south, lords are not ashamed to make music. Why, Eleanor's own grandfather was one of the most famous troubadours ever."

By this point, Rudel's companion, the man on the viol, had taken over the singing duties. One of his lines caused a round of cheers to go up around the table.

"Is he singing about the crusade too?" I asked Ermine.

"Of course. First he complained about all the false lovers and adulterers in the world, and then he said, 'Now a man may cleanse and purify himself of great blame, and if he is worthy, he may go to Edessa.' When he got to the line about Edessa, we all cheered. Unlike Jaufré, he is a commoner. No one knows anything about his background, but he calls himself Cercamon, the 'man who travels the world.' He was in Eleanor's father's service, and now he is in hers."

It wasn't the musicians but rather Eleanor's vivacity that captivated the high table. No one would ever know she had been in tears in my chamber shortly before, as she radiated youth and beauty, entrancing old men and young with her wit. Her high laugh and Raymond's answering banter could be heard above the merriment in the hall the whole evening. Well, almost the whole evening. Louis nearly ended the party single-handedly with one revelation.

"We have no money left at all," Louis said, responding to Raymond's delicately worded inquiry about the king's resources and how soon he could hire mercenaries and equip an army to retake Edessa. "Isn't that right, Thierry?"

"Yes, your majesty. We have no specie whatsoever. We spent our last penny on the ships to get here," answered Thierry de Galeran.

"We're like ordinary pilgrims—nothing but the clothes on our backs, relying for aid on Christians like yourself, Raymond," Louis said with relish.

"But surely…this is a military expedition?" Raymond responded helplessly, looking to the Templars for assistance. They might claim holiness, but their first task was to fight Muslims. He knew they would have little time for Louis's I'm-a-simple-pilgrim nonsense.

"Er, yes, money in hand has become a problem, but it can be solved with relative ease," said the second Templar, Evrard of Barres. "I have spoken to my brethren at the Temple in Antioch, and I plan to depart tomorrow for the house of the Templars in Acre to advance money on the king's behalf. We can loan Louis more than enough for him to continue his crusade."

Yes, I thought, but if Louis is funded by the Templars and in debt to the Templars, will he not be required to fight Templar battles and pursue Templar goals? What would become of the plan to free

Edessa, not to speak of what was left of the king's independence? Eleanor's worried expression suggested similar thoughts were running through her mind.

Raymond kept us busy over the next weeks, arranging one activity after another while we waited for Louis's money to arrive. One afternoon, we rode all over the slopes of the mountain south of Antioch, tracking the gazelles that roamed there, under the watch of the Templars who were refortifying the castle on its slopes. On another, we hunted with falcons for fishy-tasting crane on the buggy bank of the river that snaked through the city. And every day, Eleanor and Raymond were always side by side, laughing and trying to outdo each other. While we hunted, Louis and his companions visited religious shrines, beginning with the notable churches in Antioch and branching out to the monasteries and hermitages spread throughout the area.

Spring sun, regular food, and Raymond's solicitous care wrought their magic on Eleanor's women too, who began to recover from their Turkish ordeal. I learned the names of the ones I did not know, slowly finding out their stories, until they sorted themselves in my mind. They were not all equally devoted to Eleanor. Some of the southern women, like Mabilie, had been in Eleanor's service since her childhood and would lie down in front of a mad bull for her. But others, wives of Louis's vassals rather than of her own, blamed her for the disasters of Turkey. The weeping girl on the barge was Marie, and her husband was one of the many who had perished in the Turkish hills. As time softened the memories of the hardship that once united them, the fractures between the two groups, the Occitans and the French, began to show. They were not impolite or hostile to each other, but certain women always preferred to sit and sew, or gossip in the solar with certain women and not with others. Since I had no allegiance to either side, I tried to bridge the two cliques. But it is harder to shift a group of women who don't want another into their circle than it is to find an honest relic-seller.

A few passions united them. They all shared Eleanor's willingness to play-act at the drop of a hat, and they despised Louis's humorless chaplain, Odo, and his two Templar minders who attempted to impose disciplines of dress and austerities of behavior on everyone in the king's army. One afternoon, we returned to our quarters after hearing Odo preach a long sermon condemning crusaders who wore luxurious clothing and hunted with dogs and birds. Standing there in the silken finery given to us by her uncle, we knew his words were directed at Eleanor and the rest of us, and we were in a mutinous mood.

"Do Odo, Eleanor," said one of the women. "It always makes me laugh so when you imitate him."

This must have been a well-known trick of hers that I hadn't yet experienced. The others echoed in chorus the pleas of the first woman.

"Very well," said Eleanor, "And Alice must play my beloved husband again." This was a woman who in build and coloring was strikingly like the king. "But I don't think we can ask Marie to reprise her role as Thierry de Galeran," she said kindly as the recent widow looked relieved. Indeed it was hard to imagine the grieving woman mocking anyone.

"What about Aude?" someone said. "Maybe she could play Thierry."

I was game for that. I didn't like the man and I would enjoy mocking him. "What do I have to do?"

"Rig up some sort of costume. The three of us will discuss a few ideas, then we'll come out and play our roles," said Eleanor.

It was easy to transform ourselves into character. A black cassock turned Eleanor into the monk-chaplain, Odo and a gilt paper crown made Alice a king. All I needed was an eyepatch and a white, shapeless tunic with a prominent red cross on the front, and we were ready to perform.

We had the perfect audience, eager to be entertained and ready to laugh at the feeblest attempt at humor.

"Dear Odo," began Louis-Alice, "I must ask your advice. The queen wants to give a ball. She says it will be fun and will cheer everyone up. Her women long to dance and wear pretty dresses."

"Faugh! Dancing is sinful. Pretty dresses are not worthy of good crusaders," said Eleanor in a remarkably good imitation of Odo's sermon of earlier that day. "Instead of coming with us on our sacred mission to sit on our bottoms in Antioch eating Raymond's food, the women should have stayed home and done…whatever it is that women do. Spinning and weaving. The queen has too many balls as it is."

"Please Odo, do let us give the girls some fun. The French army hasn't had any balls in who knows how long." pleaded the king.

It was a silly double entendre, but our audience laughed anyway, enjoying the praise of Eleanor's virility at the expense of the troops. I did notice the French women were not laughing as loud as the Occitan women at the insult to the masculinity of their husbands and cousins.

It was my turn. "Thierry" crashed into the conversation.

"What's all this I hear about balls?" I thundered in his persona. "We don't need balls. What use does anyone have for balls? I haven't had any in years."

This line sent the laughing women into paroxysms of mirth, though I didn't think it was that funny. The dour French women held their sides and the Occitans wept with hilarity. Even sad Marie giggled, covering her mouth with a ladylike hand. I decided to play it up a little further.

"I have none of my own, which is why I keep a tight grip on yours, Louis," I said. "I don't have much use for them, but when I do, yours will be ready."

But the women stopped laughing. Had I gone too far? They were not even listening to me, but were nudging each other and looking beyond my left shoulder. I turned, and saw Thierry de Galeran himself standing in the doorway. We gazed at each other, eyepatch to eyepatch. Finally, he broke the spell.

"I am sent to tell you, your majesty, that the king, your husband would appreciate your company in the chapel." Without waiting for a reply, he turned and left.

"Oh you've done it now," said Berthe with ill-concealed glee. "You've created an enemy for life there. I can't believe you talked about de Galeran's balls, and he heard every word. I saw him. That was going too far." The nods and looks on her companions' faces showed they agreed with her.

I was confused. "Everyone was doing it. You all laughed. I can see why he'd be offended, but how was what I said was so much worse than Eleanor and Alice's jokes?" I asked.

Eleanor pulled the black cassock over her head, transforming herself from chaplain to queen. "Bother de Galeran. Louis doesn't want me in the chapel with him. It distracts him from his prayers. De Galeran is trying to keep me under his eye, and wants an excuse to spy on us. I'm not going. Aude, de Galeran's balls are an especially sensitive subject with him."

A snigger greeted her words.

"But why?" I asked. "I know they all love their precious jewels more than their own lives, but why must we be so careful with Thierry's? As a Templar sworn to chastity, it's not as if he uses them."

"You truly don't know?" Berthe said pityingly. "Thierry came to the kingdom of Jerusalem as a young man looking for adventure, and he joined the fledgling Templar order soon after it was created."

This much of Thierry's past I did know, but I gave no sign.

Berthe continued, "Thierry was an integral member of the new order, fighting in all its major battles. He lost his eye and was captured by the Muslims when the Christian armies failed to take Damascus. They sold him into slavery. He eventually escaped and made his way back to France, but before that, as part of his punishment, his captors castrated him. Thierry de Galeran is a eunuch."

A eunuch. I smiled grimly. Death was too good for him, but this punishment could serve as partial payment for the wrongs he did my family.

Eleanor called me away from my vengeful thoughts. "Aude, would you come back to my room and help fix my hair? Pulling that cassock off turned it into a rat's nest."

I left the others and followed her to her quarters to begin the painstaking task of untwisting, combing, then rebraiding her long hair. While I worked, she surprised me with a question.

"Why do you dislike Thierry de Galeran so?" she asked. "You were funny in the play, but I could see there was real bile behind your words."

I was wary as I finished the first braid. "Why is my lady queen interested in that."

"I hate him," she said simply. "Since the day I married Louis, he has made trouble between us. He wants Louis to take all Aquitaine's power, all its riches, for France."

Her candor goaded me to tell the truth. "The Templars killed my father," I said. "And Thierry wielded the fatal blow."

"Tell me," Eleanor said.

✠

Aude's Third Tale: Kingdom of Jerusalem, 1118

After my mother died, Father and I avoided each other as much as possible, and he spent most of his days and many of his nights with Bertulf, taking ever greater risks. Since I never knew whether he would snap at me or stroke my hair and weep, I was relieved to see him go.

When he was gone, I would spend the day exploring mother's heavy wooden chest, all that was left of her. I tried on her dresses and jewelry, and inhaled what was left of the scent of her hair on the veils that wrapped her head. One day, I saw someone else had been in the chest, because mother's headscarves, left in a tangle by me, were now folded into neat oblongs, each concealing something wrapped inside. I put on my favorite of her earrings. They dangled and were heavy, and I liked their feel on my neck. Then I picked up the biggest of the mysterious oblongs. From its shape and weight, I guessed that the veil enclosed one of my mother's icons. They had hung in the dusty little room we used as a chapel, where every stray Armenian priest that passed by our villa was invited to pray. We were off the main road, so these visits were rare, but each time she got lucky, the chapel was opened, candles were lit and we stood in a fog of incense as a black-draped man repeated words I barely understood. The icons lined the wall above our crucifix, John the Forerunner, Sergius and Bacchus, George, Grigor Lusavorich, and the biggest and most important of all, the one I was holding in my arms, the Virgin Hodegetria, Mary holding the Christ child in her arm. I hadn't gone near the chapel since her death. Father must have removed them without telling me.

My hands shook as I withdrew the golden icon from the dull black folds of cloth. Mary's face was just coming visible when a noise behind me made me start.

"What are you doing in that chest!? Who gave you leave for that!?"

Father was back early. "How dare you touch her things and wear her earrings?" He strode over and reached up to rip the piece of jewelry from my ear, almost tearing the lobe right through. My hands reached up instinctively to protect myself and the icon fell, making a sharp crack on the stone floor.

"Mother of God, no!" I cried, pain in my throbbing ear forgotten. We both dropped to the floor, racing to draw the wood from its covering. The icon was split in two pieces, right down the middle. Mary's sweet eyes looked down at emptiness now, and the Christ child, precociously adult, reached up to grasp nothing.

"Her icon," I said, starting to weep, soft at first and then sobbing more and more wildly. My father said nothing for a moment, and then he too began to cry, silent tears running down his cheeks. We both sat there on the floor weeping, not touching.

Finally he said, "This is no good. You have to go. I'm no use to you here, no use to myself, no use to anyone any more. You need to be married and I don't know how to go about it. She would have found you a fine match. It is a pity Bertulf has sworn never to marry again. That would keep you close by."

Bertulf? That shocked me out of my reverie. And wasn't I going to marry Charles some day? For the first time I had a glimmer that my fine dreams for my future might not turn out as I hoped. "Bertulf is far too old, father," was all I said. And it was true; he was even older than father.

But my father gave no sign he had heard me, and continued, "We'll go to Jerusalem and see who is available. We can arrange the contract now and you can be married at court at Easter, after the spring campaign to Egypt."

By Easter? That was scarcely six weeks away. But there was no gainsaying my father who showed an energy and determination I hadn't seen since mother's death. Even before the gash on my ear was healed, I found myself heading for Jerusalem with father, all my prettiest dresses loaded on a mule that followed our horses. Bertulf, who liked to show his face at court from time to time, came too.

I stayed with the women in the Armenian quarter in Jerusalem. Some were distant cousins and aunts, and all remembered my mother. They petted me, fed me, and compared my features to distant and long-dead relatives, none of whom I knew, then ignored me and went back to gossiping over mint tea and sweets. I listened with only half my attention and concentrated on the sweets. The talk was all about who would rule Jerusalem once King Baudoin was gone.

"Looks like we might have another Armenian queen before too long."

"What, do you mean Morfia?"

"Exactly. Her husband is thought by most to be next in line for the kingdom of Jerusalem. And with Baudoin ill and childless, our Morfia could be queen one day. Maybe soon, if this Egyptian campaign has an unhappy outcome."

"Let's hope Morfia fares better than the last one. Though I hear Arda is blissfully content in Constantinople now. I don't know what the king is thinking, traipsing through marshes and deserts on a fool's errand to Egypt. We need protection here. My own brothers were attacked in broad daylight on the Jaffa road."

When I was finally summoned to court by my father, I saw the truth of what the women had said. The king was ill. His face was grey, his hair lank under the crown, and all his robes couldn't hide the fact that his hands were shaking as if with fever. But most attention was on a group of eight men, easily recognizable because they were always found together and because each wore a long white cape emblazoned with a large red cross. Their leader, Hugh de Payens, told people that they were monks and knights, vowed to celibacy, common life, and the defense of Jerusalem.

"Balls," Bertulf scoffed. "Monk or knight. You can't be both. Doesn't make sense."

The audience was a dull affair, though a group of desert sheiks, heads covered and resplendent in silks and silver, were briefly of interest. Bored by the king before he was finished with the sheiks, my eyes wandered over the assembled knights, wondering which one might be my future husband. Not the skinny one with spots, I hoped. My speculations were interrupted when the eight mysterious white-robed men were summoned before the king.

"This bodes ill, you'll see," said Bertulf, who was standing behind me and father.

"Sir Hugh de Payens," the king called and their leader came to the front of the group and bowed deeply. Baudoin continued, "We thank God for your presence and that of your sworn companions in the Holy Land. We have considered your request for aid and offer of service. We grant your request to be allowed to freely patrol the road between Jerusalem and Jaffa to protect the pilgrims, merchants, and travelers and to apprehend the brigands and bandits that have made that road so unsafe. Furthermore we grant you a residence in our palace here on the Temple mount, and you may use the Temple of the Lord for your own services. You will henceforth be known as the Templar knights, and all those who wish to join your enterprise may swear your oath and be bound to your rule."

The hall was abuzz at this news. The king was creating a new religious order unlike any the world had known. Were they knights who were monks, or the other way around? "It's about time. That road is a disgrace in a Christian kingdom," people whispered to each other when the king had finished. As you can imagine, Bertulf and my father's reaction was quite different.

"What a disaster for us. Well, that's the end of our business," said my father, "Time to go back to raising sheep and growing chickpeas."

"Never!" said Bertulf. "Those pasty monkish knights won't get the better of us. We'll clear them out in a week."

Father gave up on the idea of a marriage for me, and we left Jerusalem for al-Lawza the same day the king and his armed host set out for Egypt. Over the next few weeks Bertulf and my father bickered over how to face the Templar threat. Bertulf argued for a quick strike against the Templars, but father worried we didn't have enough men, because several had left our service to follow the king to Egypt. Then bad news came from the Egypt expedition. The king was said to be mortally ill.

"Now is the time to strike," said Bertulf, who came to al-Lawza to persuade my father into action. "With the king out of commission, we can wipe out those white-cloaked boys with one blow. If King Baudoin recovers, who knows what further powers he'll give the Templars? Even if he dies, they'll be able to draw recruits from his army. They will only grow stronger, unless we do something."

Bertulf was right about that. Many were attracted to a life in which they could keep the worldly benefits of knighthood while attaining the spiritual rewards of monasticism. Father assented at last, and they set out, while I grumped around in my usual way, lonely and bored at al-Lawza. I retreated into my old daydreams of Charles of Denmark, composing love songs in my head that expressed my sentiments, using the popular tunes of the day and changing the lyrics. Maybe he would return to the Holy Land one day. Maybe if King Baudoin died, they would invite him to become king of Jerusalem. I conveniently ignored the local claimants to the throne.

I fell asleep to these dreams, bundled up against the chill April night, only to be woken by pounding at the gate not long before dawn. Father's back, I thought drowsily. Do I need to go down, or can I pretend I slept through it and greet him in the morning? I pulled the blankets over my head and tried to block out the sounds of horses snorting and men shouting in the courtyard. But heavy feet stamped up the stone steps the led to the second level where I was sleeping, and a fist pounded on my own wooden door.

"Set, set!" a voice pierced through my slumber. "Lady, lady!" It was Ibrahim, one of our Syrian servants. "Please come down right away. Fast, fast!"

There was no hope for it. "Yes, yes," I answered and pulled myself from my bed, shuffling around to find my shoes and wrapping myself in a thick cloak. I met him at the door. He held a lit torch and his face looked fearsome in its flickering light. "What's wrong?"

"Come! Very bad," he said and headed down the stairs in front of me. Oh dear. Was father injured again? He was getting too old for this.

The keening wails of women rose from the courtyard, an ululation of despair. More torches outside revealed a knot of men and horses at the center of the courtyard, surrounding a wooden cart. I went over to them.

"What's wrong?" I asked. Bertulf's massive bulk turned to me, blocking my view of the cart. A torch was in his hand, and his face looked grim and tight, far from his usual hearty bluster.

"Aude, your father—"

"What's wrong? Did he stop another arrow? It's time he learned to leave this to the younger men." I tried to push past Bertulf, who resisted me briefly before giving way.

I looked into the cart. Bertulf put an arm around me, gentle on my shoulder. I stared at my father's face, unearthly in the flickering light.

"Aude, he's dead. I'm sorry. We did everything we could, but it was no use."

"No! Ibrahim, fetch water. Boiling water. And cloths. He can't be dead." With shaking fingers, I moved to loosen his jerkin, which was covered in blood. That must be the site of the injury. As it came way, slowly under my fumbling fingers, I kept thinking if only mother were here, she'd heal him, if only mother were here.

Bertulf tried to stop me. "It's no sight for a lady," he said, but I pushed him, violently knocking him away. I got the jerkin open, and saw the massive sword slash through his abdomen. What a fool I was. Of course he was dead. I turned away, retching. When I stopped, Bertulf folded me into a strong embrace and let me weep.

Ibrahim knew his master was dead but brought the cloths I had demanded anyway, his wife following with a basin of hot water. I drew away from Bertulf and wiped my eyes once on my cloak, staining it with the blood on my hands. I pulled together whatever internal strength and fortitude I had managed to develop in my brief, shallow, and selfish life. "We must take him to the hall, to lie in state. I will dress him — his body — and prepare it for burial." I didn't want to, but I'd seen mother do it before, for our servants and for some of father's men who, like him, had been unlucky. I knew how it was done. And there was no one else. By the time I was done, the basin of water was dark with dirt and blood. Then, beginning at his feet, I wound a long cloth all the way around his body up to his head. The men helped by shifting and lifting him when needed.

All this time, Bertulf paced like a caged beast. When I finally covered over my father's face and sewed him entire into his long cloak for a shroud, he stopped his trek round and round the hall and gave an order. "Everyone, out. Aude and I will keep vigil. Go, the rest of you and get a bite to eat and some sleep." I was seated by this point, visibly shaking despite the warmth of my cloak. "And one of you bring a warm cup of spiced wine for Aude. Plenty of sugar."

I continued to shiver, my fingers and feet numb, pulling my cloak tighter around me. Bertulf sat beside me and did not speak, jogging his knee up and down, and mopping sweat from his forehead with his sleeve. The first fingers of dawn penetrated the hall. A servant entered bearing a large cup with steam rising from it. Bertulf took it and handed it to me, dismissing the servant. "Drink this. It will do you good."

I was in no mood for it, but my will was broken by the events of the evening so I sipped obediently. The hot, sweet wine warmed me from the inside and slowly I stopped shivering. Once I was restored, Bertulf spoke.

"Aude we are in big trouble."

"My father—," I said, and started to cry.

"Don't cry Aude, not now. We have to plan. It is far worse than your father's death."

I mopped my eyes with my sleeve, and tried to listen.

"We were attacked by those Templars, ten or fifteen of them. It was as if they knew where to find us. They did know where to find us. You remember Thierry, your father's man?"

I nodded. "Yes," I answered Bertulf, "He was among those who recently left father's service to follow King Baudoin to Egypt."

"Thierry didn't go to Egypt. He joined the Templars and then betrayed us. He showed them our lookout spot over the Jaffa road and also our two getaway paths. They attacked us from one of them, and when we tried to retreat down the other, we found we were ambushed. We managed to get your father away, but he died on the road."

Eleanor interrupted me. "So, this Thierry, the one who served then betrayed your father, is the same one who plagues me so today," she said meditatively.

I nodded. "Yes. Thierry de Galeran started his career in the Holy Land as one of my father's knights. I remember him well. In those days, he was eager to please, skinny with sandy hair and a big adam's apple. Seemed to adore my father."

"No wonder you hate him so," replied Eleanor. "Go on. What happened next?" and I picked up my story.

"Why would Thierry betray us" I asked Bertulf.

"Who knows?" Bertulf raked his fingers through his sparse hair. "Newfound religious zeal? Eagerness to curry favor with his new lords by netting them a big prize? I tried to strike back, but he fled too quickly."

"Killing him would have been good revenge, but it wouldn't bring father back to life," I said.

"Aude, revenge is not the point. Don't you see?" Bertulf got up and started pacing again. "Thierry knows who we are and where we live. The Templars don't need to attack again, all they need is to tell the next king, and he'll dispossess us. Our fiefs are held from the king. It will be easy for him to get rid of you. Without your father, all he needs to say is that your fief is too vulnerable to be held by an unmarried girl and give it to someone else."

"Wait—Bertulf, you said 'the next king.' What did you mean?"

"King Baudoin is dead. They're bringing him back to Jerusalem. They'll arrive on Palm Sunday, which is tomorrow, and then they'll bury him at Easter in the Church of the Holy Sepulcher. But that's good for us. The disorder and confusion in the kingdom will allow us to get away. No one will be able to move against us until a new king is chosen."

"What do I do?" I asked.

Bertulf stopped pacing and sat again. He took my hand in his fat paw. "We get that old Syrian priest in your village to bury your father. The words are funny, but it all means the same thing. Then, we get him to bless our marriage. And we're off. We sell what we can, here and on my estate, then we pack and we're gone before anyone in Jerusalem is the wiser. Back to Europe. To Gistel, in Flanders, where I am from.

"Marriage? To you? Never!" I pulled my hand away from his.

"What, then? Stay here alone, daughter of a dispossessed brigand? No, Aude, marriage to me is your only choice. Funny, before I came here, I swore I'd never marry again," he ruminated. "And now I find myself with a young heiress. What better sign that my sins have been forgiven by this pilgrimage, and it is time to return to Flanders?"

Under his anxiety and real grief for my father, I could tell Bertulf was excited at the prospect of marrying me and returning to his far-away home, and it sickened me. But I was tired, slayed by sadness, fearful, scarce fifteen and feeling very alone, no mother, no father, no family, and now the king was dead, no lord. Bertulf was taking charge. The path of least resistance was to let him continue.

The first night was the worst. Bertulf's men roused the village priest out of bed and brought him up to the villa, still bleary with sleep. He blessed our marriage with mumbled words and much crossing, while standing over my father's body, then accompanied the funeral procession down to the little village cemetery where peasants had been buried for centuries. I stood, dazed, as they placed my father into a hastily dug grave and tossed the clods back down onto him. The women howled, scratching their faces and rending their clothing. It was their custom. I'd seen them do the same for old village misers everyone had hated, but I envied their easy display of grief and wished I could join in. But I could not even cry. The wine had worn off, and numbness was settling back in.

Finally the last of the earth was mounded over the grave and a cairn of stones was raised over it to stop wild dogs from digging up the fresh body. We returned to the villa, which Bertulf's men had sacked in our absence. No, not sacked. Bertulf had very sensibly told them to collect everything moveable of value to bring with us. But it was a shock to see the villa turned upside down, cooking pots, weapons, bed hangings, wineskins, and flasks of olive oil, all gathered in the courtyard, waiting to be loaded on carts. And my mother's chest. The few big pieces of furniture—the beds, the big table—would have to stay. I knew the whole villa would be stripped clean the moment we left it. Already I could see a servant with a large sheep's milk cheese, sneaking out the gate.

Bertulf's men packed us in no time, and we went to his own villa nearby, to strip it in the same way. Once there, Bertulf made an announcement.

"I don't want to give the new king any chance to catch up with us. We leave at dusk and travel by night to the coast. Good thing there is a moon tonight. So, pack up, then get some rest. Aude and I will be in my chamber, and we are not to be disturbed."

The men sniggered in an unpleasant way and set to work. Bertulf took my hand in his and led me to his room. I knew what this was about. One part of me registered that the room smelled stale and rank, and the bed coverings had not been cleaned in a very long time. Maybe never.

"Take off your clothes and get into bed," he said, beginning to strip. I knew better than to resist. With trembling fingers, I pulled off my overdress and shoes, got into the bed and took off my shift. It didn't take long for Bertulf to join me. I lay on my back, still as could be and he began to paw me, gentle at first, with hot, moist hands, and then more insistent, hands between my legs prying them open, and then the big bulk of him onto of me, crushing me, pushing himself inside me, and oh, the pain, and for a moment I thought it wouldn't work, that I was made wrong, but with a tear and a thrust there he was inside of me and it was all over. He rolled off and said, triumphant, "You're the right woman for me. You don't unman me like my first wife did, that bitch." And with that, he fell straight asleep, snoring loudly, arms and legs splayed, so I had scarce room on the bed.

I huddled in one corner, pulling a cover over me for comfort, trying to forget the soreness and stickyness between my legs, the shame I felt at the violation of my body by this gross man. No wonder the priests and nuns spoke against this, and urged women to keep chaste.

I slept at last, fitfully, with sad, disconnected dreams of loss, until Bertulf shook me awake. He was already dressed. I was disoriented, dim light coming into a strange room.

"Is it dawn?" I asked, groggy.

"No, dusk. I told you we'd journey by night. Make haste." He tossed me my shift, and I put it on and then my dress, soiled and crumpled from the previous day and from their night on Bertulf's filthy floor. I had fresh clothing packed somewhere, but who knew when I'd have the chance to change? Grubby and sore, I said good-bye to the land of my youth.

✠

"My father died on the road while making a pilgrimage to Santiago de Compostela," said Eleanor, "I never saw him again. They told me it was food poisoning. In any case, he left me in the custody of my husband Louis's father, who married me off right away to his son. I was fifteen just like you. But I had no choice. I think you did have a choice."

I was almost finished with my braiding. "You're right," I admitted. "I know now that marrying Bertulf was not my only option. I should have travelled to Jerusalem and found shelter in the Armenian community. I could have mourned the old King Baudoin with them when his funeral cortege processed through the streets on Palm Sunday. I would have been there alongside them to welcome the new king, who was indeed Morfia's husband, as the Armenians had predicted. If I threw myself upon his mercy, in the exuberance of his coronation, and with the intercession of his Armenian queen, he surely would have granted me amnesty. The new king would have welcomed the chance to use my body and my lands to reward some young knight into fighting for him. But by that time, Bertulf and I were already long gone and floating on the high seas."

She turned to face me, "So why did you do it? Why fall in with Bertulf's wishes so easily?"

This was a question I had asked myself often over the years when times were difficult and I longed for the sun and warmth of my childhood. "I could claim my youth, Eleanor, or my grief, and perhaps either of those is enough. But there was another reason I fell in so meekly with Bertulf's plans, a vain, foolish reason that had nothing to do with my vulnerability at that moment. It certainly wasn't because of any secret affection for Bertulf. I knew as much about the marriage bed as any girl my age, and putting up with the sweaty fumblings of a man older than my father was no part of my maidenly dreams. No, it was because he planned to return to

Flanders. I still hadn't forgotten Charles, and I knew that Flanders was where he had come from, and that to the Flemish court he had returned. Deep in my heart, I believed this was destiny, that God was sending me to Flanders to be with Charles, to rescue me. I had been waiting for him to return to the Holy Land for so many years, but if he wouldn't come to me, I would go to him."

CHAPTER FOUR

Antioch, April–May 1148

✠

While Eleanor was being pursued by her uncle in the gardens of Antioch and the hunting grounds of its hinterland, her husband, the king, grew increasingly more fretful. At first he was content to pass his days visiting the holy people and places of Antioch while he waited for funds to come from the Templars in Acre and for the remnants of the French army to make their way on foot from Turkey. But when news arrived of other crusaders on the move and prepared to fight, Louis grew restless.

King Conrad of the Romans and the Germans had avoided the troubles that beset Louis and Eleanor in Turkey by staying in Constantinople. First, word came that he was on the move, sailing for the Holy Land, and later that he had arrived in Acre during Easter week.

"Why are we spending Eastertide at Antioch, when we could be celebrating Christ's miraculous resurrection in the very city where it took place?" Louis was heard to mutter.

"Never mind," said Eleanor at the dinner table when these revelations about Conrad surfaced in a rare moment of public speech with her husband. There were no private moments. "He'll have to turn north to Antioch anyway, since you're both sworn to help recover Edessa and this is the only place the Christian armies can muster. Once we've retaken Edessa, we will all go to Jerusalem together, and you and King Conrad can enter the holy city for the first time as heroes."

She painted a lovely picture of grateful citizens of Jerusalem waving palm branches as the two kings entered the city, a second Palm Sunday, but we soon heard that Conrad had turned south for

Jerusalem, not north for Antioch. Thierry de Galeran told us smugly that Conrad had taken up residence with the Templars in Jerusalem.

The Templars had taken over the palace on the Temple mount where Queen Arda had once lived and I had my first encounter with Charles. I fancied them enjoying Arda's fussy furnishings and eating her sweets, but I suppose her dusty luxury had been cleaned out long ago in the name of austerity and simplicity.

Thierry continued, "Now Conrad is engaged in pilgrimage while he waits for the French army to travel south to join him so both of you can sally forth in battle defending Christ's name and homeland."

"But we're not going south yet, are we?" Eleanor looked from face to face. "The Germans have to come north, to Antioch, to help us retake Edessa." Louis and his French allies stared back impassively, unwilling to discuss military matters with her. This was the first sign to Eleanor that the crusade, planned to recover Edessa—and to secure her uncle's principality—would have its target diverted.

Indeed, a campaign against Edessa seemed pointless, even to me. Its whole Armenian population had been slaughtered and the city was almost empty. Even if it could be retaken, without the walls the Turks had destroyed, it couldn't be defended. Raymond himself had begun to promote an attack on nearby Aleppo rather than an assault on Edessa.

But in truth, I cared little where the crusaders battled, as long as it didn't interfere with my own plans, and I had small curiosity about the doings of kings. I still retained the illusion of my independence then, that I could leave Eleanor's side at any time, and the only reason I remained was for the potential help she could give me, if I served her well. Once I plucked up the courage to ask her for my great favor.

And what was my plan, the favor I sought from a grateful queen? I wanted al-Lawza back, of course, the home of my youth. I dreamed of returning there since the day I left with Bertulf, a dream that gained the solidity of carved stone the day I privately took up the cross and swore an oath to return to Jerusalem, some two decades before the king and queen had made their own public vow.

Al-Lawza was mine by right, and it had been since the day my father died. Daughters could inherit from their fathers in the kingdom of Jerusalem, so long as they could supply the military service that went along with the fief. I could not fight myself, but I could hire knights. But I had been gone so many years, and the fief had long reverted to the Crown. To the best of my knowledge, it had been granted to no other knight, but whether I could claim it depended on the grace of the king of Jerusalem, and even more on his powerful mother Queen Melisende who still governed, though her son had attained his majority. I doubted that she would give me the fief based on my wit and charm alone, but with Eleanor as my advocate, I might have greater success.

I was dreaming of al-Lawza one day as we passed time in one of the pavilions that dotted the castle gardens, spinning flax into linen while Eleanor recited to us from a slim parchment volume of songs that had survived the journey through Turkey. Eve sat at my feet with her own bundle of flax, mimicking our actions, and I have to admit her finished product looked only a little worse than mine. The songs were all in Occitan, of which I could still barely understand five words in ten, and fewer when I was trying to balance distaff and spindle and create something remotely resembling thread, so my mind wandered.

In the fantasies of return to al-Lawza that had dominated my dreams for the last twenty years, I had never been alone, but now I was travelling in a group of virtual strangers, with those I loved far away. Eleanor finished a song that coincided with a heavy sigh from me.

"Did you like the song?" asked Mabilie, curious. "I thought you didn't know Occitan."

"I don't," I said in an unguarded moment. "I wasn't listening to the poem. I was thinking about my son."

"Your son?" broke in Berthe. "You never told us you had a son. What's his name? How old is he? Why isn't he with you?"

She was right, I never mentioned my son, and it was precisely because I didn't want to answer busybody questions like hers. Or reveal things that still hurt too much.

"His name is Theodore, named for my mother," I said shortly. "And I always liked to think that he was conceived right here in the Holy Land, just before I was forced to leave." Which made it all the more wrong that he wasn't where he should be, here by my side on my return.

"Tell us more," said Eleanor, putting down her book. "My voice is tired and I can't read any longer. When did you know you were pregnant?"

I wasn't ready to talk about Theodore at all, but I'd tell them another story, if I meant I could put down distaff and spindle. Still, I wasn't sure where to begin. Only Eleanor knew that Thierry de Galeran had killed my father, and I wanted to keep it that way. So I began an abbreviated version.

"My father died and I was forced to marry Bertulf and leave the Holy Land immediately for his home in Flanders. He was old — to me at least, since I was only fifteen — and brutal. Needless to say, he was not my first choice," I said, making a joke of it. The women laughed, recognizing the universal theme of a woman married too young to a man not to her taste, so I plunged into the heart of the story of how I left my sunny home for the cold and damp of northern Europe.

✠

Aude's Fourth Tale: Acre to Gistel, April–July 1118

It took me a long time to realize I was pregnant. Foolish me, I should have guessed I'd quicken soon from all the times Bertulf had his way with me, every night in the galley that took us across the Mediterranean, stinking of rotten fish and bilge water and stale vomit from my seasickness. And then every night in each flea-ridden inn and drafty monastic guest house on our way across the Alps and into France, no matter how many others shared the room with us, to my shame. Our wedding night seemed to kindle an interest in me he had never displayed before. I protested the first night on the ship, after I spent the whole day retching over the side and felt my insides were turned inside out. He smacked me with the back of his hand, knocking me down, and I complained no more. His men hooted the next day when they saw my bruised face, clapped Bertulf on his back and praised his manhood. I'd get no support from them. I submitted meekly from then on. At least Bertulf was always fast.

The less said about our journey from al-Lawza to take ship at Acre, the better. Bertulf kept us at a frantic pace, and I was sore everywhere, inside and out by the time he had haggled passage for us and our horses on the ship. In fact the less said about the entire journey the better. I was ill from the moment I set foot on the galley, and it didn't stop even after we left the big ship at Marseille for a flat-bottomed boat to take us up the Rhone. No wonder I don't like ships. I started feeling a little better once we left the water for good and began the trek north on horseback. For the first time I was able to appreciate my surroundings.

My first impression was of greenness and an untamed fertility bursting out all over, so different from the golden landscape I knew. It was June, and the whole world seemed to be coming into fruit. The rank scent of vegetation and wet earth made me feel ill. We rode through valley clefts and along river beds, the chattering of water never far from our ears, through thick woods with trees as tall as any building I had ever seen. The forests were eerie, dark even at noon and unnaturally silent. They came to life again at dusk, and that was even worse—strange shrieks and screams from unseen animals. I rode close to Bertulf.

We had shed most of our belongings in stages on the way to pay for our trip, and what we had left was loaded onto a couple of pack mules. Bertulf had tried to sell my mother's icons in Marseille but I protested so loudly that for once he gave way to my desires. The closer we got to Gistel, the more he talked about his home.

"God's balls, it will be good to see Winnoc again. Winnoc is my younger brother and he's been taking care of Gistel for me," he explained. "I've missed him more than anyone else. And little Gebirga too. She's my daughter—she's blind, poor lass. She'll be living with the nuns now, saying her prayers for her parents, but we'll see her often enough."

A daughter? This was the first I heard of her. I pictured a young girl, piously praying in a habit. Maybe it would be nice to be a stepmother.

There were more shocks to come. "I should have been teaching you Flemish the moment we left Jerusalem. That's what they speak where we're going." Flemish? But everyone in the world spoke

French, except a few Syrian peasants. From al-Lawza through France I had been able to make myself understood. He started teaching me right away, just a few simple phrases of welcome and greeting, and it was heavy going. My tongue and throat struggled to make the outlandish sounds. The men who knew the language, who had been with Bertulf since he left his home long before, began speaking Flemish with each other to help me. I was appalled by the noise they made. Truly, if I had to live among people who spoke like this, I had fallen off the end of the world. What next, sea-monsters?

"We'll get there by midday," he promised one morning. We had left the deep forests behind us and were riding through a flat, soggy landscape that stretched endlessly to a distant horizon. The sky was low and it pressed down on me as we rode through a world as alien to me as the green woods had been. Everywhere I looked, sheep nibbled emerald grass in handkerchief-sized pastures in neat squares separated by water channels. It was a hot day, and a fug of damp and the whine of insects rose from these channels, punctuated by the calls of waterbirds, drunk on minnows. Despite the heat, it could not have been more different from the dry hills and plateaus of my native land.

A lonesome bell tolled in the distance as we crept along the straight dirt track that was our road.

"Look! That's it! We're almost there," Bertulf called.

I looked where he pointed, and beyond a large willow, the only real tree for miles, I spotted a squat tower through the green haze. We rounded a corner and a woman blocked our way, tall and sturdy and trimly dressed, clinging to the lead of an enormous white dog, standing sentry. Not one of the peasants I had seen toiling in the fields. Bertulf seemed moved by some unexpressed excitement as he motioned for our horses to stop.

The woman called out to us, babbling in their language. Did I hear the name Bertulf among the strange sounds? She hadn't finished speaking before Bertulf leapt off his horse and ran to embrace her.

"Gebirga, little lass," he said to her, speaking French, stroking her hair. "I never thought to see you again. It is Bertulf, your father!

I am back from the Holy Land, back to the castle, for good. And I've brought someone home with me."

He dragged the stunned woman over to me and put her hand in mine. "This is Aude, my wife and your new mother," he said. "Come, let us all go to the castle together."

This was his daughter, this great big lump? All my fantasies of being a loving stepmother to a sweet little nun vanished. She must have been twice my age and half again my size. Of course, Bertulf had been away from the home as long as my father. Why hadn't I realized she would be much older than I? At least she understood French. She was even more shocked than I was, and obviously had no idea her long-lost father was on his way. Her face was startled, but her eyes were blank, and I remembered she was blind.

I plodded after Bertulf and his great big daughter, too tired and scared to pay attention to their chatter. We reached the gatehouse and Gebirga gibbered in their language to the sentry, a boy with wide-set eyes of blue and blond hair, just like every second person here. The youth took off his cap and bowed to Bertulf, then stared, amazed, at me.

I was not too exhausted to be horrified by the courtyard: a sea of mud with crumbling barns and wooden hovels we wouldn't keep goats in, and a manor house only stone for its first story and some sort of whitewashed mud for the rest. A woman spotted us, screamed something excitedly, before running up to one of our men. Her cry lured others from inside the hovels and behind the byres, and hugs and squeals erupted all over the courtyard as the prodigals were welcomed home.

Bertulf helped me down from the horse and brought me to his daughter in the middle of the hubbub. First shyly and then with more boldness, his subjects approached him, longing to touch and see their long-absent lord. I was tired, edgy, and scared but alert enough to pick up on the tension prickling the air around me from Winnoc, the brother, whose greeting was too hale, too hearty, punching Bertulf on the arm and launching not-so-pretend insults meant to prickle and sting. His nose was smartly put out of joint by our arrival—and who can blame him? He had ruled the roost alone here for twenty years and more.

The blind daughter was so cool with me, so impassive to her father, so competent when she chivvied our horses and our men that I felt dirtier and younger than ever, which made me waspish. I forgot all the Flemish Bertulf taught me on our journey and when the dog barked and barked, I wanted to bark too, and to howl.

"This yard is so mucky. And that dog! Make it stop," I snapped at Gebirga in French, longing to be understood by at least one person in this strange crew.

"She's just excited. She usually doesn't bark at all," said Gebirga, but she did shorten the dog's lead.

I'd only known her for a few moments, but I could tell that she loved that dog beyond reason. "I hate dogs. Horrible animals," I said, wanting to hurt someone, anyone, while I was feeling so awful.

Worst of all was Bertulf, the brutal lunk. He strode here and there, bantering and asking questions when I only wanted him to be quiet, for one moment, please. All the while, he gripped me around my waist or by a wrist, dragging me along, pinning me down. My back ached, the stink of the stable yard made me nauseous, and I wanted to lie down and sleep for a week, but I had to follow him as he inspected each cross-eyed sheep and snotty-nosed brat paraded for his approval.

Then it was dinner and at least I could sit. My throat was dry so I took a sip from the tumbler before me and almost spat it out again. It was my first taste of beer, brackish and warm, made from the barley that grew in the fields. The bread was barley too, coarse and rough, but better than the sour rye we had eaten at other stops on our journey. Would I never eat wheat bread again? My only moment of satisfaction was when Bertulf commanded his daughter to give me the big ring of keys that hung at her belt. I saw her chin shake as he humiliated her before the whole castle and, God help me, I grinned.

Then, a servant brought out the meat, offering me a platter with great pride, heaped with pinkish red slices. My stomach lurched, already queasy from the hot, airless hall and the smoking rushes behind me. He held it closer, right under my nose so I could inhale its sweetish scent. "It's our own ham, lady, we cure it ourselves and it is the pride of the region."

Ham. Pig meat. We didn't eat it at home, but I had it a few times on our journey, roast or boiled, and I'd seen the pigs, stinking and rutting in mud and filth at every inn and monastery we'd lodged at. It sickened me with its cloying sweetish-salty greasy taste. I heaved and turned and vomited in the rushes behind the bench, a thin sourish brew because I had eaten so little that day.

A woman who seemed to be a superior sort of servant, rose from her place close to the head of the table, smacked the boy holding the platter and let forth a stream of abuse against him in Flemish. She sat on the bench beside me and put her arm around me and spoke in heavily accented French. "Poor dear. With a lusty man like Lord Bertulf, odds are you are pregnant. Are your breasts sore too? And your back? When did your moon courses stop? Have you been sick often?" My eyes widened in dawning comprehension but she didn't wait for an answer. "Don't worry, it just means the baby is strong in you. You'll start feeling better soon. I am Lisebet and I will take care of you."

The boy returned and she feed me spoonfuls of gruel and sips of pear cider so I was saved the need to reply. Bertulf had no such inhibitions and took Lisebet's guess for truth. "Pregnant, Aude? Why didn't you tell me?!" He smacked my backside, almost knocking me off the bench, and then stood, toasting the hall. I recognized the words "Aude" and "Gistel." Everyone cheered and drank, and the noise level in the hall rose even higher.

Lisebet took me off to the sleeping chamber long before the feast was finished. She brought me mint tea and told me it would settle my stomach. I longed to ask her questions, and weep, but suddenly shy, I kept silent. After she left, I lay awake for a long time, thinking. A baby. That explained the seasickness that persisted on dry land, the endless tug in my gut as I bounced up and down on the horse. When Bertulf finally came to bed, I pretended to be asleep. Perhaps an infant in my belly would keep him off me, at least until it was born. That was a happy thought.

But I was wrong. No doubt excited by reclaiming his domain and the evidence of his virility, he was pushing at me the moment he lay down on the big lord's bed, and my protests only inflamed him more. After he was done, I willed myself to sleep, hoping I might never again wake up.

But inevitably, I awoke. Dust caked my eyelids and a curl of queasiness twisted my gut. The solid bulk beside me snored on while I rose weakly, putrid-mouthed. Seeking water, I stumbled out. The hall was bright, too bright. I squinted.

"What, Aude?" said Gebirga, standing haloed in dawn.

I stank of semen, sweat, and sickness.

"Water," I croaked. "Get it."

Nausea made me sour. I groped for the proffered cup and drank lustily, water dribbling down my chin. I reached the bench and flopped down, hands on splayed thighs.

"Good morning," said Gebirga.

I could tell she didn't like me, and why would she? Just as Bertulf was displacing his brother, Winnoc, I was supplanting Gebirga, who had run the castle for years alone. I didn't care. When Bertulf made her give me the big ring of household keys the night before, I grabbed at them. Mistress of the castle was my rightful place, my compensation for putting up with Bertulf in bed and out. Besides, she wasn't supposed to be in the castle at all. Hadn't Bertulf promised me she'd be safely settled into her convent? She could leave today as far as I was concerned. I had lost my home. Why shouldn't she lose hers?

She and her dog dragged me all over the castle and its yard my first morning, reeling off an endless list of duties that would be my responsibility. Dozy and stupid because of pregnancy, I barely listened, and concentrated my efforts on keeping my shoes clean. Surely there was a steward who would worry about what the chickens were eating and how many candles we had? She showed me the tapestries in the hall, rough home-spun affairs, and stood behind me, relating the stories on each one, family tales told to show me how little I belonged among these people. The one that showed Bertulf on crusade was laughable. Jerusalem looked more like one of their piddling northern forts than the grand and beautiful city it was. I told her so, and I was glad to see her face fall. She might know how to run a castle, but I had been to Jerusalem, center of the world.

I paused over another embroidered screen that showed one man cleaving another's head with an axe. "What's that about?"

"The woman who founded our line had three sons. The oldest two fought over a bride, and the middle one killed the eldest then fled. That's why my great-great grandfather, the youngest, inherited all the property. You can see him standing beside the castle."

More a hovel than a castle, but I didn't quibble. "What happened to the middle son?" I asked. I was curious about the destiny of people who lost their homes. "Did he die?"

"No," she said, "We were sea people once, and he turned back to the sea. Piracy, fishing, and trade. His descendants trouble us from time to time, but not for a while now. They're too successful to bother with stealing our sheep." I saw that the bottom corner of the tapestry showed a man in a boat. That must be the long-lost middle brother.

But Gebirga's attention had moved on. "The tapestry we finished most recently isn't here. It is already at the convent. You'll see it when we go there for my mother's feast day." There was a warning in her voice I did not understand.

"Your mother?"

"My mother. Saint Godeleva. Her bones are at the convent. My father did not tell you?" The warning was still there but I did not know what questions to ask to unlock whatever it was she was trying to tell me. I knew Bertulf had a wife before he came to the Holy Land. After all, he had this great big daughter. But I never thought about what had happened to remove her from the scene. Death in childbirth, infection and disease from living in these watery northern plains, what did it matter? But why was she a saint? That was strange. The saints in my world were all long-dead martyrs, apostles, or fathers of the church, and most of them were men. Not wives of middling landholders on the fringe of the known world.

"How did she die?" I asked finally, turning away from the tapestry. But Gebirga was gone.

I got my answer at the convent. Our arrival coincided with Bertulf's first wife's feast day, so one morning we trooped down to the small stone chapel that served the convent and crammed in there with the nuns for a festal Mass. Tangible reminders of Godeleva were everywhere, in the sturdy stone tomb that held her remains to the brilliant if crude image of her painted on the wall above it, and the altar cloth that displayed her miracles. If I understood Latin, I could have learned about the fate of my predecessor from the priest as he read the long account of her life, death and afterlife while we shifted from foot to foot, legs and backs sore from standing on a stone floor. But I knew no Latin, so I had to wait until later, when Bertulf left me with some nuns, while he arranged Gebirga's future in the convent with the abbess. I obediently sat in their parlor while they stared at me with the same mixture of caution and pity I had sensed from Gebirga.

"We hear you're pregnant," the oldest of the nuns said suddenly, clucking her tongue with dismay. The other sisters exchanged anxious glances, and one young novice came to sit beside me on my bench and took my hand.

"You're awfully brave to be married to Bertulf," she said, staring up at me earnestly.

I retrieved my hand and went straight to the heart of the matter. "Tell me about Godeleva. Why is she a saint?"

"You mean you don't know?" The nuns were incredulous and at the same time, none wanted to be the one to enlighten me. Finally the novice told me what the others feared to say.

"It is such a sad story. Godeleva always wanted to remain a virgin, like us, but her family married her against her will to Bertulf. On her wedding night, she prayed to be allowed to remain chaste. Bertulf was, er, never able to consummate the marriage though he remained capable with other women. Frustrated, he took out his anger on Godeleva, beating her regularly and trying to starve her into submission." I shivered. This sounded like the Bertulf I knew. No wonder his success on our wedding night had cheered him so. I now remembered him saying something about his first wife unmanning him.

"He locked her in a dark garret that had rats in it. Big ones," one timid sister added.

"She was a wonderful seamstress, and he chopped up an embroidered girtle she had just finished making, sliced it to bits with shears," said another nun, fingers busy sewing a shift. One by one they added to the litany of Bertulf's cruelties. If half were true, I could see why they feared for me. I feared for myself and hugged myself in my cloak against a chill that wasn't there.

"Did she do nothing?" I asked. "Didn't she try to protect herself at all?"

"She fled to her family, but they sent her straight back to her husband—"

"Which was only right and proper to my mind," a thin-faced nun broke in brusquely.

"I still think they should have taken her in. They could have saved her life."

"But then she wouldn't be a saint. It was God's will she return."

"Well, I think—"

The oldest nun broke in to halt what was obviously an often-repeated argument, and finished the tale. "Godeleva returned home to Bertulf, but his anger had hardened against her. He continued his ill-treatment of her and plotted her demise. One day while she was out walking, two of his servants seized her and drowned her in the well."

"In the river."

"In the well," the older nun repeated firmly.

There was one part of the story that still puzzled me. "If Godeleva remained ever virginal, how do you explain Gebirga?" I asked, and the oldest nun responded sternly.

"At the convent, we teach that Gebirga was an illegitimate child of Bertulf by some unknown woman." She would say no more. There was clearly something fishy about this part of the tale, but if the sisters needed me to believe that Godeleva was a virgin in order to give me their friendship and protection, then a virgin she was.

I gulped. I understood that the key to the story was sex. Deny it to Bertulf and you died. Allow it and you would live. I hope. That was the lesson I was going to take away.

It was a dreadful tale and rang true. I had already seen hints of what Bertulf was like when he was thwarted. If he turned on me, what could I do? I had no family nearby who could help. Then I thought of Charles. Might he protect me? Bruges was close, Bertulf had said, and Charles was often in Bruges. Suddenly I was doubtful. Would he even remember me?

Berthe interrupted my story to Eleanor's women. "I hope this Charles would know better than to come between a wife and her husband. The parents of this Godeleva did right to send her back to Bertulf. And I've never heard of a Saint Godeleva before anyway. Imagine making a saint of a woman who disobeyed her husband." She sniffed. "There are only two decent roles for a woman. As a wife she obeys her lord, her husband. As a nun she obeys the Lord God Himself." She looked sternly at Eleanor as she delivered this moral.

"You're lucky you had a husband," said Marie, softly. "Alone and without protection in the world, who knows how you would have fared?"

"I'm alone now, and I am doing fine," I retorted.

"A man to depend on is a fine thing," began Mabilie, but Eleanor broke in. "If you can depend on him. And if not..." We all waited for her to finish her sentence, but she was silent.

Eventually I spoke. "Whatever the merits and demerits of husbands, that day in the convent, I vowed silently to God and every single one of his saints that no matter how long it took, no matter what I had to do, some day I would return back to where I belonged. Husband or no husband, baby or no baby, I would go back to al-Lawza."

"And now you are," said Alice.

"And now I am," I agreed.

"We won't reach Jerusalem for a while yet, alas," said Eleanor, "We're sworn to help Raymond and I won't set one foot in the holy city until our vow is fulfilled."

She spoke stoutly, as if by speaking she could make it so, but it was plain to everyone that the tide of French opinion had already turned against her.

"I thought the king said we were going to Jerusalem first," Marie complained, reflecting the view that was becoming common.

Eleanor ignored her and continued, "And to help us wait, Count Raymond has invited us to visit the springs of Daphne with him this afternoon. His kitchens have prepared a feast to bring with us, and it will do us good to leave the city heat and go into the mountains."

Daphne's springs supplied the aqueducts that fed the city with running water for its fountains and baths. We'd heard of its sites, of course, the burnt remains of the temple to Apollo, sacred to his love for the water-nymph Daphne, and the churches and monasteries built there later to Christianize its pagan ruins. And as the May days lengthened, the prospect of a day in the cool was welcome, so we all packed and got ready to go.

Well, not all of us. When we were finally assembled to depart for Daphne, it seemed most of the French women, like Marie and Berthe, had elected to stay behind, leaving only myself and the Occitans, Mabilie, quiet little Ermine, Gracia, a placid non-entity, and a few more I knew less well. Raymond's wife, too, had chosen to stay behind. Or hadn't been invited in the first place. What she thought of her husband's attentions to his niece was anyone's guess.

The ride was challenging but beautiful, through craggy out-croppings and pine woods. The day was hot and insects screeched deafeningly, but the air cooled the higher we ascended. When we arrived, the servants started to set up our lunch by a waterfall in a clearing surrounded by oleander in full flower, and the count asked what we wanted to do while we waited to be fed.

"Shall we visit the shrine of Saint Babylas? Or would you rather see the temple of Apollo?"

"Oh, the temple, please," said Eleanor, "I've had enough of mar-tyr's bones."

"Very well, though there's not much to see," said Raymond.

The walk was pleasant, though the count's warning was accurate. He presented us with something that might once have been the pillar supporting a temple facade if you squinted at it the right way, and a pile of rubble that could as easily have been a fallen-down cow shed as a monument to a god.

"Look at all the bay laurel trees here. I wonder which one is Daphne herself?" mused Eleanor.

"I don't know the story of Apollo and Daphne. Someone en-lighten me, please," said Mabilie.

"Ovid tells it best," said Raymond. "Apollo was struck by one of Cupid's darts, and the next thing he knew, he was madly infatuated with the nymph, Daphne. But she'd sworn herself to chastity. He pursued her, and she ran blindly to this very grove. 'Help me my father,' she cried to the streams that flow here, 'If thy flowing streams have virtue! Cover me, O mother Earth! Destroy the beauty that has injured me, or change the body that destroys my life.' The earth heard her prayer. Bark covered her body, her hair was changed into leaves, and she became a laurel tree. When Apollo caught up with her, he caressed the tree's trunk, feeling Daphne's bosom throbbing unwillingly under the bark, and he swore then that the laurel should be evergreen."

While Raymond spoke, his hand caressed the nearest laurel in imitation of Apollo, and when he had finished, he broke off a flowering sprig of bay and tucked it behind Eleanor's ear in a gesture so intimate, the rest of us suddenly felt very awkward as Eleanor gazed up at her uncle like a rabbit about to offer itself to a hawk.

It was obvious that Raymond was intent on seducing Eleanor and that he didn't care who knew. Maybe it was nosey of me, or foolish —I had enough to concern myself with my own affairs—but I worried about her, alone and vulnerable with a husband who surrounded himself with her enemies and an uncle who seemed bent on her ruin to his own ends. I remembered her in my room, mourning her mother, and I knew that under the growing poise and charm was a young woman, with a young woman's insecurities and fears. But what could I say to stop it? All I could do was distract.

"Do you think those servants have finished getting our lunch together?" I asked brightly. The others agreed, and we walked back.

We sat under a clump of carob trees, drinking resinous wine and picking at cold delicacies with our fingers—capers, dried figs, and walnuts, salted mullet roe, cold omelets studded with mushrooms and cut in cubes, grilled meatballs, and vine leaves stuffed with rice and currants. The air was warm, and heavy with the scent of resin and early summer flowers. The wine went straight to our heads and we got very silly, reclining there in the dappled shade of the trees. Eleanor's two troubadours, Cercamon and Jaufré Rudel, sang songs very different from those crusader anthems approved of by Louis. These, so far as I could follow, were flirtatious songs of shepherds and lusty dairymaids, and sad laments of men whose beloveds resisted their charms.

When both were too tired to sing any more Raymond quizzed us with a series of hypothetical questions.

"Would you rather be eaten by lions or by ants?"

"Lions, of course, silly, if I must," said Eleanor.

"What if it were an old, toothless, clawless lion—?"

"Oh, stop!"

"Very well then, here's another." Raymond continued, "Who was more virtuous—Daphne or the Virgin Mary?"

"I'm not going to touch that one!" said one of his male companions, laughing.

But Eleanor was undaunted. "Mary, of course. Daphne was a pagan. How could she be virtuous?"

"Are you sure?" teased Raymond.

"I see what you're getting at, sir," said Ermine. "The church teaches that the greatest virtue of a woman is the preservation of her chastity. Daphne resisted, Mary did not."

"You have got it exactly right. Daphne preferred transformation into a tree rather than give up her brightest jewel."

Eleanor looked confused, "But Mary succumbed only to God, her lord. That makes it completely different."

Raymond said, "So you agree that a woman who succumbs to her lord commits no crime, but indeed may be reckoned as virtuous? You are as wise as you are beautiful, Eleanor. What Ovid said about Daphne may be truly be said about you—'Eyes like stars of sparkling fire, lips for kissing sweetest, and hands and fingers and arms, shoulders white as ivory, and whatever is not seen more beautiful must be.'"

His words seemed to both confuse and mesmerize Eleanor.

"I think it is high time we returned to Antioch," said Mabilie, breaking the spell. Her voice allowed no opposition, so Raymond gave the order to the servants to pack up our picnic, and we guests scattered to perform our ablutions before the return trip. While I was washing the greasy crumbs from lunch off my hands, I realized

Eleanor and her uncle were close by, blocked from my sight by a tamarisk bush. He was talking urgently to her, but I could not hear what they said.

I fell asleep easily after our long day and slept soundly until a thud woke me in the middle of the night. I sat straight up in bed, straining to catch the source of the disturbance over the usual eventide noises of the fountain burbling in the courtyard and the song of distant nightbirds. I decided I was imagining things and was about to settle down again, when I heard another thud. What could it be? Was someone trying to break into the queen's chambers? Or was it that pesky monkey of mine, getting into trouble again?

"Eve? Eve! Where are you?" I called, half under my breath, trying not to wake the others in my wing. There was no answer in the empty room and her lead, tied to my bedpost, was vacant. Blast the little beast. If she was gone, I'd have to find her. Last time she got away in the night, she tipped over every last perfume bottle the queen and her ladies bought in the souk the previous morning. I like perfume as much as the next woman, but she stank of jasmine and orange oil for days.

I had told Eleanor and her women that I found Eve stealing apples, and it was almost true. We stopped at a village on the Spanish coast on the way here to take on fresh water and I found some young boys stoning her in a courtyard. She was little more than a baby and when I flew at them, sickened to witness another unnecessary killing and maiming, even of an animal, after the battles I'd witnessed, they told me she had been robbing fruit. I paid them a few coins to leave her with me. Eve seemed like the right name. She was certainly good at causing mischief.

I lit an oil lamp off the brazier that kept my room warm against the spring chill, tied on a wrap, and did a quick search through my bedchamber. Not under the bed, not trapped in the clothes chest. Eve was definitely gone so I ventured out of my room to find her. The light of my lamp cast strange shadows on the walls of the courtyard outside my room as I stood, hoping to hear the sound of an adventuring monkey. There was nothing in the courtyard but the murmur of the fountain. Nonetheless, I had the uncanny sensation I was being watched by someone larger than a monkey, a vibration as if the air was displaced by an unseen lurker. I shrugged off the feeling, taking it for a night fancy, and strained all my senses to detect Eve.

There, I heard it again, this time more like a creak-creak than a thud. It was coming from the doorway that led out to the small solar where we spent our days on divans enjoying the sweet breezes of the city out of the direct sun. Had she somehow become trapped out there? She'd rip all the stuffing out of the cushions if I didn't collar her. I tiptoed around the portico, my feet making no sound on the tiled floor, then marched through the door, ready to confront her.

"You little beast, why can't you stay where you are told?…Oh!" I gasped. For it wasn't Eve the monkey captured in the light of my lamp on the divan. It was Eleanor, stark naked in the arms of her uncle, who was thrusting himself between her thighs. Their rhythmic movement halted abruptly at my words and they both looked up, startled and frozen in the lamplight.

"I am so very, very sorry, your majesty," I said, backing myself out of the room and making for my own as quickly as I could. There I found Eve curled up on my pillow fast asleep, of course. She must have crept back in when I went on my hunt.

The imprint of the two lovers burned on my memory.

"Whatever is she thinking?" I said to Eve, scritchling her neck to her delight as she stretched and luxuriated in her slumber. "Any fool knows carrying on with Raymond is a very bad idea. And Eleanor is no fool." But I couldn't condemn her. Lord knew, I had made my own share of disastrous choices when I was Eleanor's age, and older. I worried about her though. And I worried about me. Would she cast me out for discovering her secret? Or make me an accomplice?

I heard the furtive rustlings of Eleanor and Raymond leaving their love nest. The sound of their whispers, though not their words, travelled across the open courtyard. Then Eleanor's door shut and Raymond left our quarters, and the night grew silent again.

Just then I heard a faint click coming from my side of the courtyard, a door closing on one of the bed chambers adjacent to mine, where I and Eleanor's other women slept. I remembered the feeling I had of being watched. Had someone besides me spied Eleanor with her uncle in the night?

CHAPTER FIVE

Antioch, May–June 1148

✠

Eve woke me the next morning, pawing my face in hope of food. "Stop that, you little beast," I said, gently pushing her away, hoping to return to my dreams. Where had I been? But it was no use. I was wide awake, sweet dreams dispersed by my wretched monkey. Immediately my mind went to more sober thoughts, of Eleanor and Raymond intertwined the night before. Was it the first time? I thought so. I shuddered. This would not end well.

The click of that door telling me I was not the only one to discover them bothered me most. Who could that have been? I quickly ran down the list of women who lived on my side of the courtyard, mostly Frenchwomen like Berthe, Alice, and Marie, but also Ermine, from Aquitaine. How loyal were Eleanor's attendants? Would the mysterious spy share her discovery? I'd never betray the queen. I had no love for Louis and it would not serve me to have her disgraced, but more than that, I felt a bond with Eleanor that would never allow me to be an agent of her destruction. And I blamed Raymond for everything. Oh, the priests talk about wily women seducing innocent men, but his niece was young and alone, surrounded by enemies and effectively abandoned by her husband, with only a few loyal but powerless women at her side. Raymond was manipulating her for his own ends, I was sure of it. But would others see her as a victim? I was especially nervous about the French women. I covered my face with my hands and groaned. This was too big for me to handle alone.

I went to Mabilie because she'd been with Eleanor since the queen was a child. She knew the family, and I believed she'd protect the queen with her life. But it was hard to get word with her alone. We attended the queen while the servants bathed her, then we helped her dress and arranged her hair. As we worked, combing and plucking and braiding, my eyes searched out those of my fellow ladies, hoping to catch some glance, some knowing look that would betray the woman who had spied on the queen. But I saw nothing and we worked in silence broken only by Marie whose turn it was to read aloud to amuse the queen while she endured the tedious ritual of dressing.

When Eleanor, still naked in her tub, met my own eyes for the first time that morning, I returned her gaze in what I hoped was a frank and open manner. Not me, I hoped my eyes said to her, you have no reason to fear I will betray you.

Finally, Mabilie and I had a moment alone, sorting through and cleaning Eleanor's jewelry and hair ornaments.

"I'm worried about Eleanor," I began, pulling a necklace out of the carved ivory casket, one of Raymond's many gifts to Eleanor since her arrival.

"What's vexing you?" she said, scrubbing at one piece with lemon juice and salt. "The stone is loose in this brooch. Put it aside to be tightened."

I put it on a growing pile as she picked up another and went to work on it. "It's her relationship with Count Raymond. They're too close. Much too close." I knew I had to say more, but I didn't know how.

She snorted. "That girl. Though she is strong on the surface, she's always been a terrible romantic. Spent her whole childhood listening to troubadour love songs until she believed they were real. Her husband neglects her and she's a sitting duck for the charms of the count's predatory attentions. Oh, I saw the two of them together yesterday. You don't need to say any more. And I have no clue what to do. Pray her foolish husband never gets wind of it I suppose."

"Was that you last night," I said with relief. If Mabilie had been the one to spy Eleanor and Raymond together we were safe. Mabilie would never betray Eleanor.

"What do you mean, last night?" she said, mystified, and her voice suddenly sharp. "I saw them flirting in Daphne."

My heart sank. I explained the whole story to Mabilie: the noise, my silent walk around the courtyard to the solar, Eleanor and Raymond entwined. And the sense that I was not the only one to see them.

She put down the jewels she was holding and shut her eyes, as if that would help her think. Finally she opened them again. "If anyone finds out about this, anyone, the queen is ruined."

"I know."

"Raymond doesn't care about her. He has a wife, for goodness sake. He wants to use her body, and to use her to get military help for Antioch. What she won't give freely, he can now take with blackmail."

I gasped and Mabilie continued. "I'll try to talk some sense into her. She knows you saw her, and she won't mind that you told me. Much."

With that I had to be content. But a burden shared is a burden halved. I felt I had done my duty.

At least it seemed Eleanor wouldn't be kicking her heels in Antioch with too much time on her hands for long. Word came that the Templars had loaned the king 2,000 silver marks and 30,000 pounds, an astounding sum, more than half the revenues of France for a whole year. This gift would leave the king indebted to the Templars in every sense.

A council was called to discuss plans. I watched with the women from the gallery of one of the palace's many reception rooms, a vast hall with a floor of purple marble and a frescoed ceiling, fading and flaking around the edges. Like all Antioch, the rich surface you saw from a distance looked shabby when you got close. No wonder Raymond needed the crusaders.

The great barons and knights of France, Aquitaine, and Antioch sat on folding stools around the perimeter of the room while Raymond, triumphant and joyous, sat at its head. Louis, looking grim, was at his right hand, with his Templars next to him. Eleanor, claiming a place as lord of the crusader host from Aquitaine, sat on Raymond's left.

Raymond spoke first. "Avenging Edessa is what brought you here, and Edessa is our final aim. But our first goal must be the city of Aleppo. It is from Aleppo that Edessa was assaulted, and once in our hands, all the Christian lands of the east would be secure." Raymond sat down, thumbs in his belt, and waited for the king to fall in with his program.

But the king did not comply. "My Lord Raymond, count of Antioch, I am grateful for the hospitality you have shown us," he began in a voice thin and reedy, after the booming tones of the count. "But we are not going to help you take Aleppo, at least not right now. I made a vow to visit the Holy Sepulcher in Jerusalem, and it was for this reason that I took up the cross two years and more ago. My journey here has been accomplished at dire peril, and my army has suffered grave calamities. I intend to finish my pilgrimage to Jerusalem before I engage in wars of any kind. Once I visit Jerusalem and pray in the Church of the Holy Sepulcher, then I will hear you, and all the other barons of this land, and we will decide together where to direct our attack."

The king sat down, staring around the room defiantly. It took a moment for his words to sink in. When they did, Raymond's nobles and Eleanor's knights all started talking at the same time. Louis's French vassals were smug and silent. They must have been told the king's decision before the council. Raymond's voice cut through the hubbub. "And prithee, majesty, what do you expect will be the target of this future attack?" he asked Louis.

"We may well decide that our best plan is to return north and lay siege to Aleppo as you suggest." The king sounded uncomfortable.

Thierry de Galeran interrupted, and contradicted the king. "Damascus," he answered, sounding smug. "Possibly Egypt, maybe Askalon, but most likely Damascus. But not Aleppo. The Templars are agreed on that."

"The Templars? And since when does your order speak for the king of France?" demanded Raymond.

"Since we started financing the king's army, count. When you can pay for his knights, you can decide where he fights."

"But we're at peace with Damascus," Raymond responded, "They pose no threat to us. Whereas Nur ad-Din and Aleppo threatens not only my county but the whole kingdom of Jerusalem. This is a bitter way you repay my hospitality, king."

But the Templar strategy made sense to me. Why should they help Raymond enlarge his domain when by winning Damascus they could win the gratitude of the whole kingdom of Jerusalem and its queen, Melisende. And given what Raymond was doing with his wife, I thought Louis didn't owe him much at all.

Then Eleanor stood, fire in her eyes. I had never seen her look so beautiful. The entire room went silent, waiting to hear her unexpected contribution.

"Coward!" she berated Louis's brother, Robert of Dreaux.

"Spineless!" she scolded Henry of Champagne and the count of Flanders on the other side of the room.

"Ingrates, all of you!" she said, her contemptuous gaze raking all Louis's remaining vassals before turning to her husband. "And you, my lord king, are the worst of all. You are not worth a rotten pear. I may be but a woman, but I have a bigger heart than any of you French weaklings. I know how to show gratitude to my host who welcomed us with open arms when we were in the direst straits. And I know how to fight when Christendom needs me, and not to hide behind the skirts of the Templars and their money. France may shuffle off to Jerusalem with scrip and staff, but Aquitaine will stand and fight. My count," she turned to Raymond, "I will never forsake you. We are ready to help you take Aleppo." She sat, and her vassals stood and cheered their lady. The fragile peace between Aquitaine and France, founded in the marriage between their rulers, was falling apart before our eyes. Raymond smiled.

There was nothing more to say. The council, intended to create an army fired with holy zeal and united in purpose to conquer Aleppo, produced just the opposite. Eleanor's vassals massed around her, and Louis's did the same, cheering their respective rulers. At last we got her back to our own chambers, and even then she paced, round and round the solar, oblivious to the fact that while her ladies from Aquitaine were petting and supporting her, the French women were unusually silent. When she started insulting her husband for the fifth or sixth time, one by one most of the latter slipped out of the room. She didn't seem to notice, but did finally settle down on a divan, exhausted from her exertions.

Mabilie tried to reason with her. "My lady, was it wise to disagree with your husband so publicly? That is not the way we women work. Maybe some sweet words in private would bend him to your way of thinking?"

"Words in private? When have I had those since we left France?" She started to cry, silent hot tears and I passed her a handkerchief. "It's the Templars," she said, wiping her eyes. "They gave him the money, and he owes his soul to them now. He'll have us all dancing to their tune whether we want to or not, and God help France. And Aquitaine."

Ermine kneeled before her and took one of her hands. "My lady, perhaps it won't be so bad. It will be lovely to finally reach Jerusalem. Think, we'll see Christ's own tomb, and the street where he carried the Cross! Maybe then we can return here and take Aleppo like the count wants."

But Ermine's efforts at peacemaking had no effect. "Never!" Eleanor said and blew her nose loudly. "I don't care what the king does. I won't stir from Antioch unless it is to take Aleppo with the count."

This was terrible. The king would surely leave for Jerusalem and the south whatever his queen did, and what would I do, stuck in Antioch? An estranged royal couple were no part of my scheme.

"Aude," Eleanor asked urgently, surprising me, "Charles was your one true love, wasn't he?"

I was startled. I certainly hadn't expected this line of questioning, and it took me a while to recall what she meant. I hadn't thought of Charles as the love of my life for many years. "It's true that I idolized him when I was young, but —"

She didn't listen. "Did you ever see him again after you were married? I think you said you did. Did you ever have any happiness together? Please. I need to know." There was an urgency in her voice I could not withstand. The story I had to tell about me and Charles did not have the ending she hoped for, but a story might distract her from her pressing cares for a moment to give her a chance to regroup, and us a chance to talk some sense into her.

"I did see him again." I said, "Many times. But the first time was the autumn after I first arrived in Gistel."

✠

Aude's Fifth Tale: Gistel and Oudenberg, 1118

I returned often to the convent in the weeks that followed my first visit there. Although I held the keys, the household ran itself without me. Bertulf needed me only after dark—in the day he went hunting or visiting with his men. Winnoc was busy and Gebirga was cold. But the nuns greeted me with open arms every time I entered the gate, fussing over me and petting me. And best of all, they spoke French.

The castle was crowded and I sorely needed my retreats to the convent. After a life of rural isolation with only my parents and a few loyal servants, I was surrounded by strangers, and I didn't belong. But it wasn't long before the castle emptied.

Winnoc was the first to go. He made his escape with the boat that took the castle's wool to sell at the Bruges fair. I longed to go to Bruges, willing to brave more water travel if it meant I might see Charles. But Winnoc took Gebirga instead, and when she returned alone with the news that Winnoc had set out to make a new life for himself in the east and would not be coming back, Bertulf's rage was cold, silent, and more frightening than his usual bluster. He relieved it by cuffing me hard as I tried to remove his boots that evening, cutting me on the cheek with his ring deep enough to make the scar I bear to this day. Blind Gebirga could not see the wound and none of the others dared say a word against their master though they all stared at it as I held my head high over the dinner table.

Gebirga's departure was harder to endure, though not because I'd miss her company. As I was daubing at my wounded cheek that evening at table, a boy ran in to announce the arrival of men from Bruges. My foolish heart leapt. Charles, come to rescue me? What a romantic girl I was. The news could not be more different. They were messengers from the count's mother, and they wanted Gebirga, not me but Gebirga, to return with them to live at court with the count's sister, travelling with them from palace to palace, living in comfort and luxury while I remained in this flea-infested, filthy pig-sty of a castle with Bertulf alternately pawing me and hitting me. I imagined Gebirga in daily contact with the count's boon companion, Charles.

My Charles. The sting on my cheek was nothing to the rage in my heart. But I could do nothing to stop it, and Gebirga was packed and gone with the count's men before I awoke the next morning. I fled to the convent as usual, but although they salved my wounded cheek, they could do nothing for my offended heart.

The summer wore on, stinking hot, and I grew bigger. The housekeeping deteriorated after Gebirga left, but I was too listless and indifferent to bestir myself, and Bertulf didn't notice if the porridge was burnt or the linens went unchanged as long as his weapons and armor were gleaming. I let the servants do what they would, and shuffled around, belly swaying, in the same loose shift every day, napping and eating, half an ear on Bertulf and his men talking of war. They always talked of war. I yawned and rubbed my belly, feeling the baby kick. But one morning, as August turned to September, I woke to find Bertulf girding himself, a sparkle in his eye and a smile on his face.

"It's come, Aude, it's come at last," he said. "The summons to attend the count. Baldwin is calling all his vassals together. We are finally going to have war against England." He sounded overjoyed. "I leave today. We muster at the abbey in Oudenburg, down the river. We'll have a tournament tomorrow, then set out together for Normandy and war."

"War? Against whom? Why?" I asked, confused. War was a way of life in my homeland, but it seemed at odds with the tidy fields of Flanders. I had so much to learn.

"Count Baldwin is going to fight England to make William Clito duke of Normandy. Does it matter, as long as it means booty and honor for us?"

But my ears focused on one detail in his narrative. William Clito had helped Charles rescue me in Jerusalem. "Will Clito be at Oudenburg?" I asked.

"Yes, he stays close to Baldwin. Charles of Denmark will be there too. The three are inseparable, I hear." He sniggered.

I thought quickly. I must get to Oudenburg somehow. This would be my only chance to see Charles again before they all travelled off to war and who knows what. I flung myself at my husband and embraced him in a totally uncharacteristic way. "Oh Bertulf, dear

Bertulf. I can't bear for you to leave so suddenly. What if you never return? Please say I can come to Oudenburg with you, and stay for the tournament?"

I had startled him. "Aude…sweet…this is so…But, no. You are pregnant, many months gone now. You shouldn't stray from home. Stay here, and I'll be back before you know it, and we'll have a fine big boy."

"But Bertulf," I wheedled, "If I come with you, I can pray at Arnulf's tomb for a healthy boy. The nuns told me that he founded the monastery and the monks at Oudenburg want him to be raised to sainthood, so they are looking for miracles."

Bertulf was in awe of the power of the saints. "If you think it will help…"

"I do, I do!"

"Then you may come. But you must do as I say and not overexert yourself."

I went to Oudenburg by boat because there was no way to get my pregnant bulk, near seven months gone, safely there by horseback. I chafed at the slowness of the boatsmen as they leisurely punted me downstream, until Lisebet ordered me to sit down and let the men do their work. I had engaged Lisebet, who first spotted my pregnancy, to serve me and teach me Flemish. She was a long-ago cast-off mistress of Winnoc, which meant she had nice manners and ideas above her station that I was happy to exploit. "You'll swamp the boat, belly swaying like that," she ordered. "Then how will you reunite with your dear husband?"

Her voice exuded irony. Lisebet didn't know why I was so anxious to get to Oudenburg, but she knew wifely devotion played no part of it. She salved my cuts and bruises often enough to be sure of that.

The advantage of travelling slow and arriving late was that Bertulf had already secured a place for me in the abbey guesthouse. It was already full as Jerusalem at Eastertide, and Lisebet and I would have to share a bed, but it was better than sleeping outside on the ground like the men. Exhausted even by our day of easy travel, I flopped down on our pallet for a sleep before heading to the chapel to light my candle and pay my coin in front of the shrine of holy Arnulf. My prayers were sincere. Ever since I had quickened and began to feel the baby in my womb, I welcomed it. A boy would cement my position, and any child would make me feel less alone in the strange new land I was forced to call home.

Bands of young knights roamed the abbey grounds arm in arm, singing or mock fighting with each other, tipsy on beer to give them courage for the cuts and scrapes of their first tourney and the war that would follow. They gave us no trouble as we searched for Bertulf and his men, Lisebet beside me complaining of mud and flies. I was really looking for Charles. I spotted a tall man with a flash of blond hair. Was that him, over by the abbey kitchen? I tried to make out the distant man's features, when I was grabbed from behind and smacked on the bottom.

"Wife, you made it safely. Well done. Let us go to the lists. The grand melee is tomorrow, but this evening some of the younger knights will compete in single combat." Lisebet and I were drawn into the circle of Bertulf and his knights and we all went out the abbey gate together to the fields where a hastily-built barricade separated the watchers from the participants. Nowadays at a tournament there are proper stands where ladies can sit, sometimes even protected by a canopy, but back then we all milled about on foot behind the barrier. A white chevron against the red background of their shields distinguished Bertulf and his men from the other knights. One of our knights nervously took his leave from us. He was slated to fight in the single combat that was about to begin, and needed to retrieve his horse.

He hadn't been gone long before heralds announced the arrival of Count Baldwin. I scanned the men in his entourage. Was Charles among them? I recognized William Clito first of all, but I was shocked at the change to him. The black curls were still the same, but youthful exuberance had given way to a look of arrogant peevishness, and his lithe strength had been transformed by excess and indolence into a plump slackness. Was this the man for whom my husband and all these men were going to fight? And where was Charles?

It wasn't very interesting watching junior knights testing their mettle and showing their limited skill. Pair after pair bungled through awkward contests while we chattered amongst ourselves and mostly ignored the field. Our own man wasn't much better, though he did win his fight when his opponent slipped and fell on the slick ground, catcalls and insults hailing the unlucky loser. The field was a sea of churned mud and we had barely begun. I yawned, back aching and tired of standing. Perhaps I should seek out a bench and a beer somewhere inside. But the quality of the matches began to improve as we moved from the beginners to older, more tested knights. The audience started to pay more attention and cheered and whistled when their favorites came on the scene. William Clito himself took to the lists and something of the young hero he had been in Jerusalem was evident in the way he dispatched his opponent. But I was still bored.

"Is that the end?" I asked my husband.

"One more."

Sure enough two riders came out from opposite sides of the field and met in the middle where Count Baldwin stood behind the barricade. As they removed their helms to bow before their lord, I was so shocked I almost fell over. Grabbing Bertulf's forearm to steady myself, I asked, "Who's that?"

"That? It is Borsiard, he's a nephew of the chamberlain, an Erembald. One of the most important families in Flanders, they have fingers in every pie. I don't think much of his new beard though."

Beard? He'd told me about the wrong man. "No, not him. The other one."

"The tall one? That's Charles of Denmark, the count's cousin. He's a fine knight, and almost always closes out the contest. This should be good sport. Borsiard's family loathes Charles because of his friendship with Baldwin."

I released Bertulf as the two knights replaced their helms and rode back to opposite ends of the field. When the master of the joust blew his horn, they lowered their lances and rode straight for each other, cheered on by their allies. I held my breath as they passed and Charles's lance caught Borsiard's on the tip, sending pieces of it flying.

"Well done," cried my husband, "Nice technique. Instead of knocking Borsiard off his horse at once, Charles is going to give us a show."

The two men charged past each other and struggled to turn their horses around for another pass. Charles was quicker than Borsiard, and was already racing back down the field and picking up momentum before Borsiard had recovered from his own turn. He had little time to gain speed with Charles barreling down towards him and, the next time their lances clashed, Borsiard was knocked off his horse. When Charles returned to dismount, Borsiard, who had risen to his feet, lashed out at his horse, and the crowd booed this unsportsmanlike effort.

They began sword combat on foot to cries of "Erembald! and "Denmark!" from partisans in the crowd. I joined in the tumult, shouting, "Denmark! Denmark!" at the top of my lungs like a camel drover. Borsiard was better with a sword than a lance, and the blows and parries came thick from both sides. They weren't supposed to kill, or even wound severely, but with sharpened blades and heightened tempers some injury was inevitable. Blood from a scratch over Borsiard's eye mixed with the mud from his fall until he was a hideous sight, and Charles's sleeves were slashed and torn. They seemed well-matched, but soon it became clear that Charles was leading the dance, backing Borsiard closer and closer to the worst of the sea of mud. Charles feinted, Borsiard lunged, Charles turned away, and Borsiard slipped, falling headfirst into the muck. As Charles claimed the victory to the cheers of the crowd, Borsiard rose, cursing him.

"Damn you, Denmark, for a cheating catamite. You tripped me. Everyone saw."

Jeers and catcalls met this accusation, which Charles ignored. Everyone started drifting away, eager for a good place at the feast which was to follow, and few heard his last words, spoken as Charles was leaving the field.

"You'll pay for this, you cock-sucking Ganymede."

Somehow we all crammed into the guest refectory. I was in high spirits, overjoyed to have seen Charles, still the brave warrior of my dreams, and to be with elegant and sophisticated people instead of the weavers and hogwards at Gistel. Even Lisebet enjoyed herself, drinking wine in the embrace of someone's aging squire down at the low end of the table.

"Everyone is having such fun," I said to Bertulf, the wine going to my head and the baby kicking strongly in my stomach.

"Almost everyone," he answered. "The Erembalds are not having a good time." He pointed to a group, Borsiard among them, huddled together, mulish and subdued and not enjoying the feasting.

"The Erembalds?" I asked.

"I told you. Borsiard's family. Their uncle, the chamberlain, is not here—back in Bruges counting his gold coins no doubt—but the rest are over there muttering. They think Charles insulted Borsiard deliberately. He'd better watch out."

I was sure Charles would be more than a match for a whole family of Erembalds. Bertulf had promised to take me between courses to the high table to present me to Count Baldwin. With Charles seated at his right hand, surely I would be reunited with him as well. Would he remember me? I bit my lips and pinched my cheeks to give them a glow before we ascended to where the great lords sat.

"My lord Baldwin," Bertulf said, interrupting their conversation. "May I present my new bride, Aude of al-Lawza in the Holy Land." The count accepted this greeting without interest, but to my delight, Charles, who had been talking animatedly to a handsome young man sitting next to him, heard Bertulf's words over the tumult of the merrymakers and broke in.

"The Holy Land? Are you recently returned? Is the new king holding on? I fought there once, years ago."

He was addressing Bertulf but I answered. "Sire, I recall when you were there. You rescued me."

"I rescued you?" He looked at me blankly. He had no idea who I was.

But I pressed on. "Yes. From the walls of Jerusalem when I was a young girl. Remember? I had fallen."

He smiled, transforming the somber cast of his visage, and his beautiful blue eyes twinkled at me. "The heroine who stormed the walls! Of course I remember. I am delighted to see that you survived to adulthood. Welcome back to you both. May I introduce you to my friend here, Fromold." The handsome young man smiled at us politely, then the two went back to talking.

Bertulf, uncomfortable and puzzled by this familiarity, put his arm around my shoulders and escorted me back to our place. I wished him at the bottom of the sea. But I passed the rest of the feast in a haze of joy, oblivious to jesters cavorting and drunkards vomiting. Charles remembered me. And he had smiled. And maybe Bertulf would be tragically yet heroically killed in the upcoming battle with the French, and Charles would be sent to bring his battered body home to Gistel on his shield, and he would see me, brave yet grief-stricken, and…and…and…My imagination kept me happy all night long as I scarcely slept a wink.

A loud snort interrupted my tale. It was Alice. "Do you expect us to believe that you seriously thought there could be a match between you, a landless orphan, and Charles, a king's son, who had met you once when you were, what, six years old, and again when you were pregnant by another man?"

I was hurt by her words, but they caused me to reflect. Had I really believed that Charles would pine for me, would seek me out? I forced myself to think my way back into the mind of the young girl I had been then. "I was fifteen years old," I said, my voice steady. "My parents were dead, I had lost my home, and I had no one but an old man who disgusted and frightened me, who had murdered his first wife. Charles was nothing but a dream, and you could have compelled me to admit that, even back then. But it was a dream that kept me alive," I said, and as I heard the words coming out of my mouth, I realized they were true. The dream of Charles had given me hope.

"You're not so special," said Berthe. "At fourteen, I was married off to the highest bidder, a man even older than your Bertulf."

That explained a lot, I thought to myself. "Just because it happened to you and to me, doesn't mean it's right," I said fiercely.

They stared at me, incredulous, all but Eleanor. "But this is how the world works," said Ermine, sadly.

"Do you want to hear my story or not?" I asked.

"Yes," said Eleanor. "Go on."

The day after the feast was the grand melee of all the knights, divided into two teams. Bertulf and his men fought on the side of the

Erembald family, along with many more, while Charles and William of Clito battled for the opposing team.

So many were on the field, there were barely any to watch the contest. Count Baldwin watched with members of the abbey and the few of us women who had accompanied our husbands. I was drawn to a fuzzy-headed blonde girl about my age who stood with some servants.

"Is your husband among the combatants?" I asked conversationally.

Her eyes widened. "No, no. Not my husband."

"Your father?"

"No." She turned away, and I gave up. Lisebet, who knew all the gossip about everyone, was much more interesting than this shy rabbit.

The grand melee worked like the jousts of the previous day, but multiplied a hundred times. Two rows of knights, extending further than the eye could see, faced off against each other, lances ready. Much of the melee would be out of sight, but the best fighters were closest to us. I could see the Erembalds, and Charles with his allies, all wearing the insignia of the lions of Denmark. Bertulf was further down the line, opposite a skinny youth who'd be no match for his bulk behind the thrust of a lance.

The master of the joust came to the front of the lines. He raised his banner, which signaled the men to shout their war cries, a cacophony of different mottoes in at least three languages, so different from the united "Deus volt!" I heard in the Holy Land. At a sign from the count, he lowered the banner and blew on his horn. "Laissiez-les aller!" he shouted, but they were already off, lances levelled, horses charging. The two lines met in a confusion of men and horses. The lucky ones who kept their mounts rode straight through, trying to turn their horses around quickly to charge again. A knight who could unhorse more than one opponent and remain seated himself would earn extra points. Many were down already, and their squires came quickly to take their horses out of harm's way, while the knights themselves sought out others on foot to try in single combat. Others were out of the fight for good, and one of the count's men nursed a broken arm. Soon all the horses were off the field and groups of men roamed the pitch, seeking out others to fight. Borsiard and five of the Erembalds were working together and I feared they were looking for Charles, hoping as a group for the revenge that Borsiard couldn't win on his own. But Charles had slipped away to some other part of the field I couldn't see.

They found a new target in a knight wearing Charles's blue lions. It was Fromold, the man we met the previous night. Fighting alone in a corner against an opponent who quickly surrendered, he was caught off guard when Borsiard and his men surrounded him. They jeered at Fromold, shouting insults. It was more of a mockery than a battle. No match for six at once, he was quickly deprived of his sword. That should have been the end of it, but Borsiard wanted more. Someone knocked his helm off, then they grabbed him and stripped him of his hauberk. This was bad enough, but then they proceeded to strip him right down to his small clothes, ripping off each garment one by one. As each article was removed, a sniggering squire removed it from the field and out of Fromold's reach, while he bellowed and roared and his adversaries hooted at him. His adversaries left him at last, laughing, and an abashed squire ran up to him with a cloak.

The melee continued, as it would for many hours, little knots of men fighting each other for glory and honor all over the field, but I had seen enough and retreated with Lisebet to rest my pregnant self with a nap before I dressed for the feast that would end the day.

"Fromold won't let that insult go unpunished," said Lisebet. "They struck at him to attack Charles. I hope the Erembalds know what they're doing. They've made an enemy for life now."

At dinner, Charles was the hero. He won the prize, a silver-embroidered belt, for the joust the day before, and for the melee, where he unseated two knights in a row. Count Baldwin toasted him again and again while the Erembalds grumbled. Finally, Count Baldwin stood and spoke. "Today and yesterday we saw feats of arms from my most loyal cavaliers. Tomorrow we leave for battle in Normandy, to win a dukedom for my cousin and to teach our English opponents to fear the knights of Flanders."

Drunk cheers greeted this call to arms and the idiot on the bench next to me spilled red wine on my dress when he stood to holler his enthusiastic assent to his lord. When the crowd settled, Baldwin continued. "But as the priests and our host, the good abbot, warn, life is a frail and dangerous business and men's fortunes are precarious. For this reason, should anything happen to me, I commend my county of Flanders into the hands of my beloved cousin, Charles of Denmark, with the charge that he rule it and guide it as I would. I have tested his industry and his integrity and he is the only one I trust to follow in my footsteps. He will remain in Bruges and rule the county while we win honor and glory in Normandy."

Knights up and down the long tables hastily crossed themselves to avert misfortune, then applauded Baldwin's words in a sober fashion, pleased that their childless lord was looking to the uncertain future. I was spinning dreams of Bertulf far away and Charles close at hand. Might he travel to inspect his castellanies, including Gistel? One could hope.

But Baldwin hadn't finished. "And lest the brave and noble line of Denmark fade into obscurity, and lest Charles himself remain bereft of the joys and delights that can come only with feminine companionship…"

These words caused a group of young men sitting near William Clito to stamp their feet and pound on the table with their tumblers. Pretty with curled hair, elegant dress, and rude manners, they were a group of courtiers who accompanied Baldwin wherever he went. They must have known what was coming next, though I had no clue what made them react so.

A broad grin on his face, the Count gestured for them to be silent, and continued. "With these thoughts in mind, I have arranged for Charles to be married before us this evening to Marguerite de Clermont, the beautiful daughter of one of my most loyal allies. He will receive the county of Amiens as a wedding gift in the contract that has already been signed. She and her mother are with us, and may come forth now, so vows can be exchanged and the abbot can give his blessing."

Two women rose from places close to the head table, an older woman and the fluffy blonde I had conversed with so unsuccessfully at the melee. I was stunned. Was I really seeing this, Charles married to another woman before my eyes, when I had just found him again?

The hall was in a joyous uproar at this news. The two women approached the head table and Baldwin's courtiers stood and sang an obscene song called "Bedding the Bride" at the top of their lungs. It was in heavy Flemish dialect, but the rude gestures that went along with the tune made its meaning clear even to me.

I watched as Charles and then Marguerite repeated the words that bound them together for life. Charles put the ring on her finger. The tumult in the hall was so great that I could not hear them speak, nor the words of the abbot's solemn blessing. The only thing that gave me meagre solace was the look of discomfort and — dare I hope? — even disgust on Charles's face. Perhaps it was only disapproval of the antics of Baldwin's courtiers, who were playing at being shy brides and lecherous grooms, chasing each other through the hall and mock humping each other when they were captured. But maybe he shared the regret that I felt. Marguerite was shaking like a frightened rabbit, but I cared nothing for her.

The ceremony was over, Marguerite eternally bound before God and man to Charles, my Charles. I sat stunned, ignoring my neighbors while noise and feasting swirled around me, mindlessly toasting the bride and groom when called to in a hall of revelers who grew drunker and louder by the minute. When it came time to escort the new couple to bed, I pled exhaustion to Bertulf, but he refused to let me retreat to the guest house.

"There's no better luck for a pregnant woman than to see a man take a virgin bride," he said, so off I trooped with the rest across the courtyard and up to the chamber that had been allotted to Charles. We'd never all fit, of course, but it seemed to be the custom in this barbaric place to get as close to the bridal bed as possible. But when we got to the door of the chamber, we had a surprise. Charles sent Marguerite in ahead of him, and then turned to address us, his tall body completely blocking the door frame.

"This far and no further, my lords," he said.

"What? You're not going to let us in to watch?" someone called from behind me.

"No, I am not," he answered to angry murmurs, but before an organized protest could be launched, he retreated into the chamber and shut and barred the door behind him. Some tried feebly to bang on it and force it open, but the solid oak wouldn't budge and it was clear the pair would not emerge until morning so everyone wandered off to bed or more drinking.

We woke to chilly and unceasing rain. The guesthouse was chaotic as Lisebet and I tried to get ready to leave. Bertulf was out in the courtyard, seeing to his men and all their equipment. They were heading immediately to Normandy to fight the English. Charles and his new bride came into the courtyard, but the cheers that greeted them were few and distracted as men completed more pressing tasks. Their time of wedded bliss would be short. Charles was heading straight to Bruges, but Marguerite was to await her lord alone in his castle of Encre.

Bertulf and I said goodbye at the riverbank, both distracted by our separate journeys. Still, I was grateful enough that he had brought me to Oudenburg to see Charles that I spontaneously kissed his cheek.

"Take good care of my son," he said, patting my belly. "I'll be home before you know it, no longer than a fortnight I expect, long before your time comes."

A fortnight. I hoped for a longer reprieve from his attentions than that. God willing, they'd be gone for at least a month. The less time I spent with Bertulf, the less likely I was to follow the fate of my predecessor, Godeleva.

✠

"Bad husbands. Why are there so many of them?" sighed Eleanor.

"To try our souls and teach us patience so we might better merit the rewards of heaven," answered Mabilie primly. "Look what happened to Godeleva. She's a saint now."

"Yes, after Bertulf drowned her in the river. No thank you very much," I retorted. "It's worst for those who marry people from distant places, like me and Bertulf. If I had married the knight down the lane, and then we decided we didn't like each other, we could surely find some mutual ancestor a few generations back, and quick as a wink the Church would separate us to halt a consanguineous marriage. But Bertulf and I shared no common blood and so the

Church said we had to stick together for life. Which didn't turn out to be for that long, praise the Lord. In any case, there's nothing like a dash of consanguinity to get you out of a sticky situation."

"Consanguinity! That's the answer. It's so obvious, I don't know why I didn't think of it immediately. Bless you, Aude, you've solved my problem. I must go tell Raymond." Eleanor jumped up, hugged me hard and then fled the room. Mabilie and I looked at each other, confused. What scheme had my words put into her head?

CHAPTER SIX

Antioch, June 1148

✠

I soon discovered how my careless words had inspired Eleanor.

I don't know where she slept that night. I didn't want to know. She was in her chamber in the morning when we went to dress her. "The white linen tunic this morning with the gold frontal, I think. My hair in a simple braid and no jewels. Just the gold circlet. I have an audience with Louis first thing, and I want you all to attend me," she said.

She looked almost innocent when we were finished, if you ignored the excited glitter in her eyes. Trained from childhood to perform always for the public, she managed to suppress her exhilaration once we reached the doors of Louis's quarters, and fixed her features in a mien of penitent piety. She was up to something, that was certain.

She entered and we trailed in her wake, cygnets following an elegant swan. Louis was waiting, seated with the ubiquitous Templars and his chaplain, Odo. She knelt at his feet.

"If you have come to persuade me to put off my pilgrimage and fight with Raymond, my queen, I warn you that my mind is fully made up. I am going to Jerusalem, and you are coming with me," he began, defensive.

"No, my lord. I am here because my conscience is troubling me and I must speak."

"Your conscience?" Behind him, Thierry looked suddenly wary.

"It is about our union, my king. Our marriage. We are living in a state of sin my lord, and we must separate for the good of our souls."

"A state of sin? How so? Why you and I haven't even ... since we left France ... I don't understand."

"It is this. King Robert, your great-great-grandfather was my great-great-great grandfather. That puts us within four degrees of relationship on your side, and five on mine. As you well know, the Church prohibits marital unions within seven degrees of relationship. Am I right about this, Odo?" she turned to Louis's chaplain.

"Yes, technically, but I do think that in this case..."

"You see, Louis? All my nights alone have given me time to think. In the eyes of the Church, our union is a sin. Can we go on pilgrimage to Jerusalem, be shriven in the Church of the Holy Sepulcher, in this state? I, for one, cannot bear such a stain on my soul. If we do not separate, our whole pilgrimage will be wasted, all the money, and all the men who died to bring us here will have lost their lives in vain. And I fear this is why I have never been able to bear a son to you, my king. God is punishing us. There may be no heir for France unless we separate from each other."

"My great-great—what? Really?" said Louis, dazed.

"You...woman!" broke in Thierry, full of rage. I delighted to see him discomfited by my lady. "This is a plot to allow you to get your own way. May I ask what you plan to do once you and the king separate, as you say?"

"Sir, I will remain for a time with my kin, with Raymond my uncle, as long as he will have me here. I and my men may be of some assistance to his military endeavors, since the Templars are too cowardly to assist." Her voice was meek, but her words were hostile.

"Your kin, aye, your kin indeed. Much guilt can lie concealed under kinship's guise." These words startled me. While others might believe he was referring to kinship between Louis and Eleanor, I feared he meant the relationship between Raymond and Eleanor. How much did Thierry know, or guess? And what had he told the king?

The Templar levied a new attack. "My lord," he addressed the king. "It would be a terrible thing if on top of all your military defeats, you were to lose your wife as well." We gasped. Not content with attacking Eleanor, he was now insulting the king himself.

"No, no, de Galeran. Stop," said Louis, his voice full of concern. "Eleanor, dearest, what you say—is it true? Do you genuinely fear that we are in such a state of sin, our whole pilgrimage will be wasted?"

"I do, Louis. Our marriage must be annulled, as if it had never been. Indeed, forbidden by the church, it never truly was a marriage." She gazed up at him with a look on her face so mournful, so weighed down by fear of hell that I snorted, and quickly as possible turned it into a cough. Consanguinity? From a young woman who was sleeping with her own uncle? But I admired her audacity, and anything that put a look of thunder on Thierry's face was just fine by me.

Eleanor was in a jubilant mood by the time we got back to our quarters. She grabbed Mabilie round the waist and danced the older woman around the room, singing, "I'm going to be free, I'm going to be free!" while some of the other women clapped in time.

"Stop, you crazy girl, let me go. I'm going to fall over with exhaustion," said Mabilie, laughing, after they had made the circuit a few times. Eleanor let her go, both women out of breath.

We were in a rambunctious mood, but it soon became obvious that not all those who had attended the audience with us had returned. Berthe, Isabel, and even Alice, who had previously participated to the full in the queen's games, were all gone. In fact, every single one of the Frenchwomen was missing, all but shy, soft-spoken Marie. I barely knew her, despite the close quarters we shared, but it made sense that, with her husband dead and no one else to turn to, she would cling to Eleanor. The rest of the French were taking sides, and they were not choosing the queen.

Eleanor either didn't notice or didn't care about their defection. I excused myself, and made a quick circuit of the rooms around the courtyard that the Frenchwomen had used. Sure enough, each one was vacant, all their clothes and belongings gone. Even Isabel's room, which always looked as if a whirlwind had passed through it, was tidy as a tomb, her messy scarves and cosmetic pots removed along with her clothing. I felt a chill. So this wasn't a spontaneous defection by the French, a sudden reaction to Eleanor's request for an annulment from their king. This had been planned. I tried to remember if all of them had been with us at the audience with the king, and decided that already there had been a few faces missing. The rest must have drifted away when we returned to our quarters.

Eleanor and her loyal women from Aquitaine were still in high spirits when I got back. My return caused Eleanor to finally look about and see how she'd been abandoned. "Aude, you're back," she said. "Our numbers are so reduced this afternoon. Where are all the rest? Is this some French saint's feast day that I am supposed to be observing in the chapel? There are so many, I can't keep track."

"I haven't seen Berthe or Alice since daybreak," said Ermine. "They weren't here when we dressed you this morning."

"I saw servants carrying Alice's belongings out of her room this morning," said Gracia.

"All their rooms are empty," I said. "I went to check. The French-women have all left, it seems not to return."

Eleanor pursed her lips. "I had expected this, but not so soon. Never mind, at least I still have my faithful Marie." She put her arm around the woman's shoulder and gave her a tight squeeze before she spoke again. "And now Aude must tell us another story. Aude, I want to hear how you rid yourself once and for all of your miserable husband."

"Very well." What else could I say? I didn't think this was a time for listening to stories about getting rid of husbands, when we should be figuring out what the French were up to. But the next part of my story had a cautionary warning for a woman left unprotected that I hoped Eleanor would heed. And I had to admit, I was enjoying my new role as storyteller. Maybe too much. I had always been a little too chatty for my own good.

✠

Aude's Sixth Tale: Gistel, Summer 1118–Summer 1119

It was strange being mistress of the castle alone, with Winnoc, Gebirga, and now Bertulf gone. At first I was inclined to let things slide, to nap all day on soiled sheets dreaming of my lost beloved —Charles, of course, not Bertulf—while the cook served the same warmed-over barley porridge and salt beef at every meal, and the fruit rotted in the orchard. But Lisebet took me in hand.

"Stir yourself, Aude," she said, rudely shaking me out of my doze. "The pigs got into the oats again because the boys still haven't mended the fence. There's a fox in the dovecote, the lower pasture is flooded, and cook burned every last one of this week's loaves. We need you."

"Can't someone else take care of it? So many eat their heads off in my hall. Get one of them to look to it, or do it yourself. I'm tired." I rolled onto my other side, curled into as much of a ball as my belly would allow, and willed Lisebet to leave me alone. But this time she was having none of my sulks. She shook me again, hard.

"You're the mistress. You're the only one they'll all listen to. You don't want your babe to grow up in a castle that looks like a sty, do you?"

Those last words hooked me. Alone, with even Bertulf gone, I clung to the promise of my baby more and more. Someone to love, who would love me forever. I rose and reached for the nearest robe to pull it over my shift and for the first time in ages I looked at it critically. "This has seen better days, hasn't it, Lisebet. What are those laundresses up to?"

"They will be our first stop," she said grimly, and we were off. First we tackled the laundresses, who we found lolling about eating biscuits around a tepid vat of soiled linens. They stood when we entered, shocked to see me in their domain.

"No wonder my shifts return to me more soiled after cleaning than before. You, fetch more wood for this fire," I addressed one, trying to channel the voice of my mother. "And where's the soap?" I asked, opening the box and finding it empty. "Tomorrow, you make a supply for the whole castle." They groaned, but silenced themselves when I turned a cold eye onto them.

We went through every corner of the castle and its grounds. After the laundresses, we had a long interview with the steward, Lisebet whispering the right questions to ask in my ear. Over the next couple of weeks, the castle slowly returned to an approximation of what it had been in Gebirga's day. To my surprise, I enjoyed putting the castle to rights. For the first time ever, I felt I had some measure of control over my life.

I was in the orchard supervising the picking of apples and quinces when the five men came. It was late September and already unseasonably cold, so we were bringing in the harvest early. They were a poor substitute for the fresh figs, dates, and even bananas I was used to, but what could I do? The boys were putting the fruit into bins filled with sand, and I was ordering them not to let the fruit touch lest it rot in storage when I was approached from behind.

"Mevrouw—"

I turned. Before me were Bertulf's men, at least some of them, bareheaded and stone-faced, surcoats tattered and grimy. I had travelled half way across the world in their company, but they were still strangers to me.

"You're back," I said. "Is the battle over? Did we win? And where are Bertulf and the others?"

Four deferred to one delegated as their leader. "Mevrouw, the news is bad." He cleared his throat and continued. "We are all that is left from Gistel. The battle was a rout. The French never arrived and the Normans sided with the English against us. We never had a chance. And Lord Bertulf…we have him with us. But he's—"

Suddenly my ears tuned to a keening cry coming from the courtyard, a different song than that sung by the women in Palestine but unmistakable in its common meaning. I sunk to my knees holding my belly. Two of the men helped me to my feet again, and supported me on either side. "Is he badly injured then? Or…"

"He's dead, my lady." The speaker knelt and took my hand, kissing it, a courteous gesture from one I had seen only as a brute. "We brought him to be buried with his own people."

In the courtyard I found mourning women clustering around a cart for the second time in a year. This time there was no Bertulf there to hold me and protect me as I approached the figure on the cart, already sewn tight into a shroud that did not block the reek of decay rising up from the corpse. I waved them aside. "May I see his face one more time?" I asked the leader, who had followed me with the others.

"Better not. An axe cleaved his skull in two and it's not pretty."

We buried him that day. He'd already been above ground too long on the trek by cart back from Normandy. The men levered up a broad stone slab in the floor of the nun's chapel and laid him to rest in a pit dug beneath it, and the convent priest was summoned to sing the funeral mass. I'd have to find a mason to etch a record of his passing on the stone, but for now he was safe, the patron buried in the monastery he had founded.

After the Mass, the nuns clustered around me, hugging me, stroking my hair, and whispering words of comfort. I couldn't tell you which one it was who murmured to me in an undertone, "You had a lucky escape, you know. It could be you we were burying."

I knew that was true.

It was not until that evening at dinner that I thought to ask what had happened to the rest of the army.

"As we said, my lady, it was bad. Many noble knights died on that battlefield. Worst of all, Count Baldwin was sorely injured. He still breathed when we left, but might not survive."

"Might not survive? Are you certain? That means Charles of Denmark will be count."

The men looked at each other and then one spoke. "Charles of Denmark is in control in Bruges for now, but Baldwin's mother, Clemence, sent his bastard cousin, William of Ypres, to take custody of the comital regalia. She hates Charles. If Baldwin dies, William will challenge Charles for Flanders. There will be war."

"And we must support Charles," I said decisively. The men looked at each other again. Clearly they had no appetite for further war at this point. Maybe it wouldn't come to that. And we hardly had the resources to help either side very much. Five men when once we had fifteen? And no lord to lead them. Only me.

If I were a man, I'd have left the very next day to reclaim al-Lawza. The king of Jerusalem would have greeted with favor even a man in disgrace, as long as he had a strong sword arm. But I wasn't a man, I was a very pregnant young woman, due in less than two months. So while flight was my first instinct now I was free, I knew it could not be. But perhaps in the spring?

You might have thought I would fall into my old slothful ways, but the news of Bertulf's death filled me with a strange energy. Though I was bigger and more ungainly than ever, I threw all my energy into the castle. I ordered the hall swept thoroughly and new rushes laid down for winter. When the servants grumbled that changing the rushes was a spring custom, I told them I wasn't having my son born in a festering dump. Every rotten board in the pallisade was repaired, every stone fallen from the bridge was replaced, and rows of smoked hams, bins of salt beef, and tuns of good grain filled the cellar. I terrified the cook by dropping in at odd moments to count the eggs. And when I grew too big to prowl the grounds, I sat before the fire in the hearth and prepared yards and yards of linen bands for swaddling my babe so there would always be a fresh set when he soiled what he was wearing. He wasn't going to sit in filth if I could help it.

While we worked, the cold deepened until it clutched all Flanders in a frigid grip, entirely foreign to me. Some of my frenzy was a simple effort to keep warm. Frozen fog rimed the trees each morning, sparkling under an icy sun. I'd have called it beautiful, if I weren't so cold. I finally gave in to Lisebet's not so subtle hints to allow her off the pallet where she slept in my chamber and into my bed. It was the only way we could sleep without freezing. I don't know how others managed, but it's true that there was a good crop of babies the following summer. Worse than the cold was the dark. The sun barely lifted itself above the horizon before midday before it sank again, as if exhausted.

One frigid morning soon after the beginning of Advent, I woke to feel a dull pain in my back, and a damp rush between my legs. I needed the chamber pot so frequently in recent weeks and I hated to leave my warm bed for it—was it possible I had wet myself? How shameful, and it would ruin the feathers of my lovely bed, feathers newly replaced.

"Lisebet!" I pushed at her arm. "I am afraid I've wet myself, and my back is so sore. Can you help me?"

"Wet yourself?" she said. "It is probably the waters breaking. Your child has decided to be born on the coldest day of the year."

Surely, it wasn't time for my labor yet? I worked out the sums on chilled fingers, my breath visible even indoors. I had expected the baby closer to Christmas. It was my first lesson that children do not always follow the paths laid out for them. Lisebet chivvied me out of bed and told me to keep moving, warning that it might be a while before real labor began. She was right—it was evening before the pain in my back sharpened into a regular series of cramps.

The midwife came with her assistant, both clean and smiling while I sweated and grunted in pain. We worked hard all night without result as my whole world shrank down to the size of my bed chamber.

The sun rose red that day and I traced its progress, vermillion fingers of late dawn moving low in the winter sky from window slit to window slit, every time I could stop and draw breath for a few moments. Sunk deep in an eternal cycle of pain and release, only this told me that time was moving forward and not endlessly circling with me. I was drowned in pain, plunged down into crimson bands of cramp gripping and twisting my body before, mercifully, they ceased and I could rise up and breath again. As was the local custom, I pulled on a long cloth, dyed red for luck and for a boy, and knotted over a rafter, when the pain was at its height. My face was flushed hot and damp with effort but my only reward was that the cycles of pain grew shorter, with less release between cramp.

The midwife's white moon face was anxious where once it had been smiling. From a fog of pain, I heard her speak to Lisebet.

"We need Old Grettie here, and quickly."

"That witch? They wouldn't give her houseroom here. The boys have instructions to throw stones at her if she even approaches the castle."

"She's magic with a difficult birth. If you don't fetch her, I won't answer to the consequences. Take my girl with you. And be fast."

Lisebet seemed about to protest again. With mouth parched and dry, I mustered up one word in a weak voice. "Go," I said, and she did, returning unending rounds of pain later with an old woman. I saw a form approach, a shapeless shuffling heap of old clothes, clubbed staff in a gnarled fist, satchel over her back, and a wild, animal smell. Hair every which way, rheumy eyes, withered cheeks, and long yellow teeth like a horse when she spoke. Her Flemish was backwards-facing and upside down, hard for me to understand.

"Water," she said, "To a scald, not lukeish," and when the midwife's assistant brought her a basin of it, the hag took a green bit of something from her bag and sudsed her hands with it in the water. Only then did she move to inspect me, inside and out, gripping me with sure hands at the height of my contraction.

The midwife spoke to Grettie in a low voice. "The baby is coming the right way and she's fully open. But she's been laboring for hours with no result. I don't understand it."

Grettie grunted and then spoke. "I seen worse. But baby's all knotted. Won't come." She manipulated my abdomen for a moment and then called, "Fancy maid!"

"You mean me?" said Lisebet, after a pause.

"Who but? Take mistress's keys and unlock every coffer, door, and bin in this place. Don't miss a single one. May loosen her." Lisebet ran to do her bidding, eager to be away, and Grettie looked up at the rag suspended right over my head. "Which dwaas tied a rag over the bed of a birthing woman. Some boy must loosen it!"

But no boys could be found, so the midwife's girl was forced up a ladder to untie the red cloth. She left it doubled over the rafter, so I could still pull on it and I did, hard, when the next contraction rocked me. "I can't do this. I can't. It's not coming," I whined.

Grettie was unsatisfied. "Too soft and mild. You light girls fancy birthing's easy. You'll never push the babe without pain. Lazy."

Lazy? Easy? Let her lie on the bed and try it. I was furious and was about to tear a strip off the old witch, but then a contraction hit and I groaned right through it.

"That's well," she grinned. "Push with the rage. And sip on this." She unstoppered a flask she drew from her pack and I drank a bitter, foul draught. Still enraged, I pushed when the next contraction came moaning and grunting, and then again when another followed on the first, sharper and harder, and another and another with no break. I was cursing and calling out without cease and unknowing what I said, all three women between my legs.

"That's it," said the midwife, "One more, hard. And again." A slippery wetness came from within me and then a thin cry rose. "A boy," I heard her say from somewhere very far away. "A beautiful boy, lusty and strong." Grettie pulled my shift all the way up so I was bare bellied and the midwife placed the babe between my breasts and cut the cord. He stared at me, brow furrowed in worry.

"Don't be afraid," I said, "You have me. I'll take care of you." I was tired beyond hope, but elated. A boy, thank God and all His saints. How joyful Bertulf would have been. There was no mistaking it, his male parts were frighteningly large and purple for one so small. The women reassured me that was normal and Lisebet went to spread the news to the castle. I dimly heard cheers raised all over the castle yard. But I was in a world made up of only two people, me and him. They took him from me once the afterbirth was out, and I protested with my limited strength but the midwife said, "Only to bathe and swaddle the babe," and sure enough, she returned him to me and began showing us both how to nurse. "What's his name?" she asked.

I was stumped for a moment. Bertulf's family names seemed too heavy to be borne by such a new, fresh babe.

"Theodore," I said. "His name is Theodore." After my mother, Theodosia.

"It's a bit outlandish," the midwife said doubtfully. "Not a name you hear in these parts."

"Aude and Theodore," said Grettie. "You two are bound tight. Were in the womb and will always be. Well, I'm away," she finished expectantly.

I was recalled to my duties while the child suckled, a quick learner. "Yes, we must give you . . . coins?"

"No gold. Meat?" she said hungrily.

"Meat, yes. Take her to the kitchen and let her take whatever she wants."

And that's how Theodore came into the world.

The cold didn't abate, but I was lit by my own fire, of love for my new boy. Lisebet scoffed at it for a peasant custom, but I bound him to me in a long, wide linen sling, and carried him everywhere I went. It was the only way I felt sure he'd be warm enough. We'd heard of a child down by the river, frozen in his cradle one night, family none the wiser. The fresh air did him good. He had the roses of spring in his cheeks and ate enough for two. I showed him round his domain.

"Look, see those cows?" They were thin and gaunt on their winter diet. "Those are your cows. And the sheep? Your sheep. And the barn, and the keep, and all the fields around. Your fields. You are the lord and everything around us belongs to you." Unimpressed, he blew bubbles.

He smiled when we celebrated Christmas week. At least I insisted it was a smile. Lisebet said it was gas. By spring, when the lambs were born, he could roll over and hold onto his rattle and once the roses were in bloom, he could sit up by himself. In the outside world, Count Baldwin was still dangerously ill, and great men struggled to wield control, but no one disturbed our calm, while I dandled my boy and watched over my castle. I hadn't forgotten my plans to return to al-Lawza, but I put it off. Maybe in another fortnight. No later than next month. If we left now, who'd see the shearing was done properly? And if we missed Godeleva's feast day, the sisters would never forgive me. So time passed and the sun shone, and I began to heal, inside and out.

I lured a stone mason out from Bruges to inscribe Bertulf's slab, and I took him to the convent to consult on the design. He was a garrulous old fellow who spread gossip while he chipped stone.

"This won't be the last monument to that terrible Norman war, my lady. Did you hear? Count Baldwin finally passed on. They thought he was getting better, but then he up and died. And him with no wife and no heir."

"What will happen to Flanders?" I asked. "Who will rule the county?"

"We'll call Charles of Denmark, count, you mark me. Could do worse. He's pious, they say, so more work for stonemasons building churches."

"And Marguerite will be countess. Was she with him in Bruges?" I was poison green with jealousy. With Bertulf dead, I could have been countess, if Charles hadn't been forced to wed that whey-faced Marguerite. Yes, I was still dreaming. Never mind that a dowry of al-Lawza and Gistel, and all tied up in my small son, was hardly enough to tempt the ruler of one of the richest lands in Christendom, as Alice and Berthe have reminded me. Providence was on my side. Why else would God drag me half way round the world? But the devil in the shape of Count Baldwin and that dizzy ewe, Marguerite, had thwarted His plans.

The mason laughed. "That's not a man with much use for a wife. From what they say, she hasn't spent one day outside the castle of Enrce and he hasn't spent one day in it since they were wed. Or one night, if you catch my meaning."

I was such a fool with my silly dreams. Only sixteen then, and the center of my own world, I thought I was the heart of everyone else's world too. So I cared for my castle and watched my babe grow, and kept half an ear cocked for my rescue, while the days passed and no one came.

And then one day, someone did come.

I was nursing Theodore while the other women wove and spun, when we heard loud noises coming from the courtyard, shouts and cries. Before I could ask what was going on, a servant ran through the door into the hall.

"Mevrouw Aude! There are men outside on horses, with drawn swords. And a very great lady. And a man, a lord dressed rich as the sun. He wants you to come out. He shouted."

A lord? Richly dressed? My heart leapt in shock. Had Charles come after all? I ignored Hille's mention of a lady with him.

I removed a protesting Theodore and refastened my robe so I was decent for meeting guests and walked to the open door of the castle, which faced into the sun. At the base of its ladder stairs down to the courtyard, an array mounted figures surrounded a man on horseback, tall in the saddle with a halo of glowing blond hair. I squinted in the brightness. Who could it be but Charles?

"You've come for me. I knew you would," I said, triumph in my voice.

"I don't see how when we've never met," a strange voice answered. It wasn't Charles after all. "But we have all the time in the world to get acquainted."

"Who are you? And how did you pass the gatehouse into my castle?" I asked, suddenly frightened.

"Who did you think I was? And it's not your castle. Wasn't and isn't now. It's mine. I'm Christian, Bertulf's long lost cousin. Such a pleasure to finally make the acquaintance of the beloved wife of dear, deceased Bertulf. I see tales told in Bruges of your beauty were true to its reality only as the pallid moon dimly reflects the blistering glow of the sun."

His words were sweet but the mockery in his voice belied them. I climbed down the ladder with Theodore clinging to my side while the man dismounted. Now I could see that although they shared stature and hair color, this man looked nothing like Charles. A craggy face weathered by wind and battle, I was compelled to admit he was handsome. "You can stay for one night and then be gone," I said. "I want your dogs outside, and your men in the stable. I'll have pallets brought for you in the hall. We'll eat, we'll sleep, then first thing in the morning you will leave my castle."

"And a tongue as blistering as the sun too," Christian answered, unperturbed by my words. "No, Aude. Not yours. My castle. My castle, my stables, my pallets. My. Castle. If anyone leaves here tomorrow, it won't be me."

"I'll sue you at law. I'll go to the count. Charles, the count—."

"The count? Talk all you like. Bang on the doors of the castle at Bruges and demand an audience. That will get you out of my hair. But you won't get help from that quarter. Who do you think made me castellan of Gistel in the first place?"

His words cut me. Far from rescuing me, Charles had betrayed me. I was silenced.

Christian gestured to the woman on the horse beside him. "Come, beautiful and graceful bride, dismount and greet your new cousin. Aude of Gistel, meet Edith, your new mistress."

His tone was ironic and I could see why after she clumsily got off her pony and waddled over to meet me, obeying his command. Her clothing was splendid but she was dumpy and homely, flushing under her husband's cruel mockery. "Edith is an Erembald. Does that mean anything to you? I see it does."

It did. That was Borsiard's clan, from the joust, who helped him humiliate Charles's friend, Fromold. Obviously Charles awarded Christian with the castellany to keep the powerful Erembalds on his side. But I would not give up. "I know my rights," I said. "I'm a widow with a son. I can't be turned out. The land was Bertulf's and on his death it passes to his son, whoever holds the castellany. I'm his guardian, and as long as I live, I have a portion." I was clutching Theodore close in fear, and he started to whimper.

"Don't hold that babe so tightly, Aude. You'll smother the poor thing. Listen to him fuss. Yes, the land was Bertulf's, and your child will inherit. Assuming he lives to adulthood. He looks healthy, though children are sadly prone to accidents. But the castellany is the count's, to be given to someone who can defend it. Gistel is too important to be left in the hands of a woman and a weakling babe. Of course if I were single, I could have married you, wedding castellany and castle as they were in Bertulf's day. Since I already have a wife, the two of you are going to have to share me."

He leered and I realized my robe had slipped. I pulled it close and said, "Share you? How revolting!" Edith twisted her hands together at his crudity, and a mottled red flush stained her doughy face.

"Then may the best woman win," said Christian, unrepentant. "No, Aude, I'm the new castellan of Gistel. And my first task is to replace the men guarding the gate. Remiss of them to allow so many armed strangers inside. But they've been adequately punished. My men killed them."

Several of his men came forward then and dumped the broken, bloodied bodies of the men on guard duty that day, men who had given their lives to protect me. Some had survived the slaughter in Normandy and the others were boys, too young to fight the English, now killed at home by Bertulf's cousin. Floerkin and Piet from Gistel, and Claude, Hugo, Guy and the twins whose names I never got straight who came with us from Palestine, all joined in ugly death.

A chill seized my vitals. "You don't belong here. Your line was disinherited long ago, and you became pirates. You can't do this."

"Mevrouw, I already have."

He was right. The dead men at my feet were the only ones I had sworn to my service. I could do nothing.

✠

Eleanor shivered. "I hate how that story ended, Aude. It should have been Charles riding up on a big horse to rescue you, not that Christian. He sounds like a nasty piece of work."

"Oh, he had his good points too. But a woman on her own is vulnerable, as you well know. No one can stand to see an heiress enjoy her inheritance in peace. And a woman with a child is even more vulnerable, for her child can be used as a hostage against her," I replied.

Was I too pointed? Eleanor seemed to think she could be free from her distasteful marriage with no evil consequences. Even if Louis allowed it, de Galeran and the others who advised the king would not let the rich prize of Aquitaine slip through their fingers without a struggle. And Eleanor had a baby daughter left home in France while her parents went crusading. Was Eleanor content to lose her, as she surely would if she went through with this annulment?

But she gave no sign my words had made any impression. We dressed her for dinner, and she was resplendent as usual, glittering in her jewels and silks, and charming everyone from the nobles lucky enough to sit close by to the servant boys who fetched her food and drink. But was Raymond a little less attentive than usual? My misgivings about that relationship were vast. Not only was Raymond her uncle (her uncle!), but he was married, and his claim to be prince of Antioch came solely through the wife who picked at her food and watched him with a stern eye. Eleanor and Raymond could never marry, even if she were free. Did she intend to hang about in Antioch as his unofficial concubine? Had she thought this through? And would Louis really let her go? The king glumly fiddled with the enamels on his gold goblet, while his maybe-not-for-long wife sparkled. The Templars were missing from the table, and I wondered what plots they were hatching.

If she left her husband, and remained in Antioch, I would have to abandon her service. My mission was in the south, and though my reasons were different, my need to reach Jerusalem was as strong as the king's. The prospect of leaving Eleanor made me sadder than I would have expected, and I vowed I would not slip away like the cowardly Frenchwomen. I would bid farewell and be released properly. On the other hand, I would shed no tears at leaving the Antioch court. I neither liked nor trusted Raymond. True, he looked like one of the Greek gods whose marble forms still peppered the palace, ravaged by time but still stunning. He had been gracious and charming to us, but that was a veneer that would peel back the moment he didn't get his way. In truth, he recalled Christian more than Eleanor wanted to know.

I thought of other, very different, men I had known, lingering longest on the memory of grey eyes that could look serious or twinkle and a form solid like an oak tree you could shelter under, last seen on the beach at Lisbon. Those thoughts led only to pain, and I pushed them out of my mind, but I tossed and turned that night in my narrow bed, unable to sleep. Eve was restless too, and kept moving from perch to perch, probably bilious from the sweetmeats the other women insisted on feeding her at dinner. A palace was no place for a monkey, and I resolved to free her as soon as I could find monkey-kind of her own in the wild to join. Though when that would be the Lord only knew, since I had no plans to return to the land where I had found her.

I must have slept at some point, because the next thing I knew, a woman's scream woke me. I sat bolt upright in bed in the pitch dark, pulling the cover around me, but before I could cry out, intruders burst into my chamber. I gagged as they shoved a wad of cloth in my mouth. They bound it tightly with another cloth, then tossed my clothing at me. I dressed, when ordered, with much fumbling and little modesty. I heard the interlopers messing with my belongings, but whether they were ransacking them or packing them, I could not say. Once I was dressed, they rigged another cloth around my head so I'd look like I was deeply veiled and bound my wrists with a rope which they used to pull me from my chamber. Eve leapt onto my shoulder, nearly knocking me down. She had grown considerably since I rescued her as a baby.

"Get that monkey off!" a strange male voice shouted, but another refused. "Those teeth! She'll bite me." I was relieved. What could I have done if they had separated us?

They dragged me through Raymond's palace by the rope, and I struggled to keep up with my captor without tripping. From the noises around me and the scream I first heard, I assumed that all Eleanor's women had met my fate, perhaps even the queen herself. I tried to figure out where we were heading, but soon lost all sense of direction. We went down a staircase, and from the smell of stale food and then the funk of the sewers, I realized we were in parts of the palace I had never seen by the light of day. The passage narrowed and we were pressed up against each other, captors and women all together. One women put her hands between mine as if giving or seeking reassurance. I felt a flat stone ring I knew well. Eleanor.

I squeezed tightly, but before I could do more, a grinding noise and a blast of cool air before us told me we were leaving the palace.

A quick exchange of words at the town gate and the clink of coins changing hands allowed our captors to pass through with us. But which gate? I was thoroughly turned around, and with the gag in my mouth and veil over my head, I could barely breathe. They dragged us through rutted lanes until we stopped, and I heard the snort of horses. Rough hands grabbed my left foot and jammed it in a stirrup, then I was hoisted up onto the animal's back, like a wool sack tossed into a ship's hold. They wound the rope binding my wrists around the pommel before me, so that if I fell by accident or on purpose, my arms would be pulled out of their sockets. One of my captors climbed up behind me, onto a saddle that was not designed for two. Eve climbed down from my shoulder to huddle in what there was of my lap, between my bound arms. I prayed she'd hold on tight. I knew if she fell, no one would return for her and she'd be lost in whatever wastes we rode through. I clung to the pommel with my bound hands as best I could, and we rode out into what was left of the night.

CHAPTER SEVEN

The Castle of Margat, June 1148

✠

I hurtled blind through the night on that horse, wedged in front of my captor. My arms were numb, my thighs ached from the unaccustomed exercise, and the gag was beginning to choke me until I feared I'd be sick. Breathe, I told myself, keep breathing through your nose and you'll be all right. The worst was not knowing why we'd been taken, by whom, or where we were going. Oh, I had strong suspicions, and time to weigh them. The Templars were involved, I was certain.

We stopped. I'd been smelling salt for the last few miles, and after I clumsily dismounted and they released my wrists and pulled the hood off my head, I saw we were on the coast, high above the sea, the first fingers of dawn beginning to touch its surface. My captor untied my gag with fumbling fingers, and I spat the wad of cloth out of my mouth. I rubbed my wrists to get the feeling to come back into them. My travelling companion's white cloak confirmed my expectations: he was a Templar. I comforted Eve while the other women and their captors, Templars all, dismounted.

We faced a square, stone fortress of dreary black basalt blocks that spoke of dominating the countryside and terrorizing the peasantry, not brave deeds of chivalry and conquest. We were on a cliff above the sea, a barren and rocky landscape overlooking pounding surf below. There were more horses and riders than there were women, and I saw that the Templars who didn't share their horses with my companions carried bundles that I hoped contained our belongings.

One by one, the other women emerged from their bonds: Mabilie, Marie, Ermine, and Gracia. Ermine vomited the moment the gag was removed from her mouth. She was plagued with rheums that blocked her nose—she said it was a consequence of all the strange flowers and plants she was encountering on her travels—and the gag must have been a double torture for her, unable to breathe. Marie and Gracia clung together once they were released. Thierry de Galeran emerged from the fortress, a grim smile on his face.

Eleanor was the last to be freed. When they pulled the hood from her head, instead of looking scared and ill like the rest of us, she seemed oddly exultant. Her look of joy quickly changed to horror, however, when she saw Thierry de Galeran before her.

"You!" she said.

"You were expecting someone else, perhaps?"

He was right, I realized. Eleanor must have thought Raymond was stealing us away, to protect her from the wrath of her husband. Poor Eleanor, thinking she was being rescued by her beloved, only to find her worst enemy. I knew what that felt like.

"How dare you abduct us?" she cried. "How dare you set your pack of ruffians to pull us from our beds against our will and drag us to this hovel by the sea? Look at my women, what you've done to them. Ermine so ill, and the rest frightened out of their wits. Return us to Antioch immediately!"

Return us, yes, I thought. But not immediately. Our midnight ride had drained me so, I thought I'd fall over if someone didn't lead me to a bench soon.

"I, abduct you, your majesty? I had no say in this affair. I was following the orders of a man who holds every right to summon you," said Thierry, smugness dripping off him.

"Is that her?" a male voice called from within the castle portal.

Without waiting for a reply, King Louis himself emerged from the fortress, enraged to a degree I could not have imagined. He walked to Eleanor and stared at her without speaking. Then, "You slut. You slut. Your own uncle," he said. "You seduced your own uncle. And you dared to charge me with the sin of consanguinity." He slapped her face, so hard that the red marks of his fingers immediately rose on its surface, and she had to brace herself from the blow. Maybe he feared what he'd do next, for he turned around and walked quickly back into the castle.

The moment he was gone, Marie burst into hysterical weeping, shaking and blubbering, until a sharp, "Calm yourself, woman!" from Thierry made her cries fade into gasping sobs. I didn't want to weep. I wanted to hit someone too. Which of the lying, sniveling French ladies had told the king about Eleanor and Raymond after they fled her service? How could anyone who served Eleanor ever do such a thing?

Eleanor was deathly calm, despite the red welts on her face. "What next?" she asked Thierry coolly.

"We spend a few days here, and then we proceed south, first to Tripoli, where I expect we will be met by the rest of the French nobility and knighthood, and perhaps some of your men from Aquitaine. Then we continue south to Acre, where on the feast of Saint John there will be a council of all the barons to plan where to attack. You won't attend the actual council, because women have no say in the making of war."

"And Raymond of Antioch? What of him?"

"He will be invited to join us in Acre, but I fear he will not come. Poor man has too much on his plate to worry about an assault on Aleppo now. Word is that the Normans in Sicily and the Greeks are all out for his blood."

"Very well. My women and I need food and drink, perhaps a little warmed wine. We also need a place to rest, to finish the sleep so rudely stolen from us. See to it."

Without waiting for a reply, Eleanor walked into the keep, head held high and the rest of us women following close behind. I was proud of her. She wouldn't let anyone intimidate her.

We were hustled up a narrow ladder to the second story of the keep. They brought us spartan Templar food to eat, and, a little warmed wine, which we ate and drank in silence. Bundles along one wall proved to be our belongings, but we barely glanced at them before we collapsed on the straw pallets unrolled for us and one by one fell fast asleep.

I woke suddenly, and with a crick in my neck from the hard stone floor. Sun was streaming through the slit windows of the keep, but on a mid-June day it was impossible to tell what time it was—it could as easily be evening as midday. Slowly, groggily I pulled myself up, to find Mabilie already awake and staring at me. When she caught my gaze, she quickly turned away. What was that about, I wondered.

The other women also began to wake, stretching and unkinking knotted shoulders and backs. A basin of water had been left for us, and we washed as best we could, then planned what to do next.

"Are we prisoners up here? Would they allow us to leave the castle?" asked Ermine.

"Let's find out." Eleanor made for the ladder, and put an elegantly shod foot on the first rung.

"The commander thinks it would be safer for you and your women to remain upstairs today, your majesty. Just for today," a voice called from the bottom, polite but firm.

"And who are you to keep us upstairs?" Eleanor asked, but she stopped descending the ladder.

"At your service, your majesty. The commander asked me to remain here and to make sure you were not molested or disturbed in any way."

And to make sure we couldn't get out. Maybe they thought Raymond would ride after us. He must have a good idea of which direction we'd gone, and where we could be. I didn't think he'd come either for Eleanor, or for Aquitaine's army, which was large, but not quite large enough to risk open hostility with the king of France. Maybe Eleanor realized that too. Beaten, she retreated from the ladder, and the little bit of spirit she had shown was extinguished. I wondered what she was thinking. Did she hope for romantic rescue, an army storming the castle or a midnight ladder at a window and a solitary hero stealing her back again?

She spoke, though she seemed preoccupied and distracted. "If we can't leave this room, then we must entertain ourselves as best we can here. I suppose my books and things are in one of those bundles, but I don't have the heart to search through them now, and I imagine no one feels much like singing. Thank goodness we have our own entertainer with us. Aude, help us pass the time with another tale from your history. Something with a happy ending, please. We need some good news."

"No!" said Mabilie, suddenly. "We want no more of Aude's story-telling."

"What do you mean?" asked Eleanor.

"I turned this over and over in my mind during our dreadful ride through the night. One of us betrayed you to the king. We have a spy in our midst," said Mabilie. Gracia woman gasped, and the rest of us looked at each other as if the word "spy" would be suddenly emblazoned on someone's forehead.

"Whatever are you talking about, Mabilie," asked Eleanor, though she didn't sound much like she cared about the answer.

"Aude is a spy. She has been sneaking around, following you and Raymond and putting disgusting suggestions about your behavior into the king's mind. Her criticism of Thierry de Galeran is an act to make us think they are enemies. Remember, she told us she has known him since her childhood." The other women stared at me as if I was the whole Muslim army. All of a sudden, I felt very much alone.

Eleanor shrugged, as if indifferent to the question. "That seems unlikely. If there were a spy in our midst, which I do not discount, it was probably one of the Frenchwomen who left my service."

It was hardly a ringing defense, and I felt hurt. Eleanor knew how I hated de Galeran, and why. How could I have betrayed her to him?

"But your majesty, she told me she saw you with Raymond. Who else could have told Thierry? We know nothing about her. Why did she appear so conveniently on the pier in Antioch when she did? She was in Templar service from the beginning. She's not from France, she's not from Aquitaine, she's not one of us, and she didn't suffer the hardships we endured to get to Antioch. And her mother is Armenian, of all things. Who knows anything about them?"

"Leave my mother out of it!" I said, furious.

"She doesn't even deny it," said Mabilie.

"That's because it is a ridiculous accusation," I said. I was shocked and hurt that Mabilie, of all people, turned against me.

"Stop, both of you. Aude, tell us a story. Mabilie, sit down and listen with the rest."

"I don't want to listen—"

"I order you to listen." Mabilie sat down with bad grace, arms crossed over her chest as if to ward off any new lies I might tell. The other women looked equally mutinous, and Eleanor didn't even seem to be paying attention. Lovely. Did an entertainer in a tavern ever have such an unwilling audience? I wanted to snap back that I didn't care if Mabilie listened or not, but obedient to Eleanor, I kept my mouth shut.

Eleanor had walked over to the small window in the keep and was gazing out of it as if willing a rescuer to arrive. She wanted a happy ending, did she? Well, there are no happy endings, no rescuers. The sooner Eleanor learned that, the better, and I had a story to drive that message home.

✠

Aude's Seventh Tale: Gistel and Bruges, 1119–1123

Christian and Edith's arrival changed everything. The ritual of humiliation that happened when Bertulf and I came to supplant Winnoc and Gebirga replayed itself again. A lower seat at the table I could suffer—I had no choice—and walking half a pace behind Edith was endurable. But I was wiser, or more stubborn than Gebirga had been. I drew the line at my keys.

"No," I said when Christian asked for them on the very first day they arrived. I had already been around the castle with Edith and seen her grow more and more agitated as the complexities of castle life were laid out for her.

"I couldn't possibly. However do you know these things, Aude?" she said soft-voiced, wringing her hands in agitation, every time I showed her a new task. It seemed she was town bred and spoiled, even more so than I, though she was sweet where I was proud.

"No," I said again when Christian repeated his call for Edith to take my keys, a demand this time instead of a request. "Do you see in what good order you find our castle? That is due to me. I have a responsibility to protect Theodore's patrimony, and for that, I need the keys. Besides, Edith couldn't cope," I said, not caring how cruel I sounded. "Can you imagine her bossing the cook or preventing the steward from cheating us? He does, you know, unless you keep after him."

Edith looked nervous and made no protest and I marked how Christian seemed to despise her willingness to allow another woman to usurp her rightful role, pondering how I could use his contempt for his wife to regain my own place. "Very well," he said, "Aude may keep the keys and be in charge."

I smiled, tight lipped. I wasn't afraid. I may have lost the great war, but there was a battle or two I could still win.

For all Christian's eagerness to be castellan of Gistel, he still hankered after his sea-borne life. I'd find him in the hall, staring longingly at the tapestry that showed his ancestor's exile from the castle and new career on the sea.

"They got the ship all wrong," he'd say. "My grandfather's boat looked nothing like this."

"It was done long before my time," I answered, trying to ingratiate myself with my new master. "But maybe we can do a new one, showing all your fleet."

His ships still trolled the North Sea for fish and occasionally pirated the fat pickings from the merchant ships that plied between Flanders and England carrying wine, wool, and cloth. When the wind blew salt breezes from the north, he'd mumble about his fleet and be gone for weeks at a time, returning weathered, brown, and happy, with all kinds of treats, mussels we'd steam open in beer and flavor with leek, winkles to eat with a pin, tiny shrimps preserved in butter, or fresh fish to relieve our tedious Lenten and Friday diet of pickled herrings and salt cod dried into great, greyish boards. Sometimes finer things returned with him on his travels, a bolt of figured cloth, a pectoral cross studded with gems, and narwhal ivory carved into the shape of the Virgin. The first made gowns for Edith and myself, the second was a gift for the abbess, while the third found a home on the altar in the chamber below my mother's icons. It was always more peaceful when he was gone. The tension between Edith and myself eased and the servants were more relaxed, but the surprises he brought on his return made us eager for his arrival anyway.

I had to confess, Christian and Edith's arrival had other compensations. I happily accompanied Christian and Edith on their many trips to Bruges. Flanders was the wealthiest land in all Christendom at that time, and Bruges was its heart. The count had his palace there, within the walled citadel at the center of the city, and there he held court.

Sometimes we stayed with Edith's brother, Borsiard, the one Charles had beaten in combat at the tournament where I said goodbye to my husband. Borsiard's house was outside of Bruges, so more often we stayed at the house of their uncle, Bartolph, within the citadel walls. Uncle Bartolph, a celibate and childless cleric, took a deep interest in his many nephews and nieces and liked to keep them close. Bartolph was the provost of the count's church of St. Donatian, and chancellor of all Flanders. That meant he was in charge of collecting the money owed to Count Charles, the taxes on goods coming in and out of the count's towns and bought and sold at the count's markets, and from the count's estates. If Flanders was the richest land in Europe, Bartolph was its banker, and if a little money stuck to his fingers from every transaction, that was his reward for doing the count's business. He was fabulously wealthy.

Bartolph's house rivalled the count's palace. I remember him sitting in his great oaken chair on the raised dais of his hall, clad in black silks and receiving petitioners like a king. He would humiliate the most powerful men of the county by pretending not to recognize them before he heard their business.

Charles's court had changed from Count Baldwin's day. Gone were the drunken nights with bawdy courtiers creating havoc. Charles's courtiers, led by Fromold, were just as young and handsome as Baldwin's, but they were a sober, pious group, more concerned with rhetoric, law, and governance than with drinking and fighting.

The best time to find Charles was before early Mass at the church of St. Donatian, inside the castle walls. This church was round, like the Church of the Holy Sepulcher in Jerusalem, but much smaller, and heavy and graceless in construction. It was Charles's custom to ascend to the gallery that ringed the central core while the canons were chanting the office in the choir below. He repeated the seven penitential psalms while prostrate on the floor, and distributed pennies to needy paupers. Sometimes I found a moment for a word with him before he descended again to hear Mass, and I went as often as I could. He remembered me, and often had a kind word or two.

"Aude of Jerusalem," he would say with a smile. He liked me, I could tell. "We must find you a new husband one of these days."

I didn't want that. But I lived for that warmth, those brief scraps of contact. When I was in Gistel, I forgot about him, but once in Bruges, all my old feelings rushed back. Still, under his amiability was a distance even I could not ignore, a preoccupation with worries and cares he kept to himself. His wife remained cloistered in her distant castle.

Still, it was exciting being so close to court with its visiting dignitaries and excuses for new dresses. I dragged Edith around from merchant to merchant. Alas, nothing she put on made her look less like a pasty doughball. She chided me for my vanity.

"Aude, another pair of boots?" as I admired my ankles in the softest green leather at the cobblers and willed them to fit. "Those coins would be better spent on alms for the poor or a gift to the church."

"Nonsense," I replied, anticipating the sensation my feet would make at court. It was the year of our Lord, 1123, four years since Christian and Edith had arrived at Gistel, and I was twenty years old. We were all on our way to the count's audience. Envoys had recently arrived from the kingdom of Jerusalem, dragging a camel with them who shrieked and spat. Edith squealed as the beast kicked out, but I smiled to see a little bit of home in cold Bruges.

The animal was a gift for Charles, who called for his grooms to take the camel to the stables. I doubted the poor animal would last the winter. They finally got it out of the hall, but not before it spat at the Abbot of Bourbourg.

"We come with sad news," said the chief envoy. "Our king has been captured by the Turks, and is being held for ransom." We gasped. Pleased at the reaction to his words, the envoy continued. "The king of Jerusalem needs your help, O lords of Flanders. Recall the great deeds of your parents, those brave men who fought for all Christendom and retook Jerusalem from the Saracens winning worldly renown and eternal life. The battle continues against those same foes today. We need your help, and we urge you to repeat the vows made by your fathers and grandfathers to come to the aid of the Holy Land."

I was suddenly inspired. This was how I was going to get back home. "Christian!" I tugged at his sleeve and spoke under my breath. "You should go on crusade. I'll come with you. It will be wonderful!"

"Crusade?" he laughed, pulling his arm away. "That's an errand for fools like your husband. You won't catch me dying for God in a dusty desert."

I was crushed. But the envoy's next words lifted me up again.

"Count Charles, we remember how in your youth you came to our aid and fought with us. Now our king is imprisoned, our fortunes are grave, and our position is dire. Our only hope is that a new strong leader, might rise to our aid. You are that lion with a sword. We offer you the kingdom of Jerusalem. We beg you to come and be our king."

A hubbub rose in the hall, mostly of surprise, but with an audible lack of enthusiasm.

"He gets to be king of Jerusalem and we get stuck with the camel," someone behind me muttered.

Charles rose. "We thank you for your gifts and for your kind offer. We must think this over very carefully, very carefully indeed. To be king of the land where Christ walked would be indeed a splendid thing." He sounded interested. Someone at the back of the hall shouted "No!" and Charles paused, as if startled out of his dream of greatness. He continued, "But we must take council with the great men of the county before we decide."

I had no need to consult anyone. My mind was made up. Charles must go and I would go with him. My hopes of Charles, which had waned in the four years since Christian had taken over Gistel, revived once more, but took a pragmatic turn. I was a bit of an heiress in Jerusalem. If he repudiated his wife, who better to help appease his new subjects to their foreign ruler than a local queen?

I needed to reach him before men like Christian who preferred the muddy fields of Flanders to adventure and honor persuaded him to reject the offer. The next morning, before Mass, I put on my best dress, braided my hair carefully under its coif and left Theodore playing hoops in the castle courtyard with Edith and his nursemaid. I waited impatiently with the other petitioners for Charles to finish reciting each one of his psalms, while the sound of the canons droning the office wafted up from below. He was taking forever. What did he have to be so penitential about every single day? My eyes wandered over the vessels on the altar before us, gold and silver chalices and crosses covered in gems, winking in the fingers of sunlight that found their way through the slit windows of the church. The last pauper took the final coin from his outstretched hand, and he was done. He got up from the floor, and I pushed my way past the others who hoped to have a word with the count.

"My lord, may I have a word with you?" I asked.

"Why, of course, Aude." He sounded weary.

"In private, perhaps, without so many—." My eyes glanced at the others around us. He took me into a side chamber, but one of his men followed us. It was Fromold, who was always at his side. I had no wish for Fromold to overhear my words, but I plowed ahead.

"Sir, I think you should take up the offer to be crowned king of Jerusalem."

"You do?" He seemed amused.

"Yes. They need a leader and it would be a great honor, one you richly deserve. Who but a man of unimpeachable purity and valor should rule in Jerusalem? With their king imprisoned, perhaps dead already, who else in Christendom can rise to this challenge but you?"

"You are kind, Aude." He seemed receptive so I continued with the second part of my message. I put my hand on his arm.

"No, my lord. I speak only the truth. And when you go, take me with you. I long to return to my home. I left a castle there, and good servants. You can help me retake them, and I will find knights to serve you forever." If only stupid Fromold weren't standing there, smirking, I could be clearer about my intentions. I implored, "And in return, sire, I would support you with every breath in my body. My lord, I am sadly widowed. You have a wife who does not seem to please you..." I let the implication of my words hang in the air, but my meaning was unmistakable.

Charles patted my hand and removed it from his forearm. "I am so grateful for your faith in me, Aude, and your friendship. I cannot tell you. I will weigh your words with the other counsel I have received." Fromold was staring at me with pity in his eyes under his elegantly coiffed curls. Charles took his arm and said, "Come,

Fromold, I hear the Gloria and we are already late for Mass. Let us go downstairs and join the canons."

I was dismissed, and disappointed. The morning sun turned to a drizzling rain by afternoon. I spied the envoys from Jerusalem mounting their horses in the courtyard from a window in Bartolph's house, and I ran down. I feared the worst from their departure, and I was right.

"Alas, your brave count is not quite brave enough to try his hand in Jerusalem," their leader told me when asked. "He has refused us, and we return home."

"Not a moment too soon," grumbled another, with a streaming head cold.

I watched them spur their horses and leave through the castle gate. They would return to where camels were commonplace, and where the sun shone all year round. I wanted to go with them.

"Mummy!" I heard a call from the same window through which I had spied the courtiers. It was Theodore. "I am beating Lisebet. Come see!"

They were playing Wari, a game with beads and a board that the two played incessantly. I left my dreams of warmth and sun behind and went up to my son, soon to turn five, and to my real life.

The next day, doing needlework in the solar with Edith, I spoke of my frustrated hopes. I had to tell someone about them, and Edith was less likely to blab to Christian than Lisebet was.

"I think the count made a mistake not accepting the crown of Jerusalem," I said, knotting a thread. "It would have been a wonderful thing for him, and for me."

"You would have gone with him to Jerusalem?" Edith sounded mildly curious but unsurprised. She was spinning wool with a drop spindle, and paid more attention to the tension of her thread than to my words.

"Yes, to reclaim my father's estate and to give him support. And maybe more. It's clear that Charles has no use for his wife. I haven't told anyone before now, but Charles has admired me from the moment we first met in Jerusalem when I was a child. Since I came to Flanders our special understanding has grown and deepened."

A strange spluttering sound came from Edith's nose. Was that a snort? Was Edith snorting at me? She was. I could not have been more surprised if I'd seen a mouse chase a cat. Her shoulders shook, and she wiped tears of laughter from her eyes.

"Aude, you are too funny. Charles and you?"

I folded my embroidery in my lap, hands shaking. "Yes," I said in a soft voice. "Why is that so funny?"

Her sides shook, but she tried to get a grip on herself. "Aude, I am sorry. I'm not laughing at you. It's just the idea of Charles being drawn to a woman, any woman." She started to chortle again, bent double in an effort to regain her composure. I sat frozen, still as a statue.

"Why is it strange to think of Charles loving a woman?"

"Aude, I thought you knew. Everyone around here knows. I forget you weren't born here. No one talks about it, but everyone knows Charles only has eyes for men. Charles and William Clito and Count Baldwin, when he was alive, were a byword all over Christendom. They were inseparable. You remember the young rowdies Baldwin used to surround himself with? Anyway, Charles swears he has given it all up. That's why you see him so often in the church, doing penance. He fears hellfire and a curse on the county if he continues with his former behavior. But as you've rightly noticed, he gives his poor wife no time or attention, and that's why the woman stays alone in that nasty castle. And while his courtiers are better behaved that the dead count's, they are no less beautiful, as I am sure you've noticed. I wouldn't want to wager on what goes on in private."

I remembered handsome Fromold's pitying eyes on me the day before. It all started to make sense. I had known of men who preferred men, of course. Why, there had been rumors that was the reason King Baudouin became estranged from Queen Arda, my mother's friend. I remembered how Baudouin had received Charles and William when they were in the holy city. I remembered the little kindnesses Charles had shown to me in recent years, the sweet way he looked at me. I was shattered, but I couldn't let Edith know. I sniffed loudly, "I suppose that explains why he was too much of a coward to go to Jerusalem. Edith, you have a big slub in your yarn. How careless. You'd better fix it."

✠

"That is not the way your story with Charles was supposed to end," said Eleanor flatly, when I was done. Now she was cross with me too.

"No," I answered in an even voice. "But nevertheless, that's the way it did end."

"But it's all wrong. It is fine for your beloved to ignore you because he is married, or because he is cold-hearted. It is good even, because then you can fall into a decline, maybe even die, and everyone will say how romantic and true you are. But to go into a decline for a man who doesn't even like women? You look like a fool."

I was surprised. Had she only just realized that any romance between Charles and myself was doomed before it began? I thought I had given strong enough hints throughout my tale that Charles's attention did not turn to me, at least not in the way I had wanted. But I realized that Eleanor had heard what she wanted to hear. My great romance was supposed to be a model for her and Raymond, an example of what true love could be, of triumph of unlikely love over worldly adversity, the kind her southern poets sang of.

Everyone was angry with me. Eleanor because she didn't like the story, Mabilie because she thought I was a spy, and Gracia because she followed Mabilie in everything. Ermine had a headache, and who cared how Marie felt, she was so wet all the time. They weren't too fond of each other at this point either. After we snapped at each other a little more, we retreated to our own corners, and measured the time until it grew dark and we could retreat into the seclusion and solitude of sleep.

CHAPTER EIGHT

The Castle of Margat, June 1148

✠

The next few days were not pleasant. We were allowed downstairs, but though Eleanor's women were not overtly hostile to me, they spoke Occitan amongst themselves all the time now. I could understand almost all of it now, but I was slow to speak so I was effectively excluded from conversation with everyone but French Marie, and she was such a mopey mouse, I preferred to keep my own counsel. I might have talked with Eleanor, I suppose. She alone knew that Thierry de Galeran killed my father, and that I would never join with him in a plot against her. But she was withdrawn, waiting for a rescue that never came.

The keep was far too small for us, Templars, women, feuding king and queen, all picking fights or pointedly ignoring one another in its cramped quarters. "I can't breathe in here," said Eleanor one afternoon. "I'm going for a walk on the cliffs," she said defiantly and made for the door. We women followed her, though I wasn't sure we'd be allowed to leave.

"Be our guest," Thierry said, though he nodded at a few men who moved to accompany us on our stroll. Fine, they could follow, but at least we'd be out of doors. I put Eve on a lead. She needed fresh air too.

The day was muggy and overcast and the whole world seemed the same dull grey, the slate sea seamlessly merging with an oppressive sky of the same shade. Only the tawny hills where we walked showed some color. Still, I was glad to be outdoors for the first time since our forced ride from Antioch. There was hardly a breeze, but the sound of the rolling swell of the sea rose to the top of the cliffs where we walked.

Eleanor was ecstatic to be outdoors again, swinging her arms and skipping like a little girl.

"Who's up for a race?" she said, and then took off towards the distant sea.

When a queen wants a race, you race. We took off after her, our Templar guards jogging steadily behind. In our skirts and absolutely the wrong shoes, we never could have escaped their reach. I'm little but fast, and I had to keep up with Eve who was thrilled to be able to run, so I soon outpaced the others and almost caught Eleanor, despite her head start.

"This way!" she cried. "Follow me." She disappeared between a cleft in the rocks. When I reached the spot where she had vanished, I saw that it was the beginning of a path down the last stretch of cliffs to the shore. I quickly glanced behind me. The other women were flagging, slowing to a trot. Mabilie had stopped altogether. The Templars didn't seem anxious and were simply keeping pace with the women. I followed Eleanor's lead, and picked my way down the rocky path.

Once I got to the bottom, I saw why the Templars didn't care if we went down the cliff. Our route led to a small, sandy cove, inaccessible except from the path, or by sea, if we had a boat. But we had no boat. The cove must be used to supply the castle. Eleanor was sitting on a flat rock at the edge of the sea with her back to me. I stared up at the top of the cliff, shading my eyes from the weak sun. Seabirds circled above us. The other women had reached the rock cleft, and their heads bobbed just over the rim of the rock.

"Are you coming down?" I called.

"No we're not," Gracia answered. "Mabilie is exhausted, and we're taking her back to the keep. She'd never make it up and down this path." Their heads disappeared, but it was too much to hope that we'd be left alone. Two of the Templars took up watch at the top of the path. We couldn't escape, had we been so inclined, unless someone sailed up in a ship and swooped us off the shore.

"Blast them," I muttered. "I hope they get heatstroke up there. Let's give them a good long wait." Eve was fascinated by the shore and was already poking a small crab she'd found, so I let her off her lead and went to join Eleanor.

When I reached Eleanor's rock, I found she had pulled off her hose and shoes, and was dunking her feet in the sea, so I did the same. The water was cool and felt delicious. I expected Eleanor to be in the same euphoric mood she had been when we left the castle, but when I turned to her, I saw silent tears streaming down her face.

"I'm sorry," I said.

"I've been such a fool," Eleanor answered.

"We all are, at times. There will be bad weeks, maybe even months. But deep down, the king adores you. You know that. Eventually, he will forgive you. Or," I added, more honestly, "Will convince himself it never happened. And things will continue as before. Which, admittedly weren't wonderful, but…"

She buried her face in her hands and interrupted my fatuous blather. "Aude, it is so much worse than you know. He'll never be able to forget, even if he wants to."

"What—?"

"I am pregnant. It's early, so early. But I'm usually as regular as the water clock outside the palace in Antioch. I know the signs from when I was pregnant with my daughter. And it is not Louis's. It is well over a year since we even…"

If it were not Louis's child, there was only one man whose it could be. I was glad we were facing the sea, so the Templar snoops on the hill would not be able to see my face, or hers. I put my arm around her and squeezed her tight. Why was the world so unfair? There were women who couldn't bear children and desperately wanted them, while others conceived children who would spell their doom. Truly, Eve, my monkey's namesake, had cursed her line well.

I released my embrace, and she hugged her arms to her chest and held her back poker straight. "I need to figure out what to do."

"If it is so early, couldn't you and Louis…We could find some way to allow the two of you some time alone. He would never guess, if the baby were a month ahead of time. Men are foolish that way. They see what they want to see."

"Do you think I haven't tried that already? He won't come near me until he is shriven in Jerusalem, and, at the rate we're travelling that will be far too late. No, I must have the child and brazen it out. Or…get rid of it." She dissolved in weeping again, but the Templars above, if they were looking, would never know anything was amiss from her posture. I now realized why she had decided to face the sea.

Fiercely she brushed the tears from her face and turned her direct gaze on me. "Do you know anything about that, how that might be done?"

I understood then why Eleanor had chosen to confide her terrible secret in me, and not in Mabilie or one of those whom she had known for years. I was a bystander and outsider to the political drama she was born into as heiress of Aquitaine, and married into as queen of France. Child of irrelevant Armenia, and distant Flanders, I had no interest one way or another in her baby. This was not true of the women from Aquitaine. Her child with Raymond would possess the full lineage of Aquitaine from both parents, displacing the child of Eleanor and Louis, and freeing Aquitaine from French sovereignty. This child was a grave threat to France, I realized. And bastards could rule. South of where we sat, at our next stop on the journey to Jerusalem, the scion of a bastard ruled in Tripoli. When his legitimate cousin stopped there earlier in the spring on his way on Crusade and died a mysterious death, everyone knew who was to blame. Antioch had been full of the news. I feared for Eleanor's safety. Would this child be better off dead? Its life could spell death for many others, if it caused war between Aquitaine and France.

I couldn't condemn her, given the terrible mistakes I had made when I was her age. I knew what story I needed to tell her. But should I tell it? Was it wise, and did she deserve so much from me? Caution and friendship fought inside me for a moment, then friendship won, encouraged perhaps, by my own long-held need to tell at least one person a story I had never been able to reveal in full before.

"Eleanor," I said, "Any choice you make will have consequences. But I faced something similar myself once."

"Tell me."

"It's a long story. It starts right after Christian and Edith arrived at Gistel, and doesn't end until Theodore was six years old."

"Never mind, I want to hear it all."

✠

Aude's Eighth Tale: Gistel, 1119–1125

I told you how I kept control of the household and the keys the day Christian and Edith came to Gistel, but I pushed my luck too far when I sought to hold onto the bedchamber. The night they arrived, after dinner, I whispered to Lisebet that we should slip away early, and claim the bed and the lord's chamber for ourselves. Theodore was already sleeping there, in his cot as usual. She was full of misgivings, but I persuaded her. We stripped to our shifts and got in bed. I was frightened too — how could I not be after seeing how he killed our men? — but Bertulf's death had changed something inside me. I wasn't going to let anyone boss me anymore without opposition. I might lose, but I'd fight.

"Take off your shift," I said, removing mine.

"No," Lisebet replied, "What if they come in?"

"You never wear your shift in bed. It's dirty. Besides, if we're naked under the covers, they won't make us leave. Edith would die of shame."

"I hope you're right," Lisebet muttered, but she obeyed me, and we both lay there, wide awake and expecting confrontation, the dim light of a gibbous moon shining in the chamber.

Finally Christian and Edith entered. She quailed when she saw us there, but he smiled.

"Aude, get out of our bed, and take your servant with you. I am sure there is a comfortable mattress for you somewhere."

"No," I said.

Lisebet, normally so brave was shaking like a leaf beside me.

"Servant," he addressed her, "Get out of my bed or I'll turn you out of the castle naked as you are tonight." She didn't wait to be told twice. She had seen the bodies of our slaughtered guards that afternoon, and knew Christian cared nothing for my people.

"Traitor," I hissed as she wriggled out of the sheets, into her shift, and through the door, but she didn't even turn around to look at me.

"And you, Aude, wouldn't you like to follow your servant?" he asked.

"I'm not moving," I said, braver than I felt.

"Very well," he said, "This is the lord's bed, and I am the lord, but no one ever said I had to sleep alone in it. It's big enough to share."

"You wouldn't," I protested, but almost before I finished speaking, he stripped himself naked as a newt and got under the sheet beside me. I went rigid, aware of his hot, musky body beside me, a man in my bed for the first time in almost a year. What should I do now? I hadn't planned for this.

Edith still stood at the foot of the bed, wringing her hands. "Edith," he said. "Get into bed. It has been a long day."

You could tell it was second nature for her to obey any order, but it was also evident how much this one displeased her. "It's wrong," she whispered.

"Get in," he said, not loudly or with cruelty, but demanding compliance.

Slowly she removed her finery, hair diadem and girtle, slippers, garters, and hose, embroidered overtunic, then even more slowly, as if she hoped time would stop before she finished, she raised the hem of her tunic over her head. Her doughy arms shone in the moonlight as she folded her robe and laid it with the rest of her garments on the chest, to make the nurse who'd taught her neatness proud. I had wondered if her plumpness was a sign she was already with child, but from the way her shift hugged her middle, there was no baby-swelling, just puppy fat.

She got into bed, as far over to one side as possible, and removed her shift. There we were, all three side by side, Christian in the middle. I lay there, silent as a codfish, waiting for something to happen. After what seemed an age, steady breathing rose from Edith's side of the bed, punctured by an occasional soft snore. Christian took it as a signal to roll over on his side and face me.

"Aude," he whispered, so soft I wondered if I had imagined it. "So pretty." With one finger, he began to trace the length of my naked body, up and down. I squeezed my eyes tight shut. This was not what I had bargained for and I had no idea how to react. His finger continued, circling my breasts, feathering across my nipples, sweeping down my stomach, in soft steady strokes, patient, patient, before insinuating itself in the cleft between my legs. No one had ever touched me this way. I let out a soft moan without knowing what I was doing. That was the invitation he'd been waiting for. He put his whole hand between my legs which parted eagerly, inviting him, and began probing all my clefts and hollows.

"Do you want more?" he asked, as I shuddered under his fingertips, unable to answer. "I would not force you." I made no answer, but he took that for agreement. Silent, silent, he parted my legs, and climbed into my welcoming arms. He thrust himself inside me, first slow and then faster and faster. I dared not moan or squeal lest I wake Edith, though I wanted to, and in a good way.

That's how we spent every night. Sometimes he would take her, but more often it was me he wanted. Passion spent, he always lay between us, keeping us apart. We might have been sleeping at opposite ends of the castle.

Edith never spoke of what passed between her husband and myself under the covers in the dark of night in all the time I knew her, not once. When she sensed it was my turn, she would fall asleep (or feign it) as soon as her head touched the bolster. I would try to keep quiet, but she could not have mistaken the joy my body and Christian's took in each other. Or the time we took. On her nights it was different. I shut my ear to the furtive fumblings of an obligatory act over quickly with no pleasure on either side but that of duty done.

"How could you?"

Eleanor's question interrupted my story. Her tone was not outraged, merely curious. She explained. "I thought you disliked Christian. And didn't you love Charles still, in those years? And then all three of you in the same bed."

I nodded. Here she was, forcing me to dig deeper into myself again. "I did love Charles. Charles was goodness and truth. And I never even liked Christian. I suppose... I suppose I hated myself too a little bit in those days."

"I understand," said Eleanor, and kicked at some loose stones on the beach. "I suppose that's when you got pregnant again."

"Not then," I replied, and returned to my story.

As the months passed, I figured out the pattern to the nights it was Edith's turn. I discovered that he counted the days from the first onset of her menses, so he could have her when she was most fertile. Women's bodies being as they are, we were soon experiencing our moon times in the same rhythm. If she was ripe, I was too, so if he was taking her and not me, that explained why I didn't become pregnant. But for some reason, month after month as we played our games, she never conceived, and it angered him to have to do his duty with her again and again with no result. Manlike, he never asked how she felt about it.

I could have told him. The first morning we were wakened early by Theodore crying in his cot, wet and hungry. "Lisebet?" I mumbled before I remembered she was gone. I groaned inwardly. I'd have to deal with him myself. But before I could stick so much as a toe outside the covers, Edith was already up, back in her shift, and pulling Theodore out of the trundle bed where he slept beside me.

"Who's the clever boy?" she said. "Are you all uncomfortable and hungry? So sad. Auntie Edith will look after you." And then with an efficiency I still hadn't mastered in almost a year, she changed him out of his soggy linen and into new.

"You do that well," I said grudgingly.

"I had younger brothers and nurse let me help," she replied, almost apologetic.

Christian rolled over and pulled the covers over his head. "Take the brat away and let me sleep." So we did. I dressed quickly and took my clean child from Edith, but she was the one who chivvied the servants to bring him barley gruel, and she fed him with his small bone spoon, far more tidily than I usually managed. He even fed himself a few mouthfuls.

That first morning I wondered how she could do it, look after my boy so lovingly when his mother stank of her husband's sex, but eventually I realized she loved Theodore and would do anything for him. She wanted a child more than anyone I have ever known, and not just to please her husband with an heir. All that thwarted maternal love was poured into my child. If I'd been a better person, our shared love for Theodore could have been a bond between us, but instead I used her feelings as an excuse to boss her.

"Yes, you can take Theodore down to see the new kittens," I would say. "But he needs to be changed first, and his clothes are all down with the laundress, and you'll have to make sure she got the stains out this time. Then you can tell Lisebet that I need her right away—I'm not sure where she is, maybe in the orchard—and count the eggs because cook is using too many. I swear he's taking them home and feeding them to that greedy wife of his."

And off she would go, fulfilling all the tasks I, keeper of the keys, gave her to do. I was busy running the castle, and it seemed easiest to let Edith do the messier parts of raising a child and be my errand girl. But over time, it meant I missed some of the lovely parts too. She was the one who patiently taught him to stand and then walk, holding his small hands in her plump ones with the endless forbearance I did not possess, and it was to Edith he said his first word (she claimed). If her husband yearned for me, my son reached out his arms for her hugs even when I was present.

Christian shared none of Edith's love for my child, however, showing impatience at his toddling steps, and shouting at his fussiness.

"It makes him worse when you yell. He's only little," I reproved Christian, clutching the bawling boy to my chest.

"You'll keep him a baby, mollycoddling him like that. When I was not much older than he, I sailed in my father's boat and fended for myself, pulling the ropes and hauling in nets with the men, wallowing in fish guts from our catch and fighting off attackers. Your boy would need a fleet of nursemaids with him, and still he'd cry if he got splashed."

I thought time would improve Christian's attitude towards Theodore as he went from baby to boy, but he grew worse as the years passed, cuffing Theo sometimes, "trying to make a man of him." I worried about it aloud to Lisebet one day when we bent alone over an embroidery frame.

"Are you surprised?" Lisebet asked darkly, breaking off one thread and knotting another. Edith had taken Theodore to visit the nuns. They spoiled him rotten with fried honey knots and jam.

"You're not?"

"Aude, you're usually so canny. Here's our lord, month after month unable to get a child on his wife while your boy grows lustier every day."

"So what? Theodore is heir — it's good that he is strong."

"You think Christian wants to let all he is building here pass to another man's child, a man from the branch of the family that exiled him and his so many years ago? Christian hasn't turned his back on the sea towards the land just so he can pass it to Theodore one day. He loathes Theodore for what Theodore's forebears did to his own."

Her words made sense. I recalled evenings when I watched Christian stare at my boy with what looked like hate in the flickering dim of the hearth. I hadn't wanted to admit it, but Lisebet was right.

"Do you think Edith also — ?"

"No, she loves the boy. But you'd better hope that neither she nor, if you'll forgive me, you bear Christian a child."

The goings on in the lord's bedchamber must have been an open secret in the castle, but this was the first time she'd mentioned it to me.

"You think he'd harm Theodore?"

"Mark my words. Theodore is safe as long as he is the sole heir. But if either you or Edith gives birth to a healthy boy, I don't give Theodore long to live. If the boy is yours, Edith will have to watch out too. Christian will want a legitimate bond. Oh, I know he's handsome and devilish and can be charming when he gets his way. We all smile at his wit and let him pinch our bottoms and ignore the iron underneath. But I recall the ruthlessness that killed our men the first day he was here."

I was chilled. I acknowledged how drawn to Christian I had become. I preferred to see myself as a victim of his lusts so the shame of our delight could be placed squarely on him, but in truth I had been a willing participant. I still refused to admit any more than a sinful, physical bond between us, however. But if this could lead him to harm Theodore — I couldn't bear it.

I encouraged him to spend more time back on the sea — that would keep him away from us. We both refused to go with him. I'd never willingly go on the sea again, unless it was to return to Palestine. And I tried to resist him in bed. He made it clear from the start that he'd never force me. But Theodore forgive me, my flesh was young and weak and when he rolled over on his side and trailed a questing forefinger up my inner thigh, I could not deny him or myself.

I prayed and watched for the signs something had changed, but my luck held and as time passed, I decided that we were safe, that he was not going to be able to get a child from either of us.

So I spent the next four years intermittently pining after Charles and lusting after Christian, until that all changed the day I told you about, when I learned Charles had no interest in women in general or me in particular. We left Bruges that very day, to my relief, though the drizzle that had soaked the departure of the envoys from the Jerusalem envoys had turned into a driving rain.

The rain didn't stop once we got back, but I didn't care. The weather matched my mood. I had lost the dream that had sustained me since childhood, that had allowed me to survive when my dead husband pounded into me, and gave me hope after his death. I drifted around the castle while the year turned, as listless as when I had first arrived in Gistel. I didn't notice that rained had rotted the winter harvest before it could be taken in, or that the sheep had foot rot and were dying faster than they could be counted. And none of us at Gistel knew that what was happening to us was being repeated all over the county.

One bad spring will not ruin a well-run land. We had reserves and stores to last us, as did our neighbors. But the rains continued through the summer. The only time the skies cleared, we saw a blood-red eclipse. The cold stopped the seeds from sprouting, and those that did sprout rotted before they could leaf, while fruit bruised and withered on the tree. Babies born that summer in the huts and hovels around the castle fevered and coughed themselves to an early death. They were spared what followed.

I thought my first winter in Flanders was miserable, but I was not prepared for what we ever after called famine winter. Bad was the damp cold that penetrated our bones and iced our innards, but worse was the starving countryside. Peasants live off bread and beer, and with no grain, they had neither. They ate the seed corn that was supposed to grow the following year and slaughtered the animals they kept for milk and fleece. It is hard to eat your hopes for the future. They became nothing but bones, and their wide-eyed, grey-skinned children haunted the castle gate, hoping for scraps. Beggars and brigands swooped through the countryside, ransoming whole families for everything they had. We heard rumors of cannibalism when the families had nothing. Bands of the starving and desperate terrorized the country and our castle guards were on constant alert. It was not strange to find a dead man in a ditch while out riding, belly bloated and straw filling his mouth in one last, unsatisfying meal.

We fared better in the castle, though we too had nothing but precious meat to eat and water to drink. Always thin, I grew wraithlike and even Edith had lost her puppy fat. We grew tired of thin mutton broth with a few handfuls of meal to thicken it. At least we didn't starve. And Theodore stayed healthy, praise be to God. I fed him secretly out of my share, and I know Edith did the same.

Christian raged. He could not cope with this barren land that refused to bear so we sent him to sea as often as we could. At least there he might find us something to eat. But the disturbed weather made fishing difficult, and he brought the spoils of plunder more often than he brought good fish. We couldn't eat silks and silver coins. He raged at Count Charles, and in my new hurt, this was welcome to my ears.

"The count is to blame for this blight," he thundered.

I knew what he meant, and I knew that Charles himself would agree. God was punishing us for Charles's unnatural ways. With a hint of smugness I almost welcomed our suffering, if it could show Charles how wrong he was to spurn me.

"And what's worse, though he forgives the poor on his estates their taxes, he makes no allowance on the tolls he charges when we sell our cloth. He won't let anyone in the county brew beer, to save the grain for bread, and he has ordered us to plant beans and peas instead of grain this spring, because they grow more quickly. That will feed the poor, but what about the sheep?"

I knew all this was true. Charles was trying to make sure the poor, especially in the towns, had some resources. If we were hit badly in the countryside, it was even worse in the towns, where men killed each other for an egg and a woman would do anything you wanted in exchange for a crust. He needed our tolls so he could continue to distribute alms and loaves throughout the towns of Flanders. Once his generosity and protection of unfortunates would have made me love him all the more, but now I heartily agreed with Christian.

I wasn't fair. But Christian droned on and on, then complained when it was nothing but pease pottage for dinner again, so we were glad when he left for the sea once more.

Deadened by rain, cold, monotony and an insufficient diet, we carped and scraped at each other in the castle. I tried to pick fights with Edith just to stave off boredom. One day after Christian had been gone for a few weeks, I was nattering at her about her looks, trying to ignore some tumult going on outside.

"There's no excuse for getting sloppy, Edith. We may not have bread, but we have plenty of dried chamomile. A good rinse in your hair would brighten it up no end. And spare some time to take in your shifts and your tunic. You might as well make use of your new figure."

"Stop harping at me Aude. Not everyone is as obsessed with being pretty as you," she snapped back, uncharacteristically waspish.

Then the pig boy ran into the hall where we were keeping warm around the sputtering hearth. He was out of breath and frantic. "Men have broken through the gate," he gasped. "We're outnumbered."

I jumped from my stool and ran to the slit windows that looked out on the gate. I saw the rabble had broken through. They were a poor, sick desperate crew, and badly armed with staves and scythes compared to our guard, but force of numbers combined with desperation might give them the victory in the end. Besides, though Christian wouldn't leave us unprotected in these dangerous days, he took the sharpest men with him. There wasn't a single leader among the gang that remained to guard the castle.

"Quick," I shouted to the pig boy and a few of the servants who had heard his desperate cries. "Raise the ladder and bar the main door." The only access to the castle keep was from a wooden ladder that led up to the second-story hall. If we lifted it before they reached us, we'd be almost impregnable. "Edith, Lisebet, take Theodore and the other children up to the women's gallery, and don't make a sound. Try to keep them calm." Edith was already hustling the children upstairs, a baby in one arm and Theodore's hand in her fist.

I opened the strongbox that held our extra weapons. The best were in the hands of our beleaguered guard or floating uselessly on the North Sea with Christian. I cursed under my breath, and found a helm that almost fit me, a leather cuirass and a small bow. It had been a while since I had hunted with bow and arrow, but I hoped I remembered something.

"Women," I shouted, for apart from the few servants struggling with the ladder, everyone else shivering in the hall was female. "Take what weapons you can use and find a place. Those with bows, choose a window. Those with daggers, protect the main door."

I ran to where our men were struggling with the ladder. They were more fit than the rabble at the bottom, but were far fewer. I could smell the mob's stink of fear, death, and disease from where I stood.

"Scum!" I shouted. "Be gone from Gistel, or know our wrath."

They jeered and hooted, emboldened by their success at breaching our walls. One tried to climb the ladder as our people tried to pull it up. I nocked an arrow and released it at close range, striking him full in the face, and he fell backwards onto his fellows, which startled them for a moment. Our boys gained some purchase on the ladder, and I nocked another arrow, ready for a new strike, but they redoubled their efforts. All would have been lost, but then one of their number spied the cookhouse.

"Food!" he cried, and led most of the men off to plunder. This was our chance. We pulled the ladder out of reach, but our moment of success was brief. A crackle told us the fools had set fire to the cookhouse, and the gang still at the gate killed the last of our guard and ran to join their fellows at the keep.

"Fire the castle!" one called. "Smoke the bastards out!" The bottom floor of the castle was of stone, but the rest was wattle and daub. With all the rain, it should have been impossible to light, but who knew? I didn't dare close the wooden door, lest it give them a new target. They advanced with torches drawn from the fire of the cookhouse. Their flickering light gave the mob the look of ghouls from hell with the hollowed faces and filthy rags. Our servants tried to pick them off with arrows, the close range making up for their lack of skill, but they kept coming and coming. A torch was tossed inside, but was quickly put out. I heard the children crying upstairs, and longed to go to Theodore.

Then, I heard a horn. It was Christian, blessed Christian, return-ing with his men. On horseback with hard steel, they soon routed the angry mob, killing every single one without pity. Ten horsed men with swords is an army against a mob armed only with staves and short daggers, no matter how numerous they are.

When the last beggar was lying in the mud in his own blood, we set the ladder in place again and I descended.

"Thank God you arrived. We couldn't have held them much longer," I said.

"Curse all of you. How did that riffraff get into the castle? And where are those lazy serving girls? We need to bury this waste. Who knows what diseases they have brought within our gates?" he raged.

It was a rage born of fear of what might have been and I didn't hold it against him. I ordered one of the servants to call the women out of the attic and to start digging a pit for the dead outside the castle gate. I didn't even have time to give Theodore a hug before Christian took me to the gate to figure how the men got in. The faces of our dead guards looked up at me from the mud. Their own families would retrieve their bodies — no common grave for them. They had fought bravely and held out as long as they could. But Christian was furious.

"Look, there's no damage to the gate. They must have tricked our guards into opening it for them. Fools."

"But at least it means we have nothing to repair. And we'll have no trouble replacing the guards. Any number of local families will give us their sons if they know they'll be fed in exchange."

"True," he said. Danger past, he was calming down.

It was deep into the night before we could rest. Edith took charge of the inside, finally getting an over-excited Theodore and the other children to sleep. I inspected the outside. The cookhouse was a ruin, but we found the cook shivering behind the pig barn. He had been able to jump out a window before the mob could grab him. He'd be fine, but there was nothing to eat that night.

At last Christian, Edith and I found ourselves back in the bed chamber. I sat down on the edge of the bed, put my head in my hands and started to weep. I felt weak and dizzy and half in shock. Christian sat beside me and gave me a hug.

"Aude was so quick thinking and brave, Christian, she saved us all," said Edith.

"Of course she did. Look, I have a surprise for you. We won't have to go to bed hungry after all." He jumped up and broached a small wooden cask with the dagger he wore at his belt. "Look what I brought home for us."

We peered over his shoulder at a mess of palm-sized rough brownish disks.

"What are they, some kind of mussel?" asked Edith.

"Close. They're oysters. We got them on the Breton coast." He prised one open with his dagger and handed it to Edith, who looked warily at its gelid contents. "Try it. You eat them raw. Slurp it back."

Edith did so obediently. A smile spread across her face. "Ooo, it's good!"

"Do one for me!" I ordered, and Christian complied. The taste was salt and sweet, like the freshness of a North Sea breeze, beyond welcome after months of broth gruel. I wanted more, and so did Edith, so Christian opened one after another, before he remembered another prize.

"I almost forgot. I brought this too. The monks make this out of apples. Be careful, it's strong." He opened another cask, and poured out a clear brownish liquid.

I sipped and my eyes widened. The alcohol went straight to my head. "This is strong. But delicious. I can taste the apples." I took a good slug. "Whoo hoo. More," I demanded, holding my glass out

"Don't drink it all," said Edith. "I want some."

"There's plenty," he said, pouring her a cup. We drank apple spirit and ate oysters late into the night until we were beyond satisfied, sitting on our bed in the big bed chamber.

I don't know how what happened next happened. I couldn't tell you know who made the first move or how we found ourselves naked under the covers. I remember nothing more from that night except a vague and endless dizziness, like the room was spinning and I was tumbling over and over in a nest of limbs and coverlets, soft and yielding, all night long. The only thing about that night I am sure of is this: I told you how Christian always used to keep us separate, him in the middle of the bed and us on either side of him? Well, when dawn prickled my eyelids and I began to awaken, I groggily realized that the person whose arms embraced me, and who I was holding in turn, was Edith. I was in the middle of the bed.

I didn't move. I lay there like that, drifting in and out of sleep, feeling all kinds of unfamiliar sensations. Peace, I think. And safety, like her arms were a harbor, and I was home. This scared me. Edith, lumpy homely Edith. Edith the fool, Edith who couldn't even hold onto her man? But I asked myself, when I said such things about her, was I saying how I felt, or was I trying to judge her like a man would? Was it not truer to admit that she was soft and warm and gentle, not homely? That she was kind and generous, a sister to me, not a fool?

I was roused at last by Christian, swinging his legs out of the bed and dressing, whistling. After he left the chamber, slamming the door behind him, I groaned. My head hurt, like a whole troop of knights were inside my skull, trying to get out. Using swords. The room smelled like apple spirit and fish left out too long. My stomach churned, and I pulled away from Edith and sat up, waking her too.

"I do feel so ill," she said. "I think I am going to stay in bed today. One of those oyster things must have been bad last night." She rolled over and went back to sleep.

I would have liked to stay in bed also, but I was afraid to stay with her, with all these strange feelings I was having. I almost felt I hated her. Wasn't she my rival, my enemy? Weren't we in competition for the attention of the men who could protect us, not just Christian, but Charles, Bartolph, and the Erembalds, all of them who ran the world we lived in? What could two women do? Edith and I had almost lost the castle itself last night, until Christian came. I hardened my heart.

I dressed and, making my way gingerly to the hall, I was almost knocked down by Theodore barreling into me.

"Mummy! The rain has stopped. It is sunny outside, and warm!"

He was right. That's why I was having trouble keeping my eyes open. It was sunny, and the light hurt my aching head.

That turn in the weather was the beginning of the end of our hard winter. The crops didn't spring up right away, but herbs and salats for spring tonics and soups could be foraged from marshes and bogs. Maybe Charles had finally done enough penance, and God had shone his favor on us all.

The old peasant women, the ones who never came anywhere near the church, might have given another explanation for the restoration of fertility to the land if they knew about the aftermath of the raid on the castle. Though my headache faded, the upset in my belly didn't leave. It took a few weeks, but finally I realized I was pregnant.

I told no one.

Lisebet's long-ago words kept ringing in my ears—"Theodore is safe as long as he is the sole heir." But was she right? I cradled my flat, queasy stomach with my hands. What if it were a girl, a lovely girl with eyes like my mother? Wouldn't Theodore's place be secure then? But a girl could be used as bait to bring a lordly but landless boy into the family, a boy who would owe everything to Christian. What room would there be for my son then?

In the days that followed, every sharp word Christian directed at Theodore—and there were many—every cuff or smack was like a dagger in my heart. I knew what I had to do.

"Lisebet," I whispered one day when I got her alone by the kitchen garden. "Is Old Grettie still alive? Can you tell me how to find her?" Old Grettie was the crone who came when Theodore was born.

Lisebet's eyes narrowed. "Is this what I think it is about?"

There was no fooling Lisebet, but I said nothing. She continued, "Never mind. If it is, you're doing the right thing. Are you sure you don't want me to go in your stead? It's not a place for the likes of you."

"Just tell me where I can find her."

Lisebet complied, and the next morning I set out, cloaked heavily, and in my sack a precious slab of bacon winkled out of our dwindling storeroom as payment for my deadly errand.

I followed Lisebet's instructions, avoiding the well-trodden path by way of the village in favor of an overgrown route by the river. I turned down a rabbit run at an old elm tree as she had directed, and a thicket of raspberry canes rose before me, grey and dying, fruit long since scavenged by bird and man. Hawthorn and sloe stripped of berry threaded through the thicket and a knotted tangle of bindweed and convolvus matted all into an impenetrable snarl of creeper and vine and sharp thorn. Was this the place? A whiff of smoke gave promise of life at the center, so I circled around looking for an opening through the brambles. A gap between two holly bushes was uninviting, but I squeezed myself through, scratched raw and sore despite my thick wool cloak.

Inside was no pretty cottage garden but a rank, growing, dying, jumble of wort and stick and tendril, plants I knew but grown menacing, rose dense with thorn and hips, mistletoe sucking life from its oaken host, and nightshade reaching high and cloaking the hovel at the center, offering its deadly fruit, withered and blackened after the hard winter. A path of crazy flags, dying thyme in their cracks, zig zagged for no good reason to a door hung on a lunatic angle.

"Old Grettie?" I called. No answer.

I rapped on the door which swung drunkenly on its hinges. "Mistress!" I called again.

"Come in or stay out, it's no odds to me." An old voice, scratched, raw and crabbed, tired and running out of words. I had come this far. I went in.

A reek of woodsmoke undercut with a stench of acrid burning from a cauldron and fire at the hovel's heart fought with the frowst of unwashed body linen and stale food. Over it all, hung the fug of something dead for a very long time. Moist dark gloom resolved itself into shadow and I saw a form approach, a shapeless heap of old clothes shuffling, clubbed staff in a gnarled fist. The famine had touched her too. She was a wraith.

"Yes? Speak, wretch."

I had planned a pretty story of a favorite servant, pregnant in old age and needing relief. But unbidden my tongue told truth. "My moon time is late. I need—something." Maybe she wouldn't recognize me in my cloak as the women she delivered now six years before. I thought of Theodore now learning his letters with the local priest. I was doing this for him. I handed her the empty leather pouch Lisebet told me to bring.

"Something, is it? And you seek to render your something, nothing. How late? Mevrouw." With contempt she penetrated my feeble disguise.

"Maybe six weeks, on Sunday?"

"Sundays, some day. We have that for praise." Her nonsense frightened me. Had her wits fled since we last met? Maybe I should leave.

But the crone was already moving about her hovel, skittering like a black beetle from leather sack to earthenware pot, ranged around shelves of slanted boards and found wood, hung slant and threatening on the walls of her shack. Without pause she selected the scraps and shreds she needed, putting pinches of poison into leather purse, muttering words to chill the heart.

"Let's see now. Angelica root. Brown wrinkle without, white sponge within, lets slip. Puliol royal, pennyroyal for death, peppermint for flavor. Mugwort in herb and root, to root it out. Baneberry, baby's bane. Toadwort, juniper, open, shut. Shepherd's purse to collect the blood. Where is it? Yes, up here. Tansy flower, temper, twine, tie, untie."

A twist of rosemary and sage tied the pouch, a fresh sprig of feverfew jaunty in the knot, and she exchanged it for the slab of bacon I put in her grateful arms.

"You've always been generous, mistress," she crooned. "It's powerful stuff, mind. Will turn you inside out and bring on your blood. Boil it long and strong, the length of ten pater nosters, then drink, both of you."

"Both of us?"

"If he got the one, he got the other, that's always the way it is. Kill your'n, you have to kill hers too or it's no good."

Those were words to chill my heart as I made my way back to the castle, pouch full of contraband close to my skin. I hadn't thought of Edith being pregnant too. Our cycles were close. Had she bled this month or not? A child of her loins would be an even greater threat to Theodore than one of my own. She too had been feeling poorly since that fateful night. But to take her child would be an even greater sin than to take my own. Could my soul bear that burden? If she was indeed pregnant. Could I take the chance that she wasn't? Better to give it to both of us, just to be sure.

When I got back to the castle, she was sitting by the hearth stroking Theodore's hair as he showed her some new mess he had found outside, a bird's egg maybe or an odd stone. "You're back?" she said weakly. "You have such energy, Aude. All I can do is sit here, and my stomach feels so odd."

"Poor Edith," I said. "Why don't you go lie down and rest for a bit. I'll bring you a nice potion to settle your insides."

"I think I will," she said gratefully, giving Theodore a big hug before she sloped off to the bedchamber. My courage almost gave out seeing her gentleness with him. Could I take away her chance at having a child of her own at last?

She'd want me to do it, I resolved, if she knew a child of hers would cause Theodore's death. She loved Theodore too. And maybe she wasn't pregnant after all, in which case my only sin would be giving her a nasty tasting drink. Quickly, before I could change my mind, I called for water and brewed up my potion over a brazier, muttering the Our Father over and over again under my breath as Grettie had commanded. When it was done, I divided it between two pewter flagons and took it to Edith.

"What's in this, Aude? It smells foul." she said.

"Oh, different things, special herbs. And mint. Drink it down."

She did, gagging a little on the first sip, and I drank too. Truly, it was a disgusting brew, medicinal and bitter. I made sure she drank the last drop and then I took both cups away to throw their dregs on the fire. They were an unidentifiable muck, but I was taking no chances. I wondered how soon it would start working. I didn't have long to wait. A wave of hideous nausea swept over me. Was this the baby sickness, or was the witch's brew having an effect? I went back to the bed chamber to see how Edith was faring and found her rolling from side to side on the bed groaning.

"It hurts, it hurts," she said, voice faint.

I felt my gut contract in a pain sharper than labor, and sat on the bed bent double.

"What was in that drink, Aude?" she asked, sweating and shivering.

"I don't know," I lied, and lay beside her. I thought I was going to die, as the contractions continued without cease. I have no notion how long we lay there in agony, unable to give each other relief before I heard small footsteps enter the room.

"Mummy? Auntie Edie?" Theodore saw us and ran out of the room screaming. "Lisebet! Lisebet! Mummy died!"

Lisebet ran into the room and felt my cheeks. "God be praised, not dead. But cold and clammy and sweating unto death it seems." She chivvied me under the covers.

"Lise. Water?" I croaked.

"Yes, and more, but I must see to Edith first. She's fallen faint." she said, rushing to the other side of the bed, and calling for help. She smacked Edith's face a few times to try to revive her, but nothing worked until a servant brought peppermint oil, which Lisebet shoved under Edith's nose. She manhandled Edith under the covers, ignoring her groans, and then brought a cup of water over to me. I sipped gratefully, but the water caused me to heave, a thin greenish slime, all over the rushes on the floor. I could hear Edith vomiting on the other side of the bed.

We suffered like this long into the night, sliding in and out of awareness. Lisebet kept trying to get us to drink. "Water will flush the poison out," she said, worried. Christian was gone, somewhere, thank God.

At dawn, the cramping in my stomach gave way to a dull ache in my back.

"Lisebet," I whispered. She had stayed with us all through the night. "Bring me a cloth pad."

She could hear the joy in my feeble voice. "It worked?"

"It worked," I said and she hugged me close. "There will be no baby." In the morning Edith called for one too. Whether there had been a baby inside her or no, there wasn't one any more. I had been ready to curse the witch, drive her from her hovel and set it on fire for making us suffer this way. But now I could have kissed her with relief.

It wasn't over, of course. It took days before we felt our old selves again and Lisebet was wracked with guilt for, as she thought, almost killing me. Edith was silent and suspicious and kept asking me what I had put in the tincture.

"Maybe the herbs went moldy with all the wet we had this winter," I tried to convince her. "I wasn't trying to hurt you," I fibbed. "I suffered just as much as you." That at least was true.

So that's how I did it, how I betrayed Edith and took from her the one thing in life she ever really wanted, right after I found out that far, from being my enemy, she was my friend, my sister, and I loved her. I became her enemy and hardened myself against her all the more.

✠

"Angelica root, pennyroyal, baneberry," said Eleanor grimly when I finished my tale. "What else?" The horror of what she was saying struck her and she started to weep again, putting her head in her arms. "I want this baby. It is all I have left of Raymond."

I stroked her hair, remembering the words I had used about Edith in my tale. What could two women do? "I don't even know if all those herbs grow here, or where to find them," I told her. "Don't worry. We'll figure something out. I promise," I said, sounding more certain than I felt. "But come now. We've been sitting here for an age. It is time to go back to the castle before our Templar guards blame us for their sunburns."

I put my arm around Eleanor, and we made our way slowly up the cliff. I was trying to infuse her with my own strength, and yet I was filled with so many anxieties and fears. I had thought I could leave Eleanor's service when we reached Acre or even Jerusalem and make my own way to al-Lawza, but I had just bound myself even closer to her than before by giving her my greatest secret to hold in custody and vowing to help her through her own crisis. Had love led me astray yet again, love and a need to have someone listen to my story? How would I ever get to al-Lawza?

CHAPTER NINE

Tripoli and Acre, June 1148

✠

They took us by a grindingly slow and uncomfortable journey on the coastal road to Tripoli, a crusader county carved out of the edge of the sea. There, we were told, we'd join the rest of Louis's French knights and any of Eleanor's followers who hadn't gone home. We were not gagged and bound this time, but it was a hot slog on horseback under a burning sun at Templar pace. I was glad when the golden citadel of Tripoli rose before us, and even happier when most of the Templars peeled off to their own commandery.

At a feast the first evening, Ramon, Tripoli's count, entertained all the crusaders who had reached the city. Ramon's court was not French, but rather Provencal, like Antioch and Aquitaine, and I heard Occitan on all sides. I spied some of Eleanor's treacherous French former ladies-in-waiting sitting across the room with their husbands, and wondered which one was the rat who had betrayed Eleanor and left me to take the fall. I laid my wager on Berthe over there, lecturing Thierry de Galeran, who had joined us for dinner. No Templar bread and water in the commandery for him tonight.

I'd get no support from the French. But there was one woman in Tripoli who might be an ally, if I approached her the right way. This was Count Ramon's wife, Hodierna. I knew that like me, she had an Armenian mother and a crusader father, though hers had been a king while mine was only a knight. Her sister was Melisende, the powerful queen of Jerusalem, whose favor I needed to regain al-Lawza. But Hodierna hadn't greeted us on our arrival and she didn't seem to be in the hall.

There was a vacant place at the high table between Ramon and the king, and once we were seated, a woman who must have been

Hodierna came to occupy it. Veiled like a Muslim woman, but in the richest silks, only her deep brown eyes and white bejeweled hands were visible, flashing over the goblets and dishes on the table before her. Louis politely said that he regretted not meeting her when we first arrived, but she made no reply. Her husband the count answered for her.

"She's as healthy as an ox," Ramon said. "But like all women, she's not to be trusted. The Muslims have the right idea when it comes to protecting their womenfolk from their own baser impulses. I keep her sequestered in one wing of the castle at all times, and she knows that women are not to speak in public. That way, she'll never betray me. You could follow my example, your majesty, if the stories from Antioch are to be believed." He winked at Eleanor, who gazed straight ahead, stoney face, giving no indication she'd heard his remarks. So word of her and Raymond of Antioch had spread this far south. That would not help Louis and Eleanor reconcile.

The troubadours, Jaufré Rudel and Cercamon, were among those whom we met again at Tripoli. They had arrived several weeks before us. When Count Ramon seemed ready to list the wrongdoings of every woman in history beginning with Eve, Jaufré interrupted him.

"Might we entertain you all with a song?"

"Oh yes, do," said Eleanor clapping her hands, and Ramon gestured for them to begin. Jaufré stood before the dais, and Cercamon sat on a folding stool, ready to bow the viol clasped between his knees.

The song Jaufré sung was one of those we heard in Antioch, in which the Holy Land was described as a beautiful, distant woman. Now my Occitan was better, I could understand it without translation.

"Love from a distant land," Jaufré sang, "My whole self aches for you. And I can find no remedy unless I go to your call, to the lure of sweet love in a garden, behind a curtain, with my desired companion."

The song touched me. I had been torn in two directions since I left Lisbon, and now I was torn in a third, by my loyalty and, yes, genuine compassion for Eleanor. My soul was aching every which way.

Jaufré gazed at veiled Hodierna while he sang, as her breath gently raised and lowered the silk of her veil drawn over her mouth. Watching him watch her, the words of his song and passion of his singing seemed suddenly less about longing for a distant land, and more about the flesh and blood woman before him. Foolish count, I thought, did he not know that by hiding his wife, he made her desirable above all others?

Eleanor and the rest of us were summoned to Hodierna's private quarters to meet her the next day. What we found was at odds with the diffident submission she had displayed the previous night. When Eleanor prepared to make a formal movement of greeting, Hodierna pre-empted it by clasping the younger queen in a warm embrace.

"So wonderful to have you here to relieve the terrible boredom my ass of a husband subjects me to," she said in French, kissing a surprised Eleanor. "Let me take a good look at you."

While she inspected Eleanor, I examined her. In all but her liquid brown eyes, she took after her crusader father, not her Armenian mother, down to her shock of wavy blonde hair, barely restrained by a circlet. She had the dress sense of an Armenian woman, though, wearing such a profusion of silks and embroideries in every shade, you could spend an afternoon taking account of every one.

"I am surprised you go along with his restrictions," said Eleanor.

"Only when he's in town. He has a passion for hunting, and he's hardly ever in the city so I humor him while he's here. It allows us to spend as little time together as possible. My own amusements are not restricted," she said, smiling wickedly. "And it won't be for long." Her face grew hard. It struck me that this is not a woman I wanted as an enemy.

She moved from her study of Eleanor to examine each one of us ladies in turn, an inspection that took in our every article of clothing and jewelry as the well as the kind of cosmetics we used and which of us ought to leave off eating honey pastries. I was last to be scrutinized, and while Hodierna evaluated me, Eleanor gave her my name and title.

"Gistel? Never heard of it," Hodierna said. "You're not really a Frank though, are you? You're one of us."

"My father was a crusader, but like your own, my mother was Armenian."

As I hoped, my revelation created a bond between us. She smiled, and said a few words to me in our maternal tongue, to which I haltingly replied. Fortunately, she switched back to French, because I had reached the limit of my childhood memories of my language.

"And you are using the excuse of the crusade to return home," she said shrewdly. I blushed, and curtseyed to avoid a response. "Where are you from?" she continued. "Is there a castle somewhere waiting for you to reclaim it?"

Hodierna, with one well-placed question, undercut all my efforts to hide my true goal in returning to the kingdom of Jerusalem from these women. With no time to think up a good lie, I had to tell the truth.

"I wish to reclaim my father's castle of al-Lawza," I said. "I am hoping your dear sister, Queen Melisende, will view my petition with favor."

"Good luck," Hodierna replied. "She is my sister, but she can be greedy when it comes to parting with a castle in her care."

That was discouraging, and worse came after we left the countess's chamber. Mabilie pulled me aside. "Now I understand," she said. "You're here to get your castle back, and you betrayed my lady to the Templars so they would help you with your scheme." She left me, stunned, in the corridor. I easily saw how she could draw that false conclusion.

The palace at Tripoli was austere on the outside, but contained lovely gardens and courtyards within. We whiled away the time in one of these all afternoon. Cercamon and Jaufré played and sang for us in a grove of orange trees, while I sent Eve clambering up the date palms to pick us fruit. She wasn't very cooperative, and tended to stay at the top of a tree munching the fruit herself and throwing the pits down, screaming with delight when she hit someone.

The rest of us — Eleanor and her women, and a few of the knights from Aquitaine who had made their way to Tripoli — were talking and laughing and paying little attention to the singers. When Cercamon finished his turn, he joined in the jokes and chatter. Only

I, ignored and excluded by the women, and intent on making sure Eve didn't slip into one of the upstairs galleries from her perch on the date palm, still listened to Jaufré as he sang. I noticed that his head was raised, so that although a casual observer would think he was singing for those lounging in the courtyard, his voice carried best to the second-floor gallery above their heads, a gallery shrouded from the direct sun by a curtain. Then I saw a white hand emerge through the curtain and deftly toss something at Jaufré. He snatched it out of the air and slipped it into his sleeve without breaking the tempo of his refrain.

I recalled a line from his song the previous evening. Didn't it go, "Love in a garden, behind a curtain...?" Had that been a signal? The hand had emerged from the area of the palace where Hodierna's quarters lay. And now I knew she was not the shrinking violet she first seemed, I suspected she was the source of the missile. But what was it? A handkerchief? A love letter? My mind raced. Whatever it was, it made Jaufré very happy. He burst into a rollicking tune that got everyone singing and clapping.

It was our last carefree afternoon in Tripoli. I had hoped that despite our conversation on the shore, Eleanor would prove to not be pregnant. But soon after we arrived in Tripoli she became debilitated by what we called an upset stomach, which I feared was morning sickness. At first she passed it off as a reaction to the fish she ate the previous evening and stayed in her room. King Louis was still avoiding his wife, so it was no work to conceal her indisposition from him. But after she'd been ill for three days, we took counsel beside Eleanor's bed, where she lay, weak from being unable to keep food down.

"I don't think it can have been the fish after all," said Gracia, stating the obvious. "Do you think it is some kind of foreign fever? Should we call for a doctor?"

Marie had a darker suggestion. "When Ramon's cousin arrived in the Holy Land a couple of months ago, he sickened almost immediately, then died. People spoke of poison and suggested it might be the work of Hodierna and her sister, Queen Melisende. Do you suppose..."

"No, I do not," said Eleanor, a small amount of her accustomed sparkle returning to her voice. She labored to pull herself up in bed so she could speak more easily. "I know what is wrong with me, and it is not poison. It will affect us all, and it's time I told you."

Mabilie broke in quickly, "Let's send Aude down for more of that nourishing broth. You need something inside you."

Mabilie has guessed, I thought. And she doesn't want me to know because she fears I'll reveal it to the Templars, so she's trying to get me out of the room.

Eleanor took Mabilie's hand in her own, thin and frail from the weight she'd already lost. "Aude knows," she said, looking deep into the older woman's eyes. "I told her while we were at Margat."

Mabilie greeted this revelation with silence and Eleanor continued. "I think I am pregnant. No, given the way my body is reacting, I am certain I am pregnant."

No one spoke. Her own women know best how often a queen is visited in the night by her husband, and what times of any month are most favorable for conception. None of those around the bed believed this was Louis's child and thus a happy event to be celebrated with public rejoicing. Only one man who could be this child's father.

Gracia was the first to react. She cleared her throat and said brightly, as if Eleanor had not spoken a word, "My lord husband grows jealous of my continued attendance on you, and weary of the time we have spent so far in the Holy Land without engaging our enemy in battle. He wants us to go straight to Jerusalem to complete our pilgrimage and then return immediately to our home. I am afraid I will have to be released from your service."

Without waiting for the queen's reply, she made for the door of the bedchamber. "Good riddance," Eleanor said, after the door closed behind her.

"Will she tell?" asked Ermine.

"No. Her husband is one of my knights, and she has no desire to betray me, merely a strong wish to save her own skin. She already told me he was fed up and refused to fight for Louis, and wanted to go home. She made much of her own loyalty to me in her refusal to listen to him. Now I've given her the excuse to be an obedient wife."

Eleanor sounded weary. "Do any of the rest of you wish to leave? Now is the time. What comes next may not be pretty. Or safe." She plucked at the coverlet of her bed and avoided our eyes.

We all reaffirmed our desire to stay in her service. I surprised myself, a little. This was an opportunity to be quit of Eleanor and her problems, and to return to my own mission in the Holy Land. But I vowed to stay along with all the rest.

Mabilie, still holding Eleanor's hand, spoke gently, "What are you going to do about it? Does anyone else know?"

"No one but you women," Eleanor answered, and then rolled over on her side. "No more now. I need to sleep."

We left her in silence, but I was worried. If the wrong person found out that the queen was pregnant, I feared for her life. And I remembered Old Grettie and Lisebet's words to me long ago. If she didn't decide soon what to do about this baby, the decision would be taken away from her by her own body, which would not let the baby go. Maybe that was what she was hoping for. Any time we timidly tried to raise the issue in the next few days, she managed to change the subject. "Let's talk about it tomorrow, when I'm not feeling so ill and can think," she would say, and another day would pass.

Count Ramon, restless and bored, left for the hunt, and took most of the knights of Aquitaine, and even some of the French along with him. Before he left, he had declared his refusal to participate in the crusade or even attend the council that was to be held at Acre at the end of the month to strategize, and most of the lords of Aquitaine followed his lead and made plans to return home.

With Ramon gone, Hodierna emerged from her seclusion, and moved about freely in the castle without the silk veil that shrouded her features when Ramon was there. Wherever she went, Jaufré Rudel was not far behind, and the palace rang to the sound of his songs and her laughter. In public, they avoided physical contact, though many a look passed between them, but we could guess what went on in the privacy of Hodierna's own chambers. I marveled at their behavior. I knew Ramon was far from the city but surely such a jealous man would have left spies in his absence to observe his wife's actions.

One day, looking for Eve who had taken to roaming around the palace at will, I passed the portal to Hodierna's rooms and found Cercamon on a stool beside the closed door, playing a soft tune on his viol.

"I suppose they're both inside? They're going to get caught one day," I said, speaking frankly to this troubadour who stock in trade was illicit love. "What if the count returns unexpectedly from his hunt and wants to see his wife?"

"They won't get caught if I can help it," said Cercamon, without stopping his playing. "I'm the guard and my weapon is this viol. When the coast is clear, my tune is sweet, but when danger threatens, so does my song. I ring out a warning and Jaufré vanishes before anyone is the wiser."

"Good luck," I said, and told myself it wasn't my problem. I was tired of royalty taking risks and endangering others. And I was fed up with Tripoli and with keeping track of my annoying monkey who had grown large and independent. I ran down the wide staircase to the lower level, and barely noticed when five men passed me heading up the stairs. They wore turbans with the tails pulled round to cover the bottom half of their faces. Syrian Christians dressed like Muslims, and both were found in Tripoli's castle serving as mercenaries, so I didn't given them a second thought.

I stood at the bottom of the staircase trying to decide whether to go left or right to find Eve, when I heard a choked scream from the direction I had just come. I froze, my mind telling me to run, hide, but my body unable to move from the spot. A moment later came more screams, over and over, high pitched and hysterical. I heard a clatter on the stairs above me, and pressed myself into a niche as the five who had passed me earlier ran down again, and through the hall until they were lost from my sight. The screams upstairs hadn't stopped, so against my better judgment, I went up to see.

Before Hodierna's door, I found their first victim, Cercamon, eyes wide and lifeless, his shattered viol no protection for the dagger slash that had ended his life and left him in a puddle of blood. The ghastly sight swam before my eyes. It took me back to Flanders and another murder in cold blood that I was too slow to stop, one I had witnessed decades before, of a count on a cold stone floor drenched in his own blood. The sound of footsteps approaching through the halls from both directions brought me back to the present and told me others were running to help, so I left Cercamon and entered the suite. The screams were coming from Hodierna's bedchamber. There, I found a scene more appropriate to a charnel house than a bedchamber. Hodierna was propped up nude in her bed, eyes glazed, and crying out more like an animal than a human, with Jaufré's naked body sprawled over her, knife wounds covering his back in a carmine tattoo. Blood spattered the silks of the bed hangings and soaked the linen sheets. Jaufré was dead. No one could sustain that many wounds and live. Hodierna was also covered in gore, but was it all his blood, or hers?

Her whoops of agony began to die down when she saw me enter. "Are you hurt?" I called urgently.

"No…no…I don't think so. It's just Jaufré, poor Jaufré…" She began to shake and weep soundlessly, her tears diluting the blood that marked her face, rose drops falling onto the sheets as her shaking hands shrouded her face.

Others had entered the room, and one of her women handed her a vessel of what I hoped were strong spirits and then called for water to bathe the countess. Her men started to remove Jaufré's body, and began the awful work of cleaning the room.

I went to Eleanor. The whole episode had left me shaken beyond words. If I had called out to Cercamon when I first saw the men, would the result have been different?

"There was nothing you could do," said Eleanor, resting on her diwan, when I told her what I had witnessed. "Raymond told me about these men. They call themselves the Nizaris, but others call them Hashshashin, or assassins, because it is rumored they take hashish before they kill. They live in a castle in the Syrian mountains, and because they are too few to field a standing army, they achieve their goals by practicing political murder."

"Why would they kill Jaufré and Cercamon?" I asked. "And how did they get into the castle—and out again."

"I hear they sometimes do work for hire. Our charming host, Ramon, probably got word of his wife's adventures, and decided to teach her a lesson. With a safe conduct from him, no one would stop the assassins on their way in or out. Since Hodierna's sister is queen of Jerusalem, Ramon knows he can't touch her, but Queen Melisende is not going to get involved for two foreign musicians, no matter how talented."

"But that's monstrous. You should have seen them."

"I'm glad I didn't. Aude, if I am ever found dead in my bed, you'll know Louis decide to adopt his host's methods," Eleanor said with a grim laugh, arms shielding her belly, which was still flat and sleek. It struck me how different this cautious and bitter Eleanor was from the young queen I had met on the pier at Antioch. And she put into words my fear since I first saw the troubadours and Hodierna covered in blood. If he knew his wife was pregnant with another man's child, with Raymond's child, would Louis make use of the Hashashshin as Ramon had done, to kill his wayward queen—or her women? The danger that had been abstract before became vivid.

Ramon didn't return, and Jaufré and Cercamon were taken away to be buried in the Templar cemetery. We didn't see Hodierna until she summoned us into her presence several days later. She was impeccably and expensively clad, as always, but her white face and pinched forehead showed a woman whose nights had been spent in weeping, not sleep. Between her and Eleanor, it was hard to say which of the two famed beauties looked worse.

"I heard you were still unwell, Eleanor, and I wanted to see for myself," said Hodierna. Her eyes searched Eleanor's face and surveyed her form, now thin and frail because she couldn't keep any food down. Hodierna's eyes lingered longest over her breasts, incongruously swollen. She clapped her hands twice. "Servants!" she called, and her attendants sprang to attention. "Bring us refreshments. Sharbat from the kitchen, and make sure it is cold. Don't come back with any old slush—wait until they bring fresh ice to make it. And this room is a disgrace, it is so bare and empty. Bring me some cushions and hangings from elsewhere in the palace so my guests may have somewhere to sit and something to look at." In this manner, she managed to clear the room of all her attendants, so we were left alone with the countess.

"Eleanor, you're pregnant," she said once they were gone. It was not phrased as a question. "I assume the king does not know, and moreover, from the gossip that came south with you, he is not the happy father."

Eleanor remained silent, and this was all the answer Hodierna needed.

"What do you plan to do about it?" Hodierna's words were brusque, but there was compassion in her eyes.

Eleanor's hands shook, but her voice was fearless. "I am going to have the baby."

"Brave woman," answered Hodierna. "But you're not going to have it in Tripoli. It's hardly safe, as recent events have sadly proven." She laughed bitterly. "Damn them all anyway, damn them straight to hell. Now let me think."

I didn't know what to make of Hodierna taking Eleanor's problems under her wing like that. She didn't seem like the kind who would exert herself for someone else, unless there was something in it for her. But the Lord knew, Eleanor needed help from someone. Rumor was that Louis had written to his advisors in France about the advisability of a divorce from Eleanor, and was only waiting for their reply.

"You have vassals enough to protect you, but you need somewhere to go," Hodierna said. "You won't be able to keep this a secret forever, but the longer you can, the safer you'll be. It can't be in Tripoli, because, as everyone knows, I can't keep you safe." That bitter laugh again. "Best would be inside the kingdom of Jerusalem, as near Jerusalem itself as possible. No fool will allow open war to break out between Aquitaine and France with my sister Melisende to keep an eye on you."

Suddenly I got a brilliant, idea. It was the perfect bolthole for Eleanor. And I couldn't help that it was also the perfect opportunity for me. Why hadn't I thought of it sooner?

I curtseyed, "My ladies, what about my castle of al-Lawza? It is small, little more than a fortified manor, but there would be room for Eleanor, and for some of her knights, and it is only a day's ride to Jerusalem." I had sworn I would turn it into a monastery, but that could wait. "All I need is permission for it to come back into my possession."

I stared at Hodierna brazenly. She knew what I needed—permission from her sister to take back my inheritance.

"That can be arranged," said Hodierna.

So I found myself the next day on yet another sea voyage. I was bound on one of Hodierna's ships heading for the great council at Acre to discuss plans for the crusade. My objective was not the council, however, but a private audience with Queen Melisende, who was going to be there. I went armed with a letter of introduction from Hodierna. I longed to know what it said, but it was so bound up in strings and sealing wax that I let it be, keeping it close to my skin lest it get misplaced.

My ship was only one of a flotilla departing from Tripoli and other towns along the coast, all heading for the council, where the Templars hoping to gain support to shift the crusade to Damascus. King Louis had taken the long way, leaving days earlier and stopping first in Jerusalem before returning north to Acre. I was violently ill for the entire trip as usual, with my head in a bucket the whole way south, while Eve amused herself by climbing the mast and surprising the sailors.

The council met a little way out of the town, for there was no building in Acre large enough to hold all the knights, bishops, kings, and one resplendent queen who flocked to it, a veritable chess game held under tents and awnings that were little protection from the brutal June sun. It was the feast of St. John the Baptist and the patriarch of Jerusalem began the proceedings with a solemn festal mass. I could barely hear his words, since I was only a mere pawn standing far away from the rich and powerful whose decrees would spell the fate of the rest. I paid special attention to Queen Melisende, whose verdict about al-Lawza would determine both my future and Eleanor's. She played little direct role in the proceedings, seated on the dais like a statue, covered with gold and gems. I suspected her voice was heard behind the scenes.

Conrad, king of the Germans, with his intact army that not endured the ravages of Turkey as the French had, was the center of the show, not Louis, and the hand of the Templars was behind every decision. The outcome of the council was a foregone conclusion: the crusaders would launch an all-out assault on Damascus. Voices of protest were weak, since the only one who would have argued for a northern strategy was retching on her bed in Tripoli, and thus the plight of Edessa and its people, the original cause of the crusade, was forgotten for all time.

My letter from Hodierna gained me an audience with Queen Melisende, and the day after the council I came to her rooms in the citadel and presented the parchment. She loosened its seals and, without looking at it, passed it to her priest, saying, "Read it."

I cringed, dreading the prospect of its contents being read out loud at this gathering. There were at least a dozen people in the room, the queen's scribes and seneschals, as well as two of her women, and the petitioners outside her door could hear everything that went on inside. But the priest glanced at the parchment and said, "Your majesty, I'm afraid it is written in Armenian. You will have to read it yourself."

Bless Hodierna, I thought, as the queen took the letter back and slowly began to parse it, tracing its lines with her fingers and mouthing its contents. It was a long letter and surely told of more than my father's death and my claim to al-Lawza for at one point she muttered, "Ramon. That bastard. My sisters have terrible luck with husbands."

When she reached the end, she looked at me with the stern grey eyes she inherited from her crusader father. "You want al-Lawza back, eh? And you'll provide me the same number of knights your father did for its fief?"

I let a curtsey speak my assent.

"Seneschal, what do we know about al-Lawza?" she asked one of her men.

"It's been abandoned for decades. The castle is probably a ruin. The headman cheats us. Maybe Lady Aude will have better luck with him," the man replied.

"Very well, it's yours. And my sister better be grateful. Scribe, draw up a charter," she ordered, and dismissed me from her presence.

The charter was short, only a few lines long, but it was properly signed and sealed, and al-Lawza was mine again.

I was exultant. Maybe I needn't even need to return to Tripoli (I was not looking forward to another sea voyage). I could send Eleanor a letter telling her al-Lawza was mine again, and urge her to come as soon as she could. I would go straight there and get it ready to host a queen. I thought of my mother's icons back on the walls of her chapel, and smiled.

Consoled by these happy thoughts, I hurried to the convent of St. Anne where I had my lodgings and got one of the sisters to write a letter for me and seal it well. I kept the contents cryptic to avoid informing the nun-scribe of my mission, simply telling the queen that I had regained title to my castle and was going straight there to put it in order, and that I would love to entertain her there at her pleasure.

The moment the letter was dry and the parchment sealed, I snatched it up and headed for the port to find a ship bound for Tripoli to take my message. Then I would figure out how to get to al-Lawza and put it in fit shape. I had left Eve behind with the nuns the previous day while I was at the council, but I took her with me this time. Mother Superior had made it very clear to me that her convent was not to be the permanent nursery of a monkey. Preoccupied by my plans, I hurried through the twisting streets, but I was not too distracted to recognize the woman who crossed my path ahead of me despite the hood pulled over her head, unusual in the June heat.

"Why that's Marie," I said out loud to uncomprehending Eve, chattering at the end of her lead. "What's she doing in Acre, and where is she going in such a hurry?"

Some instinct stopped me from calling out her name. Instead, I decided to follow her to discover where she was heading in such a hurry. I tailed her as she returned to the part of the city I had just left, the Templar quarter where my convent was located. I think I was already half expecting it when she slipped through the portal of the massive square block that was the Templar commandery, but it took a moment for my brain to catch up with what my eyes were seeing. I made no move to follow her inside. Thierry de Galeran was there, and I didn't need him questioning me about my own purpose in Acre. Thierry de Galeran. Was Marie's business with him? Light dawned. It wasn't Berthe or Alice who had betrayed the queen's relationship with her uncle, it was Marie. Marie, who was so close to the queen, Marie whose husband had been killed in Turkey and who might well blame the queen for his death.

Marie had timed her arrival perfectly. Thierry had been travelling throughout the kingdom for the past several weeks but now because of the council and the forthcoming muster, he was fixed in Acre for a few days. And if Marie had come expressly to see him, that could mean only one thing. She was here to tell him the queen was pregnant.

I was deathly afraid for Eleanor.

CHAPTER TEN

Return to al-Lawza, July 1148

✠

There would be no sending my letter by ship. I had to return to Tripoli myself, to convince Eleanor that she was in the gravest danger and must flee for al-Lawza immediately before Thierry de Galeran decided what to do with Marie's news. There wasn't even time to return to the convent to collect my belongings. I hurried to the harbor.

Finding a ship was the easy part. Speed was a different matter. The wind was against us, so we inched up the coast, pitching and tossing in the choppy sea. My only consolation was that no other ship could beat us to Tripoli, and the way by road would take even longer. I had to reach the queen before Marie returned, and it became her word against mine. And before the Templars could put in motion whatever they decided to do about Marie's news.

As I heaved over the side of the stinking sardine boat taking me north, there were times I wondered why I was bothering so much to help a disfavored queen. I held the charter to al-Lawza free and clear. Nothing stopped me from going there directly, and leaving Eleanor to her fate with the Templars and her husband. Love. It makes you do crazy things, even when the one you love is a dear friend, not a passionate romance. I thought I was done with love, but evidently it was not yet done with me.

Once in port, I hastened to the queen's chambers in the citadel, not even pausing to brush off the traces of sardine scales that clung to my clothing. I found Eleanor and her women in the gallery that opened off her room, enjoying the sunshine. I was relieved to see Eleanor out of her bed and looking a little more energetic.

"Goodness, Aude, back so soon?" said Eleanor when I stormed into the gallery, panting and sweating. I must have looked a sight. "Did you meet Queen Melisende? Did she give you your castle back?" she continued.

I kneeled beside her and took her hand. Mabilie and Ermine pointedly ignored me and continued their stitching. "Queen Melisende agreed. I got al-Lawza back. The parchment is in my sleeve."

"Then we can leave soon," said Eleanor. "Maybe later this week, when Marie is back."

"I hate this plan," said Mabilie.

I ignored her. "Majesty, we must leave sooner than that. We should go today. Where did Marie say she was going?"

"She was ill and went up into the mountains for a few days for some fresh air," said Ermine. "She'll be back soon."

"She didn't go to the mountains. She came to Acre, and I saw her." I told them how I saw Marie entering the Templar commandery, and my fears about what she would reveal. "We must get to al-Lawza as soon as we can, with any of your knights who are still here in Tripoli. With luck, everyone will be so involved with preparations for the assault on Damascus, they won't bother to hunt us down."

A flash of pain and hurt transfixed Eleanor's face at hearing about Marie's betrayal, but only for a moment, until she was able to regain her composure. "So it is to be Damascus after all," she said. "If only I'd been able to go to Acre. Now Raymond will have to face Aleppo alone."

Mabilie said, "You're not seriously thinking of listening to Aude, are you? She's the one who betrayed you in the first place."

"It wasn't me, Mabilie. It was Marie. It was Marie all the time," I said tiredly. The moment I saw Marie, I knew I would have to face Mabilie's opposition, but that didn't make it easier.

"I don't believe you. You told Thierry about Eleanor and Raymond, and now you are trying to trick her into leaving Tripoli."

"Are you certain that's the case, Mabilie? Absolutely certain?" I asked. "Enough to risk Eleanor's life? Because those are the stakes. You saw what happened to those troubadours, and you know there is no compassion for lovers in this world." Mabilie crossed her arms and looked stubborn, so I tried another approach. "Ask yourself,

Mabilie, what do I gain by betraying Eleanor and leading her into a trap? What has she ever done to me that I would benefit from such treachery, and who would reward me for it? And why would I return here to warn you all? If I had told the Templars, surely I would go directly for al-Lawza and let them do their worst."

My words made Mabilie pause, I could tell, but it was Ermine who responded. "That's true," she said thoughtfully. "And how well do any of us know Marie? She never spoke much, after her husband died in Turkey. Who knows what grudges she harbored?'

"I thought I knew her," said Eleanor, sadly. "I thought she loved me. Maybe I am not as good as I thought at telling who truly loves me and who doesn't." I wondered if she were thinking of Raymond too. He had not lifted one finger to help nor even contacted her after she was snatched from Antioch.

The queen continued. "I know Aude didn't betray me, and the rest of her story rings true. We must leave as soon as possible." A light flush tinged her cheeks. Despite her grief at Marie's betrayal, the need to take action was bringing Eleanor, the truest queen I ever met, back to life.

Hodierna came onto the gallery. "Aude! They told me you were back. Did my sister come through for you?"

Eleanor brought her up to date on my revelations. "And we need to leave as soon as we can, preferably today. Can you help us?"

"Indeed I can," said Hodierna, all business. "I never liked your Marie. It's the quiet ones you can't trust." With a few commands, she set in motion an army of servants to pack for us and prepare our journey, and to summon Eleanor's knights. One mercy was that Hodierna decided it would be too dangerous for us to travel by sea again.

"If they find you missing from here, they will expect you at the ports. Better travel by land. I have a safe-conduct from my sister that I can give you."

We set out at dawn, all our belongings in packs, and accompanied by a goodly-sized escort of knights from Aquitaine, with some of Hodierna's own men to lead the way. It was slow riding along the narrow coastal road but everyone we met thought we were heading to the crusader muster for the assault on Damascus, and we travelled unimpeded. Still, it took the better part of a week to reach al-Lawza. Eleanor pushed hard to keep moving. I wondered if she half hoped to dislodge her baby in this manner, but the child was tenacious and stayed in her womb.

We were riding on the Jaffa road to Jerusalem when I spied the crag where we used to hunt with falcons when I was a girl. And right after that was the plain where father taught me how to ride fast without falling off. And the outcropping where Thierry de Galeran took my father's life. I was suddenly in not two places but two times at once. The country we rode through was like a manuscript scratched out and written over but on which the old writing could still be seen by the one who knew to look. One part of me was riding with Eleanor and her ladies. Another part, the part that knew the curve of the hills rising above us as we ascended from the plain better than the curves of my own face, was that girl I had once been, willful and loving. I inhaled the smell of baked earth and of grasses drying in the sun, sweeter than any perfume and more familiar. I longed to return for so many years—and postponed my return for almost as many more. What was I going to find?

"Here's the path," I said without hesitation, and turned us from the road onto the way that would take me home. The path was badly overgrown but as we ascended, for a moment I was a child again, running wild with the village children without permission.

Then we reached the top. What had I expected? What I found was a castle in decay, neglected and abandoned for decades and haunted by my memories of those who used to live here. Trees were growing out of the courtyard, breaking the patterned pavement, and someone had been using it as a midden. The table where my mother and I used to play games to pass the time was gone—maybe burnt for firewood one winter?—and only one rotted bench showed where it had been. Stones were missing from the walls, the stables where my father's horses once stood proudly was a ruined muck, and the reservoir was cracked and leaking. I thought briefly of the castle of Gistel, neat and trim, and Edith ready with a meal and warm bricks in our beds. I wanted to weep but I stopped myself when I saw the looks of horror and exhaustion on the faces of Eleanor and the other two women.

I swallowed and forced a smile. "It looks a little bleak, but we'll get it fixed up right away. You won't know the place in a day or two, I promise." I hoped this was true. The fabric looked sound, underneath the rot. And if it made them feel better, good. But it didn't help me. I was missing people, and life, not wood and stone. And they were never coming back. Al-Lawza was empty.

Well, not quite empty. It turned out that a family of squatters had taken up residence in the hall. They came out timidly when they heard us arrive. They told me their house had burned down, and they sought the castle for refuge. From the looks of their encampment, it had burned a decade ago or more and they had lived here ever since. I thought of evicting them, but I realized it might be better to keep them here and employ them to help clean out the muck and dirt of ages. At least they could cook us a simple supper.

I was worn out. I wanted to crawl to somewhere I could be alone and turn over the stones of my memories one by one in my mind, like a miser assaying his coins, but I could not. Ermine and Mabilie took charge of making the lord's chamber habitable for Eleanor, while the knights and their squires prepared the stable for our horses, and evicted a pack of wildcats that had taken residence in the chapel. That left the rest of the estate to me.

I summoned the village headman and the dragoman. They knew me right away but it took a moment and some explaining for me to see in these grey-haired and bearded village leaders two of the boys who had been my childhood playmates. With my family gone, they had colluded to keep as much of the village's surplus for themselves instead of sending it to Melisende. I couldn't blame them — all of this had belonged to them before the crusaders came and carved it up for themselves. They were clearly impressed by our knights. They offered tea and dates, we shared memories and inquired about children, and then we got down to business. They promised to send up food supplies so we could have something to eat, to get us some bedding, and even to find someone from the village who would cook for us, and they positively beamed when I pledged funds to fix the reservoir. Lord knows how I would pay for it, but castle and village both depended on its water in this dry landscape.

I was dead tired, but I had to do one more thing before I could eat the mashed chickpeas and flatbread one of the squatter women made for us. I dug in my baggage until I found what I needed, and went to see what had become of my mother's chapel. I should have been prepared for it by the state of the rest of the castle, but I wasn't. The animals were gone, but it stank of cat, the walls were grimy, and the floor was worse. I shut my eyes, and willed myself to recall my mother there, praying, but it was no use. The room was empty and I was hollow. With hands shaking, I took the icons I had brought with me and hung them on the original pegs that supported them in my mother's day. One after the other, John the Forerunner, whom I'd learned to call the Baptist, Sergius and Bacchus, George, Grigor Lusavorich, and finally the Virgin Mary holding the Christ child, crack repaired but visible, found their old places. When they were all on the wall, I stepped back to see them together, tears prickling my eyes.

Ermine slipped in behind me. "The bedding has arrived, Aude. We won't have to sleep on cold stone after all." She looked around her. "Phew, it stinks in here. Did you bring those icons?"

I nodded. "They belonged to my mother, and I kept them safe until I could return. It has taken a long time, but here I am." My voice sounded strange and flat to me and Ermine seemed out of place in this space, my old life colliding with my new.

"Are you going to stay here after Eleanor leaves?" she asked.

"Yes." My heart sank and I wasn't sure why. "My plan is to turn al-Lawza into a monastery." I didn't know why I confided even this much to Ermine. She'd be long gone by then.

"Ooo, really?" she said, walking up to the icons and looking at them one by one. "I didn't know that." She backed away from the images and looked around the whole space as if measuring it for wall hangings. "Have you decided what kind of community it will be, and which rule it will follow? Men or women?"

These questions dizzied me. I thought of Saint Godeleva's abbey and of Oudenberg. I realized I had not thought through any of this, and I told her so. I had some decisions to make, clearly, but couldn't they could be put off, at least until Eleanor gave birth? Put off like I had postponed my return home for so long.

Slowly, the castle returned to order. One by one, the villagers pledged their loyalty to me as they had done in the past to my father. Things returned to normal in other ways too. Mabilie came one morning and apologized for her suspicions of me.

"You've taken good care of Eleanor. I was so frightened for her."

I told her I understood. We'd never be as close as we could have been if her fears had not divided us, but at least we could live together in peace and harmony while we both served the queen.

Once the castle was in order, our greatest challenge was finding ways to occupy ourselves. The Templars and the king left us alone, praise be to God. Our knights could ride and hunt, and even visit Jerusalem two-by-two, but we women were without such pursuits. I think it was the first time in Eleanor's life that she was without troubadours and jesters to entertain her, and wise men to discuss poetry and philosophy with her. We had to keep her from fretting.

I taught them the game of marelles, after I got someone from the village to make the board and counters, nine in cypress and nine in sycamore, and replaced the table that had once stood in the courtyard. I hadn't played it since I was a child, but I remembered how. Mother and I played in the same place in the courtyard I sat now, shaded by the angle of the late afternoon sun. She taught me the game, and whenever father went on one of his "expeditions," we played every day until dusk, game after game. At each crack of a twig or snap of a branch beyond the sheltering court, mother would jump, hoping it was father returning home, but the rest of the time she was intent on the game as if nothing else existed in the world. I basked in her attention.

I gave Eleanor half the tokens because I knew she had the cut-throat intelligence for the game, and I showed the women how the board was incised with three concentric squares, with eight lines radiating out from the center, intersecting with the three squares. Each intersection was a fair place to leave a token. I told the queen that if she got three counters in a row, she could take whichever one of mine away she wanted. The object of the game was to be the person who had the most pieces left by the end. We began placing the wooden tokens, one by one, and then took turns, moving our pieces from intersection to intersection along the lines.

I recalled Mother saying, "Come and play Nine Turks, Aude," the moment my father left the courtyard. Sometimes she called it Turks and Armenians. I called it marelles, because that is the name they used in Jerusalem, where I played after mother died. She always attacked when she played, as if she could rout all the Muslims herself, just by moving counters of wood, while I tried feebly to prevent her from trapping my pieces. It took me many games before I figured out a defensive strategy that worked against my mother's onslaught. It was a matter of being patient and not letting her intimidate me as I drew her into the open. Then, when she grew overconfident of victory, I attacked. Sometimes, I even won.

The first time we played, Eleanor hadn't learned how to avoid being boxed in and I beat her. Nevertheless, she loved the game, and we played it over and over as the days passed, pausing only when Eve snatched tokens and hid them. Mabilie was never much good, but Ermine could give you a skilled game, and Eleanor became a formidable opponent.

But even marelles began to pall.

"Maybe you could tell us another story," said Mabilie one evening as we sat out in the cool of dusk, a welcome respite from the scorching summer heat that drove us indoors at midday.

I hadn't told any of my tales since we left Margat, and did not wish to. "What more could I tell that I haven't told already?" I asked.

"I want to hear more about you and Edith," said Eleanor softly.

"How about the siege of Lisbon?" asked Mabilie. "You always shy away from that subject."

"No," I shuddered. "Not yet."

"Very well then, tell us more about Charles," said Ermine. "Did Flanders recover from the famine? Was he rich and prosperous? Did he reconcile with his wife and have a dozen children?"

I looked at her, stunned. "But you know how things ended for Charles, don't you? Everyone knows."

Ermine and Eleanor shook their heads, and I realized that they were both too young, and too southern to have heard of the awful events that swept up Charles and Flanders, the tragedy that came so strongly to my mind when I saw Cercamon and Jaufré's murdered bodies. Light dawned in Mabilie's eyes, however. She had heard the tales. "You mean the one you knew, the one in your stories, was that Charles?"

"He was, and I not only knew him, I was there. And if I'd been a little quicker, I might have saved him. The problems began with an accusation against his chancellor," I said, and began the tale.

✠

Aude's Ninth Tale: Bruges, 1125–1127

After two long years of famine in Flanders, when a haze of green colored the fields in the spring, promising healthy crops, and bird song mixed with the sounds of well-fed children playing, we returned to the court at Bruges. It had been more than two years since I last saw Count Charles and learned that he had no interest in me, or in any woman, and I still felt awkward and resentful about him.

Bruges meant new clothes as far as I was concerned, so we fell into an orgy of cutting and pinning the beautiful fabrics Christian liberated on his sea voyages. We stayed with Edith's brother, Borsiard, in his big house outside the town. Edith adored and feared her belligerent brother who bullied, teased, and ignored her by turns. He and the Erembalds still hated Count Charles, but now their dislike matched my own feelings.

"He's a monk, not a count. He never eats meat any more, you know. He does nothing but pray, and he's thin as a rake."

"And like a monk, he's buggering all the novices," someone riposted and everyone guffawed.

They complained constantly that Charles's taxes for famine relief cut into their profits. Not that you could tell. In Borsiard's home, it felt like the famine never happened, with course after course of meats and pies and sweets. Edith's four brothers gleamed with gold chains round their necks and heavy jewels on every finger, and their wives were dressed just as richly. Even in my new brocade I felt dowdy, and I hated feeling dowdy. Christian was grumpy and silent despite the merriment around him. He disliked being beholden to the Erembald family for his place at court.

We went to court among the Erembald clan, the patriarch Bartolph at the center, and we were a formidable group. Charles had his own men too there of course. Fromold, the leader of Charles's faction, remained resentful of Borsiard for stripping and humiliating him in the melee all those years ago, and he had taken a dislike Christian too, and jibed at him every time the two men were close.

"Why has he taken against you so?" I asked one day, while we were waiting at court the first time for Charles to arrive.

"I won a large amount of gold off him at dice once. And because I am married to an Erembald, he thinks he can strike at them by attacking me. He'll learn he is mistaken."

We had been waiting for the count for a long time, and people were getting restless.

"Where is he?" someone whispered.

"At prayer. Again," came the reply.

He entered at last, and I gasped when I saw him. Ready to despise him, I was not prepared for how different he looked since we met last.

He was tall and thin and pale, but where some saw only that, I observed something more. His face was transformed to a translucent clarity as if purified by a refiner's fire, and he seemed not fully in the room with us but already hovering in the empyrean with the heavenly host, intent on deciphering the music of the spheres. He was thin beyond words but with a tensile strength like a finely drawn wire. With his blond hair and blue eyes, he looked like an angel. Or a saint.

"What has happened to the count?" I asked one of the Erembald wives.

"It is striking, isn't it? He blames himself for the famine, you know, and who's to say it isn't true? He began a regime of fasting and prayer that he has kept up to this day. He never eats meat and drinks only water. And he worked himself to the bone trying to keep all the townspeople fed. He's half way to heaven already, they say."

"Would that he'd make it the rest of the way and leave us in peace," Borsiard quipped behind us.

By some mischance, Christian and Edith had been placed beside Fromold at the feast. I was seated a little way down on the opposite side of the table, but close enough to see them, and also to observe that the count refused all the choice delicacies offered to him, while the rest of us gorged.

When I could tear my eyes away from Charles, I glanced down the table towards Christian and Edith in time to see Fromold spill a vessel of red wine on Christian's new tunic.

"Damn you, peasant," Christian jumped to his feet, towering over the other man. "That was no accident."

"Who are you calling a peasant? Get your wife's rich uncle to buy you a new one," Fromold drawled. Bartolph's hand tightened around his wine flagon. He knew Fromold's insult to Christian was directed against him. The temperature of the hall changed as the Erembalds muttered about an insult to one of their own.

"Christian of Gistel," said the count. "What is the trouble?"

"My lord. Your man, Fromold, has paid me a deliberate insult and I demand satisfaction. I challenge him to single combat, mounted on horseback."

The Erembalds cheered. Christian was a head taller than Fromold, and Fromold was a courtier, not a fighter. But Fromold seemed unfazed by the challenge. Indeed, he grinned from ear to ear as if he had hoped for this moment. He rose to address the count.

"My lord, I am unable to take up this challenge," he said as the Erembalds shouted at him for being a coward.

"Silence in my hall!" said Charles. "Sir Fromold, why will you not accept this challenge, honorably given?"

"Sire, is it not true that by your law, only a free-born man may challenge another free-born man to combat?"

"Indeed, as in all civilized lands," said Charles.

"And I and all my people are free men, attested so by generations of tradition in Flanders."

"I know this to be true."

"Then Christian of Gistel may not challenge me, because he is not free."

I was as startled as everyone else in the hall. What could he mean?

Christian protested. "Lord, I am as free as anyone at this table. My family have been free castellans at Gistel and sailors on the North Sea for longer than man can remember."

"Explain your accusation, Fromold," said the count.

"Gladly. Now, all agree that a free man loses his freedom when he marries a baseborn wife. After they have been married for a year, he takes on her servile status."

"True."

"Christian of Gistel is married to Edith of the Erembalds. All know that Erembald, her grandfather, was of servile origin and not freeborn. She and all his line inherited his status, and any man or woman who has married into their family, and every one of their progeny, is a serf."

All hell broke loose in the hall, as Erembalds rose from their seats to protest these revelations. Christian looked thunderous and Edith hugged her arms across her chest and hunched over, shuddering.

Fromold had not finished. He levied a final blow at the man who was the prime target of his attacks against Christian. "And Count Charles, given the servile status of all the Erembalds, a status for which I have clear proof, it shames all free men that one of their number is placed above us. I speak of course of Bartolph, provost and your chancellor, son of Erembald and uncle of all the brood. He must be deposed from his high position and another more worthy must take his place."

Bartolph would not endure this calumny in silence. He rose from his seat at the right hand of the count in a rustle of silks, and spoke, his voice full of confident disdain. "Your creature, Fromold, lies. He has no proof because there is no proof. My ancestors were all free, and so is my family. It is his people who are of base origins, common toll takers who enriched themselves. The count will ignore his slanders."

But when the count spoke, he did not dismiss the charges. "These are serious accusations," he said. "Grave charges that will affect many. You swear you have proof, Fromold?"

"I do," Fromold replied.

"Then our courts of law must investigate this question and come to a decision."

The feast was over. Bartolph was furious. With one glance he summoned all the Erembalds to follow him out of the hall. After a moment's thought, I followed too, though I was no kin by blood or marriage. But before I left the hall, a gentle touch on my arm made me turn around. It was Charles.

"Lady Aude, it is good to see you at our court again. I have missed you these long difficult years." His expression was sweet and warm.

I made my face as ice. "I must follow Lord Christian, my count," I said coldly, then I turned and marched out, but not before seeing Charles's smile turn to sorrow. That made me happy, but I paid for that cruel happiness many times. I still pay.

I caught up with Christian and the Erembalds, crossing the castle yard to Bartolph's house. Christian was silently furious, and Edith was in tears, pleading with him. "Christian, I swear I didn't know. It's all a lie, Christian, please believe me." Similar conversations could be heard between other couples. But once in Bartolph's hall, all were silent as the patriarch spoke.

"Charles of Denmark became count because I supported him. Now he forgets what I did for him and seeks to cast me and all my line into serfdom. Let him try. We are free, and we shall be free, and there is no man on earth who can make us serfs!" He pounded on the big oak table, and his family cheered.

If they were heartened by Bartolph's words, Christian was not. Edith huddled next to me, and Christian grabbed her arm and hissed, "Both of you! We leave for Gistel. Now."

"Ouch, Christian, you're hurting me."

He ignored her and soon we were back on the road, not even pausing to retrieve our belongings from Borsiard's house. "We'll send a man for them," he said when I protested abandoning my favorite green boots.

Christian's mood worsened as weeks passed, and Edith bore the brunt of it. He was enraged that the marriage he contracted for influence and wealth, might end in his enserfment. Edith began sleeping in the women's garret in the castle. Christian made no protest. Any child he could get by her would share their putative servile status.

To my secret joy, this changed his attitude to Theodore, whom he began to view as a worthy heir. Theodore was almost eight, ready to learn how to ride and to use weapons, and to go on the sea in Christian's ships.

I'd learned something though. Instead of capitalizing on Edith's fall from favor, her plight awakened my compassion, and I allowed myself to express the affection I had grown to feel for her, now I no longer saw her as a rival and a threat.

The suit against the Erembalds had not yet come to court when Edith's family took matters into their own hands. Borsiard and his brothers took a band of thugs to besiege Fromold in his house. They cut down and burned all the orchards that surrounded the fortified mansion, then smashed the bolts on his gate. With Bartolph's blessing, they plundered the surrounding countryside and harried Fromold's peasants, slaughtering their sheep and cattle. In revenge, Charles burned down Borsiard's great house, reducing it to its foundations.

Christian couldn't afford to cut all ties to the Erembalds, in case Fromold's suit failed. He sent Edith and me to Bruges to keep an eye on what was going on and to maintain ties with her family. He also wanted me to open lines of communication with Charles.

"He seems to like you," Christian said. "If the Erembalds sink, you must persuade him not to let us fall too." I was never going to grovel to Charles but I didn't tell Christian that.

We stayed at Bartolph's great house within the castle walls. It was late February, cold and sleety, so we remained indoors with the other Erembalds who had taken refuge there. I couldn't walk past a group of two or more without hearing vague mutterings and plottings that abruptly stopped when I drew near. Our nerves were on a knife point as we waited for the next move. Charles was in Bruges too, and we were aware of every movement he made in and out of his own castle across the way.

Word came from the count that Borsiard would get no mercy until he and all the Erembalds admitted that they were Charles's serfs. I was sure they would have to bow to the count's will and then, the evil part of my nature reminded me, when Edith and Christian were declared serfs, Theodore's inheritance would be safe forever. So for my own reasons, I kept my ears open.

One evening, I was passing Bartolph's chambers when I heard voices. No one else was in sight so I pressed myself against the door jamb to try to make out what was going on inside. I could not make out the words, but it sounded like an argument. It must have been resolved, because I heard them chant an oath together, the words distinct and clear through the thick door because spoken by so many.

"We swear vengeance against Count Charles who is working for our ruin in every way and is hastening to claim us as serfs," I heard them say. "We swear to support and aid one another until our purpose is complete."

The door began to open and I had barely hidden myself in a window seat before they came out. Protected by a tapestry that blocked the window and the dark of the hall, I hoped to avoid detection. Bartolph stormed out first and marched off, while the others milled about in the hall.

"We must plan," one cousin hissed. "Can we meet at your lodgings, Borsiard?"

"Not mine. Too many about. Let's meet at young knight Walter's lodgings."

"Very good. We'll meet there after the bell rings for Vigils and shape our plan."

The men who served the count had lodgings within the castle walls. I didn't know this Walter, but I knew where Borsiard lodged when he was in town. Would I be brave enough to hide near his rooms and follow him to their conventicle? It was the only way for me to learn their plans.

I borrowed a rough cloak and hood from the laundress when she wasn't looking, and left by way of the kitchen door. I had to loiter outside Borsiard's lodgings for what seemed an age before others turned up to collect him. I hung back in the shadows when Borsiard came out, and followed them from a discreet distance as they walked to the meeting place. But the knights' quarters were in a huddle of wooden houses and twisting lanes, and I kept losing sight of my quarry. I was edging around the side of one building to spy which way the men were going, when I slipped into a pig wallow, right up to my armpits. It was cold and wet, and the slippery mud made it hard for me to clamber out. Covered head to toe in muck, I finally made it out, but the men had vanished out of sight. They must have been in one of the dwellings that surrounded the courtyard

I found myself in. But which one? I walked slowly, ears straining for tell-tale sounds under every pair of closed wooden shutters. Finally, I found the noises I expected coming from a house at the bottom of the square. And joy of joys, the shutter was open enough that I could make out what they were saying. But I had missed much of substance because of my misadventure with the pigs.

"It's settled then, that's how we'll kill the count. Which of us will do the deed?" asked a voice from within.

Kill Count Charles? They were plotting cold blooded murder? I was horrified. Dead silence greeted his call for volunteers.

"Anyone? Are you all cowards? I have four marks for a knight who will do the deed and two for a servingman." I recognized Borsiard's voice. This was a huge sum, and a number of men promised their assistance. There were more men crammed in the small dwelling than I would have thought possible. The meeting was breaking up, so I scuttled round the side of the building and watched them leave, men with cloaked faces concealing their identities in the dark of night. My heart pounded as I stood in terror, willing them to pass without finding me. I realized I'd been a fool to come. If they'd kill a count, they would think nothing of killing me. I remained hidden long after the last plotter was gone, and the night was silent but for the distant rootling of domestic animals in straw and shed.

My mind was busy with what I had heard, and I was at war with myself. I had wanted revenge against Charles for spurning me. I blamed Charles for every mistaken turn of my life. He was the reason I had left al-Lawza and followed Bertulf to Flanders, and cause of everything bad that followed. "But not death," I whispered to myself, "Not murder." I crossed myself. The cold-blooded murder of their liege lord—for this was their plot—was a terrible thing to me, an act that would call down curses on all of them. And on me too, if I did nothing to stop it.

Unwillingly, I recalled other things. How he rescued me when I was a child. His kindness when I came to Flanders. How he always smiled when he saw me, how he always had time for me—and how I had spurned him the last time we met. Was it his fault he could not love me the way I dreamed of being loved? Perhaps he loved me in a different way. I had to tell him, to warn him of the threat against his life.

I made my way back to Bartolph's mansion, stinking of pigs and mud, planning how to approach the count with my knowledge. I knew he still attended early mass with the canons every day. I could come to him after he finished his prayers, as I used to do in earlier years. But what would I say? Thanks to my misadventure in the pigsty, I had missed hearing the details of the plot. I had no idea where or when the murder was supposed to take place. It didn't matter though. I could tell him what I knew and put him on his guard.

Once in bed and as clean I could be, with a basin of cold water in the dark, I barely slept despite my exhaustion, tossing and turning on my pallet and tense about my errand of the morrow. What if he didn't believe me? What if I didn't have a chance to speak—or worse, what if Bartolph's men overheard me? I'd have to take my chances.

CHAPTER ELEVEN

Al-Lawza, July 1148

✠

When you began your tale in Antioch, I thought the story of you and Charles was going to be like a troubadour song of passion and lost love," said Eleanor, when I drew breath. "Now it is turning into an epic, full of lords and treachery." But she didn't seem displeased. For the first time in weeks, the crease of worry between her eyes was gone.

"It's more like a saint's life," said Ermine.

"It is a saint's life," I said, beneath my breath.

"Don't stop there," commanded Mabilie. "What happened next?"

I smiled. "That's for tomorrow," I said. The Muslims tell a tale of a king who, discovering his wife's infidelity, had her put to death and then married a series of virgins, executing each one after their first night together. One wily bride avoided her fate by beginning to tell a story to the king, whose conclusion she would only tell the following night. When she finished that tale, she immediately began a new one, and thus preserved her life with a chain of stories. I decided to do the same. Every evening, I would I continue my account of the Erembalds' plot against Charles, and what came after, spinning it out as long as I could and always stop at some exciting or dramatic moment. It was not to save my life, but it might help preserve our sanity at al-Lawza. The dangers of my past seemed to distract Eleanor from worries about her future. And it would pass the time.

✠

Aude's Tenth Tale: Bruges, 1127–1128

I endured a disturbed night of horrible dreams, and when I woke, the events of the previous evening flooded back in a rush. I put on my best dress and left Bartolph's house, crossing the castle courtyard in a dense fog that smelled of the salt sea and smoke from a hundred cooking fires. It was so thick I could barely make out the buildings in the castle court. I made my way to the count's palace. There was a bigger crowd than usual for Mass that morning, a hushed group, as if muffled by the mist outside. I saw some of the Erembald hangers-on, though no one from the family. I worried I would not be able to deliver my message in secret. Fromold, Charles's favorite, passed me in a hurry and I reached out to grab his sleeve. "I have a message for the count," I hissed.

"Not now," he said, pulling away and continuing on his errand.

We walked through a second-story passageway, a rickety latticework of wood and stone that led from the palace to the church of St. Donatian, then spread ourselves around the circular upper gallery that looked down onto the main altar on the lower floor. I was pressed against one of the eight colossal piers that ringed the gallery when Charles entered accompanied by his men and the paupers who would be the recipients of the day's largesse. A balcony ran around the gallery from pier to pier. I gripped it for safety and looked down below. I could just see the altar where the relics of Saints Donatian, Basil, and Maximus were venerated. The gold, turquoise, and silver of the mosaics in St. Basil's reliquary, a gift from a long-dead crusader, made me briefly homesick. The canons were in their stalls in the sanctuary, audible in their chant, but not visible. A pile of palms decayed in one corner, awaiting Palm Sunday. It was the second week of Lent.

We shuffled around to the west end of the gallery where the shrine to the Virgin was located. Inch by inch, I wiggled myself through the crowd, until I was in the front row of those observing the count at prayer. Heavy beeswax candles burned on an altar covered in a cloth, reddish purple for Lent. Murky dawn was obscured by the colored glass of the windows in the upper gallery: blood red, poison green, and sickly yellow refracting its minimal glow. One finger of true dawn pierced the murk and traced a crimson stain on Charles's back where he lay, arms extended before him and coin filled palms turned upwards.

"Miserere mei," he chanted, blond-haloed head bent, prostrate on the cold stone floor, "Have mercy on me, Oh God, according to thy great mercy," from the fourth of the seven psalms he chanted each morning. One by one the poor, thirteen in all, tiptoed over and took one of the silver pennies he held in an outstretched hand, a performance of piety and charity for us onlookers. I was in no mood for show that day, and waited anxiously for it to be over so I could fulfill my errand.

"Deal favorably, O Lord, in thy good will with Sion, that the walls of Jerusalem may be built up," he chanted in Latin, "Then, shalt thou accept the sacrifice of justice, oblations and whole burnt offerings. Then, shall they lay calves upon thy altar." Finally, the psalm was complete. Only three more to go.

But as he began the next, I was shoved out of the way by a man I'd never seen before, tall, fearsome, and stinking. He was joined by five more from each side of the gallery, the last of whom was Borsiard. I knew this was the moment I feared, the moment I had come to warn Charles about, but my throat closed over and I could not say a word as they pulled back their cloaks to reveal swords already drawn, while those assembled gasped in horror, stunned to see bare steel in God's church. Count Charles raised his head to see the interlopers, directing clear blue eyes at Borsiard, before returning, prostrate, to his prayer. "My days vanish like smoke, my bones burn like glowing embers," he chanted, voice steady and clear.

The intruders walked to where he lay unafraid while an old woman, about to pick up one of the last pennies cried to him, "Watch out!" but still he chanted with eyes fixed on the ground. "My enemies taunt me, those who rail against me use my name as a curse," he intoned. And then they cut him down. They stabbed, they hacked, and we saw it all, and I saw it, I was right there and did nothing, nothing, for a man who had shown me only good. I cried for the men there to save the count, we wailed and shouted but no one did anything, no one came to help, no one at all, and they kept hacking and hacking until rivers of blood flowed across the stone floor, staining my slippers and the hem of my gown. When it was done, when it was over, when he was dead at last, the killers turned to face us and we all ran away, murderers and witnesses together, pushing each other and tripping in our haste to get out, to get away, to escape, and we left the count alone on the cold stone floor in his own blood.

Ermine gave a soft moan, and I stopped my story. I was shaking so much I could not have continued anyway. Speaking it out, setting the scene, and describing what happened brought it all back to me. It was too much.

"Are you all right, Aude?" asked Eleanor, softly. Mabilie handed me a cup of watered wine.

I drank deep, then spoke. "When I saw the murdered bodies of Cercamon and Jaufré in Tripoli, I recalled Charles, so many years before," I said. "His murder was the worst thing I ever saw. Not his death. No, I know we all die and it is rarely pretty. It was the cowardice, the fear. We stood there and did nothing. His best-beloved servants and courtiers were there, Fromold and the rest, and not one raised a hand to save him. Most paid for that in the end. We left him cooling in his own blood, so eager to save our own skins, we didn't so much as throw a shroud over him. Retelling it brought it all back to me."

"But what could you have done, an unarmed woman?" asked Mabilie. I had often asked myself that. I did not answer her.

"You know Charles's father met an identical fate?" I asked them. Their heads shook, no. "It's true. Charles's father was Canute the Holy, king of Denmark, and he was killed by rebellious peasants in front of the altar of St. Alban's in Odense. Charles himself saw it all."

"Like a portent of his own death," said Ermine. "Was Charles's murder the end of it?"

"It was only the beginning," I said, returning to my tale.

Though it was cowardice, we ran in good cause. Charles was the first target, but not the only one. All those loyal to Charles were slated for death that day. Throughout Flanders, at that moment, the Erembalds and their accomplices flung themselves on their enemies, hoping to be rid of them all with one blow. Some fled to the count's house after running from the church, but the Erembalds had already taken possession of it, and they found no mercy there. Word spread to Ghent where the yearly fair was taking place, and the merchants fled, even those who had come all the way from Lombardy to sell their silks and spices. Many nobles were killed but many lesser men died that day too, slaughtered without pity before their wives and children.

In the church we ran like chickens, too witless to find a way out. I saw one man hide himself in the great organ casing, and three cowered behind an altar. Fromold buried himself under the pile of palms. A castellan was hewn down where he stood. They left him to suffer for a whole day and a night until he died. Then, the traitors dragged him by his feet from the gallery to the doors of the church, where they hacked all the limbs off his body and stuck them on staves for a warning. His two sons were killed fleeing Bruges, within sight of freedom and escape.

I didn't learn of these events until later. I made it out of the church and raced across the courtyard to Bartolph's house. I ignored the crowds gathering in the hall and sought out Edith and Theodore, finding them in the solar.

I gasped, lungs pounding, "Thank God you're both here and safe." I pulled Theodore to me and embraced him fiercely, which he resisted like any normal boy his age.

"What's happening, Aude, and where have you been? The whole building is a madhouse today, people rushing around, and no one will tell me what is going on."

"Edith it is terrible, so terrible." I clutched at her. "Count Charles is dead. Murdered." I cried, great gasping sobs, for the first time since I saw Charles cut down.

"Dead? Murdered? How is that possible? You must be mistaken."

"No, I was there. In church. It was awful, Edith, dreadful. And Edith — it was your brother. It was Borsiard who did it. Slaughtered him in cold blood before the altar."

She stared at me, then for the first and last time ever, slapped my face. "You lie, Aude."

The slap pulled me back from my hysterics. "No Edith, I was there I tell you." My voice was calmer now. "I'm sorry. It was Borsiard. I saw him as plain as I see you. It was him. I'm sorry."

Her shoulder slumped. I pressed my advantage. "Edith, we can't stay here. We have to leave as soon as possible, get back to Gistel. Your family may feel triumphant after today. But they've called a terrible vengeance upon themselves. They've killed a count, Edith. A count. God won't let it go unpunished." Then more pragmatically, "And if He does, the nobles will not."

"Aude, you're mad. Do you hear the noise in the hall? If what you say is true, Bartolph can't arrange our passage to Gistel right now. Besides, where are we more safe than inside the castle walls, protected by Bartolph's men?"

What she said was logical, but I didn't care. I only knew I had to get away from Bartolph and the Erembalds. "I'm leaving, with or without you, Edith." She gave in, and Lisebet helped pack our belongings. We sought out Bartolph first, hoping for license to take our horses from his stable.

But when we reached the hall, he wasn't there. "Gone to the church," a servant said.

"He's gone to rescue my boy, my dear nephew," said a very agitated old man. I recognized him as Fromold's uncle.

Just then, Bartolph came in with a group of prisoners under armed guard, all courtiers of the count, including Fromold. The provost looked anxious, a far cry from his usual easy arrogance. He addressed his prisoners. "I will keep you here in safety, in my cellars for your own protection."

"Protection!" Fromold shouted. "You mean as your captives."

"Enough!" he said. "Fromold, I know you have been undermining my authority, trying to get the provostship away from me, and your insults lie behind the work of this day. I spare you for the moment, only for the sake of your uncle." Fromold's uncle fell to his knees and tried to kiss Bartolph's hand.

After the prisoners were taken away, for such they were, whatever Bartolph pretended, he paced the hall, wringing his hands. "May God forgive me," he cried, "I knew nothing of this, nothing."

I didn't believe him. But I could see he'd give us no help. "Come," I said. "Let's go to the stables and see what we can find."

But there was not so much as a donkey fit to ride in the stables. "Nope mevrouw, all's gone, down to the last nag and jenny," said the head groom. "You'll have to wait."

"See, Aude, it's no use," said Edith, relieved. "We'll stay here and Uncle Bartolph will take care of us."

I was not prepared to wait. "The port," I said to Edith, Theodore, and Lisebet, patiently trailing in my wake. "We'll try to get a boat. This time of year we should be able to punt to Gistel." The river between Gistel and Bruges was silting up, but in early March I hoped the winter rains had raised the level enough to allow us passage.

I bribed a stable boy to serve as our porter and the four of us set out, three frightened women, a youth, and a very young boy, impatient at being taken from his games and friends.

"But why do we have to leave?" Theodore protested, kicking a small stone with a scuffed boot.

"Shh, be a good boy and come with Mummy. Give your other hand to Edith now, and we'll all walk together."

The morning mist had not lifted and the castle yard was a frightening place. Fearsome figures loomed out of the mirk at us, swords naked and ready against their enemies, and then withdrew, seeing we were not their quarry. Shouts and cries echoed around the stone buildings, and the fog twisted sound, making their direction uncertain. When we passed the church, I spied what looked a mound of old clothes, but a flaccid bare hand in the pile told me this was where bodies were leaking the last of their lifeblood onto the straw and mud of the courtyard. I diverted Theodore's attention.

"Come quickly, Theo, all of you. No time to dawdle."

I hoped that the eastern gate, furthest from Bartolph's house would be the least guarded, and so it proved. In fact, there was no one there when we passed through it. I felt a wave of relief once we were out of the confines of the castle precinct and in the town proper. I could breathe again. Now to find a boat.

The streets leading to the port were empty and silent, fog muffling our footsteps, though we could hear the clash of distant violence. Shops that normally drew brisk business were shuttered and boarded, and no light shone from their windows, as the townsfolk huddled inside and tried to ride out whatever madness the armed men of Flanders were engaged in.

"Mummy, I'm scared," Theodore whispered.

Of course he was, poor little mite. "Nothing to be scared of. We're going to take a lovely boat ride home and then you'll see your pony and your dog. I know, let's sing a song. I'll begin and you all join in. 'Lord Halewijn took a maid for a wife, tra lee, tra la, tra lo.'"

"That's a terrible song, Aude. Halewijn kills all his wives and puts them in a cupboard. Stop!" said Edith.

I stopped, chastened. I hadn't liked the way my voice echoed in the empty streets anyway, and I needed all my attention to find the port. The mist concealed landmarks and made direction uncertain. A sudden reek of dank canal told us we were close, and soon we saw the water.

"But where are all the boats?" asked Edith. She was right. The normally busting port was silent and empty with not a boat in sight, and not so much as a hungry cat on shore.

"Maybe we haven't gone far enough," I said, so we walked a little further. But no, our first impression was correct. Boats gone, horses gone. A prickle of fear touched my spine. What were we going to do?

A whisper from above caught our attention. "Hssst! If you're looking for a boat, you're too late. They've all gone, fled or up to no good." We looked up at the round moon face of an old woman, one of the fishwives who haunted the docks in better times. "Best be going home, missees. Not safe out here for anyone." With that she slammed her shutter closed again.

"We're not going back to the castle," I warned before Edith could open her mouth.

"Then where will we go? We can't stay here."

"I know. Let me think." I paced. Horses rented at a livery stable? Surely they'd be gone like the boats were. An inn?

"We could go to my house, I suppose," Edith said reluctantly.

"Your house? What house? You never told me you had a house in Bruges."

"You never asked," Edith said. "I inherited it from my mother, and it was part of my dowry. My old nurse lives there and keeps it for me. She'd be glad to see us, but it's a little place."

How could Edith own a house and me not know anything about it? I thought I knew everything about that woman. If it were smaller than a breadbox, it would still be better than standing here in the fog, or worse, returning to the castle and becoming more deeply implicated in the Erembalds' dirty deeds. "Take us there right away," I ordered.

We hurried through the twisting streets as fast as Theodore's little legs and our overburdened page could move. Eager to reach our destination, I forgot to be wary, so I was startled when a hairy hand grabbed my arm. "What are you out here for?" A face like a lumpy rutabaga peered at me from the mist. I tried to pull myself away, but the brute was much too strong. He put a dagger up under my chin to deter me from another attempt at flight. It worked.

Edith came to where I stood. "Claes! Let her go. She's my friend."

"Lady Edith?" the ruffian unhanded me and pulled off his cap. "Your father asked me to patrol the streets, looking for our enemies. It's a bad day for them to be out. I got two who'll never bother the Erembalds again, over there." He sniggered and pointed to an alley where two pairs of boot-clad feet could just be seen. "What are you doing out here. Going to your father's house? Can I escort you?"

No, I mouthed at her, hoping he wouldn't see. We might as well have stayed with Bartolph.

"This is Claes," she said to me. "One of my brother's men." Then she turned back to my captor. "We're making our way to my house in town. And yes, you may escort us," she said, ignoring my wordless protests.

"I don't like that man," Theodore whispered.

I could not disagree, but his protection may have saved us from the other ruffians we passed, in twos and threes, roaming the streets on own their deadly errands. They couldn't all have been known to Edith. Besides, we could send our page home in Claes's care.

Edith's mysterious house was shut tight as a casket when we arrived there, and I guessed everyone inside had fled and locked the door. But after our new friend, Claes, pounded and shouted for a while, a quavering old woman's voice finally asked him his business.

"Annie, Annie, it's me," said Edith.

"Edie, my little girl! Why didn't you say so? Come in, come in."

It took a while before all the barricades she had placed against her door were taken down and we could enter. After tipping our porter and our guard, we went inside. It was apple-pie neat but small, as Edith had warned—one room below hung with hams, aging cheeses and dried bread, and one room above where there would scarcely be room for all of us to sleep stretched out, plus a tiny attic. But I was satisfied. We'd be safe here, for a time at least. There was also a small shed out back, with chickens and a goat, and a few ducks who shared the pond in the inner courtyard with the fowl from the other houses on the same court. We wouldn't starve.

Edith's Annie was hugging and kissing her and squeezing her cheeks. I jealously remembered how all my nannies had disliked me, and me them. Lisebet excused herself to settle our few belongings and make beds for us from Annie's pallets upstairs. I was surprised at her diligence until I realized she was also hoping to see what she could spy from an upper story window.

Annie set to cooking for what seemed like an entire castle. Edith pulled out her spindle and started to spin while she quizzed Theodore on his letters, which he drew in the ash on the hearth. Edith couldn't run a castle, but she had been taught a variety of pursuits as a child to make herself useful wherever she found herself. I had no such diligent training so I sat on the bench under the shuttered and barred front window, fidgeting and anxious. I had used every bit of my remaining strength to get Theodore, Edith and Lisebet out of the castle to what I hoped was safety but now that I was here, I wanted nothing in the world more than to go back. Images of Charles's broken body haunted me.

I told them I intended to go to the church and predictably, Edith protested, "Aude, stay here with us. You saw how dangerous it was out there. And what good can you do in the church?"

"I can pray," I said, and she scoffed. She knew I was not much of a one for prayer.

Surprisingly enough, Annie intervened. "Let her go. It is a terrible thing for the count to lie there, dead and unmourned by anyone after the good he did for us poor citizens in his life," she said. "And who will care for the poor now he is gone? Who will be count now?"

That was a good question, for Charles had no children. His old friend, William Clito, had a distant claim, I remembered, and there was an illegitimate cousin, William of Ypres, who had fought briefly with Charles to succeed Baldwin. I spared a thought for Charles's untouched widow. I supposed she'd be returned to her parents.

I pulled my cloak tightly around me, putting the hood up to conceal my face, and was out the door as quickly as I could move, before they came up with more reasons to stop me. I knew a wiser woman would have stayed by the fire, but I was compelled. We had walked a big circle getting to Edith's house, so it was not a long walk to the west gate through the walls. Though the sun was beginning to set, the fog had lifted a little, and it was easier to find my way. Both the bridge over the moat to the gate and the gate itself were heavily guarded by men wearing the Erembald emblem of an anchor, but they were letting a steady stream of grieving mothers and widows in to retrieve loved ones killed in the fighting, and it was easy for me to tag along.

I made my way timidly into the church, not sure what I would find. The glow of candles drew my eyes to the choir on the first floor. The canons had retrieved the count's broken corpse from the gallery, wound it in a linen sheet and placed it on a bier in the choir, a thick beeswax candle at each corner whose sweet scent fought with the stench of gore, both that of the count and of the others slaughtered there that day. If I looked too carefully in the corners, I knew I would see other signs of death, so I kept my eyes on Charles as I approached. Even here I could see the linen bands were stained with his blood. I knelt on the cold stone floor and joined the others there, all women, who had come to mourn their lost lord.

My mother died at sea, my father's body and my childhood were abandoned after a hasty funeral, and my unlamented husband needed a quick burial after being too long above ground in the summer's heat. Charles was the first love I was able to mourn properly. I tried to remember the right words, struggling to follow the Latin psalms that the other women, most local religious, muttered with authority, familiar with them through long repetition. Stumbling over my tongue, I chanted along, "I loved, because the Lord will hear the voice of my prayer," and "Out of the depths I have cried to thee, Oh Lord," and one I forget now, before I gave up, unable to follow and overcome with memories. But tears, too, are welcome at a place of mourning.

I saw myself, standing on the parapet wall, all Jerusalem at my feet, with my mother and father still alive and not a care but fulfilling my own whims in the most delightful way possible. Then the terror of my fall and the joy of rescue. Would I have loved anyone who had rescued me that day? If my hero had been plump with spots, would I have given him my heart, or did he have to be golden-haloed and blue eyed? I like to think that even as a child, younger then than Theodore, I recognized something of Charles's nobility, his true character that would feed the poor, clothe the naked, and, yes, rescue a naughty little girl from her own vanity. His sins forgiven, nay forgotten by me, I poured out all of my grief in the length of that cold night.

All night long, the women stayed and prayed, coming and going to spell each other by turns, but he was never left alone, and I stayed too, with my tears and memories. Once, when I rose and left the choir to give my aching knees a rest, I was surprised to see a familiar black-clad woman wearing a large silver pectoral cross around her neck. It was the abbess of St. Godeleva's abbey in Gistel—not the old abbess, who was there when I first arrived, and who died during the famine winter, but a younger one.

"Why Aude, I did not expect to find you here."

She had good cause to wonder. My convent-visiting habits had declined after Christian arrived in Gistel.

"Nor I you. What brings you to Bruges?"

"I hoped to get the count's help in a property dispute." She had the good grace to look uncomfortable. Any property dispute could only be with our castle. "But of course, now..." she trailed off and gestured towards the bier. "So I am come to pray for the count's soul."

"As am I. But tell me, abbess, do you return to Gistel soon? Would you send a message to the castle to let Christian know that we are trapped here without means of return? He needs to send for us, or come and get us himself. We're at Edith's house." He would know it, even if I hadn't.

"Willingly," she said. An errand to put her in the good graces of the castle was surely welcome. "And now, if you will excuse me." I let her go to pray, satisfied. Once Christian knew we were in trouble, surely he would come to our aid.

The abbess was quickly done with her turn and gone again. I kept vigil with those who remained, scarcely noticing tiredness or pangs of hunger, interrupted only by the prayers of the canons themselves as they sang their office at intervals. And throughout the long night, our watch was shadowed by armed men loyal to the Erembalds at every door, in the gallery, and up in the tower. I could not see what they were protecting or why. Every last bit of gold and silver had been looted from the church earlier in the day. The reliquary of St. Basil would never taunt me with its mosaics again.

In the morning, we were joined by the poor of Bruges, the crippled and the hungry whom Charles had protected in life. They waited for Bartolph to make the customary donation of alms they were owed after a count died. But when Bartolph arrived in the church that morning, it was not to spread largesse. Shifty and silent he paced, ignoring the clamors of the poor.

Bartolph's relief when the abbot of St. Peter's in Ghent arrived through the door suggested this was who he had been waiting for. "My lord chancellor," the abbot said, "I am here to collect the body of our dear count. My knights will carry the body and I have a litter and horses outside."

"Thanks be to God," said Bartolph, rubbing his hands together. "Let's get moving." Bartolph's motives were clear to me. If the count's body were in Ghent, the people of Bruges would not forever be reminded of his family's terrible crime.

The abbot's knights entered with a litter to bear the count away. But when they tried to pick up the bier with his body, they were overwhelmed by the canons, who refused to let them remove the count.

One of the oldest canons threatened Bartolph. "Lord provost, if they take our count, we fear the destruction of the church. With Charles's intervention, God may spare us and have pity on this place, but if he is removed, God will avenge without mercy the treachery committed here."

The canons roared their assent, but Bartolph urged the knights to hurry up with their work. At this, the canons picked up what weapons they could find to hand—broomsticks and candleholders, stools and benches. Even I picked up a stool, though it was more for defense than attack as I cowered behind a pier with some of my fellow mourners. Some moved to bar the door while others ranged themselves around the bier to protect the body. One canon ran up into the tower and rang the bells, calling on all the citizens of Bruges to defend their count. The ensuing melee inside and outside the church threatened to spill into the town streets, but before it could, a cry came from under the bier where the count lay, oblivious to the tumult he had inspired. A youth rose from the floor and shouted, "Look! A miracle! I can walk, I can walk."

The news spread. "A miracle...the count...he can walk...a sign!" and the fighting stopped on both sides. Bartolph, defeated, ordered the church doors closed. We hugged each other and cheered our victory with tears running down our faces, greeting strangers as friends. Bartolph and his nephews withdrew to plan their next move, while the abbot returned to Ghent empty-handed. The next day, Bartolph had the count buried in a reused stone sarcophagus in the upper gallery of the church after a poorly-attended Mass of the Dead in a church outside the castle walls. I think he wanted to avoid the riots of the previous day but at least the citizens of Bruges had their way. Their count—our count—would remain among us.

I say "our count" because something changed that morning in the church. We of Bruges and Flanders were a people as fragmented as any in Christendom. Lords despised merchants who loathed peasants who disdained the urban poor. Lay and religious were distanced by vocation, and we all know how men and women are at odds. But that morning, as we united to protect our count's body, the distinctions between us faded, and paupers, canons, townsfolk, and ladies like myself worked in common cause. Our success bound us in devotion to the count—and in sworn opposition to his enemies, Bartolph and all the Erembalds.

But though we longed for vengeance in the count's name, for the moment the Erembalds were in the ascendant. I returned to Edith's house the morning after our vigil exhausted but elated. She pressed me to sleep for at least a little while, but I was too excited to rest. "I wish you'd been there, Edith," I kept repeating. "We put them to flight, all of us working together. People I would never normally speak to, all united around the count. We were blessed by a miracle of healing," I said. "And the look on Bartolph's face when he saw he wouldn't get his way, and we all embraced and sang for joy, was priceless."

Edith looked uncomfortable and too late I recalled that she too was an Erembald. Though she was so gentle she shooed flies out the window rather than kill them, and hated the thought that her family were the cause of the anarchy around us, Bartolph was her uncle.

We heard word from neighbors whispering over back fences about the Erembalds' reprisals against their enemies. Here, a castellan was hanged in front of his family, there a house was burnt to the ground, and everywhere men were going into exile rather than face Erembald vengeance. The neighbors knew Edith was an Erembald, and her presence in their quarter made them feel safe. How would they feel if the tide turned against the Erembalds, I wondered? But that didn't seem possible. One by one they eliminated all their enemies and soon Bartolph would surely choose a new count, one more biddable than Charles. So though shyly, in ones and twos, the townspeople flocked to Charles's tomb for prayers and intercession, I believed Bartolph had won, and I only waited, increasingly impatient, for Christian to return us to Gistel.

But word from Gistel never came, and though boats or horses could have been hired by this point, I wanted the security of my own armed men around me as we travelled Flanders' dangerous byways. Had that hen-witted abbess failed to deliver my message? I sent another which likewise got no response. Christian was ignoring us, I realized, and I couldn't understand why, now his wife's family had triumphed over their enemies. So we stayed in Bruges, waiting for I don't know what, trying to keep Theodore entertained and Lisebet from pursuing a dangerous flirtation with a married man on our courtyard.

Meanwhile, there were stirrings of resistance against the Erembalds. Lisebet, keeping watch from her perch in the attic called, "Fire, fire!" one morning, and we all climbed the ladder to see a dot of flame and a spire of smoke in the distance.

"That must be my uncle's house burning," said Edith glumly. "Not Bartolph, another uncle." I could never keep her huge family straight. It was the first strike against the Erembalds.

The next evening, the octave of Charles's death, just as we were sitting down to eat our evening meal, a tumult arose, the sound of men shouting and the clash of steel, growing louder and louder until it seemed like it was outside our front door. I rose to make sure the shutters were fastened but before I reached the door, to make sure it was barred tightly, Theodore, slippery as an eel, raced me to it and escaped. Cooped in our house and the inner courtyard so long, he was desperate for some excitement, but I was horrified. Knowing what a mob of men could do, I ran outside and plunged into the darkened, noisy streets to look for him.

✠

There, that was a good place to stop, I thought, as I finished my story for the night. But Eleanor was onto me.

"Every time you finish your story for the night, you leave us at a moment of high suspense, and I know why," she said. "You want to distract us from the most important part of your story."

"Nonsense," I replied. Then, curious, "What is the most important part of my story?"

"That you forgave Charles for not being what you wanted him to be. At the very end, you loved him again."

I kicked at a stone in the courtyard, but said nothing. Eleanor was right.

CHAPTER TWELVE

Al-Lawza, August 1148

✠

We expected the Templars or King Louis to turn up any day at our gates, demanding entrance. But as weeks passed without contact, I grew confident and under-cautious, and thought nothing of hoofbeats heard outside one afternoon as we rested within after our midday meal. The thump of boots on the stairs stirred me from a catnap.

It was one of Eleanor's knights. "My lady, the king your husband is at the gates. What shall we do?"

"Let him in, of course," she said. "I will receive him in the hall." Mabilie hastened to the kitchens to order suitable refreshments while Ermine and I helped the queen fix her hair and put on a loose gown before her encounter with her husband. We spoke little, never uttering the questions in our minds. What was his mission here? Had he heard Marie's news? Did he intend to divorce Eleanor? And who accompanied him? Was Thierry de Galeran being entertained with the wine from our cellar?

He was not. When Eleanor finally confronted her husband in the hall, we saw that the king was accompanied only by a handful of his personal guard and his chaplain, Odo. While Odo was no friend of ours, I was relieved to see no Templar crosses sullying my castle.

"Majesty," Eleanor said to him, and curtseyed deeply.

He kissed her hand, "Eleanor, as beautiful as ever." So far so good. Except he sounded sad. In fact, now I could breathe again and look around, I saw that all the men looked somber and grim. There was something more here than a wayward queen.

Mabilie entered with a servant bearing food and drink. After he poured spiced wine and left, we remained in silence, waiting for one of the royal pair to begin.

Finally, the king spoke. "I am relieved to see you looking so well. The fresh air of the countryside suits you more than Tripoli, I think."

"Yes my lord, it does."

He shifted from small talk. "Eleanor, I know everything. Your lady, Marie, told the Templars and Thierry de Galeran told me. De Galeran took great delight in telling me," he finished bitterly.

Eleanor said nothing, and after a pause, Louis continued. "I had much time to think during our assault on Damascus—it failed spectacularly, by the way. I don't know if you got the news out here." We hadn't, but it explained his defeated demeanor.

He went on. "I know." He swallowed and looked away. "I know that you are bearing a child. I know that it would be well within my rights to put you away. But I don't want to do that." He swallowed again. "I'm not going to do that," he said with defiance. He looked directly at Eleanor again, whose own gaze did not shift from his. "I am going to take you back, and all of this...mess will be forgotten, as if it never was. The Holy Land is a hard school, but Christ has taught me forgiveness here."

I looked at Louis in a new light, with these words. I had always seen him as weak, softly pious, easily led. But ninety-nine men out of a hundred would have made their wives pay dearly for a transgression of Eleanor's nature and for him to be the hundredth needed a strength I hadn't known he possessed. I saw Odo gritting his teeth. He clearly had not been an advocate of forgiveness.

Mabilie and Ermine visibly relaxed as the king spoke. The king was willing to forgive his wandering bride and one day everything might be normal again, almost. We were so relieved that the king would forgive her, it didn't cross our minds to wonder whether Eleanor would want to be forgiven, or to go back to Louis. Nor did we consider the fate of the child to be born.

Eleanor, however, did not drop her guard. "Take me back? You mean to France? Right now?" she asked.

"No. That would never do." Louis looked uncomfortable again. "Better stay here, in this place, at least until the, the, it is born. This castle is simple and isolated, and we will say that you have retreated to the mountains for your health. Conrad returns to Germany in a matter of weeks, but I will winter in this land, using my time to visit the pilgrimage sites I have not yet seen. If I may trouble you for dinner for my men and myself, we'll leave directly after, and there is no need for you and I to meet again until…after. When do you expect to be delivered of the, um, it?"

"February, my lord."

"Very well, you and I will leave the Holy Land together in April, right after Easter."

I left for the kitchen to help the cook prepare a last-minute feast fit for a king and discovered that he had already ordered a couple of lambs to be slaughtered. It promised to be an awkward meal, but once we were seated in the hall and fed, Mabilie distracted us by asking the king about the siege of Damascus.

"How could it fail with all the flower of Christendom there?" she asked accusingly.

"It was shameful," Louis agreed shortly, and perhaps relieved to have something other than Eleanor to discuss, he plunged into the story.

"We were in good spirits as we marched north from Tiberias, along the coast of the Sea of Galilee. We drank from the waters on which Christ had walked, and we all felt invigorated being in that holy place." We nodded and smiled at this pious image.

The king took a long drink of his wine. "We reached Damascus. It is in the middle of a flat plain, surrounded in every direction by walled orchards and gardens, studded with watchtowers. Those orchards gave us fresh fruit and shade as we approached the city, but also offered shelter for our enemy to harry us every step of the way. They alone knew the twisting paths through the maze of mud walls. Still, at the cost of many men, we eventually reached the north wall of the city where the river ran. The city should have been ours for the plucking, like one of the pomegranates ripening in the trees around us."

"What happened?" asked Eleanor.

"King Conrad and I wanted to wage a full-scale assault, but we were persuaded by the local lords to move from our favorable location to the south-eastern part of the walls, an area without water and exposed to the sun but, so we were told, with only a low and easily breached city wall. When we got there, we found that the wall was strong and fortified. In a matter of days, we ran out of food and water, and the Christian army dissolved like snow in the desert. We didn't even fight," he said in anguish. "We turned tail and left."

We heard the end of his story in stunned silence. Years of planning, the immense distance travelled, and all for nothing. The men and women who had died on the road in Europe, in the mountains of Turkey, and in the orchards of Damascus, even the husband of faithless Marie. All in vain, with neither victory and nor a song of tragic valor in defeat to remember the names of those lost. I recalled Abbot Bernard's bold words of divine struggles and God's plan at Vezelay where Louis and Eleanor took the cross alongside so many more. What a terrible waste.

"But why did they tell you to move, Louis? That makes no sense. Who stood to gain from it?" said Eleanor, always alive to the political calculations of those around her. She and Louis could be a formidable team, if they would only work together.

"It was those Templars I'll wager," Ermine said angrily, and Louis smiled bitterly at her.

"Indeed it was. Thierry de Galeran, a man I thought was my friend and ally, insisted the north-western wall was impregnable and that we should move south. He said we'd never take the city where we were, but I knew that with God on our side, we would not fail. God turned His face from us because of our cowardice, and that led to our doom."

But I had my doubts. I was the last to give de Galeran the benefit of the doubt, but I trusted his appraisal of military realities on the ground over the king's hopes for divine intervention any day.

"And there's worse," continued the king. "Thierry admitted to my face that the Templars accepted bribes from the rulers of Damascus to persuade our army to move."

He looked around the table, satisfied to hear gasps of horror coming from each one of us, then continued. "He had an explanation for it. He said our army was on the verge of destruction, caught between the walls and an enemy army coming to relieve Damascus, and that the only way to persuade us to abandon the siege was to place us with no food or water so we would have to retreat before the enemy arrived. Otherwise, he said, we'd have been slaughtered. As if dying in battle on crusade had not been our fondest wish."

"But how did he explain the bribe?" asked Mabilie.

"He was proud of it. He said Damascus paid us to do something that was ultimately in own interest. They had their city, the crusaders lived to fight another day, the Templars made a profit, and everyone was happy. Everyone but God," he finished bitterly.

Once again, I could see that Thierry had a point. Why not get Damascus to pay for what you will be forced to do anyway? But I rejoiced in the rupture it had created between the Templars and the king, a rupture that might save Eleanor, the wife I knew Louis loved, in his own way.

"Profit," the king went on. "All the Templars care about is profit. Thierry had the nerve to say that the Templars needed to accept the bribe because of the loans they made to France. Sums for which my kingdom is now in hock until the Judgement Day. And for what purpose? Why, if we hadn't waited so long in Antioch for the Templar money, you and Raymond never would have...and you wouldn't be..."

He couldn't quite put it into words, but we were back to our original touchy subject, Eleanor and her adventures. The queen redirected the conversation.

"Are you going to write about Damascus in your history, Odo?" she asked the chaplain. Everyone knew that Odo was writing an account of Louis's crusade, glorifying his deeds and his piety.

Odo looked awkward. "His majesty and I have agreed that I will end my tale just before we reach Antioch. The moral of my story will be the danger of trusting the perfidious Greeks, whose treachery decimated our army. If not for them, surely we would have triumphed at Damascus. Thus, my tale will be both truthful and, er, complete." He blushed furiously, but I was pleased. Eleanor and Raymond's story would have no place in the historical record. Louis was doing his best to erase her indiscretion with her uncle in every way. For the first time, it occurred to me to wonder what he was going to do with her baby, if it were born live and hale. How would they erase it from the record? For he'd never accept it as his own, this I was sure.

Louis left, and our days fell back into routine, but his visit shifted our mood. Eleanor seemed calmer, more at peace. The new maturity I had first noticed at Tripoli had deepened and grown. She was as full of charm and passion as ever, but I thought the open, vivacious girl I had first met at Vezelay was gone forever. There was a new cynicism there. And who could blame her?

We ventured away from al-Lawza, riding carefully on the gentler plains and picnicking at the wadi, where a cluster of young gazelles, drinking and playing away from their mothers, inspired us to speculate on names for the baby.

"I was named for my mother, Aenor," she said, "I was the other Aenor, 'alia Aenor' in Latin, Eleanor. Maybe if it is a girl I could call her Eleleanor, the other other Aenor," she teased.

"Why not after one of us?" said Ermine. "Elermine or Elaude."

"You're both ridiculous," said Mabilie. "The baby will have a family name, of course. Maybe Philippa or Hildegarde."

"Or Dangereuse, after my grandfather's mistress, who was my mother's mother. This girl will be dangerous enough," riposted Eleanor.

I noticed Mabilie's suggestions were all from Eleanor's family, not Louis's. And we never considered the possibility the child would be a boy. Called Raymond or Louis? Hardly. By suggesting only feminine names, we were silently willing the child to be of the safer, female sex.

Maybe Mabilie sensed this, because she changed the subject. "You stopped in the middle of a story last time, Aude. Tell us what happened when Theo ran out of the house to the battles in the streets."

✠

Aude's Eleventh Tale: Bruges, March 1127

The sound of men fighting rose from the area around the western gates of the castle, and in the growing dusk I could just see a small boy running in that direction. "Theodore!" I called, and chased after him, catching up to him at the end of our street. The street opened into a market square which led to the main bridge that separated the town from the castle. Around the castle, a horrible melee of men fought with swords and pikes. The counterattack against the Erembalds had begun. The Erembalds were desperate to prevent knights loyal to Charles from breaching the castle. The knightly attackers were joined by a mass of citizens who had heard the tumult like us, and rejoiced at a chance to avenge the count. They carried crude weapons too, so men with hoes and kitchen knives joined the knights to assault every bridge into the castle. Smoke pouring from the far side of the castle suggested the avengers had struck there too.

"Come, Theo," I said, as a man fell, groaning and wounded, into the river that separated the castle from the town. "This is no place for us." Round-eyed with fear, he came to me but when we turned back, our way was barred by a rabble coming to join the melee at the main gate. Though I sympathized with their cause, I feared their bloodlust, and pulled Theodore into a nearby alley, barely a crack between two buildings. We were not alone. One of the wounded had been dragged here to die, fluid seeping from his gut and his throat burbling sickly. There was no way to tell which side he was on, and no hope to save him.

Men brawled all over the market square, a brutal, cheating battle owing nothing to the rules of knighthood or the order of a tournament. I saw Borsiard retreat across the bridge to the castle while arrows, stones, and spears rained down from the ramparts on his pursuers. Claes, our escort and protector to Edith's house, was captured by a mob. He had tried to escape the castle disguised as a woman. We watched as he was dragged to the center of the market and hanged on the great gallows standing there, a stick thrust through his shanks and shins and his head bent so his bare backside was turned towards the castle in full view of the men watching from the count's balcony. Theodore squealed at this horror, and finally allowed me to cover his eyes with my hands.

The dying man we shared our sanctuary with coughed and spluttered, and breathed his last. The Erembalds were beaten back into the castle, but the attackers could not breach its walls, so both sides set themselves up for a long siege. Night fell, and under the cover of darkness we made our way back to Edith's house. Cowed by our ordeal, Theodore promised to never, ever leave the house without permission. Christian would have beaten him, but there was too much violence already.

Edith unbarred the door when she was certain it was us. Theodore, clingy with delayed fright, sat on my lap and I held him close while I told Edith what we had seen. I glossed over the worst of the slaughter, but still she was distraught.

"This is terrible news, Aude. Why did I let you persuade me to leave my uncle's house? We must go back right away," she said, her hands flailing.

"Edith, are you mad?" I was proud I had foreseen the counter-attack on the Erembalds, and got us to safety before it began, and now she wanted to return to the fire at the moment when it was hottest?

"I must go. You can stay here, and Theodore and Lisebet, but I must be with my family. I can't let them fight alone." She seemed ready to leave then and there.

I was aghast. I knew what would happen if she tried to pass through the lines of besiegers and besieged. Well-known in Bruges, she'd be recognized immediately as an Erembald. I recalled Borsiard's servant Claes, twisting in the wind.

"You can't go, Edith. I forbid it. You must stay here with us. You won't help your family if you return, but you may be of use to them out here, in safety," I said in my sternest voice. Surely she would obey me—she usually did.

"Lady Aude is right," Annie intervened. "It's madness to go. You'll only be another mouth to feed in the castle." Faced with our opposition, Edith desisted.

I pressed my advantage. "No one must leave this house for any reason. No one. That includes you, Lisebet." She humphed at me. I knew I'd have trouble with her. Lonely and bored, her flirtation with the neighbor had heated up, and she wouldn't want to let it drop. She flounced upstairs to the attic garret she had colonized for her private use. I continued. "Everyone knows this is an Erembald house, but if we keep a low profile, we may be safe. Besides, Christian will come for us any day now." I didn't believe that any more. If he hadn't sought Edith out when the Erembalds were in the ascendent, why would he do so now they were under attack?

I was wakened the next morning by the sound of a wooden shutter banging against the wall. I called sleepily to Edith. "Get up and fix the shutter. It must be loose." She snored, rolled over, and pulled the cover over her head. It banged again. Annie and Theodore were fast asleep. Never mind, I would do it myself. But once I was up, I saw that the shutters on our floor were sealed tight. I heard the banging again, coming from above, so I climbed the ladder to Lisebet's tiny apartment. Her shutter was wide open and knocking on the roof in the wind. Lisebet herself was nowhere to be seen. I fastened the window tightly, then, after a moment's thought, dragged one of the heavy storage chests in front of it. If someone could go out that way, someone could also come in.

When I climbed down the ladder, Edith was awake.

"Lisebet?" she asked.

"She's gone."

"It was a matter of time. She's been chafing to leave for days."

"Has she gone to that man, or back to Gistel?"

"No doubt the man. She'll come back in a few weeks with a black eye and a baby in her belly."

Edith was right, but it made me sad. Lisebet had been my only friend for a long time.

We got used to life locked indoors. The neighbors who shared the inner court were colder now the Erembald sun was setting, but they still passed us news from the outside world. Barons and the powerful from surrounding towns like Ghent arrived and took charge of the siege from the knights. But one assault after another on the castle failed, and the siege wore on in the cold, drizzling spring, a dull war of attrition on both sides.

The citizens built siege ladders for a massive assault on the castle, and our courtyard was charged with constructing one. I did our household's share of the work so Edith wouldn't have to be among our neighbors.

The ladder was going to be massive, the height of the castle walls once complete, but we built our part in sections that would be joined together in the market square. We women were to weave green branches into a kind of lattice on either side of the ladder, to afford its climbers some measure of protection. The branches whipped and stung my soft hands, raising red welts.

One of the women saw them and laughed. "Do you good to see how the rest of us live, mevrouw." She spoke my title with contempt. When a count could be murdered in cold blood without retribution, ordinary folk could see no reason to show the old respect. I kept silent.

Then, they began to twit me about my Erembald kin.

"You're a family of murderers, you are. You'll all get what you deserve."

"I'm not an Erembald," I said. "Neither is my son."

"That fat bitch you live with is. Sister to a murderer, she is. We know."

I stopped Theodore from going outside to play with their children. He didn't mind. Children ape their parents, and the adults' taunts had made their way to him. The bloody noses he returned home with were no longer harmless play. I never saw Lisebet, though one day I thought I heard her laugh coming from the windows across the way. I hoped she was well and tried to stay inside as much as possible. At least we had our own well and didn't need the one in the courtyard.

One evening as I came from feeding the ducks, I heard male voices behind me.

"Hey, traitor."

"I'm not a traitor," I said automatically. There were four of them, and they were big.

"If you're not a traitor, then you won't care if we tell the men besieging the castle that you're living here. And your sister-in-law too, the Erembald. We'll tell and earn a big reward. They'll hang her and burn her entrails, and you too. We'll tell, unless you make it worth our while."

The speaker was a man who had fawned on us in the early days after Charles's murder, trying to curry favor with an Erembald. I didn't want him to reveal our whereabouts, but I was damned if I'd put even a penny in the hands of these bullies.

"Brave sirs," I said, batting my eyes. "We are so weak, so power-less, and you have been so good to welcome us into your midst in this courtyard. We feel so grateful for your protection and wondered only what we might do in return."

They puffed up their chests and I smiled to myself. "That's right, protection," their spokesman said. "We've been protecting you for free, and it is only right that we get something out of it. So what'll it be?"

I thought quickly. It had to be big enough, but anything too big would only make them greedy. "How about a big side of smoked bacon?" I asked. It was the right suggestion as they practically started drooling. "And a headcheese. I'll get them and bring them out."

Before they could blink, I raced inside and bolted the door firmly. Panting a little and ignoring Edith and Annie's stares, I raced to the second story and found what I needed.

I heard them getting restless below. "Where's that wench? Hey! Woman! We want our reward!"

I opened the window. "Here's the only reward you'll get from us," I said, and poured the contents of our night-time chamber pots onto their waiting heads below. As they cursed and swore, I slammed the window shutters closed.

They returned, drunk, well after dusk. "Hey, traitors!" they called, banging on our back door. "We'll burn you out like the witches you are." I peered through a knothole in the second story shutter. There were five of them now, all carrying torches.

"What do we do?" hissed Edith, terrified.

"For the moment, we wait." I watched as they fumbled with their torches. Fools. If our house caught, every single one on the court-yard would go up in flames, including their own. For the first time in my life, I was glad that Flanders was so wet. Our first story was all of stone, except for the door, and its wood was too new and too waterlogged to catch alight. They tried fruitlessly for a while, until one of them caught the sleeve of another alight and they began fighting amongst themselves. Then they turned their attention to the easier quarry of our chicken coop. They got our chickens and the last of our ducks, and they set the straw on fire so the hut became a smoldering ruin, but we were safe.

"No eggs for a while," I said. I hoped they'd be content with that, and the greater treasures offered by the castle.

I was wrong. they had one last gruesome message for us. When I woke the next morning, I peered through our knothole to survey the damage. I saw the ruined coop, then across the way, I saw what looked like a bundle of clothes—a woman's dress—hanging from an upper story, with birds perched on the top. On the skirt, I spied letters, badly made. IVDAS—Judas, the ultimate traitor. I could guess who that message was for. It looked like a kind of strawman, an effigy to warn us. As I watched, the birds flew off, scared by some cat or common signal. Then I saw that it was no effigy. It was a woman, eyeless and tongue protruding, hanged from the upper story to warn us. It was Lisebet.

My whole body shook and I couldn't speak. Edith, guessing I had seen some horror, pushed, me unresisting, from the knothole and saw it for herself. She screamed and screamed, more like an animal than a woman until I came to myself and shook her into stopping. It took both of us to keep Theodore from the window. Fortunately, he was too short to see through the knothole without aid. "They burned our chicken coop," I said firmly. "Edith is sad for the ducks."

I imagined the chain of events that led them to hang Lisebet, dear Lisebet who only wanted love and a bit of fun. Had the neighbor's wife become jealous enough that Lisebet became expendable? I preferred to believe that she had tried to intervene on our behalf, tried to protect us from some wrong they were going to do to us and paid for it with her life. But the nagging fear remained. Had Lisebet died because I wouldn't give a side of bacon?

Lisebet's murder snapped something inside Edith. She had never liked staying in the house, but as the days passed, she became increasingly frantic for us to leave, to return to Gistel on foot if necessary.

"Are we going to wait until they kill us one by one in our beds?" she asked in an undertone while Theodore was helping Annie peel turnips.

"Where can we go?" I asked. "Lisebet wouldn't have died if she had stayed here where she belonged. They haven't done anything more to us since that day, have they?" It was true. Whether they felt they had their revenge or whether they were having too much fun besieging the castle with the rest of the town, they left us alone.

But it was no consolation to Edith. She picked fights with me, and Theodore whined out of boredom, until I wanted to hurl myself into the midst of battle myself to get away from them. Thank God for Annie's good sense and her magical alchemy with a ham bone and a handful of peas keeping us all fed or I would have gone mad.

And the days passed, and we waited, hoping like everyone in Bruges for some shift in the battle.

"Why won't Christian come for us?" asked Edith for the hundredth time one afternoon, while she was spinning. It was only two and half weeks since the count's murder, but it felt like months, especially since the last half of it we had spent cloistered indoors. The noise of tumult in the city had been rising outside our front door for some time, but we had been disappointed too many times to hope that it might be some resolution to the fighting.

"Why should he?" I replied wearily, at the end of my rope and beyond. "If you die he can get another wife, a prettier younger one, and maybe a child." I could have bitten my tongue out the minute I said those cruel words.

"Don't say that to me. You're always so unkind, Aude. Did no one ever teach you kindness? Can you never be gentle or patient, like a woman is supposed to be?" Edith threw her spindle down on the ground so hard it cracked. I bent over to pick it up and she snatched it away. I couldn't have been more surprised if a lamb had grown fangs and bit me like a snake.

"Don't touch my spindle. That's mine. You always take everything of mine." She picked it up herself and threw it at my head. "Here, have it then. Take everything. Take my house, my husband, my name. My child. Oh yes, I know. I'm leaving."

She stomped to the thick oak door. The noise outside it was growing louder. She flung back the first bolt before I could reach her.

"Stop, Edith. You can't leave. It's dangerous for you to go outside, and never more so than today."

"I don't care." She pushed the door open. I hastened after her.

Edith was half way down the street, hurrying straight into the storm, when I caught up with her. "Look." I ran along beside her, trying to get her to listen, to stop, to come back to safety. "I'm sorry. I shouldn't have said that. I'm really sorry."

Maybe being outside for the first time in days that made her listen because she slowed her pace. "You said sorry, Aude. I've never heard you say sorry for anything before."

I pressed my advantage. "I am sorry. Now will you return home? You know it's not safe out here. Not for any of us, but especially not for you." People were running all around us, passing us in the street on their way to the castle, most carrying axes or short swords. Suddenly it was too much. I began to sob, soundlessly and without tears.

"Aude!" said Edith, in wonder. "You're crying! You are really worried about me."

"I'm not crying, I'm not!" I said fiercely as another sob wracked my body. I blew my nose loudly. "It's just that, I lost mother and father, and then Charles and now poor Lisebet and I can't lose you too. I can't." I collapsed into real tears and wept, while Edith pulled me into a warm embrace, holding me close, calming me with her strength and the warmth of her body.

"There, there, Aude. So strong all the time. So hard on the outside, no one can see the softness within. You love me. You really do. I always wondered."

Slowly, I calmed down. "Of course I do, you idiot," I said, voice muffled by her shoulder. "You are always there for me, you raised my son. I can't let anything happen to you."

Just then, a mob ran past us, heading towards the castle bridge, shouting and calling to others to join them. "What is going on?" I asked Edith, pulling away. "Have they taken the castle?"

A man came in the opposite direction, a small barrel under one arm, and a side of bacon in the other. I stopped a small boy passing us at a steady jog, panting. "Boy, what's happening?"

He slowed down. "It's the siege. We've finally broken it! Us, the citizens, not the knights. A band of men climbed ladders into the castle compound by night, and let the rest in at dawn through the only door the traitors hadn't blocked. Now there's a fierce battle raging, and everyone is running to help. We're going to kill every traitor we find and show the knights they can't boss us. Death to knights and nobles!" he cried, before shooting off again.

"Borsiard!" Edith cried, "My brother. We must help." She raced after the boy, and I could only follow.

Those running to the castle were outnumbered by people coming in the opposite direction with the loot they'd sacked. Mattresses, tapestries, and every manner of linen was carried by us, all kinds of chests and coffers, sacks of grain and haunches of meat. They were pulling the lead gutters off the count's buildings and the iron fittings out of his doors. One man rolled a huge barrel of beer before him. It cracked open on a stone and flooded the street. He turned back to the castle, looking for less fragile booty.

The marketplace was deserted, and everyone who could carry a weapon was inside the castle walls, fighting over the buildings. Only the church with its fortified western portal remained in the hands of the traitors. Surely it would fall too and then all the Erembalds would be wiped out. This was no place for Edith. But, frantic for news of her brothers, she could not be stopped.

"You're a fool, Edith," I said.

"Why? As you reminded me, I have no child to save my life for. I might as well die here with my brothers, loyal to my family."

Short of knocking her out and dragging her back to Annie's, I didn't know what to do. Then, on the castle walls before us, we saw that Erembald men, outnumbered by their attackers, were trying to escape by sliding down the walls. The walls were steep, without the convenient thorn bushes that saved me when I accidentally performed the same trick back in Jerusalem, and we watched in horror, as one fell head over tail to the ground.

"Gilbert!" said Edith in dismay. "That was Gilbert. One of Borsiard's vassals," she added, realizing I had no clue who she meant. "We must help him."

He looked beyond help by the time we reached him, but at least Edith was no longer clamoring to go inside. We pulled him with difficulty into a nearby shed. Edith held his hand and begged for news of her family

"Dead. Borsiard…inside the church. Walter too." This was another of Edith brothers. "Your uncles…Hacket and Wulfric." This speech cost him dearly and he gasped for air.

"What of my other uncle? What of Bartolph?" Edith asked anxiously.

"Escaped…two days ago and more." Then he closed his eyes, turned his head and was gone. The shed door open, and a man came in. "He's in here," he said, turning to his unseen fellows outside the door. Then to us he said, "You're harboring a traitor, women. Not wise."

"But he's dying," pleaded Edith.

The man, joined now by his companions, dragged poor dead Gilbert out of the shed by his feet. They tied his feet to the tail of a horse, then dragged his broken body through the streets, before decapitating him in the middle of the market square and dumping his body into the sewer. His head joined a row of others on pikes ringing the castle.

We watched all of this in silence.

"Very well Edith," I said, though she had not spoken. "You win. We return to Gistel immediately."

"How?"

"I don't know. Walk if necessary." It couldn't be more than two days away. "It will be dangerous, but no more dangerous than staying here."

We found our way back to the house, picking our way through the broken crockery, burst mattresses and occasional dead body that littered our path. It didn't take long for us to get ready. Annie refused our pleas to join us, so we left most of our belongings with her, taking only what food and water we could carry and wearing a double layer of clothing. I left my pretty buckled shoes and soft leather boots behind without a pang for once and wore my toughest walking boots. Wrapped in our cloaks, we looked like a couple of plump peasant women on an errand.

Theodore was thrilled to be outside again after a fortnight of forced confinement and would have skipped ahead, but I compelled him to hold my hand.

"Only until we're well beyond the city gate." We took back streets to the western side of town, avoiding the fighting around the castle. We were among the very few who were trying to leave. Men streamed into Bruges from every direction, coming for revenge against the traitors, or to loot the castle.

I was right to be worried. We made it through the town gate, but just as we began to breathe easier, we were stopped by a burly monster.

"Women leaving the city on this joyous day?" he inquired, pulling the veil shrouding Edith's face. "Only one loyal to the Erembalds would do that."

His words attracted the attention of others who gathered round. A short man with a slit nose said, "She is an Erembald herself! I recognize her. She's the traitor Borsiard's sister. I spent Christmas in their hall once."

Edith, frozen, was about to admit everything so I preempted her.

"Do you think an Erembald would be out here on foot in a woolen cloak? No, they're all clad in silk, dancing on Count Charles's grave back in the church."

We had drawn a crowd. "Curse the Erembalds!" someone at the back shouted and everyone cheered. I was weary of all of this anger, vengeance and hate. I'd never forgive her family for murdering Charles, but Edith was blameless as a new-born kitten. Why should she be the target of their rage?

"Erembalds, Erembalds," I said, raising my voice to make myself heard. "We never used to hear a word against them before Fromold started this fight. If he hadn't challenged their authority, Count Charles would be alive today."

For some reason, my faulty logic caught their imagination. Perhaps a new target offered fresh opportunities for booty. "That's true enough," our captor acknowledged. "The Erembalds were always generous with us."

Slit-nose agreed. "They were generous that Christmas. And it is true that we never had any troubles before Fromold stuck his finger in." The crowd rumbled its assent. While we sneaked away, they were forming two parties, one to attack Fromold's house on the other side of town, and another to go after those who had claimed the provost's house in the castle precinct. I felt no shame at redirecting their anger away from us onto Fromold. Besides, word was, he had already fled into exile.

Then we had to walk and walk. It was the journey of a single day for a strong man on foot by the main road that flanked the river, but we were two women and a boy, and I was keeping us to sheep paths and winding lanes, away from regular traffic. What's more, it was well past midday by the time we set out. Edith's energy flagged first, and then Theodore gave out. We needed a place to spend the night.

The countryside was a horror of torched fields and burned-out buildings, as different factions had used the anarchy in the county to avenge themselves against their neighbors. We spent a cold night in a roofless shed, afraid to light a fire for fear of attracting attention. Annie had provided us with salt cod pasties, but when they were gone, it would be bread and cheese until we reached Gistel.

When we awoke the next morning, Theo was ready to go, but Edith had a slight cough.

"Maybe you should go on without me," she said feebly, after we breakfasted.

I felt her forehead. She was hot and clammy. Damn. I tried to jolly her along. "Nonsense. I won't let you spend one more minute in this nasty place. Get walking and we'll soon have you in a soft bed with a warm brick to heat you." But my heart sank when I thought of the long walk still ahead of us, and who knows what reception at its end.

Theodore's feet blistered so badly he cried and it was only by sheer force of will that I got Edith as far as I did. She had a full-blown fever by then and her teeth were chattering, and her mind was rambling. We had to stop.

"Only a little further, and we'll reach the monastery of Oudenburg. Then we'll rest," I promised. I hadn't wanted to stop there or anywhere before we got to Gistel, but we had no choice.

My pledge gave Theodore and Edith the strength to make it. Fortunately, the monks welcomed us warmly, ushering us into a nearly empty guest hospice and summoning their infirmarian to attend to Edith, and to Theodore's feet. We were far enough from Bruges and close enough to Gistel that to them Edith was not a dreaded Erembald, but wife of Christian, their powerful neighbor. I feared Christian himself would not greet us so warmly.

CHAPTER THIRTEEN

Al-Lawza, Autumn 1148

✠

To my shame, I hadn't even gone back into the chapel since I rehung my mother's icons there the day we arrived, though I had seen Ermine go in from time to time. I knew that if I intended to turn the castle into a monastery, I should be more engaged with the room that would be its heart. But I kept putting it off.

One afternoon in early autumn, Ermine came out of the chapel door while Eleanor and I were in the courtyard doing nothing much. She had a smudge on her left cheek. "It's finished at last," she said. "I've worked so hard. Do come and look."

I got up reluctantly, and we followed her indoors.

She had transformed it. The whole room had been whitewashed, then distempered on the bottom few feet of the walls in a crude but pleasing imitation of marble paneling. A tracery of painted vegetation ran up the walls to the ceiling, framing the icons that marked the apse of the chapel. The old iron candlesticks had been found, cleaned, and stripped of rust, and fresh beeswax candles flickered in them. It was lovely but also strange. Like it had nothing to do with me any more.

"Is this what you have been working on so secretly in the evenings, Ermine?" I asked.

She nodded vigorously. "I borrowed help from the kitchen. I didn't want anyone to know until I finished in case it was no good. There's a part that went wrong in one corner of the altar cloth, but I was able to hang it at the back. Do you like it? I mean, all of it?"

She sounded nervous, like I might chastise her for usurping my role.

The chapel was beautiful. But it didn't feel like mine any more. "It is lovely Ermine, the whole chapel. Did you do the painting yourself?"

"The boys did the whitewashing, and one of them did the paneling. I did the wall designs myself, on a ladder."

"I had no idea you had such talent," said Eleanor.

Ermine was staring at me, twisting her hands together as if she wanted to say something more. Our praise gave her courage to speak. "I'm glad you aren't angry that I went ahead without telling you. I wanted it to be a surprise. And a kind of a gift. Aude, do you remember when you told me you were going to turn the castle into a monastery?"

"Turn the castle into a monastery?" Eleanor was surprised. "Why are you going to do that?"

Ermine wouldn't let me be distracted by Eleanor's question. "Are you still planning on doing it? Because if so—I would like to stay. Please. Here, as one of the nuns." She stared up at me with pleading eyes, hanging on my response.

"I do have plans for a monastery here, Ermine, and I'd love to have you, but I don't know—." I was about to explain how tentative and vague my ideas still were, but Ermine broke in.

"Oh, please! I would make such a good nun. I can read Latin, and my singing voice is strong. I wanted to join a community in Aquitaine, but they wouldn't have me because I had no dowry. My brothers took it all for themselves. But I'm from a very good and old family. Eleanor can tell you. I thought maybe if you were new, you wouldn't mind my lack of a dowry so much."

"I would be overjoyed to give you a dowry, for your faithful service to me," said Eleanor.

Ermine clapped her hands. "Then it's settled!" She ran out of the chapel, presumably to tell Mabilie.

We left the chapel and returned to the benches in the courtyard. I felt a little stunned. I didn't even have a monastery yet, but I already had my first nun.

"It is kind of you to agree to take her," Eleanor said.

I responded drily, "I am not entirely aware that I did agree."

Eleanor laughed. "Her brothers were terrible to her. The family is old, as she said, but not rich, and they left nothing for her. And she won't get a husband without something in return."

I understood. Ermine was as bright and sharp as cut glass, but her face was plain and her figure too unremarkable for a man to offer for her without a dowry to go along.

Eleanor continued. "I took her in because she had nowhere else to go except to live as a kind of unpaid servant to her nieces and nephews, but she's not been very happy at court. She is much more suited to life in a cloister. But Aude, tell me, why are you turning al-Lawza into a monastery?"

I massaged my forehead against a slight pain that was beginning at my temples. "It was part of a vow, Eleanor. It's the whole reason I came on this crusade in the first place."

"Ah! Am I finally going to hear the story of Lisbon?"

"No, not today. It had to do with Edith's illness when we tried to escape Bruges. I made my vow so she could be healed."

✠

Aude's Twelfth Tale: Bruges, March 1127–July 1128

When Edith, Theo and I arrived at Oudenburg, my first concern was to let Christian know we were there. I could no longer bear alone the responsibility of getting our little family home safe to Gistel.

"We'll send a message in the morning," the guest master promised. "He will come and collect you."

I was not so certain, but to my surprise the envoy returned with a terse message from Christian. "I will collect you at the monastery by Saturday." We could do nothing but wait. Edith was too ill to be moved, glassy-eyed and burning with fever despite the best efforts of the monks, every breath a labor. I was frightened, and worried that we should have stayed in Bruges. The infirmarian was kind but ignorant, and the only remedy he suggested was prayer. I thought longingly of Grettie at Gistel. I was sure she would be more help, but I couldn't get here there on my own. Blast Christian for taking so long.

Christian arrived at midday on Saturday. Seeing him all rosy and healthy inflamed my anger. I flew at him. "Where have you been? Why didn't you answer any of my messages? We could have died. Lisebet did die." I choked with emotion and tried to smack his face, but he just laughed, holding me off.

"You know that new game, chess, that we sometimes play?" he said.

I nodded. Of course I knew chess. It wasn't new to me because everyone played it like mad in Jerusalem when I was a child.

"Sometimes you need to leave a piece exposed and vulnerable for a while in order to protect it. That's what I was doing. Keeping my distance from Edith allowed me to ingratiate myself with the men who oppose the Erembalds, men who, you may have noticed, are winning right now. Besides, I knew you'd be able to protect everyone and bring them home safe. And you did."

Except for Lisebet, I thought, but Christian probably didn't even know her name. "But Christian, we're not safe. Edith is very ill. The monks fear she is dying." I started to cry.

His concern at my first words changed to skepticism as he watched my tears. "Aude, crying for Edith? It would solve some of our problems and I thought you'd only be too glad to have her breath her last."

That would have been true once, but it was true no longer. I hated him for his indifference, and me for once sharing it. Edith and I, we were bound together now, as close as me and Theo. Our time in Bruges had solidified the bond between us, nights holding each other tight at Annie's house while we listened to sounds of slaughter and destruction in the streets outside, wondering if we'd be next. I wept for her soft gentleness, her kindness, all the love she showed my son.

And worse, Christian had no immediate plans to get us to Gistel. He was on his way to Bruges, and he insisted I come along. "The barons are meeting the king of France at Arras to choose us a new count, and we Flemish knights are allying with the citizens of Bruges to make sure their choice is to our liking. Since Theodore is under-age, you will need to swear on his behalf." My helplessness enraged me. Grettie's help would have to wait. Edith would stay at the monastery, and Theodore with her.

I had barely time to say goodbye before I found myself on horseback, covering quickly the ground we had walked so painfully a few days before. We pitched tents on the great wasteland to the west of the town of Bruges, joining a sea of knights and citizens.

The next day, the knights and citizens confirmed their alliance, swearing on the relics of the saints of Bruges. I had to swear along with them, but my mind was elsewhere. It was Palm Sunday, and as we processed around the walls of Bruges with our green branches aloft, my mind was on Edith, and I prayed, "Please God, save Edith. Save her and I'll do anything."

Anything? What might that include?

"Anything, God. Truly. I'll leave her husband's bed. I'll give her the keys to the castle. Anything you want. Just save her." And I meant it. Full of the fire of my new resolution, I found a priest to hear my confession. Since it was Holy Week, many were getting shriven so they could take communion on Easter Sunday, and I waited in a long line to find one who was free. He was young and earnest, and the roof of his chapel in town had been burned in the fighting. If I promised to help pay for a new roof, maybe he'd be lenient. No such luck.

I told him the sins I had never confessed before. Not everything I told you, Eleanor, but the outline. I told him about my spiteful meanness to Edith and worse, how I had dallied with her husband, and worst of all, how I had killed my own child and maybe even hers. This caused the poor priest to mop his brow.

"A serious sin, Lady Aude." he said, looking worried.

"Too serious? Can it not be forgiven?" I was worried that if I could not do penance for my sins against her, Edith would not be saved.

"Everything can be forgiven. But it will require a very weighty penance. I wish I could talk to my bishop."

In war-torn Bruges? Not likely.

He thought a bit, then said, "I've got it. You will have to do all the things you promised — leave Christian alone, give Edith the keys to the household and be a good sister to both of them."

I heaved a sigh of relief.

"But wait, there is more. Given the burden of your sin, the only way to make up for it is the most serious penance I can apply. You have to make a pilgrimage to Jerusalem."

He took my stunned silence for dismay. "I'm sorry, Lady Aude. It is the only way. And there is more. You have to found a monastery there. Since today is the feast of Saint Theodosia, you can dedicate it to her."

Theodosia was my mother's name. "Can I found it in the Holy Land? Or does it have to be in Flanders? And do I have to return to Flanders after my pilgrimage, or can I stay there?"

"You can found it there. And if you were to spend the rest of your days in your monastery, that would be a pious act."

"I accept." I said. I could take Theo with me. But then a pang —what about Edith? She'd never leave. But it had to be done.

He was surprised that I accepted this penance so willingly. In truth, I was relieved. It would get me away from Christian at Gistel. And now I had a reason to return to Jerusalem and stay there. How soon could I leave? I thought I could get al-Lawza restored to me by promising it to some religious community as a monastery. And I could remember my mother at the same time. It all seemed meant to be.

"And if I promise all of this, Edith will get better?"

No, there was the rub. "I'm afraid no one can promise that. And you have to fulfill your vow no matter what the outcome for Edith. But I will add my prayers for her to your own, and God will surely look upon your sacrifice with pleasure."

I took the cross right there. We had no strips of cloth to use, so he removed the cross he wore around his neck, blessed it with the traditional words that protected me against both mortal and spiritual enemies, and hung it around my own, where it still hangs to this day. We parted in a happy embrace, and I sent him a splendid replacement as soon as I could.

Eleanor interrupted with a question. "Are you planning to stay here as a nun? I hardly see you as a sister."

I didn't see myself as much of a nun either.

"It was meant to be different, Eleanor, when I planned it in Flanders. My son was going to come with me and be one of al-Lawza's knights and we would be together always. I suppose I didn't think about the nun part much, just of returning home with my boy after so long. But it wasn't his home. He wanted to stay in Spain and Portugal fighting the Muslims there. I told him there were perfectly good Muslims to fight here too, if that was how he wanted to waste his life, but he wasn't interested."

Telling Eleanor all of this, I felt as lonely and rejected as I had when Theodore first told me he wouldn't be coming to al-Lawza. From Theo, my mind turned to the other man I had left in Lisbon, strong arms enfolding me and a rough cheek on my forehead. Was he why the prospect of being abbess of al-Lawza left me feeling so flat? I pushed the memory away.

Ermine returned with a well-used book in her hands. "See?" she said, opening it on the table before us. "It's my mother's psalter." Lines of heavy, dark script were on every page. "She gave it to me when she died. And look, at the back, here is the text of the night office. She used to wake up in the middle of the night and recite its prayers. I'm going to begin doing that here. Aude, would you like to join me? I could teach it to you."

I could think of nothing I wanted to do less than trip down the stairs in the dark at midnight to kneel on the cold stone of the chapel and chant psalms with Ermine every night. I said something noncommittal and worried again about whether I was cut out for this new life.

"Remember when Aude told us how Edith got so ill when they fled Bruges? Aude just told me how she swore a vow to come on crusade and found this convent so Edith would get better." said Eleanor. I could have kicked her.

"Really? That's wonderful! We should write the whole story up to use as the foundation legend of our new community," said Ermine.

It would have to be a highly expurgated version. The plan to found a monastery was appealing to me less and less.

"Our first task is to fulfill our original responsibility to serve Eleanor, and make sure her baby is born safely," I said, sounding stern.

"Oh yes, yes," said Ermine, sounding momentarily chastened. But not for long. "Did Edith get better? It would be such a wonderful miracle story on which to found our monastery. And did peace ever come back to Flanders?"

"Never mind that," said Eleanor. "I want to know why it took you so long to get here once you made your vow. Why not leave right away? It took you twenty years!"

I blushed guiltily. The truth was, though my reasons for delay seemed good at the time, there was no single valid explanation for why I hadn't come sooner. First Edith had to get better, then she needed to be taught how to run the castle. And then there was Theo. How could I take him from her? But what confessor would accept those excuses?

"It weighed on me all the time." That was also the truth. "And I'm here now, aren't I? God won't mind as long as the vow is fulfilled before my death." Then I tried to explain myself as best I could.

When we returned to the monastery, Edith was twisted up in sweaty sheets in a stuffy room, barely holding onto life. Her fevered raving frightened me. The infirmarian assured me there was hope, but I refused to leave her there one day longer. We returned to Gistel by boat to make Edith's journey easier, and when we arrived the servants helped her by stages into the lord's bed she had vacated long before, when the first accusations of the Erembalds' servile status emerged. I hadn't forgotten my promise though. I shifted all my things to the bed Edith had been using in the gallery. That was where I would sleep from then on.

Edith was half-dozing, but when she saw me remove my mother's icons from the wall she knew something was up.

"What are you doing?" she croaked, half-asleep.

"I'm not sleeping here anymore. I'm going upstairs, with the rest of the women."

She stirred restlessly. "Christian won't like that."

"He'll have to get used to it," I said grimly.

Christian didn't like it. "Who cares about your vow? I've waited for you for more than six months. Can't we go on as before?" he asked, and tried to grab me around the waist. I leapt back and held the cross around my neck out toward him, as if to ward him off.

"Do you see this, Christian?" I said, furious. "This is a sign of my sacred promise. I have to go to Jerusalem, and found a monastery in my mother's name, and if I commit a grievous sin before I am able to fulfill my vow, I will be foresworn. And you will be cursed for compelling me into sin."

He backed off, and looked for consolation elsewhere. Indeed, in our absence he'd taken up with a serving girl. She was wearing Edith's best girtle, and lording it over the other servants when we arrived home. I soon let her know that behavior wouldn't be tolerated. He could join her in her foul nest in the straw of the stable if he must, but I wouldn't have her usurp Edith's place. I became more jealous of Edith's rights, the rights I had trampled on for years, than she would ever be.

And I went to find Grettie. But the path by the old elm to her hovel was so overgrown, I wasn't sure I was even in the right place. A man ploughing in a field close by called out to me as I was peering through the weeds.

"Looking for the old woman? She hasn't been seen since the fall. You couldn't pay me to go in there." He turned his ox and headed to the opposite side of the field.

My heart sank. What should I do? Was he telling the truth? And if so, what had happened? I feared if I went in, I'd find her dead in her bed, but I couldn't leave her. I pushed my way through the brambles, feeling for the gate through the tangle of holly that guarded it and made my way to her door. I opened it and fund a riot of acorn shells on every surface, and bedding torn and ruined. Some animals had found a cozy dwelling for winter. But there was no Grettie. I looked at the shelves where she kept her medicines. The leather pouches has been gnawed and fouled, but some pots still stood intact. I shuddered. I'd feed Edith nothing from those. I left and closed the door behind me.

But somehow, Edith got better without Grettie's help. Maybe the infirmarian's prayer was more effective than I thought. All the long spring I cared for her, wiping her brow, feeding her sops of bread in broth or milk to build her strength, rejoicing when she was well enough to recognize me, and to eat, and fearful when she plunged into fever again. I visited Godeleva's convent again, clutching the cross around my neck in memory of my vow as they chanted the Latin.

News from the outside world told of the terrible revenge taken against the Erembalds. Bartolph, the one most blamed for Charles's death, was captured and executed. They dragged him through the streets of Ypres by ropes, naked but for his breeches, pulled first in one direction then another, until he could barely stay on his feet, all the while taunted, pelted with rotten vegetables, and struck with blows. They took him to the gallows in the market square and stripped him. Then, they stretched his arms out like a cross and his head was thrust through a hole in the gibbet, so the weight of his body was suffocating him. While he braced his body by the joints of his feet to put off his death—and in reality, prolong his agony—the watching mob assaulted his body with iron hooks, clubs, and stakes. When he breathed his last, they twisted a dog's guts around his neck and bound its muzzle next to his face, so that Bartolph died like the dog he was.

Christian told me that Edith's brothers were thrown from the highest battlement of the tower on the count's house, falling broken onto the ground below. Borsiard had fled the castle at the last minute but he was taken near Lille and bound to a wheel tied to a tree, while the rabble were free to break his bones. He hanged there in agony for a day and night before expiring.

And while the days grew longer, and lambs gamboled in the fields around the monastery, Edith grew steadily better, learning none of this.

"You're a good nurse, Aude," she said teasingly one morning, propped up on bolsters to make her breathing easier, "I never would have expected it." Her words ended in a paroxysm of coughing, and I passed her a cup of steeped horehound and honey.

While I had been preoccupied with Edith, Theodore turned from being my little boy to Christian's young man. Though he wasn't quite ten, he began his military training in earnest the moment the two reached Gistel. Theodore came in for the main meal every day covered in mud, bruises, and sometimes blood from the mock fights between youths in the castle yard, a light in his eyes and every word out of his mouth about horses, weapons, or battle. Sometimes he was gone for days at a time, hunting and getting up to who knows what mischief. I knew this would happen eventually, but did he have to leave me so soon? I bit my lip when he shrugged off my caresses.

Charles's old friend William Clito was count then, but he was being challenged by Dietrik of Alsace. Civil war raged again for a time, and Christian left to fight on Dietrik's side. And then, suddenly it was over. William Clito died of wounds suffered in battle. Dietrik became count. We slowly begin to rebuild, and to breath freely.

It took a generation for Flanders, once the richest jewel in Christendom, to recover from this time, but Count Dietrik took pains to reconcile both his enemies and his friends. Theodore served him later as page, then squire, and knight in Bruges. I could have left then but, well, you'll never guess. Edith finally got pregnant. She had a tiny baby girl, named Imma. How could I leave then? She would have spoiled the girl silly. So I let time slip away without fulfilling my vow to come back to Jerusalem.

That's the end of my story. Eventually, I came on crusade and here I am. There's nothing more to tell.

CHAPTER FOURTEEN

✠

We were left alone at al-Lawza most of the fall, so we were surprised one day to learn that a visitor was at the gate, a woman, with an entourage fit for a queen.

"Is it Melisende, come to count my goats and chickpeas, and make certain I am paying my taxes properly?" I wondered out loud.

It wasn't Melisende, but I was close. It was Hodierna, her sister. She kissed each of us as if we were long-lost cousins, embracing us in a cloud of silk, and filling the courtyard with a riot of colorful confusion, from her men and horses stamping impatiently, her servants bearing bedhangings, rugs, and tapestries into the hall, not to mention her own perfumed, decorated, bejeweled, jangling self. Was this to be a brief stay? I feared not.

"It is so good of you to visit," I said, hoping to elicit the reason for her arrival.

"It's more than a visit," she said. "I've come to stay, at least until Spring. You see, I am expecting a baby too, isn't that wonderful?" Her voice was brittle. "Tripoli in the winter is an insalubrious climate for a pregnant woman, so I thought I'd come here and have my baby with you, Eleanor."

Tripoli, on the coast with its fresh breezes and clean air had an ideal climate, but we knew it was a dangerous city if you crossed her husband, Count Ramon. I'm sure that was what motivated her flight.

Servants—hers not mine—brought us refreshments, and we sat in the courtyard to hear the rest of her tale while her men slowly created order out of the disorder they had brought with them.

"When are you due?" asked Eleanor, a dangerous smile lurking behind her eyes. She had already guessed the truth.

"Late March, supposedly. That's what the doctor says. But I feel very, very certain that the baby is going to come early, in February, like yours. Very certain. My family often gives birth early."

I counted months on my fingers under the table my sums led to only one possible conclusion. This was not Ramon's baby, but poor Jaufré's child. That's why she had decided to have it here. Had she planned this all along? Did she know or think she might be pregnant when we were still in Tripoli, and had she helped me reclaim al-Lawza to provide a bolthole for herself? I didn't ask. This was my payment for the help she had given Eleanor and me.

"Don't worry," she said. "You'll barely know I am here. I'll fit right into your routine, and my servants will help your own."

This was unlikely, I reflected. I dreaded adjudicating turf battles between my servants and hers in the kitchens, and I couldn't think how we were all going to fit in my small castle. Was the vocation of my future monastery to be a refuge for wayward, expectant royals?

Her presence livened things up. Everyone else was in Bethlehem, celebrating the Christmas court with Queen Melisende and her son. Louis must have been there too, though he sent no word. He wouldn't want his now visibly pregnant wife by his side.

Ermine used the season to shed her meagre finery in preparation for becoming a nun. I should be making the same transformation, I knew, especially when I heard Ermine's small feet padding downstairs in the middle of the night to pray in the chapel. How did one go about founding a monastery, anyway?

Queen Melisende herself came to visit us one day in January. She and her entourage stripped my kitchen bare, and the two sisters bickered the whole time they were together, but the visit demonstrated that we were under royal protection. And it was a change of pace. But once the excitement of Melisende's visit was over, like Eleanor, Hodierna expected to be entertained and it was cold, so we were forced to stay inside. There was even some snow in the mountains where we were. We'd all spent a little too much time at close quarters by this point, and only Eleanor and Hodierna's frequent naps allowed the rest of us to stay sane.

The two women amused themselves when awake by talking high politics. Between them, they knew how every noble family in

Christendom was related. They refought the battle of Damascus to-gether, indeed the whole of the crusade, coming up with a dozen ways it could have had a better outcome, if only they had been consulted.

"If it weren't for the conquest of Lisbon, this crusade would be a failure from beginning to end. And who cares about Lisbon anyway, stuck off there at the end of the world." said Hodierna, chewing on a dried fig. Neither woman could eat much at meals these days, so they made up for it by nibbling constantly.

Eleanor said slyly, "Aude was at Lisbon. She saw the whole siege. But she won't tell us a word about it. We keep asking but she always changes the subject."

"That's not fair. Aude, tell us everything. I want to hear all about it."

Hodierna might have a knack for getting her way, but I had no desire to satisfy her curiosity. "We sailed to Lisbon. There was a siege. We won, and took the city from the Muslims."

"Not like that," said Eleanor. "Like your other stories. Begin at the beginning."

Four faces looked at me expectantly. They weren't going to give up this time. Some losses were easier healed if you resolutely put them from your mind, I thought but I had to admit that wasn't working for me. I had not forgotten one single moment, and my losses remained sore. I had lived my life hiding from those I loved, and what had it got me? Perhaps it was time for a new approach. If I told my last story, maybe I would be rid of the memories of my recent past and I could come to terms with my new life at al-Lawza. And besides, as I asked myself so often concerning Eleanor, what other choice did I have?

✠

Aude's Thirteenth Tale: Flanders to Oporto, 1147

I shouldn't have been in Lisbon in the first place. It was not part of my, or anyone else's plans when we set out on crusade. Or so I thought.

You know I had long postponed my vow to return to Jerusalem, but after I heard the call to crusade at Vezelay, where Eleanor and

I first met, I resolved to put it off no longer. Theodore was grown, Edith was busy and Christian…was still Christian. And after the black years of the civil war and the difficult time that followed, all Flanders was ready to follow the cross, to leave, to be anywhere but there. My first plan was to go in the company of Count Dietrik, and lure Theodore to come along. But the countess decided to remain in Flanders, to rule in his absence, so I couldn't join her entourage. I couldn't travel alone, and Christian had always refused even to think of crusading, so I worried I'd have to put it off again.

Then Abbot Bernard came to Flanders, to preach and gather support. Christian heard him at Dietrik's court, and came home to Gistel with a cross on his chest.

"What's that," I asked, stupidly.

"It's a cross. I'm a crusader now, just like you." I still wore the priest's cross around my neck, a burden that was heavy at times over the years.

"If you've taken the vow, you'll have to fulfill it," I warned.

"Why? You never did. But don't worry, I will. Theodore is coming too. You'll travel with us, finally be able to remove that anchor from around your neck. And maybe then you'll be fun, like you used to be."

I hugged him close, the first time I had touched him in years. "Bless you," I said.

My blessings soon turned to curses. Christian refused to go by land, with Eleanor and King Louis.

"We have all these ships and you want to walk to Jerusalem?" he asked.

The richer he grew on land, the more ships Christian acquired, and now he had a whole fleet under his command. He called it trade, though often it was closer to piracy. He had earned a fortune taking people who feared the rule of Count Dietrick into exile in England. Civil War had broken out there too, between Stephen and Matilda, rival claimants to the throne. The Flemish supported Stephen, but I had a soft spot for Matilda's cause. Why shouldn't a woman get a chance for a change? In any case, war was good for business, and Christian continued to profit.

But while the sea might mean wealth and adventure to Christian, it was a nightmare to me. Since the awful trip that took me away from al-Lawza with Bertulf, I couldn't even take the flat-bottomed boat to Bruges without getting queasy. I was scared. And I had no notion of how one might sail from the North Sea to the shores of the Holy Land. Could these frigid northern seas really be connected to the warm, blue waters of my youth.

"Are you sure it is possible to sail the whole way there?" I asked.

"Trust me. How do you think the Normans got from the Viking lands to rule Sicily?"

We set off in May from Ostend, with half the castle of Gistel come to bid us farewell. Tears streamed down Edith's face to see us go, but she held Imma's small hand and kept a brave smile plastered on, while I was a blubbering mess when we finally said farewell.

"You've been everything to me, Edith, these years," I said, blowing my nose. "I must be mad to leave."

"You have always been a bit mad, Aude." She smiled. "You're doing the right thing. I feel it in my bones. It's time for you to have a new adventure."

She was right. She was content at Gistel but the castle was growing too small for me. And for Christian, and Theodore, who was almost thirty. We all needed an adventure.

"You'll be back one day. I have no fear," she continued. But despite my wave of grief at saying goodbye, I knew that I would never return, and neither would Theo, if I had my way. As it happened, Theodore didn't return, but I did not get my way.

I embraced her and she held me tight. But the full force of her emotions were reserved for Theodore's departure. She clung to him and stroked his face over and over. He bore it much better than if I had tried the same thing. Well, she had been his second mother over the years. Sometimes even his first.

Then our flotilla was off. The wind was light. "Almost becalmed," Christian grumbled, but I didn't mind because I stood on the small deck and felt quite the sailor as the flat shore of Flanders disappeared below the horizon.

"I do believe you're sad to leave after all," Theodore said, coming up beside me.

I shook myself out of my reverie. "Nonsense. Once you see how lovely Jerusalem is, you'll understand why." He smiled indulgently and went to scold the sailors who were making a mess with the ropes. Unlike me, the sea held no terrors for him.

We arrived in Boulogne, where a fleet of cogs and hulks and keelboats of every size and description joined us in twos and threes. To my astonishment, it seemed Christian himself was in command. What else hadn't I been told? I pestered Theodore for information, but he was taciturn. Never mind, I thought, as long as we reached Jerusalem, Christian could be papal legate for all I cared.

One delay after another slowed our departure—failure of some bit of equipment with an improbable name, adverse tides and winds, and even the hangover of our pilot one morning. At last we left Boulogne, men from all over maritime Flanders and Boulogne, and even a few women like myself. Next stop, Jerusalem, I said to myself naively.

The following morning found us skirting a hostile coast of cliffs and rocks to our north, tacking back and forth in that horrible travel-all-day-but-get-nowhere way of sea journeys. Dotted about the horizon was the rest of our fleet, keeping pace with our flagship. The boat was pitching enough to drive me below decks, but I accosted Christian before I went down.

"Where on earth are we?"

"England," he said to my shock. What were we doing there?

"Dartmouth is our next stop," he told me.

I'd never heard of it, but the next day we arrived at an undistinguished town on a deep river estuary that I was told made it an ideal harbor. It was like Acre at Eastertide—so full of ships that there was no room for even a rowboat once our ships had found berths.

A rumble of different languages assaulted us from every direction once we beached. Thousands of men, would-be crusaders from as far away as the Rhine and all over England and Normandy were milling about, picking fights and enjoying time on shore. There were so many of us that the leaders of each group had to meet outside the town. I was the only woman at the council.

A count I had never met before, Arnold of Aerschot, seemed to be in charge. He laid down the law. "To preserve order, all men on this crusade are under one of their own countrymen, and must obey his every command as if it were the word of the Lord. Rule of law is absolute, an eye for an eye, and a tooth for a tooth." Those present roared assent to each one of his provisions, after a delay when the French spoken by Arnold was translated into English, German, and Flemish.

I was bored already. My eyes wandered over the men on the dais, the leaders of the crusading host. Christian was among them, but my attention kept drifting back to another, the one they called Simon of Dover. He was a great bull of a man, muscle and bone, with flinty eyes and thick hair of the same slate shade. I caught myself wondering what it would be like to have those strong arms around me, and I blushed. I was too old for such fancies. Now, I'll be honest: separating from Christian had not turned me into a nun in the intervening years. I'd had a romance or two, nothing serious. But even I knew a crusade was not the time to start a new flirtation. Still, my eyes kept wandering back to him.

"And that our divine purpose and noble cause may be more manifest," Arnold continued, "I have asked the priest, Gilbert of Hastings, to draw up a moral code which all must obey."

He yielded the floor to a reedy, stern priest, who read from a list. "No one may wear costly garments or jewels for the length of this expedition. Or bright colors." His eyes seemed to bore right through my purple embroidered overdress. "Everyone must confess and take communion each Sunday. Each ship must have its own priest who will be obeyed, just as if the ship were his parish." I sniffed. Weekly communion and a priest? He was turning us into monks. "Finally, women must not go out in public."

I didn't like any of these rules, but I gasped when I heard the last. Not go out in public? How was that possible, over many weeks at sea on a small ship where there was no privacy? "But this is terrible," I hissed under my breath to Theodore. "We might as well have joined the Templars."

"Anyone would think this was a journey in God's name," Theo whispered in my ear, and I slapped him gently.

One leader shared my reservations. The man I had been studying so attentively, Simon, rose to speak. His voice commanded our attention through its firmness, not volume. I would not like to cross him. "What's this about each ship having its own priest? Many of our Kentish ships are small, and if we have to find priests for each, good warriors who have vowed to go on crusade may have to stay home. And should not these other commands, about behavior and dress and such, be left up to each one to follow of his own will, as God turns his mind to it?"

"Hear, hear," I cried. Everyone turned around and stared at me. I hadn't intended to speak aloud. Even Simon cast me a surprised glance.

"Small ships can band together and share a priest," Gilbert conceded.

I swore the oath of peace and friendship with the rest. After all, it was only until I arrived at Jerusalem. Then I could leave this holier-than-thou mob behind.

I didn't take the oath terribly seriously. Christian had a priest stashed somewhere on board, so that part of our duty was done—though he was a man better skilled with a mace than the Latin of the Mass. A mace would be more useful where he was going anyway. I did put away my best clothes though. No point getting them salt-stained just to make a point, and I'd need them at court in Jerusalem. But I couldn't bear to stay cooped up on ship while we waited for the last stragglers to come to port. Usually I made sure either Christian or Theo accompanied me. But one morning, I was very foolish.

I awoke to the sound of gagging and the awful stench of vomit filling our sleeping quarters. Theo was hunched over a bucket, a thin green slime issuing from his throat.

"Theo! What's is wrong? Are you ill?" I cried.

"Ow, mother, not so loud," he said feebly. That launched a new round of vomiting.

"I'll send for help," I said, pulling on my shift, and dressing quickly. "You look dreadful."

"No, mother, please—"

"You can't stop me. The village herbwoman can give me something to settle your stomach. We set sail tomorrow, if God and the winds are willing, and you don't want to be ill," I said, and swept out of the ship.

I knew where the wisewoman lived, because we needed her when one of our sailors pinched his hand between the tiller and the stern.

But when I roused the woman from her sleep, she wouldn't help. I tried to explain what was wrong, but we shared no common language. I used Flemish, since many of the words were close, but every time I said, "He is sick!" she shook her head and pointed to an alehouse across the way where sounds of revelry could be heard despite the early hour. I didn't know what she meant until exasperated she yelled, "Drunkard!" and slammed her door. Did she mean Theo? Oh damn, she was probably right, and I had woken her up to cure a simple hangover. No wonder Theo hadn't wanted help.

I passed the alehouse on my way back to the ship, and a crowd of rowdies burst from the door. "Here's a nice little pigeon for breakfast," one said and put his arm around me before I could get away.

"Let me go!" I said.

"You're pretty unfriendly for a whore." He hugged me tighter and his friends laughed.

"Me second!" another said, while I struggled.

"I'm no whore. I'm a crusader like you." I had spotted the cross on each of their breasts.

"I doubt that. Crusader women have to stay out of public places. Those were the rules. Anyone else is fair game. Don't worry, we'll pay when we're done, we're honest." The men dragged me towards the entrance of an alley, and I began to get really scared.

"Stop!" a loud voice came from behind my captors. "Let her go." They did, and I fell onto the muddy ground.

"Sorry, constable," said the man who had seized me. "We didn't realize she belonged to you."

"She doesn't. She the wife of the Flemish commander."

"Shit!" one said, and they all melted away, leaving me looking up at my rescuer. It was Simon, the man who had spoken at the council. He reached out a hand to help me up.

"Not wife," I mumbled as I got to my feet.

"What?"

"I said, I am not Christian of Gistel's wife. I am only his cousin by marriage." For some reason, I wanted him to know that. "My son is his heir."

"Oh. Well, Lady…"

"Lady Aude," I said.

"Lady Aude, you should be more careful. They're not bad men, but they've been drinking all night and that could have been ugly. I'll escort you back to your ship." I didn't object, nor did I intervene when he lectured Christian for failing to protect me properly, though between them they made me feel like a naughty novice who disobeyed her abbess, not the mature widow of station and wealth that I was. Only once he left the ship did I realize something. Simon of Dover had recognized me. He had noticed me at the council. And he had taken the time to find out who I was, albeit inaccurately. I could not say why this pleased me, but it did.

We sailed two days before the feast of the Ascension. I stayed below deck until we rounded Brittany, then I tentatively ventured into the open. When I wasn't immediately flung off the boat and into the sea by its movement, I decided it was safe to stay, and I found that by keeping my eyes on the horizon, my stomach stayed steady, so I remained above deck for the next few days.

"I think I'm beginning to get the knack of sailing," I said with some pride to my son.

"Mother, we're almost becalmed. Look at that tree on shore. We've been staring at it all morning." Still, I felt I had made great progress, and before long we spied the mountains of Spain in the distance, with hopes of a safe harbor, and fresh food and water.

But when dusk fell, the seas rose, and we were in the thick of a thundering gale. Waves pounded the boat, drenching the deck and everyone on it as the hull rolled and tossed, and Christian called out commands to shorten sail. I went down to the hold and listened to the ship's planks strain and fight against the water pressing down on them. I heaved and heaved until my guts were empty and all that came up was bitter bile. The boat crashed from side to side, shaking us like dried beans in a cauldron until I was bruised all over. I thought of my mother as I watched water seep in between the planks of the hold, first a drip then a steady stream. Even the seaman's wife who acted as my servant when I needed one, was terrified and fingered her charms and amulets against shipwreck. Those seamen not on watch mumbled their prayers and tried to sleep, before they were called on deck again to battle with the wind.

I saw Theo through the hatch, steering the ship as best he could to ride out the storm. The sight of his face, taut with strain and teeth clenched in a grimace, in the pale light of the stern lamp gave me comfort, though I knew it was illusory. One young man couldn't win against this mass of wind and water. I'd do better to pray to Mary as the seamen did.

"We are so close to land," I said to Christian who had just come off duty for a quick break. "Why don't we go aground?"

"No," he said, lurching to stay balanced as the boat pitched. "Land is the enemy in a storm. As long as we can stay out to sea, we have a chance."

The wind redoubled its efforts to convert our vessel to kindling, and he returned above deck. When our boat seemed it could take no more, one final blast rocked us, and I heard a loud crack above my head.

"All hands on deck, all hands on deck!" came the cry, and sailors raced by me up the ladder.

Did all hands on deck mean me too? I climbed the ladder and peeped my head out of the top of the hatch to see the damage. Our mast was down. That meant we could no longer steer, and worse, breaking dawn showed we were dangerously close to a shore of cliffs and rocks, and getting closer every minute.

The sailors struggled against the forces of water, wind, and stone. Their goal was no longer to avoid running aground: it was to go aground in the best possible spot on a shore of rocks and boulders.

"Now!" The cry came, and the boat lurched to the side once more, tossing me against its ribs. But that was the end. We were beached, and the boat moved no more. With shaky arms and legs, I crawled my way out of the hull, and joined the others examining the damage as dawn continued to lift.

"God damnit. God damnit all to hell," said Christian as he walked round the ship. The storm was weakening to a steady rain. There was a gash in the hull where we had scraped the rocks coming in, but even I could see it was not an insurmountable problem. And it could have been so much worse, I realized, surveying the coast, waves pounding the rocks in a brutal rhythm. We'd landed on the only spit of sand for miles. The worst damage was the mast, snapped like a twig with the sail hanging in rags.

As we paced uselessly around the boat, I looked out to the empty sea. Theodore caught my glance and said, "Everyone has been scattered by the storm. Never mind. We have a rendezvous at Oporto, on the Atlantic coast and we'll meet everyone there. If we can get this mast fixed.

"So we're all alone," I replied.

But we weren't alone. While our attention was on the ship, a band of men in drab homespun armed with sticks and staves approached us from the shore, silent as wild animals.

"Look!" I called and pointed.

Immediately our men were on guard, knives or swords drawn. We were outnumbered, but our weapons were better.

Christian called for their leader, and using dumb show, for they had no shared language, a parley was somehow arranged, in which they agreed to shelter us and help us fix the boat for a few coins and some bolts of cloth that Christian, always the merchant, had with him. Soon enough the sailor's wife and I were eating a bowl of gruel inside one of their hovels, hidden from the shore in a steep narrow fold in the cliffs which protected our hosts from enemies at land or sea. The food was hot and I was dry at last, and I wouldn't have traded it for roast pigeon in a palace.

Repairing the ship was slow work, and Christian grew more and more enervated as the days passed, pacing and urging the men to work faster.

"Never mind. We'll make it," said Theo to him.

"We'd better," Christian answered.

"Make it?" I interrupted. "You mean to Oporto for the rendezvous? Surely that doesn't matter. We can all meet in Jerusalem, if we miss them here."

Christian and Theodore made no reply, their faces a blank mask. That should have been my clue something was up.

It was late June before the boat could sail. Once they confirmed it was seaworthy, we set sail and reached Oporto a few days later to find the fleet waiting for arrival of our boat to set out again.

The moment we arrived, even before we gave thanks for our safe arrival in the cathedral which stood over the sands where our boats were beached, Christian sought out the other commanders with an urgency I couldn't understand. The first one we met was Simon of Dover, inspecting the Kentish ships. I turned my back and quickly pinched my cheeks to make them glow, but he gave me not a glance.

"Don't worry," he said drily, before Christian was able to open his mouth. "You'll get your way. We're going to Lisbon."

I saw the tension that had built in Christian since we were first wrecked on the north Spanish shore, vanish. He mopped his brow. "Thanks be to God for that." he said with relief.

"Lisbon? What's happening at Lisbon?" I asked, suspicious.

"Lady Aude, the king of the Portuguese has asked us to help him conquer the city of Lisbon from the Muslims, and we have agreed," replied Simon.

"It's a holy war," Christian explained. "And a lucrative one. We're promised a share of the spoils."

"But, what about Jerusalem," I said, faintly. "I have business in Jerusalem."

"And we have business in Lisbon. But once we have taken the city, I am sure some boat will continue to Jerusalem. Probably. Maybe," said Christian. This was outrageous. He had tricked me.

I appealed to Simon. "This is monstrous! Sire, surely you are dismayed about this deviation?"

He shrugged. "Lisbon or Jerusalem, it's all the same to me. Wherever the enemy is, I'll fight him. But I do know one thing—I'm not going back to England. I'm tired of civil war. If we capture the city, I'll take my reward in land, and stay."

He was no help. I turned to Christian again. "What about your holy crusade vow to Abbot Bernard? The one where you swore to fight for the kingdom of Jerusalem? How can you be so foresworn?"

Christian laughed. "Aude, Bernard himself suggested this venture, and proposed it to the Portuguese. The only trick was making sure the rest of our band agreed to it. And they have. You should be happy. I'll be rich and I'll buy you a silk dress when we win."

I was silent. I didn't give a fig for Abbot Bernard, but if he were behind this deviation to Lisbon, I could not stand against him. But what of my own vow?

CHAPTER FIFTEEN

Al-Lawza, February–April 1149

✠

Eleanor was the first to be brought to childbed, on a gloomy day in February. I had arranged for a midwife to live with us, and for a few women from the village to be wetnurses and nursemaids. It was her second child, and it slipped out of her almost before we had time to call the midwife up from the kitchen, where she was chatting with my cook.

"It's a girl," the midwife said, and we all released the breath we hadn't known we were holding. Mabilie and I hugged each other, and Ermine bent to her knees to look at the tiny mite cradled in the queen's arms while the midwife dealt with the afterbirth. Hodierna was nowhere near the birth chamber. "I don't do this," she said the moment Eleanor felt her first pains, so I asked her to keep an eye Eve for me. Eve was becoming a problem. She had so much freedom at al-Lawza that she was running wild, and spent more time in the olive grove pestering lizards than by my side. What place a monkey would have at my new monastery was another of the complications I was ignoring for now.

Eleanor's baby was as red and wrinkled as any newborn, but her mother thought her beautiful. "She looks like her father," she said in wonder, and Mabilie rolled her eyes. Fortunately, despite Eleanor's fond hopes, no such resemblance was evident, but what about when she grew older? Could Louis endure a constant reminder of his wife's shame at court?

Hodierna was next, a week or so after Eleanor, and this too was an easy birth and another girl.

"She's early," her mother said. "Very early."

The baby was a hefty lass, bigger than Eleanor's, but if Hodierna wanted it put about that she was early, then so be it. Though Eleanor's child looked like no one in particular, anyone who had known him would see Jaufré Rudel's nose on Hodierna's babe.

"I'll name her Melisende, after my sister. Lord knows, she deserves the honor."

Eleanor followed her lead. "I'll name mine after my sister too, Petronilla." We liked that. Saint Petronilla's cult had been much patronized by earlier French kings, and calling her after her sister gave nothing away. We called them Petra and Meli.

Though the castle had become a nursery, the women still wanted to hear about Lisbon, and about Simon too.

"And Christian," said Hodierna. "Maybe you were done with him, but it sounds like he wasn't done with you. Why else lure you to Lisbon?"

I was compelled to press forward.

✠

Aude's Fourteenth Tale: Lisbon, June 1147

I challenged Theodore about our destination when I could get a word alone with him. When pressed, he admitted that he had known all along about the deviation of our trip to Jerusalem, but had been sworn to secrecy.

"But it's on our way, Mother. We'd pass Lisbon anyway, and I'm sure you will get to Jerusalem eventually."

That was no consolation. It also emerged that he and Christian knew this coast well, and that the previous winter, when we thought they were trading with Ireland, they had been harrying the coastal settlements, taking the church plate in exchange for not burning down the villages they found.

"So you see, this is a holy mission, since we fight the Muslim enemies of God now, not the local Christians." Killing was killing and theft was theft to my mind, and I did not make the distinctions these men made with ease.

I passed the journey south in a quiet fury which Christian and Theo ignored. I was jarred out of my silent anger only on our last morning at sea when a sudden squall hit us. The storm was brief, but powerful enough that two of the smaller ships caught off guard were lost with all hands. When it was over, as quickly as it had begun, I wept with the others to see the clouds of azure, black, and grey shifting and moving in the sky, tongues of golden light shooting through them and then fading, almost as if the heavens themselves were doing battle.

We entered the wide mouth of the river, and as the clouds scudded away and the sky turned blue once more, I felt I was in a strangely familiar world. Lisbon rose up from the river to the north, encircled by walls that extended from the waterline to the hills it climbed. It had outgrown these walled boundaries however, and suburbs spilled out of them on the east and west sides of the city. City and suburbs clung tenaciously to the mountain and gleamed white in the sun, a shocking contrast to the deep blue of the river, the kind of blue you only see in southern seas. The river was mirrored in the heavens which shifted from the blue of the Virgin's veil at the horizon to deepest indigo at its highest point, its clarity interrupted only by the occasional lazy cloud drifting past, remnants of the storm that had vanished as soon as it had come.

We anchored, and Christian sent men to the shore for provisions. They returned with a strange rainbow of fresh fish and baskets of fruit, as well as casks of fresh water. Theodore was puzzled by the fruits. "What's that odd green thing?" he asked.

I took it and bit, pink seeds and juice bursting into my mouth. "It's a fig," I said once I had swallowed. "A fresh fig. The first I've eaten since I was a girl." I grinned. The air was warm and fragrant, and I realized that for the first time since I had left al-Lawza with Bertulf at my side, I was finally going home.

The figs were just the start. Almost all the foods I remembered and missed from my youth were available here in profusion: pomegranates and oranges and dates and, above all, olives and olive oil. No more food fried in rancid butter or fish oil. More to the point, the sea teeming with fish and woods full of game meant that the crusaders were in an ideal position to besiege the city and starve it into submission. We could stay as long as we liked living off the land, and waiting until their supplies ran out. We learned Lisbon was full of hungry civilians, but not many soldiers. Maybe the siege would be quick, and I could set off for Jerusalem before the winter.

At first I hoped it would be sooner. The Portuguese king, Afonso, promised us the moon and stars to help him take the city, but this wasn't enough for some. At a council on shore to determine how to respond to the king's offer, the Norman boats refused to join us. Their leader said, "We tried five years ago to help this king and there was no profit in it. Besides, the winds are perfect for a Jerusalem voyage so our eight ships are going to leave and anyone who wishes to truly fulfill their crusade vow may join with us."

"Me, me!" I said silently to myself. This was my chance.

Once the council was over, I tried to have a word with the Norman leader. I wriggled through the crowd of men milling about, trying to see over people's heads to find the ones going to Jerusalem.

A hand clamped onto my shoulder from behind. "Where do you think you're going? Trying to join the Normans?" It was Christian.

"Looking for Theo," I said, guiltily.

"A likely tale. Anyway, he's getting the boats ready. We Flemish are going to camp on the east side of the city."

"But we haven't even got a firm agreement from the king yet," I protested.

"We will get one. And by moving to the east side of the city, I can keep our people, including you, from those who would tempt them to betray the king and travel to Jerusalem."

That's how I ended up in an army camp, effectively a captive. We pulled our boats onshore and began to dig in on a height of land overlooking the city. I was in a tent with the other women who had come with the Flemish, a dull lot whose main job was to cook for the whole camp. My station excused me from that chore, so I had plenty of time to grumble, and I made the most of it, especially when Christian was around. Now we were up close, it was evident that this would be no quick victory.

The Normans caved anyway, and agreed to postpone Jerusalem, so I was trapped. The crusade leaders finally agreed to terms with the king. Christian told me about them with great satisfaction.

"You see how worthwhile this enterprise will be for us?"

I was silent and grumpy. I was spinning, which I hate, and my wool kept breaking so I ostentatiously gave it all my attention, setting the spindle in motion again and grafting together the recalcitrant fleece.

"As a pledge of his good intentions, the king has offered us twenty hostages from among his own people, bishops and lords of high estate," Christian continued. "And we have to give twenty of our own, of equal value. I have volunteered you, Aude. You'll be moved to the king's camp this afternoon. Ow!"

My spindle spun out, cracking his shins, which served him right. "A hostage? How dare you put my name forward without my permission. You're not my husband or guardian. You have no right." I was furious.

He was implacable. "It won't be dangerous, Aude. The king and I are not enemies, but allies. I thought you'd be happy. Their camp is much more comfortable than our own, and there are more women of your station there. Besides, I've promised, and one of the English constables is coming to escort you and the others." He ordered my serving woman to get my belongings ready, which she did with ill grace. She wouldn't be coming with me, and without me to serve, she'd have to help with the cooking. I sat in the tent and fumed, and lifted not a finger to help.

A while later, Christian peered through the tent flap. "Your escort is here, Aude. Time to get a move on."

I slowly rose from my stool and made my way outside. Let them wait a little. When I came out into the sunshine, my eyes blinking in the light, Simon of Dover was before me, tall on a horse, and a groom was bringing one round for me.

"It's you!" I said stupidly.

"Yes it is," he agreed. I wasn't the only one he was escorting. Nineteen others, all men, including two more Flemings and an archdeacon from Boulogne, were going to be my fellow hostages, and they waited impatiently for me to get a move on. My bags were loaded on a pack mule, I mounted the horse, and we set off.

The Portuguese camp was north of the Flemish one, only a short distance away on the same hilly ridge, which was why our camp was the last stop before our destination. My fellow hostages talked amongst themselves, which left me with Simon.

"So you're taking me to my prison," I said, trying to sound put upon, but unable to keep a flirtatious note from my voice.

He laughed. "It won't be like that at all, my lady."

I tried a few pleasantries about the weather and the local food, without getting much out of him. He seemed to have something on his mind, and when we came into sight of the Portuguese camp, he let me know what it was.

"I'm a plainspoken man and I'll make this brief. I like you, Lady Aude. You have pluck. We're going to win here in Lisbon, I can feel it. It's a matter of time. And as I told you, I'm not going back. The civil war in England has worn me out, with its treachery and double-dealing. Nowhere is immune from strife, but here seems as good as any to make a new start. After we win, I will receive a good reward from the king, and I don't want to enjoy it alone. I would like you to stay with me here, and marry me."

He stared straight ahead, and I almost fell off my horse with surprise. Marry him? Oh, it was flattering to get a marriage proposal after all these years. And he was certainly attractive, the kind of man you could lean against and be at peace with at last instead of fighting, fighting alone all the time.

"But I hardly know you," was all I said, which wasn't relevant at all, for what did knowing someone have to do with marriage? "And I have to go to Jerusalem."

"I may not know your mother's name or what you like to eat for supper, but I know what I see, and what I see, I like. You have spirit, right for making a new home in a new world."

We reached the center of the Portuguese camp. "It's good that you'll be here," he continued. "I'll have to come to the camp often, and we can get to know each other as much as you like. Don't reply now, but think about what I've said." After exchanging formalities relating to the transfer of the hostages with his opposite number on the Portuguese side, he left.

I was flustered by his words, and more than a bit dazed by the time I met the women who were to be my companions for the siege, King

Afonso's sisters. We shared a tent that put the best accommodations of Flanders to shame, and I would never admit it, but Christian was right. I was happier here than with the rough Flemish. Our tent had thick carpets, silk hangings, and folding beds that kept the bugs away. There was even a proper cook tent with an oven, instead of the open fire the Flemish were relying on. These people were used to a travelling campaign and knew how to do it in style.

I don't know what the women thought of me when I was thrust inside their silken home with my grubby belongings, and I never found out, because we spoke no common tongue. The Portuguese camp was nice, but more lonely. The male hostages had each other, but I was isolated by language from the women who were supposed to be my companions. I spent my time in embroidery, which was a big step up from spinning in my view, and I was happiest when the women sang their melodic, sad songs, a little like those sung by Eleanor's troubadours. I couldn't understand any of the words.

My isolation gave me time to think about Simon's outlandish proposal. I couldn't understand why I was being so, well, silly about him. Surely I was too old for all of this. It had been years since I had been that way about anyone, and I thought I had left all that behind me. And wouldn't he want a young bride, who could give him children? But however sternly I told myself to put Simon and his foolishness out of my mind, when I sat outside with the other women in the shade of an awning, stitchery in hand, I found I looked up every time a horseman approached to see if it were him. And sometimes, it was. He came to our camp every week or so, and once he transacted whatever business brought him, he would seek me out. The other women would smile and nudge each other as he drew me away for a walk.

We didn't talk about ourselves, or our pasts. Instead I pestered him about how the siege was progressing.

"You see down there?" He pointed as we stood on the promontory overlooking the city. "The Flemish are undermining the walls. It is slow and dangerous work — already two men have been killed in rockfalls — but if they succeed, they can light a fire in the tunnel they're digging under the walls, which will crack the foundations and breach the fortifications so our men can enter."

"How long will that take?"

"Weeks. Months," he said honestly. That was a blow. I wouldn't be in Jerusalem before the winter storms hit.

But it was peaceful being with Simon. Often we walked about the Portuguese hilltop redoubt, and didn't talk at all, enjoying the late summer sun. He would give me a hand from time to time to help me over a rough patch of ground, and one day I didn't pull my hand away from his once I was on firmer ground, but let it rest there as we walked, small and safe in his large fist.

But sieges are ghastly, five parts yawning boredom, people outside a wall waiting for people inside a wall to starve themselves to death, and one part violence, brutality, and tragedy. In the camp we had food and silk cushions, music and wine, while inside the city, they were starving. They'd eaten all the cats, we heard, and now they were turning to the rats. It was agonizing and the very slowness allowed us to dehumanize our enemies, to be willing to commit any act, no matter how foul, if it would end our wait. Nothing would happen for days, then a mine would collapse, killing a host of Flemish, or the English would capture a sortie of Muslims, stick their broken heads on pikes and wave them tauntingly before the city's defenders. Their side sent false messages of relief columns soon to liberate Lisbon, and our side brought the boats on shore and took out their masts as a sign we were going to stay the winter if need be. Loss of life was great on both sides, from arrows and stone bombardments, and the Flemish and the English built cemeteries and churches to honor their fallen. Still, inch by painful inch, it seemed we'd prevail.

It was mid-October before Christian gave the order to fire the tunnel the Flemish had been digging. All day long, I saw people from our side packing the tunnel with anything that would burn. Every so often, one would be picked off by a Muslim archer. Once they gave the command to fire, the slow but inexorable rumble of the wall collapsing was heard even up on our hill, and we all cheered. Both sides fought all night and into the next day, but the Muslim defenders prevented our side from entry. I was worried sick that Theo would manage to insert himself into the worst of the fighting. "Please God," I prayed fervently. "Don't let him do anything stupid. Please keep him safe." And Simon too, I added, under my breath.

Things were heating up on the English side of the city too, though it was harder for me to follow the action from my vantage point. They had built a massive siege engine, and used the distraction provided by the Flemish breach in the walls to pull it towards the seawall inch by inch. They also used mangonels that hurtled stones at the enemy walls. Every day the English launched an assault, raining arrows and crossbolts onto the defenders, and each night the citizens of Lisbon under the cover of darkness tried to repair the damage done by the attackers. At last, the defenders asked to parley and offered a truce, with Muslim hostages to seal the bargain.

The crusade leaders conferred with King Afonso. I spoke to Simon for one brief moment, on his way in with the other constables to speak with the king. "Is it really over at last?"

He nodded. "They have promised to give over the city and all their goods, so long as they can leave with their lives. It's a fair deal, and we are sure to agree. In a few days, they will be gone, and we will control the city." His voice lowered so the others rushing in to see the king couldn't overhear. "And, Aude, when that time comes, let's talk again about that question I asked you when the siege started." He squeezed my hand and left while I blushed furiously.

The men negotiated in the open air, and I heard them from where I sat stitching with Donna Urraca and Donna Taraja, though I wasn't paying much attention. From off in the distance, I also heard a kind of low rumble. Was there some kind of upset in the city?

The rumble grew louder, as if its source was coming closer, and I wondered if the besieged had made some kind of breakout. The other women craned their necks to locate the source of the disturbance, and I stood and shielded my eyes from the sun, trying to see what was going on.

It wasn't coming from inside the city. I spied a rabble of several hundred men, walking outside the walls towards the hill where the king was encamped. Even at this distance, I saw that many were armed with staves. The noise caught the attention of the men setting the terms of Lisbon's surrender with the king.

"It's the English!" someone cried. This was the signal for all the English constables, including Simon, and the English knights who had accompanied them to the parley to run for their horses, to head off whatever disturbance had caused their subjects to march.

This ended the formal council for the moment, and I followed to learn what was going on. Christian had brought Theo with him, so I took the chance to speak to my son.

"It's almost over, Theo. Then you and I can go to Jerusalem! Are you excited?" He mumbled or grunted whatever sons say when their mothers ask them a question, but before I could insist, some of the English lords returned, though not Simon.

King Afonso, spoke, as the council slowly came back to order. "Might we know the reason for the sudden and unwelcome interruption of my council?" he said politely.

Andrew, leader of the Londoners, spoke up. "There was a small upset among some of the men. They were distressed that the Muslim hostages had been brought to you and feared we were going to double cross them out of the booty of victory. It's all straightened out now though."

This was the wrong thing to say. The Muslim hostages, who had been ready to concede everything to save the lives of their citizens, realized that the disunity of the crusaders meant they were in a better position to make terms, and began to backtrack. They argued for hours, with Christian and the Flemings demanding the Muslims surrender in full, and the rest suggesting some compromise. I grew restless and anxious waiting for Simon to return.

"Where's Simon?" I asked, grabbing the sleeve of one of his knights. "He's not here?" he said unhelpfully. The council broke up, and we learned that all had agreed that the city would be turned over the following day. This good news should have caused me to rejoice, but I had a sleepless night, worrying about Simon no matter how many times I told myself he was sure to be fine.

I woke early and went out at dawn, scanning the horizon as if I might see him. No doubt he was back with his men, preparing for the entry into the city. Once again, I urged myself to keep calm. A voice spoke behind me. "Were you the woman who was inquiring about Simon of Dover?"

I turned. It was the knight I questioned the previous afternoon. "Yes," I said. "Is he here?"

"No, my lady. I'm sorry. I hate to be the bearer of ill tidings, but Simon, rest his soul, is dying. Indeed he may already be dead. He was assaulted in the melee yesterday and taken to his tent—one arrow to his head, and another in his arm. One of my friends saw him go down and told me, and I remembered your question."

I said nothing, dumbfounded.

"I'm sorry, my lady," he repeated, and rode away.

He was out of sight before I came to myself again, moving from numbness to panic. Dying, maybe already dead. I had to find him, to see for myself. Wildly I hoped that maybe the knight was wrong. I was about to leave, when I was stopped by one of the Portuguese cousins of the king.

"Where are you going this fine morning, Lady Aude?" he asked.

"I have an errand at the English camp," I said. "Please let me proceed."

"Have you forgotten that you are a hostage here for the good conduct of the Flemings?" he asked. "You are not permitted to leave at will."

I had forgotten that I was a hostage. Damn. "But sire," I said in beseeching tones. "Are we not all friends now. And the city will be turned over this very day. Surely my time as a hostage is finished."

"Do you hear that noise?" he asked. I heard the ring of steel against steel coming somewhere to the south of us.

He was angry. "Are you aware that at this very moment some of the Flemings are trying to break into the city, against the terms of our parley with the Muslims, while others are fighting with our own men, Portuguese Christians, for custody of the Muslims hostages from the city? Yes, of course you are aware of it. And you are not going to the English, but rather fleeing to your Flemish brethren to deny us one of the hostages they gave us in good faith, faith which they have today foresworn."

A party of Portuguese knights rode past us at a gallop to quell the disturbance. Were the Flemings really attacking? What did Christian have up his sleeve now? I could do nothing but obey the knight and dismount.

"I'll take you to the king and his sisters," he said, grasping me by the arm. "They will keep an eye on you." He pulled me to the open pavilion where the royal family gathered to wait for the Flemish to be repulsed, on a day that should have marked their triumphant entry into a glorious city.

"I caught this one trying to escape," my knight said, and they stared at me coldly, saying nothing. I found a stool at the back, and tried to fade into the wall hangings. All I could think of was Simon, broken, dying, but I had no idea how to get to get to him.

I wasn't there for long before Christian rode up, his horse in a lather. He prostrated himself before the king, chest heaving. "Pardon, your majesty!" he cried.

King Afonso let him lie there a good long time before he spoke. "Arise, Lord Christian, and speak."

He stood with hands clasped and outstretched in supplication. "Majesty, I come in penance seeking pardon for my servants who have disobeyed you. It was not by my command that they attacked the city and assaulted your men." Christian looked terrified, and I believed he was telling the truth. I wondered if the king would believe it.

The king was cold. "That your men should attack my own men is a serious crime and breach of the peace. But I reckon their assault on the city, in defiance of the treaty we concluded with its defenders, to be even more grave. I would rather not take the city at all, if I cannot do it with honor. Your men must lay down their arms, and I will associate no more with such foresworn criminals."

"It is done, my lord," said Christian, beginning to breathe a little easier.

The king also seemed to recover some of his temper. "As punishment, we will maintain the siege for one more day. Before we enter the city, each one of the crusade leaders must swear fealty to me. Also, I will need further hostages as surety for your good behavior. You can leave all of your knights here with me."

The knights who had accompanied Christian looked glum, but he was overjoyed. "I delight to be in your good favor, my lord," he said.

"Good favor might be overstating it," replied the king.

In the muddle of people leaving, I took my chance to speak to Christian.

"Christian!" I hissed. "You have to get me out of here. Trade me for one of your men. I need to go to the English camp. Simon has been hurt, maybe already dead. I need to see him."

He looked at me coldly, his humiliation before the king still fresh, and making him cruel. "I've lost enough men today as it is. I can't spare another for a useless woman. Besides, there's nothing you can do for Simon. I heard he died this morning."

He rode off, before I could challenge him again. Were his words true, or was trying to hurt me as he'd been hurt by the king? I needed to find Simon, and I had to rely on myself.

I returned to the women's tent where I had been sleeping because I knew I'd find what I needed there. Fortunately, it was empty. I'd be stopped if I tried to ride out of camp as a lady. But if I disguised myself as one of the peasant women who came in and out offering food, maybe I could slip by.

I fashioned myself a reasonable imitation of the garb of the local Muslim women from the countryside from what I found in the tent. The most distinctive part of their costume was a large scarf that wrapped around their shoulders and almost completely concealed their faces. Unless someone got a close look, I'd go unnoticed.

I slung an empty bundle over my back so it would look like I was leaving the camp after selling my goods, and then looked around the tent for the one element I was missing. I found it in the stick we used to prop the door open. It would make a perfect staff for me, and was short enough to force me to hunch over like a crone. Thus garbed, I shuffled out of the tent and towards the main gate. The guardsmen, who would have been alert to a finely dressed woman on horseback, thought nothing of a plodding grandmother on foot. We see what we expect to see. They called out something to me that sounded friendly so I waved my stick at them in what I hoped was an amiable fashion and kept walking. I was free, and breathed a sigh of relief.

The quickest route to the English camp was around the south part of the city, but that passed the Flemish camp, and I wanted to avoid any hint that I was heading there if I were stopped. Besides, if Christian found me, he'd return me to the king right away to cement their fragile relationship. I took the northern route around the base of the castle, maintaining my shuffling gate until I was well out of sight of the Portuguese guard.

Now my biggest worry were English louts, bored and annoyed that the end of the siege had been postponed for a day. I passed groups of men in twos or threes, drunk and singing rude songs. Some called out to me, but I made no response and they left me alone. Out of the camp for the first time in months, I saw the devastation wrought to the Lisbon suburbs, which I skirted as best I could, though it made my journey longer. Homes where they had raised their children, burnt out and looted; farms built up over generations, laid waste; fruit trees that took decades to grow, fired. No wonder they were ready to surrender. Distracted by these horrors, I bumped into someone whose breath smelt of drink and decay. I jumped back in surprise. He leered at me, and said something I didn't understand, making the universal gesture for "give me money" with his right hand. If I were the crone I pretended, I would have been in trouble, but I had come too far to be stopped by this ruffian. I cracked him smartly on the skull with my staff and he backed off, not prepared to brave the crazy woman with the staff a second time.

I was near the English camp by then and soon at its gates, where I asked the man on guard to direct me to Simon's tent. Perhaps startled at being addressed in fluent French by a Muslim peasant, he pointed to a sturdy canvas tent close by. I went through its door flap and surprised a couple of men eating a pick-up meal. I looked around, my eyes slowly becoming accustomed to the darkness. Simon was not to be seen.

"Wait! You can't come in here," said one of them.

"Simon. I must see Simon. Is he here? Does he still live?" I asked urgently, almost breathless after my run.

"Who's that?" a voice called from behind a partition that separated the back of the tent from the main room. A figure emerged, head and arm bandaged, but very much alive.

"Aude! What a lovely surprise. What brings you here?"

I rushed over and embraced him, almost knocking him over despite his bulk. I clung to him like a winkle on a rock, my sobs releasing all the worry and anxiety I felt.

His arms found their way around me and he began to comfort me. "There, there Aude," he said, stroking my hair like you'd do with a child. "Everything is fine now. You're safe with me. What's wrong? Is someone threatening you?"

"I thought you were dead," I said soft-voiced, looking up at him with a tearstained face, hands clinging to his chest.

"Dead?!" He laughed, then we both saw the others in the tent were watching our encounter with interested curiosity. "All right you lot, clear out," he said, and they reluctantly obeyed.

He took me behind the partition, where I found a space barely big enough for his sleeping cot. He sat us down and said, "What's all this about me being dead?"

I told him the rumor I had heard, how scared I'd been, and all my efforts to get here.

A smile broke over his face. "So you do care about me a little after all." I went red and buried my face in his chest, while he explained what happened. "I was wounded, and I did go down. Knocked cold for a few minutes, they say. Felt like an idiot when I came to. As you can see, it was a head wound, and they always bleed like hell. But it was nothing, just a scrape. The arm is worse but the barber says he got everything out. Now, can you stay for a bit? I'll send a message to the king that you're here. I don't think he'll care much either way, but it would be nice to avoid a full-scale battle over you between him and the Flemings, at least until we can take this damned city. Then you can remain here overnight and help me convalesce." He winked at me, and I am afraid I blushed.

He went to perform this errand, then returned to me. I hadn't moved from the cot. He sat beside me, cupped my head in his hands and gave me a long slow kiss. When I opened my eyes again, he said, "What is this strange costume you're wearing? You look like my aged aunt." He unwound the black cloak from my head and shoulders and then removed first my shift and then his shirt and hose.

He made love to me slowly and deliberately, eyes wide open on mine every moment and it was not brutal like Bertulf, or naughty and manipulative like Christian, or imaginary like Charles, but real and wonderful, like my favorite food for dinner and a new dress and a warm fire in the winter and coming home at last, at long long last.

We stayed like that all evening and night. When we got hungry, he found some dried fruit and a flagon of wine in his tent, and he discreetly allowed me some time alone behind the partition to use a chamber pot. We slept and woke and made love again, and then slept some more. It was well past dawn when we were woken by a timid voice entering the tent.

"Lord Simon? Sorry to bother you sir, but it's time for the entry into the city."

"Damn," he said. "Well Aude, let's go see this city we have sweated and bled for."

We dressed quickly, and he found us both horses. As we rode to catch up to the rest of the commanders and constables to receive the Muslim surrender, he said to me, "We won't do this again, not until we're properly married and all. But how could I resist last night with you turning up here and throwing yourself at me like you did?"

I shot him a quick glance and saw he was teasing. Marriage. Well, maybe I would after all. It wouldn't be so bad to stay here in Lisbon, with him.

I went through the rest of the day in a daze. Everyone was happy, rejoicing and singing hymns as we processed behind the archbishop and bishops into the city, and no one cared that one lowly hostage had vanished for the night. The king made a circuit of the castle walls on foot, and raised a banner emblazoned with the cross onto the highest tower, visible for miles around. Everyone was happy, except the people we were taking the city from. We ventured into the main mosque. Its endless rows of parallel columns made me feel like I was walking in a forest of stone, but we left quickly. It had been used as a hospice for the sick and dying, and smelled like a charnel house. The ordinary citizens owned only the clothing on their backs, and whatever food they could carry. All their other property would be divided amongst the crusaders. They left in a silent and angry procession, migrating out of the city they had lived in for centuries, to parts unknown.

✠

"So you all lived happily ever after?" said Hodierna. "Well, all except the Muslims, but they're supposed to be our enemies, aren't they."

"Sieges are ugly things." Ermine shuddered.

They asked more about Lisbon, and I told them about the house Christian was given, where we lived until I sailed for Jerusalem. But when they asked me about Simon, and what happened there, I told them it didn't work out in the end. "My vow was more important to me than any man," I said primly, trying to leave the impression of a woman who couldn't care less.

I thought I had convinced them, until one day when Eleanor and I were alone together. She was nursing little Petra, an odd thing for a queen, but for some reason she insisted, dismissing the wetnurse I had so diligently interviewed and hired. Out of the blue, she said, "Why are you here with me? Why aren't you in Lisbon with Simon?"

"I told you, we found we didn't care enough for each other, and I needed to come here to reclaim al-Lawza."

"Nonsense. You dressed like a peasant and escaped from camp to see him and then you found you didn't really like him after all? I don't believe you. Tell me what really happened."

If she had stayed like that, demanding and pushing, I would have stuck to my story. But her voice changed, turning soft and sad. "If I had a beloved, someone who loved me, I would do anything for him," she said, looking far into the distance. "Give up being queen, being duchess. Go anywhere, live in a hovel. Anything."

She stroked little Petra's cheek and the baby greedily suckled. I felt a pang for this woman and all she had suffered so silently and I did what I resolved I never would. I told the truth.

✠

Aude's Last Tale

After the king took control of the city, Simon was busy dividing the spoils, so I went back to the Flemish camp and didn't see him for a few days. I explained my plans to Christian and Theo.

Theo was thrilled. "That's wonderful, mother! Congratulations." he said, giving me a big hug and then left me and Christian to go off on some errand. I was happy but not surprised by his reaction. He was probably relieved that someone else would care for his mother so he wouldn't have to.

Christian said nothing, but a range of emotions passed across his face, none of them pleasant.

"Aren't you going to congratulate me too?" I said eventually.

"No Aude, I don't think I am. Because you're not going to get married to Simon or to anyone else. Have you forgotten your vow? Your promise to found a monastery in Jerusalem? The vow that kept you out of my bed after we had enjoyed ourselves there for so many years?"

I was stunned. That was years ago, and after I refused Christian, he found comfort elsewhere with a series of serving girls who remained the same age while he grew older and older. He had no interest in me himself, I believed then, though maybe Hodierna is right to suggest that he did. I was sure he was being a dog in the manger, jealous of someone getting something he didn't even want. I was furious.

"You can't stop me." I said.

"True. I can't stop you. But I can make it so Simon will stop himself. Do you suppose Simon will be interested in a woman who was so degraded as to enjoy carnal knowledge with her husband's cousin? And his wife? At the same time? I think the moment Simon learns of your sordid past, and realizes he's taking my leavings, you'll find you no longer have a groom. Far better to turn him down and go to Jerusalem as planned and build your little convent and stay there, a good penitential nun."

I was sickened. Unless I told Simon I wouldn't have him, Christian would make sure he wouldn't have me. I had a sleepless night as I tried to figure out what to do. Was there a way to explain my past to Simon so he'd understand? The heavy cross I had received from the priest in Bruges when I made my confession weighed on me too as I lay there in my cot. True, I hadn't promised the priest I'd never marry again, but it was always my intention to stay at al-Lawza once it was a monastery, either as one of the nuns or as a consecrated widow. Perhaps I had been wrong to even think of marriage, and this was my punishment.

The next day I told Simon I wouldn't have him after all. He was on the beach, supervising the move of the English to their new homes within the city. I handled it badly. I couldn't tell him about Christian's threats, of course, so I blamed it on my vow.

"I have to go to Jerusalem."

"But why? The bishop told us that we fulfilled our crusade vows by fighting in Lisbon. That means you too."

"I have to go. It's a separate vow."

"Fine then, go to Jerusalem. And then return to Lisbon and marry me. I'll wait."

My heart twisted. If only. "No," I said firmly. "This is the end. I won't be coming back. I'm sorry." I wanted to tell him I'd miss him, but then I would cry and he would take me in his arms, and I would all be undone.

"Maybe you found you didn't care for me quite as much as you thought? Heat of the battle and all that. Too elegant for me, I suppose. No desire to tie yourself to a simple English soldier when you can flutter around the royal court in Jerusalem." His voice was bitter.

I wanted to deny it all, but I said nothing.

"That's your final decision?" His face was like cut stone. I nodded. "Well, that's that then."

I didn't see Simon again. The king gave him property in the country-side as well as houses in Lisbon. He left to inspect it the following day, and divided the rest of his time between there and the king's court at Coimbra. I could have gone to court over Christmas with the rest but I was afraid Simon would try to change my mind—and more afraid he wouldn't bother. He made no effort to seek me out over the three months I stayed in Lisbon after the conquest. Who knows? He and Christian were still much together on the king's business, and Christian may have told him about my past as a pre-ventative measure in case I did think to return to Lisbon someday.

I put all my hopes and energy back into my original plan, trying to recover my old enthusiasm for returning to my childhood home with my son, and almost succeeding. "You just wait, Theo. If you think it is lovely here, Jerusalem is ten times more beautiful, and there are all kinds of opportunities for a man of your family background and skill. We'll find a nice bride for you, maybe an Armenian like my mother. It's more than time you married." Theo never said much when I went on like this, and that should have been my warning.

It was early February before the seas were calm enough and I found a boat that could take us where we wanted to go. Christian was not among our number. He had plans to return to Flanders later in the spring and I was relieved. The two of us were barely speaking, which was difficult when we lived in the same house.

I was packed days before we left, and I kept nagging Theo to get ready. Finally, my bags were stowed on the ship, and Theo and I were ferried out to it in a small boat. I climbed the ladder up to the deck, rejoicing for the first and last time in my life to be on a ship. I couldn't wait to leave Lisbon. I called down to Theo. "Come on! Climb up after me. They're almost ready to set sail."

He said something. The wind was picking up, flapping at my shift and wrestling with my hair, no longer neat under its tight coif. I stood on the foredeck and tried to understand his words.

"I'm not coming."

"What?" The wind blew his words away from me.

"I said, I'm not coming. I'm staying here. In Lisbon."

"What do you mean you're not coming?" I demanded. "We had it all planned."

"You had it all planned. I never wanted to come. There are enough battles here to last me a lifetime and more. I'm going to fight with the Castilian king in the spring, and then, who knows? Maybe I'll come to Jerusalem later. Or you can come back here."

"But why didn't you tell me?" The sailors were already starting to lift the anchors. The winds and tide were perfect, and they weren't going to wait.

"I tried. I wanted to. But I didn't think you'd listen. May the winds be with you, mother. And come back some time."

We pulled away and his last words were swallowed up by the wind and the surf. I was so full of grief, I didn't know what to do with myself, so I turned it into anger, anger with Theo for abandoning me, anger with Simon for not sweeping me onto the back of his horse and riding away with me despite my words, and anger with Christian above all. I sailed in a white heat of self-righteous fury that only abated for one brief moment when I rescued a monkey off the Spanish coast.

And that's how I ended up on the dock in Antioch where we met, no husband, no son, nothing but a naughty monkey named Eve. The story comes full circle, and I truly have nothing more to tell.

CHAPTER SIXTEEN

Al-Lawza, April 1149

✠

It wasn't the end of the story as far as Eleanor was concerned. A part of her still wanted to believe that true love would win out in the end, like it did in her songs.

"You've fulfilled your vow, now go back to Simon," she said. "If he truly loves you, he won't care about your past."

"If he truly loves me," I agreed, suppressing the tiny flutter of hope awakened by her words. "But he made no move to persuade me to stay after our first conversation."

"That's because he thought you didn't love him. Men are proud that way. If you return he'll know you do love him. But if you don't go back for Simon, then at least send for Theo and tell him to come live with you."

"I was wrong about Theo. I see that now. He has his own destiny, and it is not to travel in his mother's wake. As long as he is still lives." I crossed myself quickly. "I think I will see him again some-day. When he's ready."

She didn't give up but tried a new tack. "Very well, if you don't want to go back to Lisbon, don't stay here. Not right away. Make Ermine prioress, and put her in charge. You know she's dying to do it. Then come with me, at least until we get back to Europe. I know you don't want to be buried here, not just yet."

She struck a nerve. No, I wasn't ready to settle down, a contented widow at al-Lawza, though I cursed my perverse will for tempting me to turn my back on the home I had longed to return to for so many years. But it took time and persuasion for me to give in to her wishes.

"Please, Aude. I need you. Mabilie is old and doesn't understand everything. Please. Just until we reach Italy. Then I won't nag you any more, I promise. You can return here if you want, or stay with me and come to France. Or even go back to Lisbon."

I knew I wouldn't do the latter, but at last I consented to her wheedling, signing myself up for yet another unwanted sea voyage. Perhaps a nasty journey by ship would resign me to a lifetime of prayer at al-Lawza. And in truth, I was worried about Eleanor. Everyone expected Louis to accept her baby without question as part of his family, but I had my doubts, and I'd be easier in my mind if could see the two settled together.

Eleanor was summoned to court that Easter to attend the celebrations with the husband she hadn't seen since the previous autumn. Hodierna would be there too, with her sister, before she returned home to Tripoli to face her husband's wrath.

We stayed in Bethany outside the city, at the monastery of Lazarus where Hodierna's other sister, Joveta, was abbess. The day before Easter was the feast of St. Theodosia, and that morning al-Lawza was made a priory under the auspices of St. Lazarus, and Ermine became its prioress. Joveta promised to send her a few novices.

At midday, we arrived at the royal palace of Jerusalem, now in the ancient palace of King David. There, Louis and Eleanor met in public for the first time in months. I watched warily, but Louis's behavior was everything it should be, the very model of how a king was supposed to greet his spouse after a long absence. Baby Petra wasn't with us, and maybe that helped. She had been baptized that morning, and we left her with the nuns in Bethany.

We departed the palace in a great procession, Latin and Greek abbots and their monks in the front carrying crosses and singing hymns, and the royal party bringing up the rear, including Louis, Eleanor, Hodierna, and Queen Melisende with her son. We filed through the narrow streets that lead to the church of the Holy Sepulcher, each with an unlit taper to be fired by the mystical flame that unfailingly descended upon Christ's tomb every Eastertide.

I barely recognized the church of my youth. What had been a series of disconnected sacred spaces was being gathered under one roof built in a European style. Each nook and corner of it was crammed with people from every part of the world when our procession arrived, and soldiers cleared a path for our entry using more force than persuasion. A few people suffocated in the church every year at Easter and I could see why mother had always refused to bring me when I was a little girl, no matter how hard I begged.

"You'll have plenty of chances to go when you're a bigger," she had said, but those chances never came until now. I wondered awestruck with the rest at the press of humanity, the mingled aromas of unwashed bodies, incense and beeswax, the cloth of purple and gold worn by the queen, and the rags of the paupers. Somehow we made our way to the high altar in the rotunda, facing the Anastasis, the place where Christ rose from the dead. Our arrival was the signal for the Greek and Latin clergy to begin chanting vespers, which they did in their own languages, each side trying to drown out the other in a cacophony of praise. When they got to the first lesson from Scripture, the Latin patriarch went down from the altar to look through the grill into the Anastasis to see if a flame had been kindled yet in the oil lamps that were left there on the lid of the empty tomb. When it was clear he saw nothing, an audible groan rose from those waiting and watching. The next time he went to look, the crowd spontaneously started chanting "Kyrie eleison—Christ have mercy," drowning out the recitation of the lesson. The roof of the rotunda was open and a light rain began to fall on all of us waiting for our scheduled yearly miracle. Suddenly a reddish glow lit the Anastasis from within. The chanting stopped abruptly and once again the congregation cried, "Kyrie eleison," over and over, this time with joy, as the living flame was passed from taper to taper and the whole church was slowly illuminated.

Most left the church at this point, returning to their homes and churches to kindle the lamps extinguished on Good Friday with the sacred flame. We remained in the church, however, for the baptism of Hodierna's baby Melisende, with her royal namesake as godmother. I had to admire Hodierna's bravado, christening her baby of dubious parentage in the most important church in all Christendom on the most sacred day of the year. She was daring anyone to say that the baby was not what she seemed, the legitimate child of herself and Ramon.

At the end of April, we left al-Lawza in Ermine's capable hands and met the king in Acre to depart from the Holy Land, two ships all that remained of the huge army that left France two years before.

Mabilie and I were to sail with Louis and Eleanor in one ship. We reached Acre in the morning, and the king was already waiting impatiently. The nursemaid's hands were full of the crucial things a baby needs that cannot be packed away in the hold, so I found myself holding Petra. Although Eve on her lead was jealous of the attention the child was getting from me, I didn't mind. Petra was at that lovely age where babies smile and interact with the world, but before they are mobile enough to do damage, or vocal enough to be annoying. She burbled and cooed over my shoulder, a tuft of hair, red like her mother's, peeking over the edge of her blanket. Such a small person, it was hard to believe she could cause all this fuss. But after Louis greeted us and saw the baby in my arms, he had eyes only for her.

I have never seen such icy cold loathing as I saw in his eyes when he gazed upon little Petra. Reflexively, I held her tighter against my body.

"What is that?" he pointed, voice like iron.

"You know, Louis," said Eleanor, puzzled. "It's the baby."

He shooed everyone back so only Eleanor, Mabilie, and I could hear his next words.

"What is it—"

"She," corrected Eleanor.

"What is she doing here?" he demanded.

I stroked Petra's sleeping head, glad she couldn't hear his words or understand his tone.

"But Louis, I don't understand. Why are you so angry. You said you'd take us back. You promised." Eleanor sounded bewildered, and reached to put a protective hand on her baby's curved back where it nestled in my arms.

"I said I'd take you back. You. Not that." His finger jabbed in my direction again. "Eleanor, listen to me. We have two ships. I will sail in one, and you sail in the other. And when we meet again in Sicily, that baby will not be with you. Do you understand? I don't care what you do, but that baby will no longer be with you."

He turned without waiting for a reply and gave orders to change the passenger list for each ship. Louis and the French would all sail together on the biggest ship, and Eleanor and her entourage and remaining followers from Aquitaine would sail on the smaller. One of her men would give orders to the captain.

By the time we got Eleanor to the main cabin of our vessel, she was hysterical.

"He wants me to kill my baby. He wants me to throw her over the side." she cried.

"No, no," soothed Mabilie. "He didn't mean that. You can find a nice convent that will take her on one of the islands we pass."

"I could send her back to al-Lawza to be with Ermine. Or take her myself," I pondered.

"No! No one is going to take my baby away from me," Eleanor cried, and was inconsolable until we both swore we'd find a way for her to keep Petra. But what could we do against the king's will?

Most Europe-bound ships tried to depart the Holy Land in the autumn, but we were leaving in the fickle spring. Eve enjoyed exploring the masts and rigging the first day we were out, but the second day all of us including her stayed below decks as we were beset by a wave of storms from the north that lasted almost a week and pushed us far off course. Because our ship was small and light, it did poorly close to the wind, and we found ourselves bobbing around the north African coast alone, the king's ship nowhere in sight. What's more, we had suffered enough damage because of the high winds that we had to put into shore at a dusty little port to do repairs that took an endless amount of time. The sky had by now cleared of course, and it would have been perfect sailing weather.

"Maybe there are Christians here," said Mabilie. "We might be able to find a nice convent for Petra." The look Eleanor gave her shut her up right away, and she never mentioned this possibility again.

By the time we could resume our journey, the winds had shifted again. Now high hot gusts from the south mixed with the sea currents, bringing us gale force winds and heavy rainstorms. We were pushed north and found ourselves wandering almost blind in the Greek islands. We had been travelling for two months and more, with nothing to show for it.

"It's like there's an invisible line in the middle of the sea that we are powerless to cross," said Mabilie. "What will King Louis think? He must be in Sicily already."

"It's God's will," Eleanor said, tickling Petra's tummy, who was sitting on her lap. "I know what we need to do." Later that day I saw her arguing with her ship master, and though she wouldn't tell me why, by her look of exultation, I could tell she had won.

It didn't take long to discover what was up. I may be a fool when it comes to seafaring, unable to tell my bow from my stern, but I do know that the sun rises in the east, and when I saw it ascending the heavens in front of us the following morning, I realized we were not heading west, to Sicily, but in the exact opposite direction, back where we came from.

I confronted her the moment she appeared on deck.

She laughed. "I wondered how long it would take you and Mabilie to figure it out. Neither of you pays a bit of attention to where we're going. Yes, I ordered them to head east."

"But why? What are you going to do? Leave Petra with Ermine after all? Throw yourself on the mercy of Queen Melisende?" Neither option seemed plausible.

"No, better than that. I'm taking Petra to her father. I am taking her to Antioch. I gave orders for us to sail there, and we should arrive in a few days."

I was flabbergasted. "Antioch. But Eleanor, he has a wife. And children." And he's your uncle, I thought to myself silently. "He won't want you."

She turned on me angrily. "He will want me. Yes, there will be difficulties, but we can sort them out. I should have planned this from the beginning. Some may be too cowardly to reach out for true love, but I'm not."

Her last words hurt. I decided to stop arguing with her, and went to tackle Mabilie. She was as appalled as I, but her pleas met with equal resistance. So we continued to drift eastward, enjoying good winds and fair skies at last. Whatever was in charge of the weather appeared to favor Eleanor's rash scheme.

Or so it seemed until the morning we woke to find three ships bearing down on us. "They're Greek," said the captain scanning the banners they carried. He sounded worried.

"That's no problem," said Eleanor. "France has no quarrel with the Greeks."

"France may have no quarrel with them, your majesty, but this ship is Sicilian, and we are at war with Byzantium and the Greeks."

There was no way to outrun them. Each one carried twice the sail of our little vessel, so we surrendered immediately and allowed them to board. When the captain told the leader of the conquering invaders about his royal cargo, he was delighted. "The governor of Cyprus will be eager to meet you," he told his valuable captive. Eleanor was furious at having her identity betrayed, but I knew that if they believed she was worth something, she'd be safer—and so would we.

When we reached Cyprus, all the women, including Petra and her nurse, were removed from the ship to the governor's palace in Limassol, while the rest stayed on board, including Eve who had befriended a few of the sailors. We were treated well, and allowed to wash and change before we were taken down to the governor.

Even in this distant outpost of the Byzantine Empire, the famed Greek court ceremony was in evidence. We were taken past a line of courtiers with impassive faces, all in the same costume, a wall of solid color. It was calculated to intimidate us, but Eleanor does not intimidate easily, though the governor refused to bow to her. He seemed to think that being the servant of an emperor made him superior to any mere queen.

"We are grateful that you have decided to visit our humble shore," he said, sounding not at all humble.

"It was not our wish, but rather that of your servants that we should be wrongfully detained and diverted from the proper course of our journey," replied Eleanor.

"Those who travel in the ships of our enemies will be treated as our enemies."

"My husband and I were one year ago the honored guests of your emperor. He will not be pleased when he learns how I have been obstructed."

"But you are my honored guests now," the governor said in a voice filled with smarm. "And as soon as we have investigated the contents of your ship and made sure that no wicked person has transported on it that which he should not, you will be free to resume your journey to Sicily. Tonight, you will join me in a feast, and you may resume your voyage in a few days. I will send a pilot with you to take you out of the harbor and send you to Sicily. We expect your husband to be so grateful to have you restored to his loving care that he will know the Greeks are his true friends."

Eleanor's shoulders relaxed, but the tone of her voice did not change. "Very well, but Sicily is not our destination. When we were so rudely stopped and boarded, we were on our way to Antioch."

The governor must have known some of this already. His captains had surely told him that when they caught us we were heading east, nowhere near Sicily, even if they didn't know our precise destination.

"Dear me no." The governor chuckled. "You are not going to Antioch. Your husband would be most distressed if he found we had sent you there. Besides, I don't think you will be well received In Antioch at this time. You see, they are all in deep mourning. So sad."

"What do you mean?" Eleanor said, suddenly wary.

"Such a tragedy," said the governor, smiling broadly. "Nur ad-Din invaded the county of Antioch and besieged the castle of Inab. Raymond of Antioch rode out to relieve the castle, and Nur ad-Din withdrew, but stayed close. That night, he and his army encircled Raymond's forces, and the battle was over almost before it began. They say he put Raymond's head in a silver box and sent it to the caliph of Baghdad as a prize. The news is all over Christendom. I'm surprised you hadn't already heard."

It was as if someone had extinguished the light inside Eleanor, but she stood very straight and spoke in measured tones. "We had not heard. Then, indeed, we shall go to Sicily." She swallowed. "You said something about a banquet? My women and I must go get ready." We were dismissed, though there was very little getting ready to be done, since we were already in our best clothing. Eleanor held Petra in the rooms they had given us, rocking the child slowly in her arms, staring into space.

We suffered through a slow dinner of too much food and heavy resinous wine. Fortunately Byzantine protocol did not require Eleanor to say very much because she sat like stone the whole time, staring straight in front of her and eating almost nothing. The governor ignored the insult to his kitchen and beamed with pleasure, well aware of the upset he had caused.

I don't know if Eleanor slept. I certainly didn't. The next morning, she gazed out the window at the waves crashing on the rocks and sand below. The sea was so blue it was almost painful to look at. I was playing with Petra, bouncing her on my knees as she giggled and I wondered what was going to be this little mite's future, when a maid came in, bringing us bread and curd milk for breakfast.

"Is this your baby?" she asked in Greek. "Pretty, pretty."

I didn't have the Greek to explain whose baby it was though I got the gist of her words, so I just smiled and she left the room.

"What did that woman say?" asked Eleanor, listlessly. These were the first real words she had spoken to me since finding out about Raymond's death the previous day.

"Silly woman, she thought Petra was my baby," I said, handing the girl to her mother. "I couldn't figure out how to tell her she wasn't, so we may start a new rumor."

Eleanor stroked Petra's back and stared at the ceiling, a thoughtful look on her face. I wondered what new plot she was hatching.

"That's it," she said. "We'll pass off Petra as your child. It's the only thing that makes any sense."

It didn't make sense to me. "What? At the French court? I don't think anyone is going to be persuaded by that."

"No," Eleanor agreed sadly. "And you won't be able to go to the kingdom of Jerusalem either for my story is too well known there, and you are too closely associated with me. I won't send Petra anywhere where she'll become a political pawn. You'll have to go somewhere new and fresh where your story won't be questioned. Somewhere distant and a little isolated. You must take her back to Lisbon and live with her there. It's perfect, because you can pass her off as your and Simon's child. He can take you back and Petra will have both mother and father. People see what they expect to see. No one will suspect a thing."

This was possibly the worst idea she, a woman well known for bad ideas, ever had.

"Even if you are right, and you may well be, that we could fool people in Lisbon, how am I going to fool Simon? He can count on his fingers as well as anyone, and he will know that Petra isn't his, can't be his. Besides, he showed no sign of wanting me when I left.

He'll hardly be more enthusiastic if I return with another man's child in tow, asking him to claim it as his own," I said, a touch of despair creeping into my voice.

But Eleanor was wholly given over to her vision of my future. "You're proud, Aude, too proud. You wanted him to love you, but you didn't want him to really know you. What could he do but withdraw when you cast him aside so coldly? If you go back to him, he'll take you, I promise."

"But what do I say? What do I tell him?" I asked, helpless, already being won over to Eleanor's dream.

She knew she had half-persuaded me. "Tell him everything. Everything. Yes, even who Petra's real parents are. He'll have to know, and if you can trust him, I can too. But don't only tell him that. Tell him about yourself too, who you are and who you've been. Tell him about when you were a little girl in Jerusalem, and your life in Flanders, and all the stories you have told us since we met. Then it won't matter what Christian said to him. I'll find a ship to take you from Cyprus to Lisbon, and something to write on, and Simon can read it for himself and know you, and understand. You'll see."

✠

And so, Simon, that is why I am about to land on your doorstep in Portugal with a stack of this paper they use for parchment now in one arm, and a baby girl in the other. Eleanor was as good as her word, and before we parted she found passage for me on a ship bound for Lisbon and the North Sea. We also released Petra's nursemaid, who spoke only Syriac, finding passage for her back to her home, and engaged a new nursemaid who spoke only Greek.

Then Eleanor set out with Mabilie for Sicily, and an uncertain future with her husband. She held Petra close one more time before passing her off to me.

"Be good to my girl," she said.

"Maybe it won't be forever," I said softly, but she just smiled and walked to the rowboat that would take her and Mabilie to the ship where the men were already hoisting sail. I held Petra up to see her mother one last time while Eleanor climbed into the ship, the boat lifted anchor, and sailed. We watched until it was a dot on the horizon, then I found my own vessel, an English ship out of Hastings.

We're becalmed off the south coast of Spain right now, though the captain says the wind is changing and we'll be able to set out on the final leg for Lisbon by tomorrow morning. I hear the monkeys chattering in the trees on shore, and Eve hears them too and chatters back, looking for but unable to see her mysterious brethren. Once I finish this, I will pay a boy to row me to shore with Eve, and if Eve wants, she can go and join her cousins in the trees. She's more than half wild now after months of near freedom at al-Lawza, and though she'd have a longer life at the end of a chain with me, I find I cannot do that to her.

In a few days, we'll land at Lisbon, and in my dreams, Simon, you're waiting on the dock to enfold us in your arms and take Petra and me home. I know this is just a dream. You won't be there because you have no idea I'm on my way. But I will find you wherever you are, and give you my stack of papers and you can read them and make your decision. If you don't take me back, I'll live in Lisbon with Petra, and maybe even Theo when he pauses from fighting the Moors and we'll brazen out any scandal. But I think you will take me back. I think you will.

Poitiers, 1169

✠

Eleanor, by the grace of God duchess of Aquitaine and Normandy, and Queen of the English, rubbed the bridge of her nose, warding off a headache. Eight pregnancies in fifteen years to her now not-so-new husband, Henry, king of England, had not diminished her looks, but she did get tired, especially since John, her youngest, was only two.

"One more set of accounts and then we're done," promised the steward who attended her in the solar of the palace. "Now, the abbot of le Merci-Dieu has petitioned—"

A knock at the door interrupted his words. "Come in," said the queen. Anything for a distraction. It was Isabelle de Talmont who had served as Eleanor's chief lady-in-waiting since the death of her beloved Mabilie, five years before. "There's a young woman who insists on seeing you. She can sing. And she says you knew her mother."

They all said that. Since Eleanor moved from England back to Aquitaine the year before to help her fool husband rule the duchy, she had been beset by a plague of young women who wanted to enter her service. Mabilie would have been better at dissuading them, but Isabelle let every girl with nice manners through, and it was Eleanor who had to disappoint them by telling them there was no room.

"Very well," she said to Isabelle. "Tell her to come in. Steward, we are done for the day." He rolled up his parchments and followed Isabelle out of the room, and a young woman of about twenty entered, alone.

She was tall, almost as tall as Eleanor herself, with a curl of auburn hair escaping from her tight coif, and Eleanor had the strange sense of recognition she sometimes felt when she saw a young woman who reminded her of her own lost youth.

"What is your name, girl?"

"Petronille de Leiria."

"Never heard of you. Now, Petronille, the Dame de Talmont told me I knew your mother, but I don't know any Portuguese women at all and I have all the ladies I can cope with now anyway, so no matter that she sent you, you'll have to tell her—."

"My mother didn't send me."

"What?"

"My mother is dead. She died last year. And she is not Portuguese. Neither is my father, though that is where we live. It was my father who sent me. He told me he promised my mother before she died, that he would send me to you. I don't know why. He swore it on the cross she wore around her neck. It was a deathbed promise. She even wrote a letter. I have it here."

Eleanor, despite herself, took the parchment, folded and sealed, that the young girl held out to her. She broke the seal with a sharp thumbnail, opened it up and read. It was one line, written in a shaky hand. 'I return what I borrowed,' signed with a single letter, A.

A chill shot through her body.

The queen looked up from the parchment at the girl, trying to see the past in her features, faces long gone, and innocence that she herself lost long before.

"Would you like to live here with me?" she asked the girl, suddenly shy. No matter the promise, the choice must be hers.

"All Christendom speaks of your court, your majesty, and how you attract poets and troubadours and scholars to your side, and how women learn here alongside men and even write poetry of their own. I could think of nothing better."

"Isabelle tells me you can sing. Sing something for me."

The girl began to sing, a slow sad song in the language that had become her native one. While she sang, memories came to Eleanor one by one, of a monkey on a pier, a grove of laurel, a castle by the sea, the sun slanting into a courtyard.

When she was done, Eleanor said, "Well Petra — Petronille —"

The girl smiled. "You did know my mother after all! Petra was her name for me."

"I did know your mother. I knew her well. I thought the years had taken her away from me forever, but now she returns in the shape of you."

"Then I may stay?"

"You may stay with me as long as you wish."

Author's Note

Are you like me? When you read a historical novel in a period that is new to you do you get not much further than page three before you flip to the back to see if there is an author's note that will tell you what is true and what is invented about what you are reading? Truth is complicated in historical fiction, and more so the further you go back, when our only sources report rumors as facts and write to argue for a position rather than to convey information in a disinterested way. But here are a few details that you might be wondering about.

Aude is my creation but she moves through a landscape of mostly real people, places, and events. The histories of the kingdom of Jerusalem, Flanders and what happened to Count Charles, the siege of Lisbon, and the Second Crusade are all much as described in these pages. I've altered a name or two, choosing different spellings to differentiate historical characters, so if you want to find out more about Bartolph Erembald, seek him under Bertulf, and Dietrik of Alsace is better known by his French name, Thierry.

The best known of all my historical characters is Eleanor of Aquitaine, though her early life is its least well-known part, which leaves lots of room for the historical novelist. Her participation in the Second Crusade is well-documented from the call to crusade at Vezelay, though the misadventures in Turkey, until she encounters her handsome uncle Raymond in Antioch. Rumours about their relationship swirled among her contemporaries and are documented by several historians. But the narrative breaks off and we have no idea what Eleanor was doing or where she was for almost a year. We know she and Louis VII, her husband, left on separate ships, that they both ran afoul of the Greeks, and that Pope Eugenius tried a spot of marriage counselling when they arrived in Italy. That gap in Eleanor's history is a field where a historical novelist can play, and its events and their outcome are the product of my imagination.

I invite curious readers to visit my homepage lucypick.com to learn more about the history and fiction of the events that inspired *The Queen's Companion*.

www.ingramcontent.com/pod-product-compliance
Lightning Source LLC
Chambersburg PA
CBHW050603190726
48283CB00007B/2264